I0772316

THE
HAPPY HARROW
MURDER TRILOGY

Murder to Music
Murdered Mothers
Murder in Marriage

B. F. CAYZER

ARPress
45 Dan Road Suite 5
Canton MA 02021

Hotline: 1(800) 220-7660
Fax: 1(855) 752-6001

Ordering Information:
Quantity sales. Special discounts are available on quantity purchases by corporations, associations, and others. For details, contact the publisher at the address above.

Printed in the United States of America.

ISBN-13:   Paperback   979-8-89389-492-9
           eBook   979-8-89389-660-2
           Hardback   979-8-89389-659-6

Library of Congress Control Number: 2024921777

This book is dedicated to Marianne Castle. I am in awe
of her hands-on work for many charities, opening her home for
them, where President John F. Kennedy vacationed in his early years.

CONTENTS

RACECOURSE SETTINGS

Ascot, in Berkshire England

Flemington, the site of the Melbourne Cup, managed by Victoria Racing Club, Australia

Santa Anita, a few miles from Los Angeles, California

Calder, in Miami, Florida

Churchill Downs, the home of the Kentucky Derby, Louisville, Kentucky

Nad Al Sheba, Dubai's race course, which pays the largest purses for winners anywhere in the world

Cagnes sur Mer, in southern France

Lingfield, in southern England

Beverley, in northern England

MURDER TO MUSIC

CHARACTERS IN MURDER TO MUSIC

Rick Harrow, narrator, who is a British trainer of racehorses

Hillary a/k/a Happy Harrow, his wife, an apprentice jockey and talented sleuth

Tim Harrow, the Harrow's 3-year-old son

Dorothy Harrow, the Harrow's 18-month-old daughter

Carla Purcell, a famous soprano, half of the Purcell Sisters Duo

Fran Purcell, the contralto half of the duo. Both sisters earn over 20 million a year

Heidi Wahner, Carla's understudy, who plays Madame Butterfly's maid in Sydney, Australia

Kotski, a British-based Russian émigré tycoon, who joins Rick's stable

HM Queen Elizabeth II, one of the greatest and most knowledgeable of racehorse owners

Sybil Sykes, formerly a Hollywood star; now big on the London stage; an owner in Rick's yard

Filipa Grant, and her husband Rus. Filipa sings duets with Fran, makes millions, is a new owner in Rick's stable. Her husband, Rus, flirts with Happy

"Little Betty," the sick child that Filipa and Rus try to have cured by Happy

Munchie, a singer who goes to Australia to practice for the role of Elizabeth in Pride and Prejudice; has hopes of joining Rick's stable

"Paw" Riley, Happy's father; a pillar of Kentucky hills' traditional way of life

Captain and Mrs. Ainsley, who profited greatly by taking over Feathers, Hal's great horse he sold to them out of kindness

Colonel Flyte, Rick's most difficult owner, who seesaws between stables

Goofy Howe, a saxophone musician who was a boyfriend of Fran's

Nelson Polk, a Hollywood gaffer, Fran's newest boyfriend, who picks her up at the Santa Anita races

Leila, a big musical comedy star, an import from Hollywood, who competes with Fran for fans

Bell Natchez, Leila's husband, a tenor who had originally been Fran's boyfriend

Honore Boudin, a wily Frenchman, another of Fran's cast-off boyfriends

Prince Albert II of Monaco, an opera enthusiast

Paul Peters, a pizza delivery boy

Tom, Rick's Head Lad in his yard

Mrs. Rea, longtime housekeeper for the Harrows with some jurisdiction over the "chillun"

Perry Coulis, producer of comedies on the London stage

Virgo, a reporter with CNN; a constant friend to the Harrows in any hour of need

Ellie Grace, the aristocratic friend who has helped launch Happy into county society

The Hon. Jeremy Grace, heir to his Earl uncle, who rides to hounds as a cover, but has a mysterious past

CHAPTER 1

"Always a bridesmaid, never a bride," Col. Flyte complained in his disgruntled baritone, when once again his now-sluggish racehorse disgraced my yard.

I'm Rick Harrow, a British racehorse Trainer based at Epsom, home of the Derby, although my yard has never yet had a horse that rated being in that race. I'm six feet three inches tall, heavy, with carrot red hair from my Irish mother, and brown eyes from my Norman blood. In case you're interested, Norman blood used to mean something in England.

With my little blond wife, Happy, an apprentice jockey born in eastern Kentucky, we'd tried all through 2006 to convince Col. Flyte that we had his horse Broadback's best interests close to our hearts.

Col. Flyte was a difficult owner to please. We'd won a good race at Doncaster at the beginning of the 2006 season, but Broadback had trained off after the unusually sultry summer. But, tell that to Col. Flyte? Not on your Nellie! A tiny man, who holds himself extremely erect by throwing his backside out for balance, he'd never been one of my favorites. I guess I don't suffer complainers gladly.

Poor Broadback! If he'd been sent to grass, I could have hoped to win again with him the next flat season. But, no. Greedy Col. Flyte demanded we race him again and again, until Broadback shuddered with distress when we loaded him into a horsebox for yet another drive to yet another racecourse.

Col. Flyte, the younger son of a minor Baron, prided himself on his family's ancestry. He thought because Broadback came from a distinguished racing lineage Broadback could run forever. Not true. If he'd read up on Broadback's lineage properly he'd have noticed that both dam and sire had raced only twice as two-year-olds. I needed Col. Flyte to remain in my yard. Death, two murders, and financial problems had thinned my list of owners. If I wanted to stay in business I needed to woo Flyte, or go bankrupt.

Thanks to Happy's Kentucky hillbilly accent, we'd acquired an exciting new owner, Sybil Sykes, a Hollywood singing star who'd been recruited to play Daisy Mae in a musical featuring the Lil' Abner hillbillies.

Sybil wanted to win big. She contracted me to buy two colts and a filly for her, the best horseflesh available. "Ah'm goin' t'show them shits at Santa Anita what Ah'm made of!" she declared several times on each visit to our yard, in her awful fake Kentucky drawl. She always practiced it around Happy, hoping my wife would correct any mistakes, but Happy kept her mouth shut like a mousetrap after the mouse is caught. Happy knew better than to try to correct Sybil's ghastly four letter language. When they'd first met, Happy had gently veered Sybil into her own prim Baptist wordage. But it was shit, fuck and hump still with Sybil off-stage. I suspected Sybil's years of couch-casting for her film roles had over-broadened Sybil's vocabulary.

Daisy Mae Hog Town II was transferred from Broadway to the London theatre district, where Sybil was a huge hit. Her swelling boobs and tiny waist mimicked the original Daisy Mae character, and she wore her hair in the same long blonde single pig-tail.

A greater boon came about around Christmas, when I'd been wondering how to buy gifts for a homesick wife, and two infants who'd been introduced to designer clothes and toys. Sybil brought a pair of singer twins to my yard, the famous Purcell girls, Carla and Fran.

"Yo-all's made fo' one anothuh," Sybil whooped. "They's both into hoss's. Wants yo' t'train winnuhs fo' them."

The twins, supposedly identical, weren't.

Carla had bouncing boobs, Fran had none, to bounce or to show off. Fran was totally flat-chested.

Moreover, their voices were different. Carla was a soprano, Fran a contralto. The way their voices melded had gained them their fortunes They'd started out creating magic with the bell song from *Lakmé*, and the flower song from *Madama Butterfly*; but, like with Charlotte Church's career, the really stupendous millions flowed in when they switched to rap.

Fran, seemingly the more retiring of the two, whispered, "Andrew Lloyd Webber's wife got us interested in horseflesh. Only, we want racehorses. Can you find us some that will win?"

You bet! Politely, I said, "I'll try. Do my best. Would you like to see some of the yearlings I've got in my yard?"

Carla, in her high soprano lilt, shouted out, "Not interested in No-hopers. Don't try shoving off on us some useless nags."

I didn't. Only the best for the Purcell sisters! Because they could afford the best. Their combined earnings annually exceeded twenty million pounds sterling. Placating Carla, I said, "Come see, and judge for yourselves." I led them to our stalls for yearlings.

Fran gasped with delight when I brought out a chestnut.

I said, "This character has Homing blood. We call him Home Alone. Homing was the late Lord Rotherwick's best horse, won him the Queen Elizabeth II stakes at Ascot. Born Robin Cayzer, he bred his own champions before he came into the Rotherwick title. His father had been an MFH, and Robin Cayzer was MFH of the Bicester hounds. He bred a very fine filly that won the Irish Oaks, and then Homing. This colt has a sweet manner until he's with others of his age, then he makes out like a killer until he heads them all."

Carla sneered, "I don't like his name. Home Alone, sounds stolen from the film."

No smart-ass reply from me. I needed these twins as owners, and so I kept with the placating mode. "You could change the name. Though it's said to be unlucky, changing names."

Sweetly, in her famous contralto, Fran demurred. "I love the name. *Home Alone* was a big hit as a film. And so were its follow-ups. Lucky name."

Quickly I gained the impression that these twins were not too fond of each other. Too bound together, they may have found that being a twin was as smothering as chocolate sauce on scoops of ice cream.

Moreover, I sensed Fran was smothering some characteristic that was frowned on by Carla.

Fran bought Home Alone. Carla chose a filly from the late Lord Carnarvon's Highclere breeding, an over-sized seventeen-hand giant she called Sweet Song.

My other new owner, the Russian-Brit magnate Kotski, wasn't pleased when he heard about that filly's name. "I own a gelding.by the same sire as Soviet Song. I might have wanted another of that breeding, a filly, and used that name."

Arrogant and bossy, he strutted around my yard like a rooster.

It was after Happy had celebrated Thanksgiving that we had a very different type of visit from Kotski. A changed man, he was in an hysterical mood. From a serious, bright businessman he'd mutated into a shivering wreck. He'd lost his straight back posture and bent over as if he'd been crippled by osteoporosis. His eyes and cheeks were sunken, He seemed to have lost a lot of hair. Perhaps formerly he'd worn a toupée which now he'd discarded.

He came down to our Epsom cottage gibbering like an ape. "They murdered him! Will I be the next to have a nuclear bomb in my stomach? Holy Mother of God, save me from them!" He made the sign of the cross three times.

"Sit down, have a brandy," I handed Kotski a full tumbler. "Who's them? They? A nuclear bomb in your stomach! Come on, sir. Pull yourself together."

Kotski, his teeth chattering making a noise like castanets, looked furtively into the shadows around our tiny hearth. He whispered, "Those former KGB officers. They got Alexander Litvinenko, right there in central London in a crowded hotel. Terrible slow death, poor soul. His father flew from Russia to London to be at his bedside at University Hospital. And what did Walter Litvinenko say? He said, said, yes, he said, 'My son died, and he was killed by a little nuclear bomb.' He was referring to radiation from an alpha isotope, polonium-210. One, of three ex-KGB officer-hosts, dosed his tea during a meeting at the Millenium Hotel."

Kotski had downed his brandy in two chugs, like a viking quaffing mead from a tunneled cow's horn.

Happy, my extra-cognizant wife, said,"Let me give you dinner. Y'all feel better." She placed bowls of soup on our dinette's table. Kotski couldn't handle a soup spoon full of tomato bisque. His trembling fingers spilled it all over his shirt. Happy tried a different tactic. "Ah'll bring y'all yo'r soup in a cup." But he made the cup clatter so badly in its saucer that the soup grew cold.

Kotski said, "Mrs. Harrow, Happy . . . I understand that you solved the murders of seven people. Help me. Help . . ."

Happy thought quietly for a time before answering Kotski's plea. "Y'all had any dealings with ex-officers of the KGB? If not, I could offer y'all a plan."

"No. I swear I'm a simple businessman, who made his money in finance. No political deals. None. Not involved in oil, diamonds, smuggling. Nothing like that."

I interrupted. "Mr. Kotski, I've been following the Litvinenko story in my morning tabloids. Litvinenko took twenty-two days to die, in excruciating pain. As you said, his death was caused by alpha radiation from polonium-210 planted inside his body. Surely, you're not going to breathe or swallow polonium-210."

Kotski, shakily cleaning soup from his shirt, spoke through slivers of lobster stuck in his teeth. "One by one Litvinenko's vital organs were attacked—his liver, his spleen, his kidneys. Finally, his blood pressure dropped to nothing. All caused by a speck of that polonium-210, no bigger than the head of a pin. How can I avoid that? You can't even see it. Nor taste it if it's in your tea." ' He eyed what remained of his soup as if it contained poison. "Because I make my living in England, I'll be killed here as a traitor."

Happy said, "Mr. Kotski, the Russians may have 50,000 tons of chemical weapons left over from the Cold War, but they're in Russia. Not here. That big amount of chemical weapons is mostly for spreading diseases—plague, smallpox, anthrax, like that. Oh, Ah read in the tabloids that there have been thefts of polonium-210. But it cain't be easy to transport that stuff. Not even a quantity the size of a pinhead. Now listen up to my plan. When Hal Murphy wanted publicity, we got a PR man for him. We'll get one for you. He should write a series of articles about what a patriot y'all are, how y'all love yo'r homeland, but yo'r business keeps you from living where yo'r heart is." She spoke with the sincerity of a Kentucky woman who misses her native hills. "Then nobody's going to call y'all a traitor, and order yo'r death."

Kotski glared at her. "Those three ex-KGB officers, now working for its successor the FSB, left traces of radiation all over London. Seventeen innocent people, waiters and waitresses and such, were found to have been exposed by them to polonium-210. A restaurant that Litvinenko used is sealed to the public. A hotel bedroom too. Even a seat in a British Airways plane that flew them out from Moscow. That plane had a seat that sent a Geiger counter into orbit. Yet all three assassins made it back to Russia. Oh, they can get at me, don't you doubt it."

Happy placed a comforting hand on his free arm. "The British doctors found out what poison it was that killed Litvinenko."

"But, too late," Kotski screeched. "He died hours before the doctors pinpointed polonium-210."

"Surely other victims have lived to tell the tale." I tried to reason with him.

"One case. But it wasn't polonium-210 that was used. The weapon of choice was radioactive thalium. That hit was against Nikolai Khoklov, like Litvinenko an ex-KGB agent living abroad, who was criticizing the government. Thalium was put in his coffee during a conference in Frankfurt. He was lucky, though, because American doctors at the military hospital there found out it was thalium and saved his life."

"Well, there. See? There's hope after all."

"The hell there is! Take another case, that concerned a businessman, a simple businessman like me. Not a former KGB man, or a critic of the government. In the 1990s Ivan Kivelidi, an entrepreneur in Moscow, had the receiver of his telephone dusted with a chemical weapon. He died. You bet he died."

Happy served a pot roast from kitchenware. Kotski eyed it doubtfully. "I think I'll go back to London now," he said lamely. "I'll be writing to you."

The approach of Christmas put an end to any bickering over a name for Kotski's gelding. Before a partridge could sing in a pear tree, Kotski wrote us that he was emigrating to Canada. He ordered me to sell his horse.

I contacted Tattersall's, and made the arrangements. We'd lost Kotski from our stable. One owner less!

England's Christmas season meant that every town and village had its streets festooned with lights. Shops competed to produce the best window displays of toys and clothes appropriate to the season. Annual Christmas parties took over from computers and printers at offices, where employees got well and truly pissed.

Schools exchanged classes for nativity plays. Morris Dancers jangled their belled socks on village greens. Geese were fattened, the smart ones escaping into any protective woods. Trees were flattened to provide the traditional yule logs.

Cities emptied when anyone who could afford a rail ticket moved to a village where a friend or relative could provide a bed. The village churches, empty for most of the year, filled to capacity on December 24th for midnight services. Carol singers charmed householders out of cash sorely needed for gifts and turkeys for their families.

Kotski would be celebrating Christmas in Canada, two weeks later due to his Russian Orthodox calendar leanings. I secretly wondered what fabulous present he'd be giving to my ex-paramour, Irina. She'd ended our too-brief one night stand relationship after the Arc weekend in Paris, so I wasn't expected to ante up a gift for her. But I do think that Kotski could have sent us at least a card, if no gifts. But then again, maybe a card would have given away a secret new address.

Happy and my infants were overwhelmed with presents like an avalanche had descended on our little cottage. The Purcell twins brought their own platinum records. Our generous local aristocratic neighbor Ellie sent a large Christmas hamper of food from Harrods. Sybil Sykes motored down from her London theatre with videos of her films. Captain and Mrs. Ainsley chose clothes for both kids. Hal Murphy mail-ordered a toy fire engine that could be driven by my toddler Timothy and a four-feet tall teddy bear for Dorothy's room.

Col. Flyte sent nothing, an ominous indication that he'd be removing Broadback from my yard.

It felt heartwarming to be surrounded by friends like Ellie, Sybil and the Ainsleys on Christmas Day. Our hearth could barely contain them. After mulled wine came the Kentucky-style fare that Happy cooked.

My Brit friends were polite if not thrilled by fried chicken and grits for Christmas, but the plum pudding from Selfridge's went down well enough. The entire group went with me to feed carrots and apples to our horses.

My stable lads had placed wreaths on the horses' stalls. These were good boys and Happy gave each a watch and a bottle of booze. They had slices of the plum pudding and a platter of roast turkey with turnips and new potatoes; their own preference in the foods department.

Boxing Day was lonely. All our friends had gone to their various flats and houses to unwrap gifts or set aside some to recycle for next Christmas. Like after the end of a school holiday, there was a feeling of let-down.

But that was as nothing compared to what emotions drowned any remnants of Christmas joy on December 27.

Our telephone rang early in the morning. Fran's contralto filled our hearth with a din of misery. "Carla's been killed. Murdered. Strangled! The police are here now. Nothing can be done for her. I had the ambulance men quickly, as soon as I found Carla turned purple in our living room. Dead." There came a pause while Fran wheezed into the receiver. Her tone changed. "What's to become of Carla's horse? Sweet Song was a name for a horse that brought trouble from the start! I said so! Now Carla's gone, I'll soon be broke without a singing partner. No one's going to want me," she wailed, choking on each word. "A contralto, without my soprano twin. I'll have to sell Home Alone."

Trying to calm her, I said, "Surely not. Terrible about your sister, but - - " It was then that I learned what characteristic Fran had kept under wraps around Carla — a use of foul four-letter words. "Fuck that! You're an asshole."

CHAPTER 2

Fran didn't sell Home Alone, and when Carla's estate was settled Fran kept Sweet Song. Fran was no longer earning a half share of twenty million. But she could pay her racing bills and plenty others after she graduated Carla's understudy Heidi Wahner to fill Carla's place in order to continue producing saleable music.

The duets they produced weren't as popular. Heidi worked hard enough to offer a decent soprano. The effect simply wasn't magic. It was merely workhorse.

Because they called themselves The Purcell Singers they managed to cut a new record. The notoriety connected with Carla's strangling had actually helped sell their music.

Rap wasn't as demanding as opera had been in those first challenging years of Fran's career. Fran told us there was not so much emphasis on Bel Canto and dexterity of the vocal chords. With rap, Fran embellished their act by displaying imagination and repeating lines in the slower movements. Fran was less pleased by Heidi's theatrical manner that put off some record producers, who refused to work with the new duo. Heidi's tempo fluctuations were painful, and although Fran displayed professional ease, it was Heidi's inexperience as a top performer that lost them new contracts, or so we learned from a long letter posted from London. Fran's downturn in the popularity ratings continued. Heidi's harsh notes were a serious put-off.

The lyricism of good songwriters was often absent. And Heidi suffered from a lack of musical understanding. It became obvious that her role as Carla's understudy had worked as long as Heidi hadn't been called on to perform in front of a mike.

In mid-January Fran telephoned Happy and begged her to come to London to her Chelsea apartment "I'm so lonely," she wailed down the wire, "please make the trip. I know you have those two small infants, but I need to see you here."

Happy responded ably, "Ah knows how y'all feels. When Ah lost mah Mammy, Ah'd have given up on lahfe if it hadn't been fo' mah love o' horses. How about if'n Ah brings Miss Ellie? She lost huh boy-friend from a shot-gun acceedent. She'll unnerstand."

Ellie's boyfriend had killed himself with his shotgun when poisoned aspirin gave him the idea he had inoperable cancer. Happy didn't elaborate.

Happy and Ellie went on the first train from Epsom to London, after Happy settled our two infants with the housekeeper-cum-nanny.

From London they took a taxi, Ellie paying.

The block of flats that contained Fran's home was dilapidated. Built from poor materials too soon after World War II, it needed serious repairs. Where before there must have been a Porters' lodge, now a gaping hole contained nothing but a hand—written sign on cardboard warning no human voice would attend to visitors. An arrow pointed to a metal plaque containing push-buttons alongside individual slots for calling cards. Several of the name plates were empty of cards. Among them, Fran Purcell's. Above these calling cards was a circular grill for speaking to the tenants.

Ellie said, "My Mater knows a duke who lives in this block of flats. Impoverished duke, is the polite way of saying he's on hard times. No calling card here for him. Too grand, I suppose. Let's try some of the single ladies listed, and see if they'll press the buzzer to let us get inside."

First, Happy tried buzzing two of the empty slots. "Who they hell is this? Go away!" came a furious male voice in the over-cultured tones of someone too special to have gone to a public school and had been educated by tutors. The circular grill had vibrated from his tone. Happy guessed the voice belonged to the duke. She tried the other blank slot.

Nothing.

"Ah supposes thet means this'un belongs to Fran." She pressed the push-button again.

Again, nothing.

Ellie said, "Oh do let's try one of the old women." She buzzed Miss Alice Kohl.

A quavering, frail but very eager voice trembled through the grill. "Yes? Is it you? Dear, Mary! Here to visit?" The buzzer for the door sounded almost simultaneously. Happy and Ellie were inside quicker than thoroughbreds enter the Winners' Circle.

There was no lift. This was a walk-up.

Ellie led the way upstairs, like a schoolchild about to go home. "I think she said she was on the Third floor, over on the right."

When they arrived, Happy pushed the doorbell. Nothing. She knocked and shouted "Fran, it's Us'n. Open up."

Fran recognized Happy's hillbilly accent. Her steel-lined door opened slowly.

"Oh!" Happy couldn't suppress her shock at the disastrous change in Fran's looks.

Fran, her face heavily wrinkled, her eye area with bags pulling down the reddened lower lids, her teeth coated with yellow goo, gave an effect that was pathetic.

Happy felt saddened at Fran's deteriorated looks. But there was more. The formerly elegant singing star had given up on her image. Fran stood there in a very tired night dress, her feet in dirty worn slippers. Her hair was in curlers, her face had no makeup.

For a young woman in her mid-twenties, she had premature grey hair. Which was a mess.

Ellie thought, "There's practically no resemblance to the girl on the front cover of her albums."

Fran said, "Want a drink? I've got everything over on the bar. Coke? Speed?"

Happy chose a bottle of Diet Cola. Ellie shook her head, she knew she couldn't swallow whatever Fran would have poured out. Neither woman was into drugs.

The cocaine she'd stashed in an open bowl. There were finger tip marks in the powder, obviously from recent use.

Fran patted seat cushions on a costly sofa. All the furniture was expensive. Curtains and accessories had certainly been supplied by famous interior designers. A collector's oriental carpet had an ugly brown stain. Fran noticed that Happy's eyes had seen the spot.

She said to both women, "You think that strangling would be a clean business. Well, it wasn't. The things that made me realize something was gravely wrong was the busted door lock and then an awful stink of poop. Poor Carla's bowels made the mess on this carpet. My Bolivian maid didn't want to clean it up. I did my best with Genie soap."

Happy said, "Mebbe y'all should move. Git a fresh lahfe in a newer buildin' so's yo' c'n erase turrible mem'ries."

Ellie echoed, "Yes. Move out of here! It may not even be safe for you to remain in this flat."

"Safe enough. Police told me this was not a random killing. Carla's death was pre-meditated. Police said the killer wore gloves—no fingerprints."

"Nowadays most professionals wear gloves."

"There were also no footprints in the thick carpet in my hallway. Couldn't tell if the killer was male or female because the shoes worn made no marks. Knew where Carla kept her famous jewelry. That, yes. But no DNA left. No hairs, no clothing threads. No fingerprints or footprints other than mine and Heidi's."

"Heidi's?"

"Heidi's because she works with me here most days." Fran interrupted herself in huge, hard gasps to weep. Ellie wondered if so much weeping could affect her contralto.

She said nothing.

Happy stayed quiet too. Her eyes took in much of the visible aspects of this large room. She saw that Fran owned an apartment, not just a flat, because it took up much of the third floor and contained a stairwell that rose to the next stage, making it a duplex.

When Fran stopped weeping, Happy asked, "How did the thief entuh yo'r home?"

"Broke the front lock. Not difficult, cheap lock. My Mum owned this flat from way back. We sisters grew up here. Never changed much. Just a few expensive touches."

Ellie spoke out, "I imagine the killer got in same way we did, by buzzing some older tenant, lonely for company."

"I thought of that too. Police think the person knew about Carla's jewelry. After all, she always wore so much bling, and that was part of her image. Written up a lot in newspapers, mentioned on TV. She may have come home from shopping, noticed the broken lock and charged in to stop a burglar from taking her jewels. Part of her capital, you know. And Carla was never cowardly. She'd have kicked, bitten, done anything to stop losing her diamonds."

Ellie nodded. She averted her eyes from the poop stain, but her facial expression altered and Fran guessed what her next comment would have been if Ellie's tutors hadn't brought her up to act delicately as the grand-daughter of an Earl.

"Wondering if Carla was raped? Yes, that's what you're wondering. I can see it in your face. No. Not raped. Police checked for that. Poor Carla was the subject of an automatic autopsy."

Ellie blushed. She thought, "Thank God no autopsy for my Ivor. Unnecessary with a shotgun shooting all its pellets into the throat."

Happy tactfully changed the subject. "Ah heard y'all on the new record y'all cut. Sang that James Blunt ballad from his *Back to Bedlam* album."

In a doleful tone, Fran agreed. "Yes. I liked "No Bravery" best. Where it goes 'Old men kneel and accept their fate. Wives and daughters cut and raped/A generation drenched in hate.' He wrote that after serving with the British army in Kosovo. Suits my mood at this time."

Ellie said, "I prefer 'You're Beautiful'."

Happy murmured, "Blunt cut that album in LA. Now *Back to Bedlam*'s into Britain's top ten. Ah's read somewheres Blunt said, 'When both the next single and the album went to number one, I was in a state of shock.'"

Fran moaned, "Wish I could be in that kind of state of shock. Instead of this!" She used her hands to make a sweeping gesture that included the awful brown stain.

Happy couldn't resist staring at her tiny hands. Happy thought, "Ah don't know hows Ah c'n be so wicked c'nsiderin' Fran's a friend t'mull ovuh any idea she might be the killuh, but Ah cain't help thet. Except now Ah've looked real good at them, Ah c'n see how huh hands be too small fo' stranglin' Carla. A chicken, mebbe. Not a grown woman."

Fran washed away Happy's suspicious thoughts as expertly as a channel swimmer hits waves. She said, "I'm concerned I'm going to lose Heidi as a partner. There's been no offers for us to cut another record."

Ellie didn't delay asking, "Has Heidi any back-up money? How will she pay her expenses with no cash coming in?"

"Can't imagine how. Carla never paid her much. Understudies don't get on the gravy train. I shared our record money. Don't know how long that will last her."

Happy said, "Ah b'lieves as Ah saw somethin' writ in a noospapuh thet Heidi's bin considered fo' *Daisy Mae*. Not Sybil's starrin' role. But as 'nuthuh such hillbilly. She'll have t'learn the lingo. Talks too fancy raght now."

Fran agreed. "Yes. I read that too. I need her, God knows. But if she's in dire straits, Happy maybe you should have a word with Sybil to help her get in the cast."

Happy drank up what remained in the Diet Cola bottle. She said to herself, "With all the millions Fran has, Ah'd think she'd help out Heidi."

Ellie said, "Is there no one you know of who could replace Heidi to make up your duo?"

Fran blushed, and sheepishly muttered, "I have been trying out some other sopranos. Sybil's understudy has a super voice. She's an Australian, and would be easier to work with than Heidi. Her name's Filipa Grant. Very pretty, her face would complement mine on an album's cover. She's on her way to my flat right now. I wanted to talk to you two first. Learn what you think."

"Does her voice blend well with yours? That's prima," Ellie said. "Yes. Better than Heidi's, for sure."

Happy chimed in, while collecting her handbag and gloves. "If Heidi gets thet job in *Daisy Mae*, Ah c'n coach her in how to speak Kentucky-lahke. We'll all be bettuh off. You, Fran, with this Filipa as your duet partner. And Heidi singin' in a honest-to-God music'l com'dy. Then, hopefully, Ah gits me a payin' student if Heidi hires me to teach her."

Looking brighter, Fran saw us to her door which had had the broken lock, now repaired. On the hall table was a lipstick. Fran outlined her lips, improving her image considerably.

Happy hugged Fran and invited her to come to houseguest in our Epsom cottage. "Y'all c'n stay long as y'all lahke. But don't need bring no likker. Rick keeps plenty in the cupbo'd."

Fran nodded her thanks, although she guessed "no likker" contained a warning not to bring cocaine. "Soon. I'll be down with you soon." Her glance fell on the bowl of cocaine in her living room. Fran shuddered. She wondered if she could stand three days without a line.

Outside, going down the stairs to the street, Ellie complained to Happy, "You've forgotten all you ever learned in your Elocution Lessons. Really, you must try harder. No more double negatives, Happy! Please!"

Neither woman wanted to comment on their visit to Fran. Happy hailed a taxi, keeping her thoughts to herself.

CHAPTER 3

F ran turned up on our doorstep for our Twelfth Night party. Her appearance had totally changed. Fran wore a couture suit under a mink coat. Her handbag was Gucci, her shoes Jimmy Choo. Cosmetics of various kinds enhanced her skin, eyes, and mouth.

Next to Fran's Louis Vuitton luggage stood a tall, stunning blonde.

Younger than Fran, barely out of her teens, this girl brought no luggage.

Happy noted the no-luggage with relief. She didn't want two house guests. Their cottage could never house two prima-donnas. And it was very apparent from the start that this younger woman was a prima-donna.

"Meet Filipa Grant, my new singing partner," Fran chirped. "We signed our contracts this morning. Now that Heidi got that job in *Daisy Mae*, no problem."

But there were problems in our cottage. Several. From chirping on arrival, Fran fell into a disagreeable humor within minutes. I'd offered to show the two women our colts. We'd headed for my stables.

The afternoon was glorious. The weather that had been threatening had undergone a miracle into summer breezes and bright sunshine. I removed my jacket and continued down the manure-strewn path in my shirtsleeves. Filipa Grant picked her away around the horses' messes as if she'd never been in the countryside before. She grumbled, she whispered complaints at Fran's side.

What did she have to complain about? When her whispers grew louder, I heard her say, "I can't believe I came all the way to Epsom just to walk through manure." After reaching my tidy yard Filipa put up her nose at colt after colt as my grooms brought them out and put them through their paces. If I'd had any illusions that this young singer would become one of my owners, I could forget them.

She spat, "If I ever have enough spare money to buy a racehorse, you can be very sure I'll send him to Harold East to train."

Harold East! His name is anathema in my establishment. His horses had bumped mine in any number of races, his stable jockey had twice whipped mine in the face.

I said nothing. But soon Fran also had plenty to grumble about. Filipa's nastiness proved highly contagious. Fran swore, "Shit, I never thought the day would come when I hated the sight of my filly. Poor Carla, maybe it's lucky she never saw how her colt has turned out. No class. No class at all."

I wondered on what Fran based her opinion. She'd shown little knowledge of a horse's conformation. Her expertise was in the realm of microphones, hand-held or clipped to her clothes.

Both Sweet Song and Home Alone had never looked better. Their coats shone, their eyes were alight, their ears pricked and they neighed joyfully savoring the pre-spring sunshine.

Fran neglected to tip the grooms, and tried to forego giving carrots to her two racehorses. On the latter, I insisted. I knew the colt and the filly wouldn't forget they'd been given no treats by their owner.

Back at our cottage, Happy tried to improve the atmosphere by providing a surprisingly adequate tea. Her teas were usually on the very poor side. In her Kentucky home, I believe moonshine liquor took precedence over tea.

"Where's the whiskey?" demanded Filipa..

Fran echoed, "Yes. Whiskey. Too damned hot for tea."

Happy's elaborate tea would have gone to waste. Only a surprise appearance by Ellie put paid to that. Ellie sat down to our battered refectory-style table to munch through all the scones and pasties, savoring each and complimenting Happy as she did.

To Fran, Ellie said, "So, all's well that ended well as regards you having the right singing partner."

That comment brought out a smile. Fran, chirping again, said, "Filipa's going to reverse all the bad reviews I've been getting. And even better, she'll get sales up. For me, that's even more important."

Filipa put paid to that hope. Waiting for the taxi to take her back to London, she said, "I've got to go back to Australia, soon as this album's ready. I've a sick baby at home in Melbourne."

When our local taxi collected Filipa and we did the wave-off thing to watch the vehicle slide over the manure down our lane, I said to Fran, "We've got this party on for later. I hope that won't disturb you if you came for a rest. But we need to entertain our neighbors. We've been here about a year now, and we're still considered the 'new arrivals.'"

Happy laughed. "Ah don't mahnd if they's feelin' lahke we's new. In pawhts o' Kentucky, folks as is in a house a hundred yeahs is thought t'be new by the folks what's families bin theah two hundred yeahs." Happy hadn't lost her good humor when Filipa had been rude about our horses. Somehow Happy accepted the girl's bad manners when she heard there was a sick baby alone back in Australia.

I hustled Fran to our spare bedroom. I felt slightly embarrassed when I opened the armoire and saw my Dad's corduroy trousers airing there, but Fran simply shrugged and put her couture clothes on the hangers without a word.

Much as I admire my Happy as a jockey and a mother, I didn't rely on her non-existent culinary talents to provide a proper Twelfth Night feast for our snobbish neighbors. And, in addition to them, I had dared to add some of my owners to the guest list. Costly as the decision was, making a real dent in our budget, I'd hired a catering firm to do the job.

Called The Right People, it turned out to be an all-male group. Not all the males were obviously male, some arrived wearing high heels and lipstick. They unloaded a high-end van, carrying in to our very modest kitchen elegant copper pans and antique serving platters.

These snooty caterers put up their collective noses at the meager facilities in our tiny kitchen. Nevertheless, delicious smells began emerging from the pantry door.

I found Fran fiddling with the knobs of our TV, probing to find the channel for the evening news.

She complained, "I never hear any mention now about Carla's murder. It's ignored. Seems like it's a stale item."

I helped her find BBC1. "Yes. After the inquest turned up nothing new, even the police seem resigned to believing it was a burglary gone wrong."

"Wrong? Not for the burglar. He's got her jewelry, hasn't he? None of it's turned up. Probably in some Arab country by now, the diamonds reset in geometric designs."

A newscaster appeared on the screen. A different face than usually heralded all of the world's current disasters. His most important announcement was that he'd replaced the newscaster of the past three years. Carla's death didn't get even a postscript. He ended by inviting his viewers to go to Dubai in late March for the big prize races there.

I said hesitatingly, "Think about that, Fran. Are you interested in going to Dubai?"

"Can't. I haven't got a two-year-old to run. Both horses are yearlings." "No. As of January First all horses are one year older, no matter when foaled. Yearlings last week are now two-year-olds."

"You mean to tell me all colts and fillies are judged as of the same age?" "Those, in the Northern Hemisphere, are a year older, yes. But that doesn't mean all will run as if foaled simultaneously. Of course not. That's why we speak of late foals, early foals, etc. Sweet Song was foaled in January 2006, so she'll be very advanced. Home Alone, foaled last July, will not be. From what I've seen of her action, I believe Sweet Song could possibly win a maiden in Dubai."

"Don't you hate that place after your wife was abducted there last year?" My eyebrows knitted. I guessed that Fran was a regular devotee of the evening news and had followed Happy's abduction ordeal as had hundreds of thousands of other viewers.

I groaned. "It was terrible for Happy. But she remembers the joy of welcoming our baby daughter there. In a clean, up-to-date hospital. State of the art equipment."

"She had a second C-section," Fran spat out, as if she envied Happy.

"Yes. And thank God the hospital's located within minutes of the Nad Al Sheba racetrack. Built to service injured jockeys. Happy was over nine months pregnant when she was sequestered, but because she'd been a jockey she was able to escape her second set of abductors by grabbing a nag and rode it to the racetrack. The ride caused her water to burst. I believe you know the rest of the story. No, I don't hold any grudge against Dubai. I'm ready to return to race my string there."

"I'll think about sending Sweet Song."

"Can't think about it too long. She'll have to be entered in the right race."

"Doesn't anybody consider what I'm going through? I have to think about this, I have to think about that. I'll go crazy," Fran whined. "I can't take much more."

Happy entered the hall. She placed a warm arm around Fran's shoulders. "Ah's heard thet. We cares. We do. We wants t'help."

"Help? How? Will you read all my filthy e-mails and the disgusting letters that come every day from sickos? Necrophiliacs who say they want Carla's body to do horrible things?"

I heard guests arriving up the driveway. Happy changed her expression to take on a wide grin like a chatelaine ready to greet tourists.

To Fran, she whispered, "You needs a stiff drink. Ah'll give yo' some o' mah Pappy's special moonshine Ah's brought from Kentucky."

Happy and I threw open our front door and eased in Col. Flyte, my most irascible owner. Neither of us guessed from his party manner that he intended to have a damned good dinner and then spring on us the news he was quitting my yard.

Behind difficult Col. Flyte came dear Ellie, escorted by the heir to the family earldom, Jeremy Grace. Last November both flew to Dubai to help me try to find Happy after her abduction—real 'friends in need who were friends indeed.'

Another surprise during the evening was the amount of attention Jeremy proceeded to douse over Fran, like a schoolboy who had a crush on his music teacher. He never stopped touching either her hand, her elbow, or her shoulders talking her up big time. I wouldn't have judged Jeremy as the type of aristocrat who falls for a star in the entertainment world. That galaxy was so far removed from his own quiet hearth, surrounded as he is by family portraits and heirloom silver.

Fran perked up considerably. She reminded me of a Labrador we'd had. That labrador dragged his rear legs and seemed ready to die until a female lab was purchased by a neighbor. When the female went into heat, there was no more dragging his legs by our fellow. This situation was in reverse, except that after the initial three hours of Jeremy's wooing, Fran seemed to be in heat.

I'd read somewhere that Fran never sang on her own. She was strictly a duet star. But that Twelfth Night, Fran sang. And sang. And sang. There was no stopping her.

Maybe it was Pappy's Kentucky moonshine that prompted her. Fran warbled the old Steven Foster favorites, "Swanee River", and "Jeannie With the Light Brown Hair," combining that repertoire with James Blunt's "You're Beautiful." Happy accompanied her on an old guitar, strumming it like a medieval troubadour.

Our snobbish neighbors loved the music. They ate every morsel provided by The Right People, and didn't leave for home until every drop of booze had vanished down their gullets. My kind owners Captain and Mrs. Ainsley ate their fair share of what was on offer, and also hit Pappy's moonshine. I'd never seen either Ainsley tipsy before, but that night they excelled themselves in that department so much that I asked Jeremy to drive them home. They'd have been breathalized for sure, and maybe lost their licenses, no matter who was at the wheel.

Jeremy seemed abashed at having to leave in order to give the Ainsleys a safe journey. He obviously didn't want to part from Fran, not a minute too early. He asked her, "Will I see you tomorrow? The local hunt may come this way. I'm cubbying. But whether or not the hounds wheel us this way, I'll be on the doorstep if you're willing."

Fran, still high on moonshine, quoted Dickins. " 'Barcus is willin'.''

Dear Happy, pleased that her party had turned out exceedingly well, hurried upstairs to get her purse to pay The Right People. She was still upstairs trying to find where she'd hidden her money, when Col. Flyte dropped his nasty news. "I'll be sending for Broadback in the morning. He's going to Harold East's yard."

Happy couldn't fathom the reason why I looked so dour. We saw Fran to her room, turned out the lights downstairs, and doused the fire in the hearth. Then I took Happy in my arms for comfort. I needed the feel of her to help me through the pain of losing Broadback. I sighed. "Happy, we've lost Flyte. Permanently. He's sending Broadback to East's yard."

We held on to each other like Hansel and Gretel lost in the woods. Only Fran had come out of the evening with a plus.

CHAPTER 4

Good to his word, Jeremy appeared in his hunting togs early the next morning. He arrived mounted on a superb gray hunter that I judged could be made into a champion steeplechaser.

Jeremy's tan-topped-boots, velvet cap, finely tailored pink jacket and tight jodhpurs really sent Fran into orbit.

She astonished me by appearing at dawn in a traditional tweed skirt, twin set and pearls. Her makeup was demure. Her hair arranged in a county style that was severe yet flattering. What a transformation! Was I seeing the next Countess?

Fran certainly thought so. She took on airs, treating us with *noblesse oblige*. When I returned from early morning stables Fran said grandly, "I don't suppose you have time with all your other interests to follow the threat to hunting!"

"Actually, I have. In fact I was part of the hunting enthusiasts group who protested in front of Parliament, and were beaten away by Blair's police with night sticks. I slipped from their onslaught and cut my cheek. See, scar?"

Fran inspected my scar. She grunted. "I'll be going back to my apartment tonight. After Jeremy's evening visit."

The name Jeremy hung in the air like the final note of a violinist's dirge. It hit Ellie in the face as she appeared in our kitchen, prepared for one of Happy's fry-ups. Dear Ellie's gentle mouth, usually stretched into a half-moon smile, now turned downwards. She didn't take her usual place at our kitchen table, preferring like a boxer under pressure to keep to a corner. "You're seeing Jeremy this evening?"

"Yes, yes. I certainly am. And he's coming up to London day after tomorrow when there's no cubbying. He's taking me to the Dorchester. I sang with Carla there once, long ago. Before we got our platinum."

Ellie said nothing. But her thundercloud expression spoke volumes.

I busied myself sorting the leftovers from last night's feast. I chose Chilean melon and Hawaiian pineapple slices for my breakfast, not being partial to Happy's Kentucky fry-ups.

Happy galloped into the unspoken row between Ellie and Fran. "Ah'll be goin' up tomorrow too. Heidi has hired me t'tutor huh in Kentucky talk."

"If you don't stay too long, you can come and call on me first thing. Jeremy's arriving at seven."

As if the Ice-Age had returned, Ellie bit out, "I'll come too."

The following morning all three went up to London with their own projects foremost. Fran intended to snare Jeremy. Happy wanted to secure a steady job with Heidi. Ellie was determined to end any budding romance between a singer and her family's future Earl.

Left alone with my children, the nanny-housekeeper and my horses the estate seemed almost too quiet. That, of course, is a manner of speaking when two hearty infants let go with their lungs every so often. But all in all it was a happy day for me, seeing my infants and my horses in good health and progressing in their learning cycles.

It wasn't such a good day for Happy. She and Ellie took the train again, and a taxi to Fran's Chelsea digs. This time they knew which name slot's push button to buzz. The lobby door opened, they went in, climbed the stairs to the Third Floor, and found Fran on the threshold of her renovated apartment. Everywhere there were pre-Spring flowers. She'd sprayed additional scent from Harrods housewares. New, fresh pillows were scattered in armchairs and on the imposing sofa.

Wherever space allowed, Fran had added chic Elsie de Wolfe-style pillows with their tangy remarks. "Never miss out on a good thing," "Love only comes once," "Have sex as often as you like it," "Have a heart," and such like.

Wordlessly, Ellie strode around the main room reading each and every legend. Her facial expression never stopped thundering until she took in the bowl of cocaine still in its allotted place, its contents considerably less than when they had visited here earlier. Now Ellie's eyes threw bolts like tornados.

Still without a word Ellie pointed out the cocaine to Happy, while Fran was occupying herself preparing drinks at her bar.

Ellie prodded Happy's elbow. They exchanged meaningful glances. While Fran served up diet colas, Happy said, "Dear Fran, Ah thinks it'd be wise-like if'n yo'd flush thet cocaine powduh down the terlet. Jeremy shouldn't see thet."

"Have you any idea what cocaine costs? 'Down the toilet?' I might give it to my agent to flog around to his other clients. But, throw it away? It would be like flushing gold dust."

Happy considered warning Fran that should she 'flog' her cocaine, she would be committing a serious crime. In addition to 'singing star' the word 'Drug Dealer' would be added to her name. Drug dealing could cost years in prison . . But why did Fran count what she'd lose by flushing? Fran was a multi-millionaire. Why did she always hog her shillings? Happy knew that Fran had neither tipped the grooms nor the nanny-housekeeper after her Epsom visit. Sitting in Fran's mother's apartment, Happy knew that Fran had not suffered from a deprived childhood. What was it with her?

Like the proverbial Dutch boy, Ellie put a finger in the conversation "dike" stopping possible wordage. Briefly, she said, "Let's go, Happy dear. You need to be on time for Heidi. I have shopping to do."

They didn't drink the Diet Colas Fran had served. They had nothing more to say after her refusal to flush her cocaine.

Happy needn't have hurried to her appointment with Heidi. Her student had flown. A curt note greeted Happy, "Forget any tutoring." Poor Happy's expensive journey to and from London hadn't paid off.

Ellie's trip was far more rewarding. After shopping, she went to the Dorchester and found Jeremy waiting early for Fran's appearance. Ellie knew her cousin would be ahead of time, he often was.

He ordered a White Lady for Ellie, and she told him about Fran's cocaine habit. He said, "I'll help her quit. It can be done. You know the old saying, 'Love Conquers All.'"

"No. Maybe Fran would quit for a while. Go to the Priory or some place where they specialize in addictions. But the cocaine habit always comes back. Even if the customer doesn't want to buy it, the dealer makes certain he doesn't lose business. I've read about all kinds of tricks the drug dealers play to restart a habit."

She'd silenced poor Jeremy. Conflicting emotions played over his gentle face, until finally he took Ellie's outstretched hands, and said, "I want healthy children. I'm sorry for Fran. She sings so beautifully and is such fun. But I do want healthy children. I've a friend who lost the septum of his nose, sniffing line after line. He told me that raw cocaine is processed with sulfuric acid. It eats the nose, it can eat the brain. He's in a mental hospital now." Jeremy sighed deeply. "I suppose the best thing is to leave a note of apology to Fran for standing her up. We'll take the train home together."

CHAPTER 5

Fran didn't take well to being dumped. The next weekend, high on cocaine, she came raging down to our stables and threatened to sell both horses, or send them to Harold East's yard. Her addiction was very apparent. Mood swings came and went according to whether she'd secretly taken a line.

This visit, she arrived with a stash of dealers' envelopes. If Fran didn't have her line every few hours, her language grew lethal "I'm leaving you. Take my horses and go to East." Or, "I'll tell everyone in the Rap World you're a flop as a Trainer."

I didn't want to lose Fran as an owner. Her two horses were superb. And I could commiserate with her over an addiction. Wasn't I addicted to Happy? I tried calming Fran. I didn't press her to take yet another line, but I tried almost everything else. I even suggested we go next door and call on Jeremy.

"That son of a bitch? Who needs him! I've got a real guy. He plays the sax in a band I use. His name's Goofy Howe, and I adore him."

Lucky she left when she did. The weather changed. From mock-Spring our yard fell into deep winter. In Britain, much of the climate depends on the prevailing winds. When they come from Africa, buds sprout too early on trees. When the winds come from the arctic, sleet and snow kill the buds, which is horrible. Like when a neighbor's preschool child is killed by a car, we mourned our buds. The manure strewn driveway became covered with thick snow which developed an ice cover. When old cars dripped their oil into the road, we got black ice. Lethal. I tried to go into town for baby food, but my pick-up was caught by the black ice and rotated as if on a record player.

The cold hit my horses. An epidemic of coughing grabbed the two-year-olds. I decided to separate my older string from them. I fitted out an old hay barn with individual stalls, and had an electrician put a lit bulb in each to add warmth.

With the arctic weather reaching into every nook of our home, the central heating couldn't cope. Happy and the children huddled near the hearth, with Mrs. Rea, our housekeeper, complaining she couldn't get near enough.

I spent most of my time working on the yard's books. In late January it was almost too tardy to enter some of our prime movers into the right races. I went to the stables to check on our two-year-olds' temperatures and see that they took their medicine.

I went into the hay barn to supervise the feeding and grooming of our three-year-olds. With no grass available to them, we had to add more hay to their menu of oats.

My generous Canadian owner, Hal Murphy sent a crate of honey from Harrods for his Arrow. "Our grooms c'n enjoy that honey," Happy chortled. "They'll never give the honey to the hosses."

Arrow didn't cause me any concern. He was in prime condition. I was more anxious for Feathers.

Many a filly when she turns three becomes broody. Not Feathers, she didn't want a stallion, she wanted to race. Like the great Dahlia, who won some of the racing world's best prizes at five, Feathers whinnied with desire to get back on to the gallops. But I couldn't risk it. With so much ice on top of the snow, she could easily break a leg. I drove her to a covered exercise building where she could gallop, but it was really too small for her needs. She tugged at her reins, and once reared up against them until I feared she'd snap her neck as had my childhood's pet filly, Colonel's Lady.

It was on the first show of improvement in the weather that we had another surprise visit from Fran.

Instead of Goofy, she brought Heidi Thomas, her dead twin's ex-understudy, who was now a singing star almost on a par in *Daisy Mae* with Sybil.

Happy and I had never met Heidi. Happy had hoped to tutor her in Kentucky-talk but was cancelled out before she had a chance to strut her stuff. Happy and Heidi had spoken by telephone, but there had been no sighting of this shooting star who was gaining precedence over other members of the *Daisy Mae* cast, a/k/a *Hogtown II*.

Fran wasn't high on cocaine. She arrived sporting sedate county-correct clothes, a tweed coat with matching skirt and cashmere sweater. "I never wear jewelry, except the occasional string of fake pearls," she explained the lack of bling. "Poor Carla, she was the one who loved diamonds. But in her case they certainly weren't 'a girl's best friend.'"

Heidi nodded, like a college professor listening to a student's thesis. Heidi appeared in what was generally thought of as a Hollywood-style outfit, fur-trimmed parka over sequin studded wide trousers. The trousers would have been suitable in a nightclub for a star wooing an audience, but hardly suitable for a walk down our manure-strewn lane.

Everything about Heidi was extra-large. The parka ballooned. Her trousers swirled like a concubine's in a harem. Her hair was over-teased. Her hands were huge. Her feet, almost hidden by those immense trousers, peeked out of size 10 boots. Was her soprano voice as over-powering? I wondered about this amazon.

It seemed odd that Carla had chosen such a larger-than-life understudy! I remembered her as a very gentle person.

In her first words to us, Heidi made it clear that she had no intention to be a friend. "Oh, hello, you're the dreadful Rick. You're the hillbilly, Happy. And this is where Fran hangs out? I'd expected things to be a lot better than this."

Like Filipa before her, she disdained our home, the yard's horses, and their facilities. She didn't turn her nose up at our booze. She tasted Pappy's moonshine, my best whiskey, and the champagne left over from our Twelfth Night party. No favorable comments, just glass after glass downed.

Heidi didn't get tipsy. Like everything else about Heidi, her gut must have been over-sized because she could certainly hold her liquor.

She was over-sexed, too. I can vouch for that because from her first appearance in our home, she ran her big fingers up my neck and then down toward my nether regions, whether Happy was in the room or not.

"Ah thinks we'd best git yo' both safely up t'town," voiced a very concerned Happy. She'd seen that type of behavior before when my fellow Trainer, Hassan, had introduced sultry Sirena to our hearth in 2007. Happy jingled our car keys. "Ah'll do the drivin' not to worry Rick. He's needed down in the stables."

Usually, we sent our guests to their homes by train. Happy had no intention of leaving Heidi to her wiles a minute longer.

A frantic knocking at our front door interrupted Happy's plan. It was Tom, my head groom, at the door. "Mister Rick, somethin' awful's happened. Feathers has disappeared."

"Calm down, Tom. There will be a logical explanation. Maybe Burt has taken her out for a gallop, now the weather's marginally better."

"No, Sir. T'was Bert who found the little lady'd gone missing." Tom accepted a glass of whiskey from Happy and downed it in three gulps. "Her bridle's gone. Favorite saddle too. She's been kidnapped."

CHAPTER 6

The Epsom police were not too interested in Feathers' disappearance. After my 999 telephone call I was made to go in person to the police station and give a deposition.

No patrol cars went zooming out on to the local highways to see if they could spot our filly. It was left to Tom and me to scour the countryside. We didn't find Feathers. With night approaching, we had to give up our search.

My home seemed empty without Happy cooing to our children. Mrs. Rea produced an awful English supper of over-cooked lamb with greasy sauce, tasteless boiled potatoes and gray spinach. Even Kentucky fried chicken would have been better.

Happy telephoned from London to ask if Feathers had been located, gasping with worry like a mother whose child has gone missing

She said, "Ah wasn't told nothin' by Feathers thet she meant t'take off. Y'all knows she'd a' tole me if'n that were huh idea. She's done bin stolen bah a rustler."

I knew Happy talked to our horses. I believed they communicated with her. I said, "I suppose you're right."

Happy didn't waste time in London. She sped back to Epsom, and – as I know how Happy drives—I'll bet that most of the time she was on the wrong side of the road, left-handed, Kentucky-side. Coming through our front door, Happy was already shouting to me what we could do to retrieve Feathers.

"Git on to our CNN friend, Virgo. Tell him t'broadcast t'the whole world thet our Feathers done bin stolen."

I recognized the validity of her suggestion. Within seconds I was on the blower to Virgo, who was grateful for the story because this end of January was bereft of news, except for the daily suicide bombings in Iraq.

Virgo saw the PR possibilities right away. "This story's worth a mint. Your filly will be world-famous within the next hour. I guarantee it. She won't need to win the Oaks to be wooed for breeding." His voice lowered. "You are certain you didn't set up this horse hi-jack yourself?"

"Damn you, Virgo. Get serious. She's American-bred, that will sell the story to your USA viewers. She has Northern Dancer blood, that will claw into the brains of your Canadians. Became a three-year-old just this month. A baby, still. Gentle. Friendly. Too friendly, it seems. Letting herself be towed away! A winner, as a two-year-old. We'd planned to send her to Dubai in March, expecting her to win a big purse there."

"E-mail me her breeding. And a recent photograph, if you have one," Virgo said. "I'm running to the office. It's eleven p.m. in Atlanta, at our headquarters, and I might just make the tail end of the eleven o'clock news there."

He did. Happy and I sat in front of the TV as if we were in our saddles racing for the Finish line. Virgo delivered just as he'd promised. There on the TV screen was the photograph I'd taken only days earlier of our Feathers resplendent in the snow. And then her fantastic breeding rolled, with emphasis mentioned of her Northern Dancer connection.

The phone rang. It was Jeremy Grace on the blower. "Hello, Jeremy, I guess you saw the CNN news."

"Yes. But that's not why I'm calling. Rick, my grey hunter has been stolen!"

"That very valuable gray?"

"That's right. So it's not an isolated incident regarding Feathers. Nor has it anything to do with enmity against you, or Feathers' owner. There's someone, or a gang, out in our line of country, who knows the price of these horses. I swear we'll hear about more robberies by morning." He rang off. Poor Jeremy was certain to go out on the same highways where

Tom and I had ventured, and with the same result. Worse for him, being in the stygian night, without the brilliant sunset that had accompanied our search.

Ellie telephoned next. She'd watched CNN, and also heard from Jeremy. "Rick! What can we do?"

"Plenty. First things first, though. I must do the painful thing, and telephone my Canadian owner. Hal Murphy has been so good to me, and now he's got this problem with Feathers. Remember how he reacted when Happy was abducted? I'm certain he'll get into full swing in the morning and send private detectives and who knows what to solve this situation."

The next morning dawned as one of the most lyrical I could remember. The sky was a perfect blue dome, sunlight streaking through the boughs of trees, turning their last mantle of snow into a decoration like diamond-encrusted ermine. Birds, returning from their winter quarters in Africa, perched on budding bushes. I looked out my window and met eye to eye with a robin. He looked at me and I blinked at him. We were one in a magnificent universe of colleagues sharing this scintillating weather.

Reluctantly I parted from my friendly robin to check my e-mails.

What came next was such a contrast from the idyllic moment I'd shared with that robin. In my computer were too many e-mails to read them all. There were condolences for my new ordeal, but there were hate messages too, condemning me for training horses to race, when they should "be allowed to roam free" or some such. Nothing from Hal Murphy.

I tried to telephone him and got his answering machine. I heard the customary "Please call later." Where was he? And then I recalled he'd alerted me that he was going shooting into the wilds of the Canadian Rockies. Did that mean I couldn't reach him for a week or more? Please God, help me on this!

It was time for early morning stables. Generally I'd have welcomed this daily job with the enthusiasm of a priest saying Mass. But today, it was with a very heavy heart that I joined my two grooms to lead out our reduced string. Without Feathers to dazzle us with her outstanding gallops, the beauty of the morning was definitely soured.

Back in my kitchen, joining Happy for a breakfast of eggs and bacon, I could barely manage to eat a forkful of the greasy mess. The telephone rang constantly. Happy and I decided to leave it on the answering mode.

We hadn't the heart to listen to hate calls today, and we both knew they'd swarm in. We could screen the calls on the machine to listen to any that might promise help.

There weren't many of those. I was still lingering over my coffee when Ellie appeared at our door. "I couldn't get through on the phone. I decided to come and sit with you, hoping we can come up with some ideas to end this situation. I'm so VERY sorry about Feathers!"

Dear Ellie, she never mentioned her cousin Jeremy's prize gray hunter. It was OUR filly she'd come to sympathize with us about.

"Hal Murphy proved to be unreachable. I think I should hire private detectives on his behalf."

"Definitely. I know just the firm. Try Pete Lagger, terrible name, good heart." Ellie borrowed our much thumbed telephone directory and located his number. Too early. No answer. Again we made use of an answering machine, and left a message.

Happy had turned very quiet. I knew she was suffering a personal loss, like an auntie who mourns a favorite niece. She couldn't eat her bacon and eggs, her cast-iron stomach could handle the grease but her emotions wouldn't permit swallowing. I took her shoulders and squeezed them tenderly. She looked up and met my eyes, hers brimming with tears. We shook our heads, wordlessly.

Ellie had sat down in front of my computer and was reading the e-mails. "Maybe we should take up this offer, sent yesterday," she said more brightly. "It's from Sybil Sykes, inviting us to see *Daisy Mae, Hogtown Two* tomorrow night. It says she'd left tickets for the three of us at the theatre's Box Office. What do you say? Shall we take a break and go to London?"

To my surprise, Happy agreed. "Yes'm. Ah'm all fo' thet. Mebbe we c'd stop in t'the Jockey Club on Portman Square and enlist its help, befo'e we goes to the the-a-tuh."

Wonderful Happy! She'd come up trumps with a solid idea. I went to the computer, and made use of e-mail to accept the offer of tickets. I also sent an e-mail to the Jockey Club, although it was with mixed feelings, loath to do the wrong thing.

All day long we kept confined to the house, wasting the glorious weather outside. We reached Pete Lagger, I hired him, and gave all of Feathers' specifications: Height, seventeen hands, color chestnut brown, long neck, short ears, white socks on her forelegs. Most importantly, I added the numbers tattooed on her upper lip. I faxed a photo of her.

When it was time for evening stables, I was truly ready for them, although I felt a sharp pang in my heart when passing Feathers' empty stall.

Neither Happy nor I slept that night. We cradled each other in each other's arms. Later, I pressed my knees into her back for the position that usually brought slumber. Nothing helped. Not even an attempt at sex, that failed not for lack of need but because we were both suffering too much over Feathers.

The next morning there was no robin at my window. The skies had returned to their usual misty gray, and after early stables we packed for London.

Ellie collected us in her family's vintage Rolls, a 1956 Silver Cloud, its tired upholstery the original green leather and its pristine sparkle-added color still a forceful red.

I felt grateful for that red color when we found ourselves caught in dense fog. The lights of a 1956 Rolls didn't pierce the pea-souper as well as collagen lamps on a modern Volvo could, so we had a near miss with one. The Volvo's owner called out, "Motherfuckers," but didn't summon the police after we pronged his new vehicle. His reason? Nefarious, no doubt.

Ellie had neglected to call ahead for a number that would gain us legal entry into Mayor Ken Livingston's fee-paying Central London, but she shrugged and said, "It's Mater's car, and she'll pay the fine gladly if this visit to London helps find Feathers."

Somehow we reached London, and by steering for Selfridge's Department Store, a target Ellie knew well, we managed to find Portman Square. I did what I thought right, spoke to authorities there, and later we headed for the theatre district. Bright lights cut the fog, and we parked in a very expensive NCP lot, to gain easy access to Chinatown. Customarily I loved going under its light-festooned Chinese archway to prowl its narrow streets to select one from its myriad restaurants. Today we were weren't in a laughing mood. We settled for the Mah Jong Restaurant that featured spits roasting ducks in its window. We ate in silence. The food was tasty, but none of us had a welcoming palate.

Daisy Mae was wonderful. An enthusiastic audience—a full house— applauded passionately each individual song. The acoustics of its

Victorian-era theater were fabulous. Sybil's acting prowess and Kentucky-speak were equaled by her crystal voice. Less professional was Heidi's.

"She ain't lahke no Kentucky-gal," Happy whispered disgustedly. "Heidi should 'a took mah lessons. Walks wrong. Uses huh hands too much. 'N what she thinks she's doin' wigglin' huh behind? She ain't supposed t'be the town whoor."

Heidi's voice was big. Like all of her, and she used it to its full potential. I said, *sotto voce*, "Heidi's huge soprano must have drowned out Fran's contralto. No wonder they came to the parting of ways."

There were flowers thrown at Sybil, Heidi, and the girl who played the town "whoor" character, Munchie Young. Six curtain calls. They received an avalanche of applause, and the ovation continued until the curtain came down with finality.

Ellie said, "We've been invited to go backstage. We should go to the stage door and we'll be let in."

A stream of chorus girls and boy dancers, thrusting through the back alley, impeded a prompt entry for us. We lingered watching them, as they laughed with relief that another successful performance had ended well, flirting among themselves, and saw them head for a favorite pub. I was startled to see how poverty-stricken they looked. Their clothes were past tired, their shoes very worn. They smelled as if they could use fresh bars of soap. This was no exodus of debutantes or Eton students. I wondered at the disparity between the fees London musicals pay a star, and the pittance for the members of a chorus.

Eventually, when the flood of performers and musicians eased and we could gain admittance, we passed through the Stage Door area to inquire the way to Sybil's dressing room. We were led there by her dresser, a gray-haired dour-mouthed cripple who looked pained that there might be a delay for her to go home.

"I'll knock," she said plaintively, in a hurry now to get rid of unwanted visitors. "Miss Sybil don't like for to be seen in grease paint 'n no clothes on."

No response.

She knocked again.

Still, nothing.

Happy, her hackles rising, slowly prodded open the dressing room door.

Sybil lay on the floor, dead.

The silk belt of her Chinese negligée was tight around her neck. She'd been strangled. Her famous Hollywood looks were gone. In their place was a wizened old hag's. Like the pseudo-Tibetans, in the film "Lost Horizon," she had aged thirty years.

Ellie said, "Call 999. Is there a phone in here? No? Find one."

Happy unwound the silk belt and placed her cheek against the bloated, blackened cheek that only minutes before had been pink with appreciation for applause garnered. Happy's tears smeared Sybil's greasepaint. In between gasps, she moaned, "Ah remembuhs so well thet fust tahme Ah seen huh, theah in the Hotel Carlyle in Noo Yahk. So beautiful!"

The dresser whined, "What's to become of me? I'll have no job. That nasty Heidi won't have me, calls me an ugly cripple."

I had no comforting words for the dresser. I gave her a hefty tip, the amount the dresser might have garnered at Easter or Christmas from Sybil, had she remained alive.

Privately, and ashamed as I am to admit this, I wondered what was to become of Sybil's three two-year-olds! Who were her heirs? I knew she'd been married three times, but never had any children. She never mentioned a sister or brother. Her parents were probably dead, or they'd have traveled to London to see her star in *Daisy Mae*. No family had come. Sybil's bloodstock could remain in my yard and run in the name of The Estate of the late Sybil Sykes. But would they be permitted to by any heirs?

I thought, "That makes four of my American-breds out of commission. Poor Sybil, dead, just when her filly looked so promising that I've entered her to run in Dubai."

Happy spoke up. She was very specific. She asked the crippled dresser, "If'n Miss Sybil was known to not lahke stranguhs see huh in greasepaint, how come she'd opened huh do'r earlier, to huh killuh?"

Ellie said, "Please answer that. You made so much fuss when we wanted to come in. Had to knock. Had to call in."

Sybil's skinny dresser, limping in an exaggerated way, playing for sympathy so as not to lose her last train home, whined, "She wouldn't let no stranguh in, I swear to that."

The police arrived. A sketch was made of Sybil's position on the floor. Her body was placed in what looked like an over-sized garbage bag, and removed.

Poor Sybil, I thought again.

All of us present were told not to leave. A Mayfair Police Station Detective Sergeant arrived. He barked various orders. When he heard that my Happy had removed the silk belt from around Sybil's neck, he gave her a verbal thrashing, clocking up her misdemeanors, endangering the search for DNA and such.

Happy spoke up. "Ah did what Ah thought was propuh. Sybil was a good friend, 'n had been a guest in mah home. Ah couldn't leave huh with that silk belt chokin' huh."

Mayfair Police are much tougher than Chelsea's. But then they had no reason to consider this murder a random crime. Nothing had been stolen. Sybil Sykes was murdered for a reason, and this narrow-eyed Sergeant was very determined to find out why. He threw his weight around some more, giving me a once-over, and then collected his ammunition to shoot it at Happy. He demanded to know what she was doing here in the dressing room so late at night.

Ellie answered that. She drew out a copy of Sybil's e-mailed invitation to come to the theatre. "We three were asked by Sybil to come. I suggested we go backstage. Unfortunately, fatally as it turned out, we were delayed outside and didn't arrive in time to save Sybil from her assassin. But we have to go now, we'll lose my reservations at the Lansdowne Club if we don't appear there before midnight."

"Too bad. Forget getting anywhere before midnight. I'm thinking of taking you three to the station. And who's this fourth person?"

Sybil's crippled dresser had made herself nearly invisible. Crouching behind the door, she'd ogled what was happening to the three of us and wisely determined to stay out of the searchlight. Now, it put its full glare on her when the sergeant growled that she must come forward and answer questions.

"I'm, I *was* Miss Sykes' dresser. Yes, sir, ever since she came from Hollywood, or Broadway or whatever fancy place she was starring in. We got on fine. Not a difficult lady. Turrible language she used, but other than that, well I guess you could call her a lady."

The skinny dresser, limping with greater showmanship, sent a pleading look to the sergeant, exaggerated her limp, and played hard on his sympathy. "I'm handicapped. I have to take the train, can't climb into no bus."

Handicapped is a big word in England. It opens all kinds of doors. Like Senior Citizen, it has its own very special appeal. I've sometimes wondered if politicians have counted up the amount of votes they could get by pandering to the handicapped and to Senior Citizens.

Mayfair police may be tougher than Chelsea's but this sergeant took the hint and gave the go-ahead for the dresser to leave. "You come to the station tomorrow. Sorry, but I'll have to insist we take your fingerprints and a mug shot." He didn't add what was obvious, that her DNA would be all over the room and its contents.

TV sitcoms: "The Blue Line" and "The Bill" have made their mark on Britishers. Fans of these sitcoms soon crowded toward the taped off door of Sybil's dressing room. I recognized the face of the soprano who'd played Stupefyin' Jones, Munchie Young . . Behind her, ogling everything was a hushed Heidi, her huge eyes bulging.

The theatre's manager was summoned to come inside the room. He ducked under the yellow situation tape and faced up to the sergeant. Dressed in black tie, preparing to end the evening with an after-theatre supper party, he looked annoyed rather than sympathetic. He was dry-eyed. Apparently there had been no love lost between him and Hollywood's Sybil.

His replies to the sergeant were curt, brief, and discreet. He didn't want any unfavorable publicity to harm this show or his theatre. With no reporters present, he didn't need to play to an audience.

The sergeant must have been a musicals buff, because suddenly he asked, "Who will replace Sybil Sykes in the role of Daisy Mae? I saw her here last week. She was very good."

The manager bit one side of his lips. "Her understudy will have to take over for a few days. Understudies are nothing but shit, but this is an emergency."

Heidi's big voice startled us, coming from the hall outside. "Mr. Baines, I know all her lines. All the songs. And, I'm a soprano."

Baines shrugged ungraciously. "No go, Heidi. To fill the house we'll need another big star. A name."

All of us turned to watch Heidi's face as Mr. Baines answered. He spoke carefully, as if he didn't want to lose two of his principal actresses in one evening. "Heidi, we love you. You're perfect in the role you have. But no, my dear. Don't ask to be Daisy Mae. You can't project innocence."

The play's producer now elbowed his way toward the yellow tape. It was lowered for him.

Called Perry Coulis, he was a British born Greek, said to have made millions in tourism. Perry was short for Pericles.

He looked dismayed at the sight of the dressing room emptied of his star. "Is it true?" he asked, his face crumpled with worry. "We've lost our Sybil?"

Perry Coulis had ignored Heidi when he passed her in the corridor. No love lost there. He hadn't given her a flicker of recognition. Perry turned back toward the corridor and called out to the big-breasted girl who'd played Stupefyin' Jones. "Miss Young, will you come in here please?" Thinking no doubt of the cost of costumes, although they were skimpy in *Daisy Mae*, he personally lowered the yellow tape for Munchie Young.

As she entered the room all of us could see that Munchie Young was exactly the right size to fit into Sybil's costumes. Another plus: it turned out that she knew Kentucky-speak.

"Ah'm truly shocked-lahke, thet lovely Sybil Sykes bin done in," she gargled between tears. Happy, delighted to discover a fellow American, hugged her and lent her a handkerchief.

"Y'all's from Kentucky?"

"No. Cain't lay claim to thet. Ah'm from Tennessee. Nashville, most lately. Ah've bin tryin' t'break into the country music world. No luck so far. But y'all could say Ah've bettuh luck than po'r Miss Sykes." Her shoulders heaved.

"Y'all talks So'thern, not real Kintuck speak. We-alls No'th o' the Mason Dixon lahne, different kahnd o' speak."

"Not too different. When some o' yourn Kentucky minuhs done got killed, it was So'thern talk on TV just lahke when describin' one of ourn Tennessee tornados. Mah hometown's Gallatin, and we's just suffered somethin' turrible from a tornado. Twelve folks daid. Gas leaked 'n leveled houses. Had to have a curfew t'stop the lootin'.'"

While Happy and Munchie were bonding, Perry Coulis faced up to a Police Inspector who had arrived.

Perry said, "I can't have my cast messing up. Can't you clear the corridor?"

The theatre manager tried to calm Perry. "Most of the cast left before the news leaked that Sybil Sykes was dead. Nobody in the corridor's making any trouble. We've got important issues to discuss, Coulis. First things first. Try to come up with a star who can carry this show. I don't want an empty theatre."

"How about Liza Minelli? If we can get her!"

"Good voice. Great voice, really. But she's just not a Daisy Mae. Short, cropped black hair, dark eyes. No way."

"She could wear a wig, and tinted contact lenses."

"Get anyone you like. You get enough bums on seats to fill my theatre and I don't care. A star's a star, I suppose."

The Police Inspector interrupted, braying that everyone involved in the play or employed by the theatre should help further inquiries. He demanded that everyone present on the premises must come to his precinct in the morning.

We filed out of the dressing room like inmates of a holocaust-concentration camp going to the gas chambers.

In the line alongside Happy, her new friend Munchie said, "Could y'all let me sleep wheah's y'all's goin'? Ah's mahty fraided. Don't cahe t'sleep alone in mah rented appahtment."

Ellie, loping behind Happy, answered for her. "We're heading for the Lansdowne Club. You're most certainly welcome to take a room there if they have any left. We may have lost our reservations by now. It's being past midnight."

Ellie left her Rolls Royce in the locked parking lot. Midnight had been the last chance to retrieve it before the place closed. We'd walked there and now had some difficulty hailing a taxi, but eventually a bleary-eyed driver pulled up to the curb outside the parking lot. We had no night clothes, not even toothbrushes, all locked up inside Ellie's mother's Rolls.

But there was a place at the Inn. The Lansdowne's night porter welcomed us. "Too late for the reservations clerk. But I can give you the forms to fill out."

We were allotted three rooms, a double and two singles. Officially we were Ellie's mother's guests. I'd let my out-of-town membership lapse when

I lived in the USA. But I was familiar with the facilities. I led Ellie, Happy and Munchie into the octagonal room that had been the favorite of the original Marquis of Lansdowne.I pointed out the framed copy signed by Benjamin Franklin of The Treaty of Paris, that sealed an end to America's Revolutionary War.

There was no waiter on duty to serve drinks in the grand Adam-decorated room next door. We parted company, Ellie and Munchie took the lift that led to the old building's grander premises. Happy and I went down a short flight of steps past a barrel ceilinged ballroom to enter a 1950's style annex. We had trouble locating our room, and when we did we learned that it was necessary to share a bathroom with the occupant of the single bedroom from the hall opposite. We had to wait our turn to use what Happy calls "the terlet."

"Don't mattuh," Happy sighed. "Ah was hopin' fo' a bath. Ah hates sleepin' in mah unduhclothes. Wohse without no bath. But, Rick, what's it mattuh? When yo' thinks o' po'r Sybil. Murdered!"

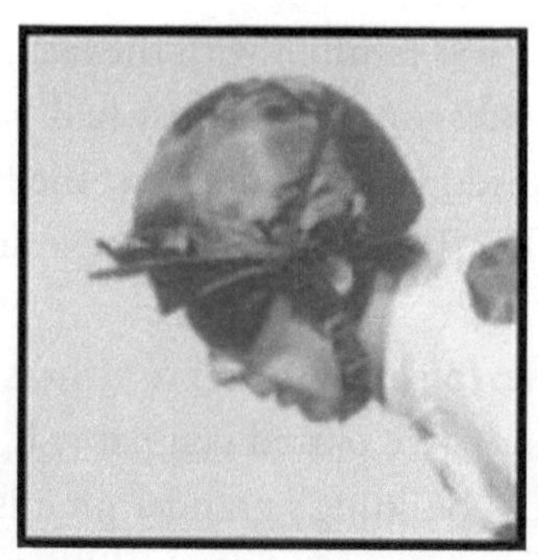

CHAPTER 7

I love having sex in a city's club or hotel. It was wonderful for me that night to take Happy in my arms, relieve her of that tired underwear, and have sex.

I was under a terrific strain from undergoing the stress of another murder that concerned one of my owners. Happy, too, needed that time-honored wonderful remedy against stress.

We both took baths once the facility had emptied, and later fell asleep in each other's arms.

Morning brought no easing of the pain brought on by Sybil's murder. With Happy still sleeping soundly, I went to the club's basement and looked for the Olympic-size swimming pool I remembered was there since my university days. I passed the old squash court. Two middle-aged paunchy individuals were sending a harassed ball to outdo each other. Next door I saw two fencers practicing their graceful swordsmanship.

I bought a pair of swimming trunks, lucky because the club's shop was already open. I found a clean towel in the men's changing room and ventured to the pool. The last time I'd been in it the water had been heated to 80 degrees. I dove in. Good God, the water wasn't heated above 50! I managed two laps before the marrow in my bones complained and I dashed for the hot showers.

Feeling human again, I returned to the room, where Happy had been peering down the corridor in her slip, anxious as to where I'd been going.

Early morning tea was served by a flunky, who in a surly manner indicated that if we wanted a "proper breakfast" we'd need to go downstairs to the first floor to the club's dining hall.

"Do we-all have tahme?" Happy worried. "We's got t'be at the po-o-lice station early. "N what about Ellie and Miss Munchie?"

"We'll take time."

Ellie and Munchie were in the dining hall, eating large breakfasts. Ellie had eggs on halibut, croissants and jam with Earl Grey tea. Munchie welcomed the American dishes on offer, waffles with maple syrup, brown bread, and coffee.

"Waffles?" Happy followed Munchie's lead. I copied Ellie's.

The club's uniformed porter hailed a taxi circling Berkeley Square. It drew up to the curb at Fitzmaurice Place. The driver didn't look pleased when we instructed him to take us to the Mayfair Police Station.

"Wha' fo', Guv?" he said in an anxious tone. "T'do with last night's murder where *Daisy Mae*'s playing?"

Ellie answered for me. In her crystal Heathfield Girls' School accent, she said, "Just drive on."

The Inspector was waiting for us.

Trembling in her wrinkled skin, Sybil's dresser crouched beside him. She was whining. "I don't like coming to London daytimes. Only for matinees. That's twice a week. Not fair t'make me come here now."

"You were the last person to see Sybil Sykes alive." The Inspector growled.

"No. I wasn't. I'd gone out for a ciggie, when she was toweling off her makeup. The theatre don't allow smoking inside the place. Have to go to the sidewalk. I wasn't long, just one ciggie. But when I come back into the room I noticed a perfume smell. Someone else was there, or had been there. Whoever that person was, I'll swear must be the last person to've seen her alive."

"What kind of perfume? You'd recognize it again!"

"Cheap. A freebie. Lots of the girls in the cast got it. From a shop across the road. A promotion. Same for the men, smelled different. But they got their freebies too."

"The men's scent can't have been the same as what's sold for women."
"I didn't say they were the same. Just not very different. Some kind of spice in both."

The Inspector took note, and sent a lackey to the theatre to collect samples of the freebies for both men and women.

I wished we hadn't hurried through our breakfasts, since the Inspector seemed too preoccupied with the dresser to bother with any of us.

The dresser had played her limp for all it was worth, but the Inspector didn't show any compassion. He pushed for every glimmer of information. "Is there a screen in the room where a person could have hidden?"

"Not a screen. But them curtains are from King Edward's times and would cover up anyone, not even shoes would show. Come to think of it, I do seem to remember hearing some heavy breathing behind one of them drapes."

The Inspector's lips curled in disbelief. He evidently thought she was inventing as she went along. "And why did you go out of the room again, leaving Sybil Sykes alone?"

"Another ciggie. I can't shake the habit for the life of me. Look, Mister Inspector. Look at the tips of me fingers, stained brown, from tobacco. Teeth brown too."

She offered her arthritic hands, and bared her lips to show her teeth. "That'll do. Go into the next office and sign your declaration." He turned his back on the dresser, who scuttled out like a cockroach smelling garbage. Happy asked him, "Shouldn't we ask huh if Sybil ever entertained a man at the the-a-tuh? A boyfriend?"

"You're going to teach me my job?" The Inspector thundered. He softened to add, "We'd already asked her that question before you arrived. If you'd been here promptly at nine you'd have heard her say that Sybil Sykes had no man in her life. At least, she'd never spoken of one nor entertained one in her dresser's presence."

Happy nodded. "Sorry. 'Scuse me. Just curious. She nevuh tole me o' none, neither. The only men I evah saw near huh was huh agent, huh limo drivuh, o' huh cout'rier. Ah knows she'd had three husbands. Mebbe them's was enuf."

I was keeping tight-lipped. "Never volunteer" was what I'd learned in the cavalry. I was ready for him when the Inspector sized me up.

"You trained horses for Sybil Sykes! Was she a difficult owner? Bad-tempered? Mean?"

"Nice person. Paid her bills on time. Tipped the grooms, remembered them at Christmas. Gave my children super presents from Santa. Never bad-tempered. Did do the 'Hollywood Star act' sometimes. Not often."

My description was cut short by Munchie, who wanted to get in a word. She'd been pushing my elbow all the time I spoke. She said, "Inspector, Ah nevuh went across the road fo' a freebie perfume. Ah've been loyal all my life to Estee Lauder's Youth Dew, since mah teens. Here, smell! Ah've put some on mah wrist. Smell! Nothin' lahke that freebie stuff."

"Could you differentiate between the freebies given to the women and those for the men? Give us ten minutes. My men have gone to the theatre to collect samples."

Munchie agreed to wait. She was determined to establish that her perfume wasn't what the dresser had noticed those decisive minutes before Sybil's murder. Munchie gave her calling card to Happy, added a hug, and broke into tears.

Ellie snapped at the Inspector, "Does that mean we can go?" She didn't wait for a reply. She took Happy's arm and marched her outside the station, where she asked me to hail a cab. "We'll go collect my Mater's Rolls from the parking lot, and head home."

We did.

The return drive to Epsom had none of the lilt we'd shared on the way to London yesterday.

CHAPTER 8

I n our double bed that night Happy cuddled close, but instead of initiating lovemaking she said, "Ah needs t'heah one o' them stories o' yourn."

I wanted sex, but there was nothing for it but to give with a tale of racing lore before I could hope for more than a cuddle.

"As you're still mourning Sybil, I'm sorry to give you a sad tale, but I think it's necessary. I need you to put on your thinking cap and plan what else we can do to find Feathers."

"Go ahead. Ah'm listenin' up."

"In 1982, before you were born, a great horse called Shergar was kidnapped. He'd won the Derby and other prestigious races in the Aga Khan's racing colors. By 1981 it was decided to send him to stud in County Kildare, he'd earned his fun. Syndicated to a group of thirty-nine top racing owners, Shergar was sent to the Aga Khan's stud farm in Ireland, an estate which had been in that family for fifty years. On February 9, the BBC announced that Shergar had been snatched. The Head Groom, James Fitzgerald, was taken with Shergar, but released forty miles away from the stud farm. The kidnapping had happened on the night before, when masked men pushed their way into Fitzgerald's home and demanded at gunpoint that he help them load Shergar into a horsebox." "The poor Trainer! Who was he?"

"Michael Stout. It was he who'd brought Shergar to those heights of glory. He was quoted as saying, 'Shergar was the best horse I ever trained. I hope nothing has happened to him.'"

"Was Shergar insured?"

"Oh yes, during his racing career by Lloyds of London. But when a ransom note finally appeared, the kidnappers demanded millions."

"That wouldn't have been too much for the Aga Khan to pay. One o' the world's richest men."

"Ah, but the Aga Khan didn't own Shergar outright any more. Remember, Shergar'd been syndicated, and other members of that syndicate balked at paying a ransom, to deter the kidnapping of other racehorses. No millions from them for the kidnappers."

"What about Shergar's insurers?"

"When months, then years passed with no sighting of Shergar, the insurers refused to pay up because there had been no dead horse to view."

"Why evah not? Somethin' happened to him!"

"I think he was eaten."

"Y'all don't mean thet!"

"Eaten, yes. I'm afraid I do. Because a dead horse is not easy to dispose of. A very large hole would have needed to be dug. It was February, remember, the ground would have been very hard. Removing earth would have caused suspicion. New turf would have been noticed. Ireland's not a big country. People know what's going on. Eaten, easiest."

"No one evuh heard whut happ'ned?"

"Lots of conjectures. Some said he'd been flown away in a private plane from a hidden airfield. Or shipped out on a large yacht. To America? To Tokyo? But the most compelling version came from a former IRA man called O'Callahan, who wrote about the Shergar saga in his book, *The Informer*. O'Callahan alleged that Shergar had proved too difficult to control. The kidnappers could not handle him because of his ferocious behavior and they killed him."

"Rick, we cain't let thet happen to Feathers."

"Put on your thinking cap, Happy," I repeated, giving up on any hope for sex that night, and rolled over to my side of the bed to sleep.

At dawn Ellie arrived, weeping like a bride who lost her husband on their honeymoon. "Jeremy's grey has been killed," she wailed. "And I never got to hunt him."

Very bad news. Did it mean our Feathers was dead too? I put an arm around Ellie. "How do you know?"

"Jeremy's had an e-mail from the anti-bloodsport people. Boasting. The antis say he'll get a hoof in the post. A hoof with his grey's distinctive long white sock!"

Happy produced a cup of tea with biscuits for Ellie. To me, she whispered, "Go check ourn e-mails."

Feathers hadn't been kidnapped by the antis, even though the two crimes had occurred within twenty-four hours one of the other.

I knew, because there WAS an e-mail for us with a thug's ransom demand for 2 million dollars. I was showing it to Ellie and Happy, when another unexpected caller arrived with tears on his face It was Tom, the groom responsible for Feathers.

"Bumbles has run away," he groaned. "She's pregnant, sir. About to have her kittens any moment. Cleaned her dish of cat food, somethin' she never did before, preferrin' t'lick at it all night. She must have had a plan to go look for Feathers. Missed him somethin' awful."

Happy did the English thing. She offered Tom a cup of tea from the pot prepared for Ellie. "We's goin' t'fahnd huh," she said. "Ellie, git on t'the BBC."

BBC and CNN both told us that a cat missing was not a story for TV. Ellie suggested making copies of a photograph of Bumbles and putting it on the internet and in local newspapers with the offer of a reward of 100 pounds. "Make enough copies," she added, "And I'll distribute them to the green grocer's, the butcher's and the local dress shops."

Happy was good at making copies on our fax cum printer. She handed some of the photographs to Ellie, and others she kept herself. "In Kentucky we'uns nail our reward offuhs t'trees."

Both women took their cars and sped away to spread the offer of the one hundred pounds reward for Bumbles.

And the ploy worked. Within hours a shrewd-sounding woman telephoned to ask if I had the 100 pounds in cash. "I've had a cat arrive at my stables, went into one of the stalls, and proceeded to have kittens. If it's your cat, please collect her and the kittens. Very unsanitary."

"Did you say 'stables'?"

"I have a livery business some twenty miles from you, Mr. Harrow. I know where you are. But you can't expect me to use my gas to drive all that way with your cat and kittens. *You* should come to see if this is your cat."

No contest. Within half an hour I was at the livery stables. The tiger-striped cat was my Bumbles. She was on the straw nursing her kittens. Bumbles looked very pleased with herself, cozily encamped next to a black filly.

The filly was Feathers, with her coat dyed black.

The livery owner brought a cardboard box for Bumbles and her kittens. She seemed unaware of my recognition of Feathers. She wanted her 100 pounds reward for alerting me to the presence of Bumbles in her stables, and had no concern otherwise.

On my mobile I telephoned the Epsom police, Wetherby's, and the Jockey Club. I asked the racing authorities to fax Feathers' particulars to the Epsom police . .

The livery's owner listened in amazement. "What's going on? Why are you making trouble? I've done you a favor. Where's my 100 pounds?"

I paid her, feeling as abashed as if I'd paid the thirty pieces of silver to Judas. There was no point spelling out the situation until the police arrived with copies of Feathers' papers.

After the police brought everything necessary, including the number of her tattoo proving her identity, the livery owner still balked at releasing Feathers. She grunted, "This is a black filly, the papers definitely describe your Feathers as a chestnut."

"Dyed black." I wet the tip of my index finger, and off came black dye. She insisted, "Not your filly. She belongs to an American. He had a chip put into her neck that identifies her. If he were here, and not in America, he'd see you off pretty fast."

An Epsom police officer interrupted, "If you don't want to be had up for handling stolen property, you'd best stop here and now. And it's up to Mr. Harrow if he'll be preferring charges."

Tom had left with Bumbles and her kittens, but returned within the hour with our horsebox for Feathers. Under police supervision we loaded her carefully. I paid the livery woman, who counted every single one pound note.

The trip home to my stables was laden with delight. The craggy verges on either side of the winding road had exchanged Old Man's Beard for glistening buds. Robins and crows picked at the buds, a butterfly or two probed at the few thrusting flowers.

By mobile phone I could give Happy the brilliant news of Feathers and Bumbles safe recapture.

Ellie drove Happy to meet our horsebox halfway and provide an escort to our yard.

"Ah sho' thanks God," chirped my little Baptist. "Aftuh thet story y'all tole me about Shergar, Ah was so 'fraid Feathers had been eaten. Cannibal-lahke."

Back at my desk, my first duty was to inform Hal Murphy by e-mail that there was no need to contemplate paying a ransom. Feathers was in her stall in my yard. It was about two a.m. in the Canadian Rockies, I couldn't telephone him with the great news. He'd have to wait until he opened his laptop for his e-mails.

I informed my contacts at both the BBC and CNN that Feathers had been found. I didn't implicate the livery woman by name, although I swore I was going to follow up on the hint that an American had done the deed. I doubted that an American had been involved. I'd learned from Happy's offer of lessons in Kentucky-speak how easy it is to fake the accent.

To put closure to this case was high on my list of priorities, which included hiring a bodyguard to protect Feathers in future.

Virgo, at CNN, now loved the story of Bumbles playing an active part in our finding Feathers. Her kittens were on the news every hour, alongside Bumbles and Feathers nuzzling. My e-mails improved, because Britain and the rest of the world have a penchant for cats and kittens.

In my recent life it seemed that whenever I had an upper there was soon to be a downer to follow. Among the hate e-mails, two suggested I had killed Carla and Sybil detailing the similarities of the two cases, that they both had horses in my stable, both women were sopranos of note, and they were both strangled. I'd managed to keep my mind free of hate mail, but at six that same evening when Happy put on the news, we heard of another murder.

A BBC newscaster started the news hour with "Singing star Fran Purcell, one of the Purcell Duo, called police to her Chelsea flat this afternoon when she returned there to find her boyfriend strangled. The boyfriend's name was Goofy, no surname, who played saxophone in the Dirty Digs rap band." Still pictures of Fran and Goofy followed, while a voice-over added, "Only a few short weeks ago Fran Purcell lost her twin sister in the same Chelsea flat by strangulation. That murder is still unsolved."

Awful that we'd be close to yet another murder, and yet there was some consolation when the e-mails stopped that had been accusing me. Now the strangled victims in London included a male, who neither had horses in my stable nor was a singer. And I'd been near Epsom searching for Feathers at the time of his killing.

Happy turned off the news. She couldn't listen further. "Po' Fran! Turrible fo' huh. Ah tole huh not t'stay in thet apartment."

The telephone was jangling. I answered with a heavy heart, like a criminal on the run expecting his lawyer to tell him he'd been convicted *in absentia* The voice was a soprano's, high but gentle - Munchie's.

"Y'all hu'rd the evenin' news? Ah's sca-y-ed. C'n Ah come down 'n stay with y'all?"

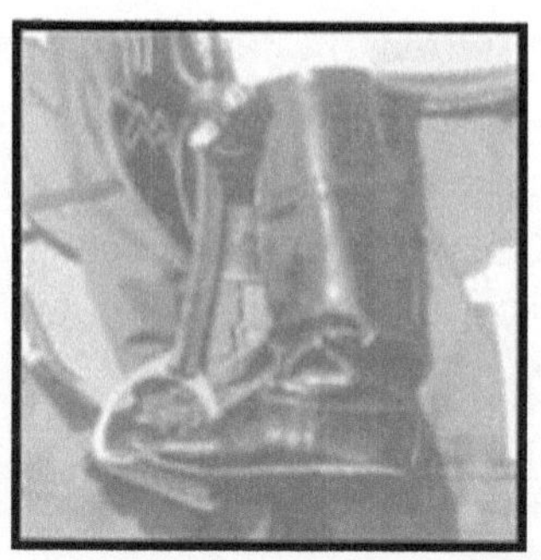

CHAPTER 9

Munchie had undergone a favorable metamorphosis since she'd taken on the starring role of Daisy Mae. Like a late-season butterfly, she'd grown important wings.

She arrived to take up residence in our tiny guest room with a pile of Louis Vuitton luggage, three coats, and a new puppy. I like dogs, love puppies in particular, but this little fellow proceeded to cock his leg on the guest bed's skirts and then jumped up on it to leave a worse card on its eiderdown.

"Ain't Skippy cute?"

With fewer owners than Ivor had left me, I couldn't argue with Munchie. She'd bought a yearling and I was to school it for next year's races. I would have preferred to call her puppy Shitty instead of Skippy, but that might have offended this latest of my owners.

Happy provided the perfect meal for Munchie - grits, hushpuppies and fried chicken. I downed that mess with good grace, but once I escaped to the stables I shared the grooms' food.

Munchie wanted to inspect her yearling, but it was too late for that after dinner. We watched the late news, hearing more details about Goofy's murder. I turned off the TV at midnight, I knew Happy would have nightmares if she listened to more grizzly facts.

The morning brought heavy rain. We three were closeted all day with my tots and the nanny cum housekeeper, Mrs. Rea. The lunch cooked up by Mrs. Rea was far from Munchie's taste. She ate little, and after lunch insisted on switching channels to hear everything on offer on the various channels regarding Goofy.

Happy said, "Ah thinks it be hah tahme we called Fran. She must be goin' crazy."

Fran was beyond desperate. "I'm the only one to mourn dear, darling Goofy. Oh, shit, no that's not quite true. He had a pal, the saxophone artist who'd been helping Goofy in his career, Jimmy Halpern. Jimmy brought his antique 1923 saxophone to the morgue and played 'Beautiful Liar.' If I hadn't been weepy before, I just about died listening to that. Beautiful music, terrible about poor Goofy."

Down the wire we could hear her sobs, she could scarcely manage a full sentence. "All my fault. I'm like a bird of death. Those close to me die." Cocaine had aggravated her emotional mess.

I said, "Come down to us. We want you here. Do you good to see the horses."

Fran came. Amazingly she brought a new boyfriend with her. It was only three days since Goofy's murder, and Fran had already warmed up to a new man, singer Bell Natchez. A tenor, he seemed too feminine to be a boyfriend, but that evidently wasn't Fran's perception.

At the stables, in our dining room, beside the hearth, wherever, Fran wound her arms around Bell's narrow girth. She kissed him on the mouth, eyes, hands and shoulders totally oblivious of our presence. He didn't kiss Fran. He wasn't oblivious of our presence, but neither was he embarrassed. To my dread, he aimed his own flirtatious tricks at my Happy. Perhaps I over-reacted, but I felt a real shiver of apprehension.

Happy ignored him, at first. She had been shocked at Fran's rapid recovery from her period of mourning. Three days!

Ellie's frowning face showed she joined in Happy's repugnance at Fran's present indifference to the tragedy that had overtaken Goofy. Ellie was still mourning her dead Ivor, although it was two years since he'd shot his head away.

Bell's tricks were unusual. No touching, no European-style hand kissing. None of those old, passé wiles. He sang. And as he was singing he directed every word, every note to Happy. He stared at her, his eyes drilling into hers, absorbing their light and their sweetness. His tricks were a hypnotist's.

I felt bullocked.

How to defend our marriage? I trusted my little Baptist, but only as far as you could throw a church. What woman can resist hypnosis, if she's predisposed to being hypnotized!

Ellie noticed what was happening. And she didn't like it. She resented Bell's intrusion into our lives, and was truly shocked at his dismissal of Fran's overtures. Fran had brought him to our home. He was Fran's boy toy. But Bell had developed a different idea. He was totally taken by my Happy.

"I love your Southern American accent," Bell crooned, when he stopped singing to her.

Happy had heard that comment from other Britishers, and always before she had sharply corrected them with, "Not So'thern. Ah's from Kentucky. Thet's No'th o' the Mason Dixon Lahne." No correction came for Bell. With her eyes fastened by his, Happy smiled blissfully. I hadn't seen her eyes behave so erotically since the early days of our courting. During our hours of sex, Happy habitually closed her eyes so I'd had no opportunity to view this reaction since 2004 in Kentucky.

I cut short Fran's visit. After her brief inspection of her horses, and a "yes" as to sending Sweet Song to Dubai, I gave her and Bell the door. Their chauffeur-driven car started up the drive, but not before Bell unlocked his hypnotic eyes from Happy's. From the car, Bell waved his handkerchief to her like a girl off to boarding school leaving her mother.

Deciding to give prominence to the situation, I spent hours planning my maneuvers to eradicate Bell from our lives. The plan I settled on was to introduce Bell to a stunner he would trade for Happy. But where was I going to find such a stunner? Not in my stables, not among the gentry in the grander houses outside Epsom.

Munchie solved the problem. On the Monday before Valentine's Day, when I should have been working on next month's trip to the Dubai races, Munchie telephoned with news that was soothing for her and doubly soothing to me. "Rick, Ah've been replaced as Daisy Mae. Mr. Coulis, our produsah has finally contracted fo' a new soprano, a big Hollywood star lahke Sybil was, she's called Leila Forbes, and she's gorgeous. She stahts in de show next week. Ah'm back to being Stupefyin' Jones. We're rehearsin' togethuh, but we could come down to y'all on Sat'day. No mo'e worryin' thet Ah's goin' t'be strangled lahke po'r Sybil."

I was on the blower the next minute to Fran. I invited her to bring Bell for Saturday lunch, nothing more. In case my plan didn't work, I didn't want Bell and Fran around any longer than strictly necessary.

Saturday gave us ideal weather. The spring-like breezes anticipated by a month the best of Britain's countryside joys. I heard an early cuckoo, I saw butterflies. Tulips were blooming, wisteria still offered a generous purple mantle, and daffodils unfurled their scalloped upturned bells.

In our stables all the two-year-olds had stopped coughing and were straining to go out and play. Their elders, our three and four-year-olds neighed for their gallops. Brass fittings were highly polished because the grooms had plenty of time before the flat racing season started. All was pristine clean and perfect for showing off to my lady owners.

Munchie was overly attentive to Miss Leila Forbes. But what a disappointment as far as solving my problem or redeeming my marriage. Leila was ugly. She had a prominent nose, narrow crooked lips, and yellow eyeballs. Her figure was appealing, with the huge boobs associated with the cartoon character, Daisy Mae. Her eyes were blue and her hair an appropriate yellow, but I couldn't imagine how Mr. Coulis could have hired her to portray Daisy Mae, Li'l Abner's delectable girlfriend.

Leila's conversation was interesting, but one-sided; all about Hollywood. She constantly dropped names of producers and screenwriters, none of which any of us recognized. Bell paid attention, but continued to do his hypnosis act, mesmerizing my Happy.

Lunch ended, Leila picked up Happy's guitar, and then came about such a transformation as only a true star can achieve. Leila began to sing, interspersing well-known lyrics with smart-ass comments about everyone in the room. Leila became Barbra Streisand and Judy Garland and Whitney Houston and Emmylou Harris and Joni Mitchell and Madonna. The magic that is terrific music performed by a trooper now changed Bell's pole of attraction. His hypnotic eyes swiveled to magnetize Leila's. Game, set, and match. I'd won. Happy was released to snuggle close to me to revel in Leila's great singing.

Just as I'd hoped, Leila and Bell left together. Fran stayed on close to our hearth, warming her bum next to Munchie. Our leather-covered bum-warmer had never before had two famous singers' asses hanging in there, toasting at our fire.

For the remainder of the weekend I concentrated on oiling my two lady owners. I drove them to Cheltenham to learn about jumpers, although it wasn't my policy to train horses over the sticks. It was the atmosphere I wanted them to savor. As a prelude to the flat racing season, a golden afternoon with Cheltenham's enthusiastic crowds is hard to beat.

I didn't see Leila Forbes again. She became an item with Bell, and their names were entwined in gossip columns and on the evening news when they announced their engagement.

The reason I never saw her again was that she decided to buy a colt from my nemesis, Harold East. That suited me, because it meant that Bell wouldn't be near my Happy until that colt began to compete against our horses. That could take the better part of a year.

In spite of needing more owners, and having had first bite at Leila, I didn't regret arranging that definitive meeting between her and Bell. God knows, it was a million times more important to me to use her as a lure to entice Bell away from Happy.

Mayfair police hadn't forgotten us. Newer tests with mitochondrial DNA, which allows the testing of cells without a nucleus, including cells from a hair shaft, brought about a change of heart with our friendly police. The Sybil Sykes case had heated up due to the discovery of a fragment of hair from the person who had strangled her.

Sybil's poor crippled dresser had to give samples of hair. In my opinion, the old dear hadn't the strength in her arthritic hands to strangle a chicken, The Inspector told me, "Stranger surprises have happened in the annals of crime. Hate gives strength like you wouldn't believe."

Happy and I gave cuttings from our hair. Ellie, too. Negative, of course. There was a suggestion that all members of the *Daisy Mae* cast, the musicians, and the theatre's employees should give samples too, but that was over-ruled after complaints by their unions.

That DNA found under Sybil's fingernails helped the case damn-all if there was nothing to offer a match.

A month and a half went by, and there was no more talk of solving Sybil's murder.

Happy and I busily prepared for our trip to Dubai. This time in addition to Tom and the fillies, we took a bodyguard.

CHAPTER 10

I t was just my luck that Bell and Leila were on the same plane to Dubai. Married earlier that morning, Bell had chosen Dubai as a cheaper venue for a honeymoon in the sun. He reckoned it would prove less expensive than St. Bart's in the Caribbean or the Hotel du Cap at St. Jean Cap Ferrat.

In the airline's magazine there was a big spread about Leila's taking the starring role in *Daisy Mae*. Amazingly, she looked absolutely beautiful in the PR pictures. Her large nose had vanished under highlighted brown makeup contrasting cleverly with the bright blush-on rounding her cheeks. Extraordinary what cosmetics can do! I looked down the aisle at the live new bride and saw the same ugly face. She glared at me, not at all pleased that we'd be going to Dubai too.

Dubai felt different this year. It was more like an old shoe, familiar if uncomfortable. I was not going to be amazed that there was no betting nor alcoholic drinks at the racetrack.

Happy had come prepared for the annual hats' competition, bringing a huge cardboard hat-box stuffed with three varying-style hats. The hats competition compensated for her dreadful memories of her abduction, and later the C-section necessitated by Dorothy arriving backside first in Dubai's jockeys hospital.

We'd chosen to go to a different hotel this year. That disgusting hotel manager that had been so offensive and unhelpful during Happy's abduction and Sirena's murder, caring more for the blood on his carpet and the bad PR than for human victims, had been our reason to pay more and go to the best. Unfortunately, Bell and Leila were checking in for the bridal suite when we arrived at the Reception desk. Both honeymooners snubbed us, acting as if we were invisible.

Who cares? Happy and I went to our little double room and had great sex, as we always did in a foreign city's hotel. I was willing to bet that Bell wouldn't get anything near it from sulky Leila.

Very early next morning I left Happy sleeping soundly and hailed a taxi to collect our bodyguard, Dick Prentice, from his cheaper hotel. Together we went to the nearby stables for horses being prepared for the big races. I found Tom already busily cleaning out yesterday's straw from the two fillies' stalls. We helped him load the hay nets and bring in the English water we'd brought with the hay from England. The fillies had managed the trip well. Feathers reacted like an old trouper because she'd been here before.

I left Dick with Tom, because I wanted to make absolutely certain that no dirty business stopped the fillies from running. Back at my hotel I went to the newspaper shop to buy a paper, and to my surprise I found Bell there. He'd grabbed every English newspaper on offer for the accounts of his wedding. I noticed that he told the shop's owner to put them on his suite's bill, which showed me that Leila was paying for everything on this honeymoon. He hadn't needed to choose a cheap venue for the honeymoon..

Bell was fully dressed in jacket and tie, right down to white socks for his loafers. While I was at Eton, white socks had been the mark of a homosexual. Was Bell gay? He hadn't come to the lobby in a T-shirt and slacks, outfitted as if he intended to return immediately to the marital bed.

In a grouchy voice, he said, "Look here at the *Daily Mail*. Hardly a mention of my wedding. A picture of Leila, not of me, and gives only the info we'd taken two unknowns to the Registry Office."

It was not the tone of a man who had been a guest in my home, where he'd met his bride.

Obeying his pointing finger, I peered at the offending article. It seemed quite normal to me, but I'm not in the entertainment world where anything written is okay as long as your name's spelled right. More is best.

I left Bell ordering other newspapers, and took my *Sporting Life* upstairs. I didn't get to it right away to study the entries of fillies in our two races. I went back to our marital bed, where Happy was now awake and making the cooing noise that meant she was hungry for sex. Lucky me!

By lunchtime we were both very hungry. Sex always brings me an avalanche of ideas for food. Our telephone had rung, inviting us downstairs to eat with a pal of Happy's, Gail Brophy, a former Kentucky Derby winning owner. She'd been part of a syndicate in 1991 that took the roses with Strike The Gold. Her story was one that Happy didn't favor. Gail had been invited to rejoin the syndicate for the following year's derby, but she hadn't believed that lightning could strike twice. With another gold-named horse, the syndicate had won the roses again, but that time without Gail.

She was seated in the main restaurant, wearing an extraordinary hat with a five-inch brim totally covered in gold net flowers. She explained, "I'm trying out hats every day to choose what to wear to the track. I'm going to win the hat contest, or die."

Happy looked dismayed. "Ah's brought only weensy teensy hats. No brims."

"You'll be fine. Tiny hats for a tiny woman," Gail laughed. She was in a much more cheerful mood this year than last, when she was worrying about the health of her ex-husband, Giles. And Giles had died shortly after the 2006 Dubai races. He'd gone to Camden, South Carolina to visit his two-year-olds and died there April 9 of leukemia at the age of sixty-eight. Giles had been managing partner of the syndicate when Strike The Gold took the roses.

Why do women care so much about the hats they wear to big races?

I thought, "That sounds like a line that Professor Higgins might have said in *My Fair Lady*."

Whispering, looking around the restaurant as if Leila might appear any minute, Gail asked, "Is it true the honeymooners are here in this hotel?"

I answered for Happy. "I saw Bell earlier today devouring the English newspapers for comments on the wedding. Not too many write-ups. Not enough to satisfy Bell's ego."

"Who do you suppose is paying the bills at this, Dubai's most expensive hotel?"

"Leila. Bell hasn't got a job at the moment. He cut a disc with nine other tenors, but it hasn't gone up very high in the charts. He'll have to start touring very soon to help push up sales. Leila won't like that."

It seems that whenever a name comes up the person named duly appears. Bell strode into the restaurant alone. He didn't wave at us or ask to join our table. He scrunched up his shoulders and indicated to the Maitre D' that he wanted to be hidden in the far corner, away from any windows. We ate slowly, lingering over our puddings, curious to see if Leila would join him. She didn't.

Because we couldn't talk about the honeymooners with Bell within ear shot, Gail changed the subject. "All the talk here concerns Michael Jackson. Will he or won't he come to the races? Sad man, once the pop-music king, and now practically a bankrupt."

"Ah's read wheah he closed his California ranch, 'Neverland' and folks complained his zoo animals weren't bein' propuh-lahke fed."

"I read that too. But Michael Jackson owns fifty percent of a song catalogue that includes Beatles' hits. That catalogue could sell for a billion. No poorhouse for Michael Jackson quite yet."

After cups of Arabian coffee, our little party of three split up because I needed to go to the airport to meet my owner, Fran. But I didn't leave our hotel without asking Happy to stay in our room. She'd wanted to go to the souks with Gail, but considering last year's abduction, I didn't want her to risk another such.

Fran's arrival didn't bring out the photographers or paparazzi in any numbers comparable to what Leila's appearance had harvested. If she looked disappointed at a lack of fans at the airport, that was nothing to what she experienced at the races.

Fran had traveled without any cocaine in her possession, wary of customs and sniffer dogs. She ordered a stiff whiskey at the races, and couldn't believe that there was no alcohol served publicly in Dubai. She complained loudly about that, and again when she learned she couldn't place a bet on her own filly. No betting permitted in Dubai either. Too bad we couldn't put a muzzle on Fran like they do on camels in Dubai!

But her worst moment came when we went to the five-star restaurant's huge buffet and all heads swiveled to stare at Leila's appearance there, while she was abysmally ignored.

As soon as she finished eating her expensive but mainly untouched meal, I rushed her to sit in front of one of the racetrack's large screens where she could watch the runners even when they were at the far end of the course. No interest. Fran couldn't care less about these runners because they didn't include her own.

I led Fran to the round table for VIPS but she wouldn't sit there when she saw Leila queening the area. On the top floor we sat on a balcony with a great view of the panorama, but Fran was listless." I want to go to a casino and do some gambling," she whined. "This is a bore."

"No casinos here, Fran. Sorry."

She stared at the mix of Europeans, Arabs, Japanese, and Africans. "Now I understand why there was such awful food on the buffet, catering to all these different kinds of people. And these women! Half in burkhas, the others wearing crazy hats over French fashions."

"Ah thinks it's mostly the older women wearin' those capes and veils," Happy said. She wasn't missing the races, not my Happy!

When an Arab owner won the last race, Fran said, "I'm ready to go home to England. Seems like all the winning horses belong to Arabs. My Sweet Song won't stand a chance. Didn't last year's big winner belong to Dubai's ruler, Sheik Mohammed?"

"Yes. And he wins a lot of the main races in England too."

A Japanese race-goer in the next seat to Fran's said, "Lady, he only became ruler when older brother die. He big racing man, everywhere."

"You want to make a personal bet with me that he'll win my race? Come to our hotel and we can lay our bets in cash. How about it?"

"Ten thousand dollars, you did say your horse Sweet Song!"

The Japanese gambler followed us to our hotel and produced the cash, as did Fran.

And Sweet Song won her race next day. Fran went home to England a happier songbird.

We stayed on because Feathers still had her race to run.

The big race before ours was taken by an American-bred, said to be a contender for the 2007 Kentucky Derby.

Joy! Our American-bred won too.

I didn't go home in a great mood though, even if both my entries had won their races.

A telephone call from Ellie in England, where she'd been overseeing Mrs. Rea's care of my tots, brought disgusting news. "Rick, someone's been mutilating horses in our line of country. So far, it's been hunters had their ears and tails chopped off, but it could be racehorses tomorrow. Better hurry back."

CHAPTER 11

E llie's dire prediction came true faster than anyone could have predicted.

Two racehorses were blinded by red hot poker within miles of my yard.

Britain's variable weather had brought full springtime by March 21. Racehorses were permitted to enjoy the fresh new grass. The flat season was upon us, and it was the late foals that were turned out to grass while their elders prepared for races soon to take place. The two blinded horses belonged to Harold East's yard. I disliked the man, but as a fellow Trainer I truly felt compassion for what had happened there.

I took major precautions to prevent a copycat crime in my yard. My Canadian owner, Hal Murphy, went along with my idea to keep on our two bodyguards, including the one I took to Dubai. But their presence failed to stem the horror.

On March 22 one of my youngest fillies had her neck scorched with a poker. The intruder must have been frightened off because the poker's flame was headed toward her eyes. The burn on her neck surely was done by error, in haste.

Happy, with tears in her eyes, groaned. "Ah declares Ah feels as bad as if'n mah daughter had been raped."

She gritted her teeth and promised she'd do her utmost to track down the criminal who had committed this dastardly deed, nicknamed by the press as 'the pokerman.'

Our attention was drawn away from the crime scene by the unexpected arrival at our yard of one of my owners, Munchie. She'd come to sign the papers to get ownership of Home Alone. Munchie looked anxious. "Will our fillies git their eyes burned out?"

"Not if I can help it," I groaned.

Only two miles away, the 'pokerman' was counting the tips he'd earned the night previous.

Name: Paul Peters. Age: 19. Weight: 150 pounds. Height: five eleven. Character: nil.

Paul Peters earned a minimal salary as the delivery boy for a pizza parlour. He couldn't drive a van. He had no license. He rode a bicycle with a basket arrangement on the rear wheel.

His maternal grandfather supplied him with a bed and the use of his hovel's one bathroom. The toilet was a 'Chick Sales' outside. Paul had rarely lived with his parents. He hated his mother. She took money for sex, and Paul had peeked in at several of her graceless couplings. Paul's father, an army corporal, had been posted for years in Germany, never rising above his early rating, and preferred to spend his off-base hours with the local girl with whom he'd fathered an illegitimate son.

Paul had grown up in Germany until he was seven, never understanding why his parents referred to faraway England as 'home' and never accepting that he was a foreigner in the land where he was born, Germany. When sent to his grandfather's and entered into a British council school, he was mocked for his accent and made no friends.

A neuter as regarded sex, his only pleasure came from masturbation after killing mice.

As an early teenager he tried to kill rats and foxes, but they bared sharp teeth which frightened Paul. He tried slitting the throats of sheep he found grazing near the hill where he lived. But the sheep's wool protected them from his blunted kitchen knife. He went into a nearby field to slice at cows, but a ferocious bull did for that plan. It was only recently that Paul discovered he could safely approach horses.

The unexpectedly warm pre-spring weather brought out the hunters into fields. Some wore protective blankets, but he could still reach their ears and tails when the horses came to their fences or turned to leave. He chopped and severed flesh, enjoying the rush of blood.

Racehorses were more protected. However, the spring weather appealed to their grooms, and Harold East's yard had distant fields where his two were maimed beyond any dream of ever racing again.

I called on Harold East to give sincere condolences. I inspected his field where the deed was done. So did the Epsom police. But there was no give-away trail to the criminal. A local newsman scouring the police records caught hold of the story and it was soon taken up by the major broadsheets. One tabloid ran the story as its headline. "Harold East's Racehorses Mutilated." TV spread it on the news with the gory details of eyes burned down to their sockets.

In all this turmoil we had another unexpected visitor, Fran Purcell, who'd come to sign away Home Alone. I was miles away, at Doncaster. Happy had stayed with our infants because Mrs. Rea had her "time off" and left the kitchen emptied to take all our food with her.

Happy greeted Fran warmly, glad not to be totally alone with our kids. She said, "Ah's so pleased t'see yuh. How's the love lahfe? Tell me all!" She settled Fran in our kitchen, with some tea, which was about all that was left in the larder.

"Nothing to fuck tell," Fran complained sourly. "No man in my life. Remember when Jeremy acted like he loved me? And I believe he really did, until he found out about my cocaine habit. At that time, when I was missing my twin a lot, I think I must have exuded a need for love. Because along came Goofy, who was on speed so he couldn't care less if I took a line, and we had a great love affair. Not just sex! Love affair. Then he was murdered, and I found Bell. Don't know if it was love with him. Tenors? I guess you know about them. He was awfully crude about sex. Once said to me, 'when you want to get laid, call me.' But Leila took him away, so I never found out his real feelings."

"What y'want t'eat? Ah c'n tel'phone fo' Chinese, or an Indian tikkoo, or a pizza."

"I like Chinese, but not take-away Chinese. Hate tikka. Let's go for pizza."

Happy, who had never before ordered food delivered, drummed her fingers through the business pages of our local directory and came up with the number of a pizza parlor. It was the one where Paul Peters worked as delivery boy. Within a half hour Paul arrived at our back door. He wore the red and white uniform almost universally accepted as identifying pizza delivery personnel. The uniform was supposed to offer customers a level of security.

Fran had moved into our sitting room to be close to the fire. The evening had drawn in bringing cold air. She crouched on the bum-warmer stirring the logs with a poker for more warmth. Happy asked the pizza boy to place the box on the hearth's coffee table while she returned to the kitchen for money with which to pay.

Grabbing her chance to have a line, Fran went into the downstairs loo.

Paul, left alone waiting for the pizza money and his tip, stole our poker. With its red-hot tip, he couldn't hide it under his clothes. He whirled to face the open back door and tossed it outside.

Happy returned, paid up and added the tip. Paul left after her polite "goodbye." She placed our own knives and forks alongside the two cardboard plates provided and proceeded to slice the pizza.

Fran came back to the fire, Happy added glasses for Pappy's moonshine, and then remembered to close the back door. The two girls settled on either side of the coffee table to eat their slices of pizza, when Happy noticed her poker was missing.

Accustomed to checking on the horses' tack, Happy had a quick eye for missing items. "Thet d'livery boy. He's stolen mah pokuh." She jumped away from the table, uncurling her legs to stride to the back door.

She could just see a flickering bicycle light retreating into the distance. Happy didn't hesitate. She knew immediately that Paul was the criminal who'd maimed horses. She yelled, "Fran, y'all listen up fo' mah kids. Ah's goin' t'the stables. Git a hoss."

At the stables both grooms were eating a Chinese take-away. "Git me Rick's saddle hoss." Tom was quick, but not fast enough for Happy. She took a running jump like Frankie Dettori does to alight when he wins major races and, bareback, sped out of the stable yard.

The area wasn't as pitch dark as the desert had been when she rode a nag to freedom from her abductors in Dubai. The rosy glow from Epsom helped her locate a viable path where she could gallop to follow Paul's bicycle's flickering light.

Paul wasn't heading for Epsom.

Happy had guessed that he wouldn't, now that he was armed with a red-hot poker. Behind her, she could hear the hooves of Tom's saddle horse that he rode for morning and evening gallops with their string. That sound was very heartening. Happy didn't want to be facing Paul alone with his knife and her red-hot poker.

Paul stopped in front of a field where two fillies had been left at grass. He switched off his bicycle light and approached the two fillies.

They were startled, and disliked this intruder. Their ears pricked and they neighed. Trouble was something that horses can recognize in advance. Fear made them canter alongside the fence. Paul kept up with the smaller of the two, the red-hot poker outstretched

Happy caught up, galloped alongside Paul, and neatly avoided two thrusts with the red-hot poker. She had nothing with which to hit at him; no stirrups, no whip. The nose band on her saddle horse could be ripped off, but then how would she control him?

She used an old Kentucky weapon, her horse's hooves. She reared her mount and had his hooves descend on Paul's head. He dropped the red-hot poker and screamed.

He was still screaming when Tom rode up, brandished his whip, and cowed Paul into a kneeling position. Within seconds, Tom was on his mobile, summoning the Epsom police. Happy, dismounted, had relieved Paul of her poker and his knife.

"We c'n sho' git his finguhprints off o' these. Yeah man! And settle this case."

CHAPTER 12

When I returned home from Doncaster I found Happy and Fran celebrating. Pappy's moonshine was going down a treat. "You'll be able to stock up on more moonshine," I chortled after I'd heard the end of the Paul saga. "We're going to Kentucky next week, you can see your Pappy. Then we're heading for California and the Santa Anita races." I didn't want to cross the Pond without a stop in Kentucky, because Happy and I always had our best sex in Pappy's homestead.

Fran interrupted my lyrical thoughts of sex in that Kentucky homestead." Can I come too? You'll be running my Sweet Song, won't you?"

I'd had my doubts about the suitability of taking Sweet Song to Santa Anita. She wasn't a maiden now, and she'd come up against other prize-winning fillies of international stature.

Happy answered for me. "Yeah man! We's only too pleased t'take Sweet Song." The moonshine had hit her and she would have taken a saddle horse if asked.

Fran wasn't the only one of our friendly female owners who wanted to come to Santa Anita with her filly.

Munchie was on the blower that same evening with stunning news. *Daisy Mae* had closed. The theatre was dark without a replacement show. Coulis had closed down the whole operation when Leila's prolonged honeymoon sent the gate crashing down to bankruptcy status. No star, no profitable gate. "Ah didn't want t'play Daisy Mae ag'in, 'n mebbe git mahself killed. Heidi took on the job, but she's so hopeless in the role that the theatre's bin empty the last few weeks. Ah needs t'go t'Hollywood 'n renew mah contacts theah. How about it? C'n Ah come with y'all, 'n bring Home Alone?"

What can you say to a beautiful, unemployed soprano who wants an excuse to go to her homeland? I said, "Yes," mainly to please my darling wife, who likes Munchie almost as much as she loves me. I think!

The two singers, soprano Munchie and our contralto owner Fran, had arrived in L.A. while we were still enjoying our sex trip to Pappy's homestead. Hal Murphy, our so generous Canadian owner, declared his intention to join us in L.A. to oversee Anchor's race, and offered to pay for us to stay at the Bel Air.

What Hal Murphy didn't want to do was to pay the two bodyguards in our yard while his Anchor was in California. He intended to hire a bodyguard to sleep at the Santa Anita stables for visiting horses.

The Ainsleys, although they'd earned a goodly sum on their horse, still were not keen to pay a bodyguard at our yard, and neither would my Doncaster owner. I doubled Tom's salary to assure he would look after the string.

We decided to take Dick with us to California.

He made the trip over the Arctic Circle, the fastest and best way to go. Our stopover in Kentucky could have cost me dear, because when I'd had my surfeit of sex and flew on to L.A., I found Fran and Munchie squabbling like a dolphin fighting a shark. As my old Dad would have said, "They weren't acting like ladies."

There had always been a frisson of professional jealousy between these two. Fran had her platinum album under her belt. Munchie, younger and prettier, had more offers of work in today's difficult entertainment market.

California's balmy weather entranced me and brought on another wave of needy sex. Seeing all the bikini-clad starlets lounging by our hotel's pool had made me hornier than ever. My Canadian owner was overly generous with the drinks, and I discovered I liked Bourbon. If I hadn't had my string to worry about, I would have lain with Happy for sex hour after hour.

I needed to oversee the early morning gallops. Fran came with me, high on coke. Munchie lolled in her bed back at the Bel Air, trading movie magazines with my star-crazy Happy. How different this stay in California was for her, from when I was working as Assistant Trainer to Bono Munoz and Happy made do with a tiny cottage. Then she'd reveled in having two past-their-sell date actresses as neighbors. This trip, with Munchie in tow, Happy had an entrée to the sparkling best of Hollywood. "Munchie, Ah doesn't know how to thank y'all 'nuf fo' takin' me to all the fancy doin's heah. Ah nevuh had so much fun!"

Munchie paid little attention to Happy's rapids of thanks. She'd been listening to them ever since the two had joined up to prowl Hollywood's bling places. For Munchie, this was work time. She needed a new job, and had to be picky about what she chose. She knew her future career hung on her next move. She left Happy reading while she telephoned agents.

Happy opened a new page of her magazine. "Munchie! Lookee heah. Sez thet Leila's going t'star in a Broadway musical called *Fannie*, based on the lahfe o' Fannie Brice. Who were she?"

"Big star. Before our tahme. A puhfect role fo' Leila. Fannie Brice were famed fo' huh big nose." Huge laugh from Munchie. "More important is the next article. Sez Heidi's desperate fo' work. Aftuh she flopped as Daisy Mae, none o' the impresarios wants huh."

Happy's big heart beat for all the people she knew, although beating more for some than it did for others. "Po'r Heidi. Cain't say as Ah lahkes huh much. But it's sho' tough not t'have work. Ah don't see much o' Filipa with Fran these heah days. Mebbe Fran could take on Heidi ag'in."

"Don't bet on it," Munchie's tone was very professional. "Truth is, Heidi's got a lousy voice. Cain't sing a damn. Filipa? She done gone t'Australia. Huh home. Don't say much fo' huh fondness fo' Fran."

Fran had serious worries outside of her singing career. She'd received threatening letters. And Fran saw that her filly needed a lot more preparation for her race.

Munchie wasn't aware of problems with Home Alone, she was too busy catching up on Hollywood gossip.

"Sez on t'next page thet Heidi's bein' auditioned fo' a Documentary 'bout Al Capp."

"'N who he be?"

"Yo-all don't knows? He be the fella what wrote Lil Abner, the comic strip."

I interrupted the two girls to invite them to go poolside for cool drinks. And whom should we see first thing there? Heidi, of course! Didn't I always believe that the person you talk about shows up within minutes?

Heidi looked totally different, unlike when in London, she hadn't tried to adopt the Daisy Mae image. She was a Marilyn Monroe, a Doris Day, a Rita Hayworth. She slinked up to us and in a sultry tone said, "You people have nothing better to do than hang around a pool?"

Munchie knew how to answer that one. "We's got hosses runnin' at Santa Anita. We's just takin' tahme off'n ourn busy programs fo' the Spo't o' Kings."

Heidi laughed. She'd heard through the Hollywood grapevine that neither Fran nor Munchie had any work. "Ho, ho, ho," she roared in her huge voice, but it was not with the famous Santa Claus intonation. "See you at Sardi's, where I'm lunching with my producer."

That was true. Confirming her story, Happy and I took my two owners to the Beverly Wiltshire. It was crowded with wannabes. When Heidi entered with a plump, greasy-faced older man, all eyes swiveled to him and forced smiles cracked expensive plastic jobs. I'd never seen him before, he was the nearly invisible backer whose money – Howard Hughes like – bankrolled the film industry. Again Heidi had changed her appearance. Like the clever actress she hoped to become, this time Heidi looked more of a Bette Davis type. I thought, "Heidi's certainly hung up on old classic movies."

She snubbed us and followed the Maitre D' to the best table. We'd been seated in "Siberia."

But, in case our voices carried, we didn't talk about Heidi. Munchie started another subject. "Po'r lil Filipa. Ah heah's huh baby's sick."

"Oh! Thet sick baby!" Happy sounded emotional. "But she ain't got no husband to help her?"

"Yup, she has an Aus-tra-lian husband."

I said, "She's only a teenager, nineteen. Must have been seventeen when she got pregnant. That's barbaric."

Hurt, my Happy chimed in to defend her own background. "We Kentucky gals git wedded 'n has babies when we's teenaguhs. Ah did. Good ole Kin-tuck custom. Ah knows some gals wut got stahted at fo'teen."

Fran chimed in, "And in Britain, as well. I read somewhere that there are more fourteen-year-old unwed mothers in the UK than forty-year-old first time mothers."

I'd been shot down. I couldn't help thinking I could hear my old Dad tut-tutting all the way from Warwickshire.

When Heidi and her producer left the restaurant, Fran started in with the really vicious gossip." I read how Heidi got picked for this Al Capp documentary. No, not on the producer's casting couch, although I wouldn't rule that out. According to a magazine that's trying to copycat the *Enquirer*, Heidi got the role because there had been a girl who tattled on Al Capp's sexual life, and Heidi looks something like that girl."

"We-all want t'heah all 'bout thet!" Munchie chortled, her eyes dancing like fireflies on a hot summer night.

"Well, it seems that Al Capp had lost a leg when he was a kid. Been sitting on a curb when a bus or some other vehicle drove right over his leg. He lost it and ever since had psychological hang-ups. Later in life, sexual problems. He needed a real fuck more than all the money and fame."

"Oh, oh!" Happy didn't like the way Fran had returned to four letter language.

"One day he met a young female journalist who wanted him to read the manuscript of a book she'd been trying unsuccessfully to sell. Since by that time Al Capp was so famous that his style was being taught in colleges, she took her book up to his apartment, thinking she'd drop it off and he'd read it. Like shit, he did! Instead, he unscrewed his leg, and tried to screw her!"

Munchie gloated, "And that's the role Heidi got! The unsuccessful journalist!"

"There's more. Not so juicy, but interesting. When Al Capp couldn't get into her cunt, he waited until she'd believe he'd have read the manuscript, and then he returned it to her marked 'unread' with a bill for two hundred dollars for having it Xeroxed."

"Sounds like Al Capp and Heidi were made for each other," I said, grinning. When I paid for our lunches, I stopped grinning. Our Sardi's stopover had taken one hell of a dent in my budget. Driving home, I returned to the unpopular subject of Fran's dallying. "She certainly changes boyfriends frequently."

Happy agreed. "Yeah man. Boyfriends wut don't lahke thet she's hooked on cocaine. Othuhs what don't lahke huh penny-pinchin' ways. Not an ole-fashioned chu'ch-goin' gal, our Fran. Nevuh gives nothin' t'charities."

Nodding, I grumbled, "When on Christmas I asked her if she wanted to go to church with us, she sneered, 'When I'm on stage, that's when I feel I'm in church. Don't fuck need any other.'"

That evening, when Hal Murphy arrived, Happy and I loaded up on a really huge dinner.

We could breakfast on the freebie coffee in our room but I knew I'd have to cut corners here in Hollywood as regarded entertaining. And I didn't want to sponge off of Hal too often.

Santa Anita Racetrack has a very different atmosphere from our courses in England. It was somewhat like Churchill Downs, but the Kentucky women looked nothing like the Hollywood types that thronged Santa Anita. Maybe I could compare the women to some I'd seen in Paris at Longchamp's Arc race: expensive clothes, expensive face lifts, expensive escorts, but no really knowledgeable race-goers like I'd found in France. Under all the attention-trapping devices used by both Hollywood and Parisian women, in France if you scratched under the surface you'd have discovered these women knew the breeding and past performances of all the horses in every race.

Anchor ran in the Arcadia Handicap on the day before the Santa Anita Derby. It had a purse of $150,000 guaranteed. Very poignant for me was that the horse I'd trained for Bono, Nile, trying to get him to perform at a Mile, won. He beat Anchor into Second.

My kind owner, Hal Murphy, accepted the Second money in good grace, delighted to have at last seen his horse in action.

"Well done, Rick my boy. I imagine you must feel elated that NILE did his thing. All due to your original preparation, I'm sure."

Santa Anita is laid over 320 acres. It has a 1100 foot long grandstand that can accommodate 26,000 viewers. The park around it can hold 50,000 guests. There are 61 barns able to house 2000 horses. It also has a fine equine hospital.

Arriving, you approach the main building by passing an important fountain that sprays a high jet of water. Nearby are ancient palm trees dating from the 1930s, and these tower at the height of a five-story building. Opened in 1934, the facility was designed by the same architect who built Colorado's Hoover Dam, Gordon Kaufman.

We headed for the Turf Club, where a strict dress code is observed. I felt a trifle anxious that my flamboyant owner, Hal, might be stopped because he wore an awful tartan jacket and a turtleneck shirt without a tie. But he passed muster and we enjoyed a walk through the Paddock Gardens before looking to get the best food at a track famous for its restaurants. Hal treated Happy and me to the Front Runner, where we had a table overlooking the Finish Line at its 300 foot long glass-enclosed facility. We weren't alone to watch Anchor's and Nile's run. There were at least 525 other diners. Happy passed up the Kentucky Fried Chicken for the crab cakes, a First, for her.

Santa Anita Park is located in a town called Arcadia, fourteen miles from downtown L.A., although most Californians prefer to think of it as L.A.'s track.

I received a cold nod from Nile's Trainer, the former Head Lad who'd replaced Bono at the helm when Bono was murdered by Hassan. When he'd been Head Lad I'd always treated him with fairness and courtesy, but I guess he simply resented being with a former boss at his moment of glory.

Another member of our group drew an extremely hot look. It was Fran, and within hours she was in love again. She'd picked up a gaffer from Universal Studios, a man who admired her for herself, who'd never heard her voice, and knew nothing of the Purcell Girls duo. He introduced himself at the rail of the six furlong training track, where I'd led my group to watch Home Alone do her gallops. No mention that Fran was a racehorse owner. He fell for her looks. And she certainly went for his. "I'm Nelson Polk, I work at Universal. Who're you?"

Nelson ignored the rest of my group. He was interested in Fran, only Fran. Nelson was short, pug-nosed, had red hair and very freckled skin. He wore a business suit with no tie, and an open shirt that revealed a thatch of red curly hairs climbing from chest to neck.

Without being asked he attached himself to my group, grabbing Fran's elbow as if he'd known her for years. We went to see the seven furlong turf course, that I thought I could use next year for a two-year-old sprinter that looked promising at home. But would she perform at Santa Anita?

Sweet Song didn't. She was a dismal failure. Home Alone won her race, but Fran didn't seem to care that her own filly lost, while the one she'd sold to Munchie was the big winner. Fran cared about nothing except that she'd found a man who was attracted to her. They exchanged packets of cocaine. Fran was ecstatic that she'd entered California's cocaine culture. Nelson didn't notice that Fran was very miserly with money. He didn't know about her twenty million. He thought she was a temporarily unemployed singer who'd lost the soprano of her duo. Fran hadn't monopolized their conversation by talking about her own career, she very astutely asked questions about his.

"I was born in Canada, got involved in the movie business through a Brit called Hoare. When the jobs dried up in Canada, I came to L.A., and made a good living here. Could support a wife." He said that last bit with great emphasis. He certainly had fallen for Fran!

At first, Fran was slightly dismayed, and made fun of his name. "Poke? Or did you say P-o-l-k?" The joke about poke stopped after an hour. I think Fran had already dreamed about a poke from Nelson.

Hal liked his fellow Canadian. He welcomed him into our circle and gladly paid for his lunch.

Happy dragged me across the infield to see the children's playground, Anita Chiquita. She examined all the facilities in case they were dangerous for our children, the three year-old and the one year-old. Satisfied, she said, "Love this place. Next yeah, us'n c'n bring the kids!"

When it came time to quit the racetrack, Nelson stayed as close as a tick to Fran. He had no intention of leaving her. Instead of asking, "Your place, or mine?" Nelson steered Fran to his beat-up old chevrolet and drove off with her. Lucky Fran, she didn't need to explain away the fact that she was staying at the most expensive hotel.

Fran wouldn't want to have had to invite him to "my place."

Of course all our dinner talk was about Fran and Nelson. Munchie voiced what was uppermost in our minds. "Will Nelson be strangled? Ah sho recall thet Goofy was!"

Fran must have been thinking along the same lines, because the next day when we met up for the Santa Anita Derby, the first thing she said was, "I'm selling my apartment in Chelsea. Nelson has never been to London, but he has an ancient auntie who owns a place near Hurlingham. We're going to stay with her when I have reason to return to London."

I said nothing. I needed her to keep her Sweet Song in my yard, I didn't want her to remain too long in California and decide to sell the filly. Sweet Song hadn't won at Santa Anita, but that didn't mean she couldn't perform well on her native heath.

Happy gave a huge hug to Fran, she felt truly pleased that her friend had a new love in her life.

We had a long wait in a queue to enter the racetrack on derby day. As in my group were neither owners nor I a Trainer of horseflesh acting in races that day, we paid our entry fees and joined the huge crowd swirling for box seats.

Hal Murphy was better dressed for the derby. He'd taken a cue from other race-goers the day before. Nelson wore the same business suit, but this time he'd buttoned up his shirt to hide the thrusting red curls on his chest. Fran must have given him a hint that she didn't want to share his persona with strangers.

We had a light lunch. I didn't want to stick Hal with another huge meal-bill. Munchie had offered to invite us all to champagne, but I knew she couldn't afford such a luxury. The six of us had taken a table close to the panoramic windows, and were thoroughly enjoying ourselves.

The derby was a splendid dash. I loved watching some of the finest colts in the world compete for its $750,000 prize. Happy shouted home the winner. She hadn't bet on him, but she'd guessed which horse would pass the Finish Post first. While the trophy was being given, Happy turned to Munchie, and said, "Too bad y'all didn't win big money lahke this'n. Gawd knows y'need it, with no wo'k fo' y'all."

When Nelson heard that Munchie was unemployed, he said, "I've heard about a part going in a horror movie we're making. It's taken out of a true story from last year's news. Remember that would-be cannibal who killed a neighbor's ten-year-old girl to eat her flesh? That type of story goes over big in Hollywood. One film made $40 million with a similar focus."

"I remembuh," Munchie groaned, her color rising to paint her cheeks like a sunset tinting peach blossoms. "His name wuz Kevin Ray Underwood. He done wrote in his blog thet all he wanted in lahfe was to be able to live lahke a normal puhson.' Some normal puhson! He joked in his diary he had an elab'rate plan to eat human flesh. Wrote how when he didn't take his med'cation he had 'dangerous and weird fantasies.' The po-lice found a big plastic tub in his closet in his home, and in the tub they found the li'l girl's unclothed body along with a towel to soak up blood."

Nelson continued the info. "Underwood lived in an apartment immediately below where the little girl lived with her father. Little girl's name was Jamie Rose Bolin. When the police found Jamie's body in the bedroom closet in a tub in his apartment, Underwood confessed to FBI agents, 'Go ahead and arrest me. She is in there. I chopped her up.'"

Shuddering, Munchie asked, "Does Ah have to be in thet kind o' movie?"

"You'd be great as Underwood's mother, Connie. She wept a lot, and offered apologies to Jamie's family. You've got the right face for that. Yes. Connie wasn't a great mother, though. She produced a loser. Kevin Underwood was nothing but a grocery store stocker. Neither old, nor a youngster, he's twenty-six. These folks lived in a small town forty miles from Oklahoma City. Real good for footage of a neat hometown. My studio loves that kind of background. Underwood killed Jamie when he tracked her going to a library. He took her to his apartment, where he beat and smothered her, before dismembering her body. Make a super horror film. The police found meat tenderizer and barbecue skewers to use when he roasted parts of her body, but I don't think any producer will want to add that fact to the film, because copycat crime always follows that kind of input."

Heidi and her producer entered the restaurant. Suddenly we felt as chilled as if hail had beaten down on the flowers of our garden.

They'd taken a table beside ours and heard the pertinent parts of Nelson's idea.

Heidi leaned toward Munchie, and said, "Forget it. That movie won't be made. The story's a year too late."

"Why? What do y'all mean?"

"Renée Zellweger signed a year ago to star in a similar horror thriller called *Case 39*. About a social worker who saves an abused 10-year-old girl from her parents. And then shit-all happens when the parents turn out to be horrible. What chance would a film you'd make have against that kind of competition? Renee Zellweger is an Oscar winner."

Hal Murphy put an end to that line of talk. He said, "I can help you out, Munchie, with the payments for the keep of Home Alone."

Nelson, quick on the up-take, now realized that there were racehorse owners in my group. He asked Munchie, "You own Home Alone? The winner of yesterday's fillies race?"

Munchie nodded. She was quick on the up-take too, and guessed that Fran had kept hidden her own position as an owner and a successful singer. Loyal Munchie didn't want to spoil Fran's budding love affair. But she didn't want to lie. Nodding was all she would do.

Heidi, at the next table, also guessed that Fran had kept quiet about her wealth and her status as an owner. With her booming voice, Heidi interrupted. "Fran owns the other filly, Sweet Song. Fran's so rich *she can* help out Munchie until there's work for her."

Heidi's producer wanted her attention. He ordered a bottle of champagne. With the bubbly in their hands, those two finally left our table to our own devices. The afternoon was ruined for us. Fran's sheepish half-smile had owned up that she was an owner, and Nelson took the news with a sour look.

"What else haven't you told me? Rich! You can produce a movie for your friend!" He stood up and would have left our table, but Heidi overplayed her hand.

From the next table, grinning through the bubbles of her champagne, she added, "There's loads that Fran hasn't told you, I'll bet. Little tidbits like the fact her twin was murdered in the apartment they shared, and later her boyfriend Goofy was murdered there too."

Nelson returned to his seat. With intense compassion, he took Fran's hands between his freckled paws. "Precious, wonderful Fran, I'm here for you. You could have told me why you didn't want to return to the apartment you own in London. You didn't, and that's the way it is. I'm going to have to learn to understand you."

Heidi's voice boomed out, "And to count Fran's shekels."

We left the restaurant. At the racetrack's exit gate there was a surge of humanity pushing to get the cars from the valets collecting them. Hal brought out a ticket to have his limo called, and we decided to leave our cheap rental Honda to return with him to the Bel Air.

Fran didn't object to letting Nelson know she was living at the Bel Air. No point to that now. They drove behind us in his battered Chevrolet. Arriving at the Bel Air he hesitated giving his Chevrolet to a parking attendant, Nelson wasn't accustomed to using parking attendants. Fran tipped the boy in advance and pushed Nelson into the hotel's lobby. "Now it's not your place. It's mine," she said, leaving the four of us in the lobby while leading Nelson to the bank of elevators to go upstairs to her suite.

"They'll be all right," Hal muttered. "It's not that tough to have a girlfriend who's loaded."

CHAPTER 13

Our Epsom home didn't expand well for house guests. But we made an exception for Munchie. With no job, and frightened to sleep alone in her London flat, she needed us. We'd returned from L.A. without Fran or Hal, and the three of us hired a minicab for the drive to Epsom, cheaper than a registered black taxi or a limo.

The minicab's Pakistani driver would have done well to keep his mouth shut, however when he guessed he had a singing star in his cab, he gave with a torrent of comments." Very nice play, that *Daisy Mae*. My wife and I went to see. Poor people, those Dogpatch people, poorer than in Pakistan. But loveable. Don't you think so? What role did you play?"

Munchie didn't want to admit to having been Stupefyin' Jones, the town whore. "Ah understudied fo' Sybil Sykes, so Ah took on the role of Daisy Mae after she were killed."

"No. We saw it with a big Hollywood star. I remember now, you were Stupefyin' Jones," he contradicted her in his sing song accent. "That star, she gone on to Broadway. Playing Fannie Brice. My wife and I thought we fly to America to see. But Leila Forbes mix up with Neil Young, who like mix politics with music."

"And is that so bad?"

"Bad, yes bad. In his album, *Living With War*, he ruminate on war in Iraq and call for impeachment of President Bush. She joined in a

100-voice choir for backdrop singing flip flop. Not good. We not go to Broadway now."

Munchie, hooked on gossip as surely as Fran was on cocaine, lapped up the news that Leila Forbes was in a spot of trouble. Munchie was sorry to leave the Pakistani's minicab, she'd harvested such a tasty bit of gossip from him.

Happy, overjoyed to be reunited with our babies, hurried Munchie to the guest bedroom and was done with her. Happy needed to pay some attention to Ellie, who had given up her own life to oversee Mrs. Rea's care of our children.

Ellie looked as exhausted as a midwife who'd delivered triplets. She accepted the gifts Happy had bought for her in Pasadena and L.A., and then hurried to her parents' home. She missed having a personal maid, a butler, and a chauffeur in attendance.

True that I take enormous pleasure in sex during trips to faraway lands, or really in any hotel room. And yet the sex in my own double bed at home in Epsom was terrific, too. I always achieve a huge erection when I see that Happy gets a satisfactory orgasm, and that night we both reveled in the best sex for a week.

As so often happens in my life, when one aspect of it goes well then something dramatically awful follows. This time my joy in returning to my own bed with my wife was cut short by a telephone call from Tom, my head groom. "The two-year-olds are coughin' somethin' terrible, Mr. Harrow. Even the three-year-olds seem to have got a fever. Better come down, and call the vet to meet you here."

On a balmy April morning, when Springtime was in full burst with the azaleas opening and the migrant birds using our garden as an inn, my horses were as sick as if in the midst of a winter's tempest. Our vet didn't like the look of them. "Need a second opinion, Mr. Harrow. But I'm afraid most of your horses have pneumonia."

When people get pneumonia, their lungs ache. When horses get it, they stop standing tall and lie down in their straw. The most beautiful, really magnificent horses in my string were moaning and prostrated on straw.

My plans to take the best of my string to Newmarket for the Guineas meeting came to naught. I'd isolated my two fillies and Anchor when they arrived back home from California, and I decided to give the two fillies a chance to show off at the cradle of racing.

On a warm day the first week of May I bundled them into a horsebox. I drove North up that sublime road lined with cherry blossom trees until I reached the Jockey Club Rooms in Newmarket where I settled in while Tom took the horsebox to unload the horses beyond the town.

I reveled in the gracious atmosphere of that fine old building, with its paintings by Stubbs and its faded photos of the great contenders of yesterday. Rising early, I heard neighing from horses in fields nearby, and smelled the grass fed by centuries of manure provided by the best racehorses of this nation.

Of the three in my string that were free of pneumonia, it was Sweet Song that gave my yard a win. I'd brought her along just in case, because I thought she might be a contender for the One Thousand Guineas of 2008, and wanted to try her out on Newmarket's heath. Living at Epsom, I should have aimed her for The Oaks, but I doubted she'd handle that uphill run. The pity of it was that Fran had stayed in California with Nelson and had not seen her filly win.

Munchie did have the joy of being present for Home Alone's taking a prize at Kempton. I had the chance to see its recently installed all-weather track and make a decision if I should run any of my two-year-olds there. What a performance Munchie gave when she accepted the trophy for Home Alone. She was Queen Victoria, at the moment of becoming Empress of India, she was Marilyn Monroe singing Happy Birthday to President Kennedy in Madison Square Garden, she was Keira Knightley at the Oscars. The trophy was a large crystal rose bowl. Few racecourses give silver except for the classics because few racehorse owners want to spend time cleaning silver. Munchie was one of those, and was quite content not to have a silver ornament gathering a black patina on her mantelpiece.

I took Anchor to May Ascot races and he came in Second in the White Rose Stakes, no mean achievement. Sweet Song ran badly in a fillies' race at Epsom on Derby Day, proving I was right about her reluctance to gallop uphill.

My Arkansas-bred filly and my Kentucky-born wife had a special relationship. Happy gave up the excitement of racecourses to stay with Feathers and nurse her back to health. She hand-fed her carrots and apples.

She spooned in the hay to her net and changed her water every few hours. Eventually Feathers began to show improvement and I could dream of entering her for an Ascot race.

With Royal Ascot approaching, Fran reappeared in England. She had attended that event every year since she was eighteen, and had no intention of foregoing that pleasure on Nelson's account.

Happy and I were invited to join them for lunch at the Hurlingham Club, within a few blocks of Nelson's auntie's house. We went there on a cloudy day, threatening rain, but sat outside on the club's terrace to watch the tennis players. Fran's face was as cloudy as the sky above. She looked to me as if she was about to cry. When I was left alone with Nelson, because the two girls had disappeared to the ladies' loo, I got an earful from him. His red hair the color of flames erupting from a volcano, his face ashen, he said, "Fran wants to get married. What the hell! Why do these babes always want a wedding ring just because they're getting screwed? The only reason I'll ever get hitched is if I go broke and need the gal's money."

In the ladies' loo, tarted up with dried flowers and botanical prints, Fran had finally burst into tears. "Happy, you're a married woman. Tell me what to do." Between gasps she continued without waiting for input from Happy, "He wants unprotected sex. Says it's like being in sunshine and wearing a raincoat when I insist on a condom. But what if he has Aids?"

"Can't you say you want to git wedded? 'N find a place what won't give a license without an Aids test?"

"Tried that. He said no way did he want to get married. We'd be fine together as we are if I'd just agree to no more condoms."

Happy was speechless. When she would have given some input, she was put off by the entry into the loo of an elderly club member who took an inconsiderate amount of time in the W.C. Happy waited until she'd washed her hands and left.

"Cain't urge y'all to give up on condoms. Not 'lessen he takes a test. But what makes y'all think he might have Aids? Looks healthy enough,"

"You saw how he picked me up at the Santa Anita track? Oh, shit. He tries to pick up women in front of me, now. No shame. Flirts with waitresses, hat check girls, anybody."

"Mebbe y'all should move back into yo' apartment. Y'all could be the one in control."

"Nelson won't do that. I asked him to. Said 'no way.' I think he gets an erotic kick out of his old auntie listening to us fucking. Happy, what am I to do? I still love him."

Happy put her arms around Fran, and felt her trembling. "Ah don't thinks as he deserves yo'r love."

When Fran returned to our table on the terrace the rain began and we needed to go inside the clubhouse. There was no opportunity there to pursue this sex subject. No doubt the members used condoms but they didn't speak about them in the club precincts.

To my astonishment and discomfort, Nelson arrived on our Epsom doorstep that night, without Fran and with a suitcase. There was no mistaking his intention. Having seen Happy in action with our two infants, and judging that she and I enjoyed sex without condoms, he came to woo my Happy.

He didn't know that she'd been fully alerted to his impending break-up with Fran over the use of condoms. Nelson flashed his pearly implants, enhanced by Listerine's whitening mouthwash. He complemented Happy on her taste in decorating, her excellent mothership with two well-behaved infants, and even had the gall to tell her she was a superb cook. Our décor had suffered from Feathers' soiled nosebags dumped on the furniture. Our infants wailed loudly all evening. Happy made her usual ghastly greasy Kentucky fry-ups. Nelson's wide smile and compliments continued, thanks to his expensive California dentist and even more expensive California shrink.

Happy stayed true. When I went down to my yard for early morning stables and Nelson promptly appeared at our bedroom door to gain entry, he was given short shrift by my loyal little Baptist wife.

Nelson was on the noon train for London.

Happy and I went up to London a few days later for the privilege of watching Munchie in her new role. She had been hired by the D'Oyly Carte opera company to be in *The Mikado*. With two others she sang the time-honored Three Little Girls From School Are We, and brought down accolades from all over the house.

Our blond friend from Tennessee wore a black wig and brown-tinted contact lenses to play a Japanese maiden. Her voice was perfect for that exquisite medley of girls' voices.

After the show we didn't go back stage. Happy deemed that unlucky, considering that the last time we'd done that we'd walked into a murder. On the late train home, Happy asked, "Why don't Munchie cut a record with Fran? Seems lahke tahme's a-wastin' fo' Fran t'git back t'wuck."

"Ask Munchie why she hasn't."

Happy did. The following week, when Happy went back to London to raid the shops for her Royal Ascot hats, she met Munchie in Chinatown for tea between Munchie's appearance in a matinée and an evening performance.

"Munchkins," Happy used a favorite nickname, "what's stoppin' y'all from cuttin' a reco'd with Fran?"

"Cain't. Wouldn't be right t'do thet to Filipa." "Meanin' she' done got a contract with Fran."

"Thet, too. But Ah wouldn't anyways. Not mah style t'poke in wheah Ah's not invited.'

"Speakin' o' poke. Did y'all know thet Fran 'n Nelson done split up?" "No surprahse. He tried t'make out with me, early on-lahke, in Cal'for-ni-a."

"She thinks he maht-a had AIDS."

"Gawd amahty. No sweat? Ain't we-all the lucky ones, t'turn him off. Po'r Fran!"

"Yeah man, she done give him the boot. Now she's alone ag'in."

"Fran needs t'git smaht. In this entertainment bus'ness y'all gotta keep in the public eye."

"Ain't thet easy!"

"Nope. Ain't. Got t'git busy. Lahke Beyonce 'n thet Co-lomb-ian gal Shakira, they dun got busy singin' a duet wut got 'em mentioned in the Latin Music Awards."

"Thet be impo'tant?"

"'Nuf. Mahnd y'all, Ah c'n give huh a great ideah. Michael Jackson's doin' anothuh recordin'. Yo-all remembuh he did one fo' hurr'cane victims in Lou-si-anna? Now he's preparing anothuh."

"How c'n Fran get in on thet?"

"Not easy. But could be done. Jackson's raght heah in London. The record's to be released end o' this yeah. Jackson was quoted sayin', 'I am incredibly excited about my new venture and I am enjoying being back in the studio making music,' Jackson done said thet to promote this record fo' a label, 2 Seas Records. Owned by a Bahrain prince called Sheik Abdullah bin Hamad Al Khalifa. Long name, big money. Record label's based in Bahrain. Richest li'l piece o' land most anywheahs. This Sheik's into music, not lahke the Dubai Sheiks, what owns race hosses."

"And Fran?"

"Ah've met this Sheik. He come backstage t'othuh night. He gimme his cahd. Ah'll introduce Fran. The rest's up to huh."

CHAPTER 14

Fran found another boyfriend, but he wasn't a Sheik. More of a shakedown artist. His name was Honoré Boudin, a Frenchman, who claimed he was a Count but I think he was one of those my old Dad referred to as Counts of no-account.

Fran, dazzled by the phony title, having wanted to be a Countess way back when she fell for Jeremy, was urged to return to the stage by this new guy.

She was on the blower to Australia day after day, pleading with Filipa to return to London to cut a record. Fran could hear Filipa's infant squalling in the background during each and every call. Happy, still suspicious of Filipa, claimed that Filipa might have pinched the baby to make it cry when Fran called.

Not true. Filipa's baby girl was seriously ill.

Filipa had this crisis on her mind, prima. She'd bought a horse in Harold East's yard, but had never seen it run. A gelding, there didn't seem to be any urgency for it to win a race, because it could never be used for breeding. East's horses and mine continued to compete against one another. At a Kempton meeting, East told me about Filipa's baby's illness. It seems she was semi-paralyzed, with useless legs.

When I passed on this info to Happy, she almost wept. Her big heart embraced so many people and horses, but she always seemed to have room in it for one more needy character, equine or human. She gulped, and said, "Po'r Filipa. Only nahneteen and havin' to cope with a sick baby. We-all should help. We-all could call up the Marston Children's Hospital and get advice for wut ails her."

We did. Or rather, Happy did. She had our own pediatrician do the donkey work, checking data and such. I called Australia and jotted down the baby girl's symptoms and the local doctor's diagnosis. Happy relayed all of this to our pediatrician and he met with one of the top people at the Marston. All the reports led to the diagnosis that Filipa's baby had suffered from polio; her high fever and subsequent paralysis seemed to indicate the doctors were right.

"Mah Mammy had polio." Happy declared, " 'N Ah don't think thet now'days as folks gits it ennymo'e. They's thet Salk vaccine. Sho' thing Filipa must'a not given thet chile the vaccine." We checked, and she had.

Happy's no doctor, but she's so often right about a lot of problems. I said, "I know what you're thinking. We should go to Melbourne." "Yup."

"Not now. But when Royal Ascot's behind us, I'll think about making the trip."

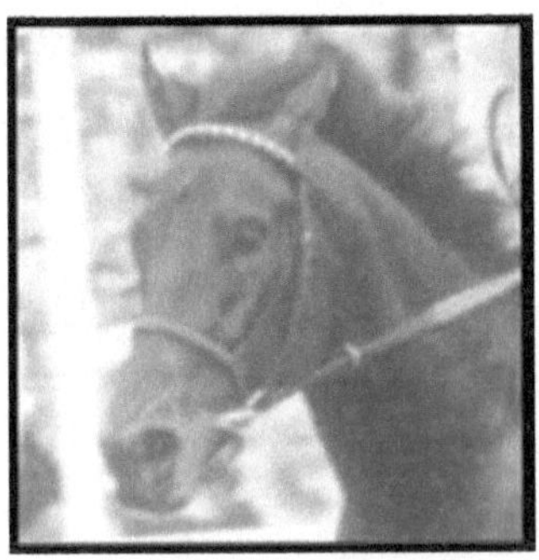

CHAPTER 15

We couldn't miss Royal Ascot.

That meeting was very important in so many ways. For owners like Col. Flyte and Captain Ainsley its social prestige counted very high in their annual calenders. They wanted to see and be seen there.

For more serious horsemen, winning its races would add luster to any member of the equine world. The future great mares and stallions would win here. Winning a Royal Ascot race counts high in the breeding tables.

For Trainers, Royal Ascot took precedence over anything except perhaps the Derby, the two Guineas, and the St. Leger. But while a Triple Crown was the ultimate to yearn for, among some of us, we know that for social caché our owners usually prefer to win at Royal Ascot.

As that all-important week loomed, I could be relaxed so far as my kids were concerned. They were fine.

Happy turned over their care to our housekeeper and like an ultra-feminine debutante she concentrated on what to wear at Royal Ascot. She bought four new hats for the Ascot meeting, but made do with only one new outfit, a silk coat and dress to match.

She decided to rely on old shoes for comfort. "No thenk y'all." Happy summed up her opinion of the season's five-inch heels.

This year we drove ourselves in a cheap rental car, nothing as grand as Father's 1956 Bentley that had motored us to Ascot in 2006. Too bad that Father didn't accompany us in 2007. He'd have had little to complain about. Millions of pounds from the queen's private purse had been spent to eradicate last year's disasters. The landscaping had been improved with over-sized Versailles boxes spotted in favored places, their tops rounded with hydrangeas. The lawns were better appointed, and the General Admission folk had been neatly sidelined to go through their own entrance leaving the Royal Enclosure members to mingle with one another. Still no gypsies with lucky white heather for sale, but a tidy area had been reserved for a polite vendor of cornflowers for buttonholes.

HM The Queen was beautifully turned-out. I've always thought she saved the best of her wardrobe for Royal Ascot. She came down the course in a parade of antique landaus filled with her relations and best friends. She smiled and waved, but there was more to her persona on the opening day of Royal Ascot, that smile and those waves were based on a feeling of well-being. In spite of being eighty-one years old, she was like a young woman on her way to a holiday party.

Happy thoroughly appreciated the scene, although as she was so tiny she needed to locate one of the huge screens on the far side of the gallops to view The Sovereign. And that was thanks to modern technology.

"Ah declahs, Ah was supposed t'be impressed when at Santa Anita them's race touts rolled off all them names of movie stahs whut went to that track in yeahs gone by, Charlie Chaplin, Clark Gable, Cary Grant and Bing Crosby. 'N y'all knows how Ah loves movie stars. But, tell y'all truth-lahke, Ah thinks the Queen o' England beats it fo' glitz ovah all them film people."

I listened attentively. Any favorable remark about my native land's monarch was like honey on my toast.

Royal Ascot's my favorite meeting of the year, and I had three runners liable to win their races. The weather, very different from Royal Ascot's in 2006, veered from milky sun to sharp showers. My mudder liked the showers.

All my runners were entered in Group Three events, those which prepare horses to eventually run in a Group One or Group Two.

In spite of all Happy's personalized nursing, Feathers was still not well enough to run. It was Home Again and Sweet Song that both won early in the week. Sadly for Munchie, who was in a matinee on the Wednesday, she didn't see her filly romp across the Finish Line.

Fran was cheered on to shout out for her horses by that doubtful French count.

Hal Murphy arrived just in time to see his Anchor win on the Saturday. Happy and I didn't get any of Royal Ascot's well-served catered meals until Hal arrived, Fran still pinching pennies and too mean to celebrate her wins with a bottle of champagne.

I didn't produce a winner for Captain Ainsley, but I had hopes to earn him some prize money in late July on the King George VI and Queen Elizabeth day, not for its big international event, but a smaller one later in the day.

With the 2007 Royal Ascot week over, the Northern owners of Billandbea kept insisting I give their horse an airing. I waited until a small race at Lingfield that looked easy. I felt like a student who cheats in an exam by peering over the nearest shoulder.

But picking an easy race worked. I sent him to victory there. I couldn't hope to keep all my owners if I only catered to the stars in my yard.

On the King George and Queen Elizabeth day we were back at Ascot, but this time Happy wore her last year's hat. It was a dullweather afternoon, with heat but no sparkling sunshine. Mess from yesterday's charity event at Ascot had left a debris of torn programs and tickets. Elderly minions in green velvet knee-length jackets for livery worked in the suffocating heat to eradicate the mess. Their black silk toppers embossed with royal crests showed they were doing their job for our monarch, not searching like homeless men for something of value.

I wanted to win for Captain Ainsley. He and his wife had repeatedly backed me up during bad times and I felt truly ashamed when their jockey broke a finger while mounting and had to abandon their race. No reflection on the status of their horse, but it would be some months before the Festival of Racing would give their horse another opportunity to show his very real talent.

CHAPTER 16

Fran and Filipa had corralled us with invitations in late July. Fran, sidelined temporarily from the more lucrative rap world, had accepted to sing as Musetta at Covent Garden Opera House in *La Boheme*. Filipa had won the starring role of Mimi.

Their three day engagement coincided with a milestone in racing, the transfer of important duties from the Jockey Club to the British Racing Authority. I felt I should combine a trip to the opera with a visit to the Turf Club to listen to what other Trainers felt about this development.

I drove to London in the Volvo with Happy. We were so looking forward to this day that we sang excerpts from *Madama Butterfly* as I headed down Park Lane to take a left into Piccadilly, and then turn towards Haymarket.

"Lookee theah!" Happy pointed out a restaurant she loved. "Some crazy drivuh has left his ve-hi-cle on the sidewalk in front of Tiger Tiger."

Eyeing the restaurant and illegally-parked car, I almost missed the entrance to Jermyn Street, but managed to reach Fortnum & Mason's rear door to deposit Happy there. She wanted to buy specialty foods for the next time we'd entertain our owners.

From Bury Street, I turned in at Pall Mall to go on to the Turf Club, where I found a perch at the bar to listen in on conversations between several retired trainers.

Ian Balding said, "We'll have to wait and see how it turns out now that the Jockey Club has handed over so many duties to the BHA. Personally, I've always thought the Jockey Club did a fine job. Maybe we didn't need this change."

"Hear, hear!" Voices agreed all over the room.

By noon, Happy joined me at the club to go upstairs to the Ladies Dining Room. We sat there, under its marvelous skylight, and enjoyed looking at the great oil paintings while ordering from the luscious selections on its menu. Happy left the table while waiting for our food to arrive. She stared long and hard at a very old oil of a jockey on his mount. "Sakes alahve, if it ain't thet famous jockey, Fred Archer," she whispered in an ecstatic tone.

We'd been given matinée tickets to *La Boheme*. The cheapest, because Fran continued to pinch pennies.

Both Filipa and Fran were in good voice. Their costumes suited them, and they acted well, although Fran over-played the Musetta role during her restaurant scene, flirting with every man on stage, when she should have restricted herself to two only. Was Fran's boyfriend not measuring up?

At the interval, I invited Happy for champagne and smoked salmon sandwiches in the newly built two-story glass hall. We camped on tall seats near cages holding figurines costumed in the luxurious silks of a bygone opera era. We didn't attempt the two-storey escalators reaching up to a penthouse restaurant, although I would have enjoyed the celebrated view from there of Covent Garden's street players, mimes and buskers.

Returning to our seats for Mimi's death scene, I admired the way the opera house had been refreshed and restored without damaging its late Victorian atmosphere. There was still the great semi-circular frieze containing Queen Victoria's image, and the gold -backed figures of lyre players. The architects had even retained the half-torsos of naked women holding up candelabra in front of each box.

Of course, we weren't in a box. Fran's penny-pinching had merely provided gallery perches. However, we had a good look into what had been King Edward VII's box; where, when Prince of Wales, he entertained the singing stars on his couch there during the intervals. I told Happy, "In a book I read, it said that Queen Victoria had a toilet installed in the Prince of Wales's box, because after all his dallying with easy women, she didn't want to share hers with him."

Happy had to strangle her laughter. A bearded professor in the row in front had turned around to glare.

We drove home singing songs from *La Boheme*.

Sex was great that night, and I nibbled Happy's ear while crowing, "This time when we went to hear music in one of London's great venues, it wasn't like when we walked into Sybil's murder. No horrors."

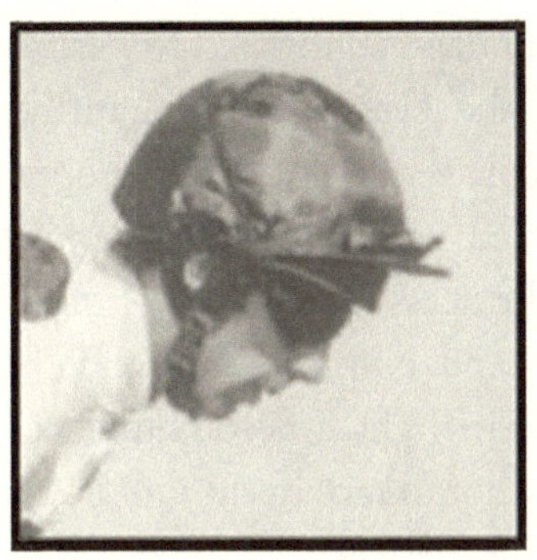

CHAPTER 17

How wrong I was about the horrors. When the tabloids arrived on our doorstep the following morning, even before early stables, Happy and I were dismayed by the headlines. "Two Cars Packed With Explosives at Top Sites in London" and "Detonators Failed to Trigger Explosions in Front of Tiger Tiger Restaurant and on Park Lane."

"Rick!" Happy recognized the car pictured on the front page. "Thet's the ve-hi-cle us'n saw parked illegally. Lookee heah, the noospapuh says theah was a party goin' on at Tiger Tiger for the birthday of a duke's daughter. And also, we must have passed the car parked bad on Park Lane. Thet's two narrow escapes."

"Yeah." I agreed, peering at the newspaper over Happy's shoulder. "And look how it describes the agony suffered by the tow-truck guy whose job it had been to take that Park Lane car to be held at a pound. When told what he'd been towing, he fainted."

"Why do y'all suppose the bombs didn't go off?"

"The terrorists must have been amateurs. But the police are trailing them. They have information about the escape car."

"Ah hopes they nails them terr-or-ists befo'e us'n goes to Fran's next singin' job."

Didn't happen.

Fran and Filipa had been contracted to perform a medley of Puccini arias near Glasgow, at the Ayshire estate, Lanfine. The system of using grand stately homes as the venues for opera or operetta evenings had been successful since it started with *The Mikado*, performed by the D'Oyly Carte professionals at Princess Diana's early home, Althorpe.

I'd promised Fran and Filipa we'd attend the medley evening and accompany them on their flight. I needed to check out the course at Ayr in case I could send Anchor to race in the Gold Cup there. It didn't appear to portend a near-death experience.

But we'd forgotten that the car-bomb terrorists had still not been caught. Happy and I were carrying Fran and Filipa's overnight bags through the concourse of Glasgow's airport, and had almost reached its front doors with our two singers, when a large vehicle smashed past the bollards supposedly protecting this airport. Within seconds the vehicle had stopped near us, flames pouring from all four windows. One terrorist ran for his life. The second terrorist, trapped in the vehicle, was burning like a torch on a fireworks night. Local heroes downed the first terrorist, securing him until airport police arrived. The second terrorist was attended to by compassionate doctors, who overlooked the slaughter these terrorists had attempted.

When the vehicle's flames were doused, explosives were found inside it similar to the ones that failed to ignite on Park Lane and in Piccadilly. There were enormous quantities of bomb material coupled with chains and nails planned to produce the worst carnage.

I thought my three ladies would collapse. Not at all. Happy led the two singers to our rental car, her face grim but determined. Our two singers, who had merely screeched a bit from nerves, calmed down when we stopped at a roadside Big Chef restaurant and I plied them with coffees.

At the restaurant was a TV tuned to comments on events at the Glasgow Terminal. We learned that the two terrorists were both medical doctors employed by England's National Health.

Muslims, they had been recruited to produce havoc in Britain by killing as many innocents as they could reach with the three vehicles they had packed with explosives.

"Britain should be 'shamed fo' takin' in those doctors." Filipa said, when she heard that these two doctors had been turned down by Australia when they'd applied for work there.

I'd doubted that our two singing stars would be able to give their evening concert of Puccini arias. Again, I was wrong. Those two troopers had their faults, but missing a performance wasn't one of them.

Fran remarked, "I think the Americans invented the expression 'The Show Must Go On'."

We drove past Lanfine's eerie mist-covered lake to pass the stately home and enter the area allotted to parking. The lot was almost empty.

When we left the singers in their dressing rooms, Happy and I took our cheap seats to find the singers had been snubbed. Their audience was exceptionally thin. Terrorists at Glasgow Airport had proved a mighty excuse for opera enthusiasts to stay home. Although the tickets had sold out, less than half the seats were occupied. Fran had sneered during our visit to her dressing room, "I'll bet most of these folks who've turned up are the servants or gamekeepers on the Scottish estates of the fraidy-cats who'd bought the tickets."

But the two girls sang at their best no matter who formed the audience. We heard the *One Fine Day* aria from Madama Butterfly; Mimi's introduction giving her name from La Boheme, *Mi Ciamano Mimi*, Nessun Dorma from Turandot, and Don Giovanni's cemetery song. The two singers alternated as soloists or gave us duets. They had chosen early Nineteen Hundred's gowns in a style that divas wore during the zenith. of Puccini's career. In matching white silk with balloon sleeves and long trains, they looked fantastic.

It was Happy who buckled. My valiant wife, so brave when faced with death during her abduction in Dubai, had a late-reaction during the interval. She got the shakes, and had to find a seat while her knees were wobbling. She choked out, "Our chillun could have been made or-phans today."

Dourly, I agreed. The terrorists' attempts to kill innocent passengers at Glasgow's busy airport had come close to making orphans of our two tots.

CHAPTER 18

Happy and I were back at Ascot for the Shergar Cup for the next time we entertained there. Owners send some of the best jockeys from the rest of the world for this cup, but I didn't place a horse in the race because I get the shudders every time the name Shergar is mentioned. Feathers, when she was kidnapped could have suffered his same fate! Eaten?

The Ascot Festival in the next to last week of September brought the mighty landowners back from their shooting lodges and country mansions to join in with race-goers again. Col. Flyte was not disappointed. His horse did win a small race in heavy rain during the three day meeting which tolls the end of the 2007 flat racing season. The Festival antes up over 1 million pounds in prize money, with no less than six Group races.

Hal Murphy didn't come over for the Festival. He telephoned. "Rick my boy, I've been thinking I should save my energy to go to Australia for the Melbourne Cup. Are you game? I'll pay your and Happy's trips, hotel rooms, and you deliver Anchor in stupendous condition so that I can add an Australian race to his roster. A deal?"

"A deal!"

When I told Happy of our plans, her immediate response concerned Filipa and her ailing baby. "Thank God. Ah've bin prayin' we's goin' thet-a-way. Ah's got ideas on how t'cure thet baby."

"Do you believe I could win a race there with Anchor?" "Naw. Good hoss, not a great hoss. Why not take Feathuhs?" "But is she fit? Hasn't she lost a lot of condition?"

"Fit, yeah man. Lost condition, but don't worry huh none. Feathuhs c'd win awraght."

I was on the blower immediately to Hal, and suggested we take Feathers instead of Anchor. "I think Anchor needs a rest. He's had a lot of racing. We don't want to put him off the job."

Hal agreed, as he almost always does. What a nice guy! If I believed in having men friends, he'd be top of the list. I admired much in Hal, but that didn't stop me from noticing his appalling lack of taste in clothing. At Royal Ascot he'd appeared in a brown top hat, brown morning tail coat and brown striped trousers. If he wanted to be noticed, he succeeded. Wasn't it Beau Brummel who said, 'Never brown in town.!' " I wondered what outfit he'd produce for the Melbourne Cup. It's a national holiday in Australia for the Melbourne Cup, and I worried that dear Hal would turn up there dressed as a clown in a circus.

The next day I was concentrating on faxing my entries, when Happy rushed into my office. She looked terribly upset. "Ah's awful bothuhed," she cried.

I stood up from my desk and held her shaking shoulders. "What is it, darling?"

"Y'all knows Ah'm no worse fo' gossip than most, but Munchkins just 'phoned me with news Ah knows y'all don't want t'heah."

I felt temporarily relieved to learn that it was gossip and not the lives of our infants that had so disturbed poor Happy, "Are you sworn to silence?" I asked with a small laugh.

"This ain't no laughin' mattuh. Listen up. Ellie, our Ellie has the hots fo' Harold East. They's got engaged. Romance bin goin' on since Ascot, 'n we nevuh guessed."

"Harold East!" I felt stunned. My nemesis, the nearby Trainer who beat our horses regularly—and worse—hadn't fired his stable jockey after he whipped ours in the face reaching a Finish Line.

"You're sure? This isn't just Munchie making up a whopper." "She sez lahke an announcement be in The Times t'morrow."

"Oh!" I sat down and collected my thoughts. I didn't need to read an announcement in the broadsheets to realize that Munchie's news was spot on. I knew the facts. They were planted right into the marrow of my bones. How Ellie had been so pleased to stay in our house to watch over Mrs. Rea's supervision of our infants, with Harold East's yard within walking distance. Like Lizzie in *Pride and Prejudice*, she'd have stalked the moors between our gallops to reach the home of her beloved. And I knew she needed a man. It was over two years now since Ivor had blown out his brains. She'd mourned him properly and the time had now come to move on to a new romance. She liked the aura of a Trainer's yard, she certainly spent enough time in ours to prove that. Dear Ellie, after the first shock, I thought, "I wish her happiness."

"The's mo'e."

"Like . . .?"

"Ellie's goin' t'Aus-tra-li-a with Harold East fo' the Melbourne Cup."

I groaned. "Damn, that means he'll be running those blasted fillies of his against ours."

"Yeah man."

There was no advantage in blaming Munchie, and when she telephoned to invite us to The Berkeley for Sunday lunch, we accepted.

London's streets were painted orange and rust and dull red from masses of leaves that covered the tarmac like a heavy snowfall. Street sweepers were not in evidence. I parked unwittingly on a yellow line because the leaves were so thick I couldn't see its warning streak. Ticket! And tow job costing £150.

Munchie's invite didn't include the top-rated restaurant. We settled in sofas near the bar, overlooking the lobby. A crackling fire cheered the lobby, with tourists swirling around in unsuitably thin clothes. A taxi drew up to the hotel's front steps and we watched as a shooting man emerged with his long gun case, his moor boots, and wearing the tweed jacket he no doubt expected to use on the next day's shoot. He didn't tip the taxi driver nor the doorman, and I couldn't help to wonder at that, knowing that a day's shooting could cost in the thousands.

Munchie distracted my thoughts, "What y'all goin' t'eat?"

Happy chose the least expensive item on the bar menu, "Chick'n sandwich. Ah'd love a root beah, but Ah don't expect lahke as this'n ho-tel would have enny."

"Take a fresh orange juice. Pricey, but good heah. 'N you, Rick?"

"Same. Chicken sandwich will do just fine. And a beer. Miller's Light will do."

The menu sorted, Munchie dove immediately into the Ellie-plus-Harold East affair. "They's bin sleepin' t'gethuh fo' months."

I groaned: "As they'd say in Australia, 'good on her.' She's been awfully lonely, pouring her love into my children and some leftover for her cousin Jeremy. Not healthy."

My little Baptist wife objected. "Ah's not agreein' t'thet kind o' talk. Ah sez they should git wedded. Soonest, best."

"Accordin' to the *Daily Mail*, their weddin' is set fo' December 26. Wut yo Brits call Boxin' Day. Sho' nuf. Ah c'd come to thet. No puhfo'mance fo' mah new job on Boxin' Day."

"New job? Tell us, you've been so full of the Ellie story we haven't heard that news." I was keenly interested. Anything in Munchie's career moves was noted because she was the owner of one of my best fillies, and there had been so many strange stories that year. One of the worst equine flu epidemics had erupted in Australia in August, causing the authorities to close down all its racecourses for seventy-two hours. At the time, I'd doubted I'd take the best of my string to Australia unless the flu scare ended promptly.

Munchie was bouncing with her news. "Yeah man. Ah's got t'paht o' Elizabeth in a musical version o' *Prahde 'N Prejudice*. Suits me fahne. Ah was so tahed o' bein' a Jap'nese. Them brown-tinted contact lenses made me feel blind."

I wondered how her Tennessee accent would work for a County English character. Maybe she'd go to the same elocution lessons place that tried to weed out my Happy's jargon. We ate our sandwiches, I drank my beer, Munchie talked on. I knew she lived alone, and I figured she must want an audience for her thoughts, not just an audience in a theatre.

"Ah wants t'go with y'all to Aus-tra-li-a 'n see mah filly run. *Prahde 'N Prejudice* don't open until mid-Decembuh. No rehu'sals fo'e couple weeks.

Male lead ain't contracted yet. What y'all think?"

"She may not win. Australia's a long way to go to watch her come in second, or nowhere."

"So why're you sendin' huh?"

"Because she might win. And it's only fair to her to give her that chance. The best stallions in the world will accept to have her if she wins on Melbourne Cup Day."

"Ah've anothuh tidbit o' gossip. Want t'heah?"

"Sho' thing," Happy agreed, eyes shining as if she was about to meet a movie star.

"Fran, she done moved back into huh ole' apahtment." "Two murders didn't stop her?"

"Didn't stop huh Honoré guy. Thet Frenchman, he wanted a bettuh address. 'N she weren't able to lease it, no tenants wanted t'sleep theah. Too scary. 'N y'all knows how Fran pinches pennies. Hated t'waste prime real estate. They done moved in yestuhday."

"Fran doesn't need to pinch pennies. She's got excellent investments." "Don't mattuh. Got a good job too. Ain't y'all clued in? Fran changed huh image. Like Marilyn Monroe became a comedienne. Lahke Cliff Robertson switched from hero roles in films, *PT-109*, fo' instance wheah he plays a young John F. Kennedy, then changes persona t'be Uncle Ben Parker in *Spiderman I, II*, and *III*."

"Don't know as Ah learned me none o' thet kahnd o' change about Fran." "Yeah man, Happy. She's singin' in a nightclub. Dirty stuff. Thet rap whut folks don't want their kids t'heah. She wants t'cut a reco'd o' them filthy lyrics. Ah promise y'all, she'll be panned in Tennessee."

"I know she doesn't need the money. What's the Frenchman get out of this?" I asked. "Must be Honoré who's put her up to it."

"Ah thinks she just got fed up waitin' fo' Filipa t'come back heah fo' their duo."

Happy didn't agree. "No. The's mo'e to it than thet. Anyways, we's goin' t'be in Melbourne in November 'n we c'n talk to Filipa in puhson."

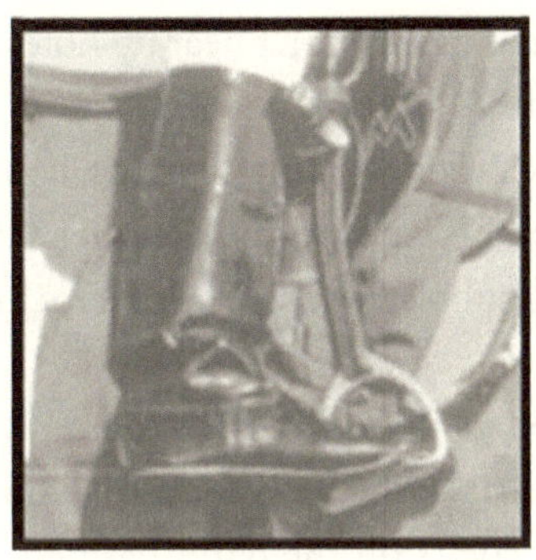

CHAPTER 19

When November came around, we did.

Exhausted as we were after that over long flight to Australia, we winkled out Filipa first thing. We'd flown, with Munchie in tow, directly to Melbourne.

We found Filipa's tiny bungalow in the unfashionable outskirts. It was a very ugly house, much like cottages built in the 1930s in the Midlands. An untidy garden, bordering an unkempt lawn, surrounded the place. Filipa was waiting beside the front gate, the gate was half off its hinges.

"Thank God you've come," Filipa said, hugging Happy and Munchie in that order.

Happy wanted to examine her baby, a little girl called Betty. I wanted to know what chance there was that Filipa would honor her contract to cut a record with Fran.

We were stalled from furthering any of our plans by the very abrupt appearance of Filipa's husband. "Good on ye'," he said, but didn't make any gestures of welcoming us into the home. It was his house, this untidy monstrosity, which had the look of a place used for holiday lets rather than a home base. "My name's Russell Brent."

"Russell, lahke Russell Crowe?" Happy asked, still movie star-smitten. "Naw. Rus, like Rus Brent." His sole connection to Russell Crowe was the lack of having shaved that day. "I don't beat up hotel employees. Don't beat up anybody. Want beers?"

With that semi-invitation we finally made it inside the bungalow. It was worse inside than out. No décor, you couldn't call the beat-up flowered sofa with its cat-clawed upholstery, nor the one rocking chair with its back struts missing, a décor.

Then Filipa ushered us into the baby's room. What a transformation. Here all was costly materials, the newest custom-built furniture, pushcart and crib, original watercolors on the hand-painted walls, and the deepest carpeting to minimize noise.

"This is Betty, my baby," Filipa said wistfully, hoping a miracle might be produced by Happy.

Little Betty wore iron braces on her paralyzed legs. The braces were removed, *immediately*, by Happy. "Mah Mammy had polio. Mah Pappy wouldn't wed huh lessen they's was taken off."

Filipa didn't object to the removal of the braces. It seemed she'd been waiting for Happy, sure from a woman's instinct that Happy would bring about a cure for her little girl. "Do what you want. Rus won't let me take Betty to a doctor. He's a Christian Scientist, she's only been seen by Medical practitioners. You know, alternative medicine types."

Happy frowned. "In Kentucky, next do'r to us'n, they was a l'il boy wut his Mom thought had polio. Mah Mammy took one look at his l'il laigs, and declahed, 'rheumatic fevuh' nothin' else."

Without the constricting braces, little Betty was kicking wildly, like a puppy right out of the womb. "You really think that's it?"

"Easy way t'fahnd out. We goes t'hospital, doctors take a sed'-mentation rate. Blood sep'rates. They knows."

A rough voice interrupted Happy. We all turned to listen to Rus. We expected him to shout at Happy and tell her to get lost. Instead, he mellowed. He forced a friendly smile and said, "Happy, you and me will go to the hospital. We got one near here." He dismissed Filipa as if she was a lowly employee, not worthy of mention.

Once he'd left the house with Happy cradling Betty in her arms, there was a favorable change in Filipa. She pushed on us the beers promised but not delivered by Rus. She settled me in the broken back rocking chair, and collected pillows for Munchie for the sofa.

In a relaxed, gossipy tone she turned to Munchie, "Did you know that Heidi's in Australia?"

I was the one to be upset by her news. "Not. Heidi! Not here, in Melbourne."

"Actually no, not today, not in Melbourne. She's based in Sydney. Got a job in the Sydney Opera House warbling in *Madama Butterfly*. Munchie's role, can you beat that?"

"You have similar voices?" I asked Munchie.

"Naw. Heidi's got a much bigguh one. Yo'all c'd heah huh up in the last row of the top tier of an opry house. She can have thet role in Butterfly. Ah's fed up bein' dressed as a Jap'nese."

"Heidi coming to Melbourne?"

"No, thanks to the fact she's singing all that way away in Sydney. Too far to come for an afternoon race, when she may have a matinée and other days most certainly will have the curtain go up by eight." Filipa laughed. "Everyone else who can possibly get here will come for the Melbourne Cup. It's a National Holiday here so's everyone who can come, DOES."

I was worried for Fran, and wanted to be put at ease. I didn't like the fact that Fran was singing in a nightclub, and had made a demo tape being peddled around London by Honoré. "Filipa, are you going to come back to London and work as a duo with Fran?"

"Rus doesn't want to leave Australia. And anyway, I'm no Joan Sutherland, no Kiri Te Kanawa, no Nicole Kidman. I know that now. A talent scout plucked me out of my Queensland choir, helped me become a professional at the age of fourteen. Like with Charlotte Church, but I haven't made her kind of money."

Russell and Happy returned victorious from the local hospital, the corks bouncing on Russell's swagman's hat. Both Russell and Happy were radiant with joy. And something more. Was sexual excitement rearing its head for them?

Rus said "Betty's okay. It WAS rheumatic fever, the fever was brought on by a strep throat. Just like Happy believed."

"Rus, I'm so very delighted for you and Filipa. Doe this mean you can travel to England, and she can continue with her duo with Fran?"

Filipa, cooing to her baby, looked skeptical when I questioned Rus about a possible trip.

To our amazement, he said, "Sure. Any time you say, after the Melbourne Cup."

Ominous! Why did he agree so quickly? Filipa said he wouldn't go to doctors. But he went to them with Happy. Filipa said he wouldn't travel, but he'd agreed readily to a trip to England where Happy will be. And I noticed a look he gave my Happy and I guessed I was going to be up against another suitor lusting after my wife.

I was prepared for that, what I wasn't prepared for was another murder in our circle.

CHAPTER 20

Munchie was strangled on the morning of Melbourne Cup Day. Her Home Alone had won the previous afternoon. So our favorite owner had decided to forego watching other people's horses, to stay in her hotel suite and work on singing her songs for the role of Elizabeth in *Pride and Prejudice*, scheduled to open in New York within weeks.

I'd watched our two contenders from the Trainers' stand, but Happy reneged on attending the races. She was mourning Munchie as she'd mourned Sybil, and even Carla. No point saying she'd mourned Goofy, although knowing what a big heart Happy has, maybe she did.

Our Melbourne hotel room was dismal. Happy had the TV on music that sounded like a Requiem Mass by Mozart, and probably was, although I'm not canny enough about music to know. There were no whoops of joy from Happy when I handed her the two trophies won that afternoon.

"Don't 'spect me t'go out on t'town. No drinkin' no dancin' not with Munchie lyin' in a metal drawer down at t'morgue."

"Were you asked to identify her?"

"Yuh. Awful. Mah pretty Tennessee songbi'd with a pu'ple face and red ma'ks on huh neck."

"Did the police say there were other murders? Seems like a great day for crime, when the whole entire nation goes on holiday watching the races in person or on TV."

"No robbery in Munchie's hotel. Nothin' disturb'd. But the maid cum in and found huh when t'was tahme to change towels. C'ld girl. Stahted screamin' 'n screamin', said lahke Munchie's eyes all bulgin' with the veins bursted from the stranglin'. Makes me want t'puke."

I asked, "How come Munchie didn't hear the murderer enter?"

"Police told me lahke she was playin' t'piano 'n singin' some song from *Pride and Prejudice*. Called 'Darcy.' Practicin' fo' huh new mus'cal play in New York. Them po-lice saw the sheet music on her piano."

When a scarlet sunset faded into sapphire night, I thought it might be a good idea to go for our customary habit of testing a foreign hotel's bed for glorified sex.

Disaster. *I* couldn't make love. Happy didn't want to make love. Munchie, strangled, haunted me with that description of bursting veins in bulging eyes. Munchie, so dear to both of us and such a successful owner having only one filly and winning repeatedly. Why did her life end this way?

Early next morning our telephone was jingling. Happy didn't answer. She liked her sleep more than I do and as I was up readying for the stables, I took the call.

It was Rus, asking for Happy. I said, "She's asleep!"

"No Ah'm not," Happy called lustily across the double bed, "Ah heahs. 'N Ah'll take t'call."

It was impossible not to listen to their conversation with the telephone receiver's wire stretched between me next to the night table and Happy sitting up on the far side of the bed.

Rus asked, "G'day, Happy, could you, uh, would you come with me to see the local gardens? We've got some beauts in Melbourne."

"Sho' thing. Ah could come. Ah'd love t'come."

Happy was dressed and outside the hotel quicker than I could manage to get downstairs. Rus had a beaten-up pick-up and was waving from the near side, the British side's window. He was wearing a soft wide-brimmed hat that had strings with corks hanging from them all around the brim.

Happy climbed into the seat beside him like a practiced jockey. They sped off without a wave.

Ten hours later Happy returned to our bedroom with a crimson sunburn. While she dabbed cream all over her burned face, Happy hummed "Dancing Matilda" until she broke into dollops of talk. "We wuz all ovah. Gahdens fuhst, then went to a village of Ab-o-riginals.

"Do you have to keep singing that song?"

"'Dancin' Matilda' thet's lahke this Aus-tra-lia's unofficial national anthem. It's about a banjo playuh who roamed t'hinterland wearin' his swagman's hat."

"Swagman's hat? Is that what Rus calls what he had on his head? With all those cut-up corks jogging?"

"Yeah man. Great ideah. We-all should introduce thet t'England. The corks keep the flies away."

'I hope that's the last we'll see of Rus."

"Don't count on thet. Rus sez he's willin' lahke t'drive us to Sydney t'go see Heidi in Madama Butterfly. How about thet?"

"But Sydney's ten hours away by car."

"He sez lahke he drives all ovah Aus-tra-lia. Even went to a place called Alice Springs wheah the Ab-o-riginals worship a huge red stone, big as a mountain."

"I'll bet he never did that. More likely that he saw the movie with Meryl Streep that plays in Alice Springs, where supposedly dingo dogs stole a human baby."

"Yup, he tol' me about thet. Lady got acquitted aftuh yeahs in prison. Wish Ah'd seen the film. Ah love Meryl Streep movies. Ah c'n rent t'video and save us the trip. But Sydney, thet's somethin' else. Ah feels Ah needs t'go to Sydney."

Happy brushed her teeth, chose a nothing-special nightgown from her suitcase, put it on, got into bed and turned out the light.

No sex that night, either.

On the dot of nine, when an unseen church clock chimed the hour, Rus appeared wearing his swagman hat, an open tartan cotton shirt, and cords. That was his dress code for an evening at the opera. "G'day. Sorry, but my pick-up hasn't any air-conditioning." He placed Happy in the front seat beside him, and left me to arrange my long legs and aching knees in the back on a cattle-dung-covered floor. There was no seat in the rear of his pick-up. I felt like a bull being driven to market to be slaughtered. Worse. The bull didn't know it was going to be slaughtered.

Attempting to tolerate the smell of manure, the bumps in the road and the intermittent rain I read a much-fingered paperback novel by Agatha Christie, *Death On The Nile*. I'd found the book under the bed at our hotel. That was the only plus from that bed during our stay. The murder was based on an intricate plot, and I thought, "How simple all the stranglings have been that we've suffered over. There must be a simple answer to all of them."

It was dark when we reached Sydney's outlying suburbs. They weren't much different from many I'd seen in UK cities. With winter approaching a few had curling smoke from fireplaces but most houses must have had fake gas-fed fires producing no smoke.

Which was lucky because most of these bungalows were square cement squares with no chimneys.

Approaching Sydney's famous lopsided giant-winged opera house I'd hoped to see its splendor. But I suppose it must be viewed from the bay, or else by airplane. All I saw was the street leading to a car park and the walls of the building before entering its box-office.

"Yes, there are a few tickets remaining in the top row of the gallery," the box-office girl said, after the traditional " G'day," which she said although by now it was nighttime. We filed to the lifts and crammed ourselves into our narrow seats on the top row.

Dear Munchie had been spot-on about Heidi's huge voice. It certainly reached uninhibited to the sky-high region of our top gallery. She over-acted. Heidi smiled too broadly and made hideous grimaces, totally out of character for a geisha's maid. But at the end of the performance she received a spattering of applause and a small bouquet while the star was bunched with half-a-dozen armfuls of local flowers.

The stage door guardian let us pass, but Heidi wasn't in a private dressing room. She'd been made to share with other female singers who had minor parts in Butterfly. "Gosh, it's wonderful to see you," she said to Happy. She gave a very brief nod to me, and waited to be introduced to Rus. They exchanged huge handshakes, suitable to both, but not much in the way of new-found friendship.

"Ah jus' had t'come see y'all in Sydney," Happy said.

For her, that was very non-committal.

"Too bad I couldn't have met you in Melbourne. Would have been so great to see the running of the Melbourne Cup. But it's so far away. And I have evening performances every night."

"Mebbe a frien' c'd 'ave brought y'all."

"I don't know anyone in Australia. It's been awfully lonely here for me," Heidi complained loudly, meaningfully, telling the other girl singers she resented they hadn't been more friendly.

It wasn't true that she didn't know anybody here. Heidi'd given us short shrift, and when we were rushed out to the stage door, we heard a bearded man telling the guardian, "You must let me in. Miss Heidi and I have a dinner date, and we'll lose our reservations at my club if we don't get there soon."

We'd booked rooms at a moderately-priced hotel. I'd thought of going to the Shangri-La, but it cost $1,826 a night for just a single, and I didn't want to over-drain Hal's generosity. It was dreary when we arrived after midnight. Half the lights had been dimmed to save on electricity. This time Happy had brought no nightgown. She slept in her slip. Again no sex, although we were in a new city and at a different hotel.

In the morning Rus suggested we take in some of Sydney's more famous sights, and that we try the shorter Harbor cruise. He insisted we see the Aquarium, which fascinated Happy, although she wasn't that keen on viewing sharks close up. We went to the wildlife park. We saw kangaroos, koala bears, emus, wombats and dingo dogs. I sipped champagne instead of coffee among the kangaroos. Apparently that's usual for visitors here. I had a chance to examine a platypus in close quarters. I found the funny little creature quite adorable, with its duck-bill and webbed feet. We ended with an early lunch at a popular place called Doyle's, where fish and chips are served with the local wines. I could get the wine cheaper in London, and most certainly get a better bargain on our British staple fish and chips.

I hadn't offered to lease a rental car for our return to Melbourne, because the opera tickets had proved so expensive at over $300 each.

The long drive back to Melbourne seemed endless. Ten hours in a bouncing pick-up the day before our over-night trip to England was almost more than I could tolerate. I couldn't sleep in the rear of the pick-up. Rain had dampened the manure and made the pungent stink even worse. Before checking out of the hotel I'd bought a few newspapers to read, but I ended by sitting on them to keep out the damp and ease the bumps.

From up front in their seats came non-stop claps of laughter. Happy and Rus howled after every one of each other's short phrases. When the two up front weren't laughing, they were singing. Their preferred songs came from the soundtracks of movies they'd admired. Happy was overjoyed to find a fellow movie buff who knew all the music from their mutual favorite films. She couldn't sing any better than a Kentucky hog-caller, but she echoed the words and the cadence and kept up with Rus.

We interrupted all this superb music a few times on the route to buy petrol and ghastly sandwiches provided at roadside comfort stops. Each time Rus managed to put both his arms around Happy to help her down from the pick-up's seat. Many times, during her career as an apprentice jockey in the USA, I'd watched as Happy bolted out of saddles to land with no trouble at all. But on this day she played the Southern Belle and smiled archly every time he put arms around her waist.

Was my little Baptist going to be unfaithful? Or, had she already become an adulteress during that ten-hour disappearance the day after the Melbourne Cup?

I decided to act the complacent husband and generously bit into our budget by suggesting we all three go to one of Melbourne's finest restaurants.

With me smelling of cattle manure, and the enamored couple both dripping with sweat like Olympic athletes due to the lack of air-conditioning in the pick-up, it came as no surprise that we were turned away by the Maitre D', who excused the lack of hospitality by the late hour of our arrival. " G'day, sorry. But we've had the last serving tonight."

We took the last ride on the Colonial Tramcar to enjoy *its* restaurant, although we didn't see much of the sights that daytime tourists like. Rus was in a talkative mood between swilling beers. "Good on you, girl," he started, directly himself exclusively to Happy. "You want to know about my childhood? Well, I lived in the outback, on a small parcel. We were poor. Our bungalow didn't have a toilet. We had to go outside to a hut where there was a wood plank, with a large hole, perched over a barrel. Not much fun cleaning out that barrel every other week. The worst was when a snake decided to live in the barrel, we'd see its eyes looking up at us. I took to crapping in the woods."

Great peals of laughter.

"Yeah man, we'd got one o' them Chick Sales too. Was y'all evuh friendly with the Aboriginals?"

"Sure. They taught me how to paint my face like they did for their tribal dances.I thought the world of them Pamagirri dancers."

"What about crocodiles? Evuh meet up with one?"

"Sure, many. I'd have lost a leg once if I hadn't made buddies with the tribe. Croc killer came and saved me."

I thought, "I'll bet that story's straight out of 'Crocodile Dundee II."

Rus went on until the restaurant closed. "I could take you to the Maruku, where you'd see some Aboriginal art. Wonderful stuff. Or better, take you to caves where there's ancient paintings on the walls."

Happy was growing tired. She gave Rus a short goodbye at our hotel. Hal had booked us into the Langham Hotel on the river-front. I was feeling terribly horny despite all the discomfort of our pick-up rides. Joy! Happy drew me into the shower with her to soap each other. Then she produced an engaging nightgown she'd bought in the Sydney hotel's boutique, and she did her entrancing striptease for me, and finally we had great sex.

I knew that Happy could enjoy daily sex, so I wasn't feeling too secure when she announced she wasn't going to watch Feathers in her race on the Australian Oaks Day. She would go to early morning stables and have a serious talk with Feathers, but in the afternoon she'd be sightseeing again with Rus.

"Feathuhs needs t'be tole' thet Second ain't good 'nuf. We congratulat'd huh befo'e when we shouldn't 'a done. She needs t'be taught t'pass t'othuh hosses. Not be so p'lite! Ah's gonna have a wo'd with huh."

When she returned from the stables Happy took a great deal of care with her makeup and chose a pair of tight fitting jeans and T-shirt causing me to remember greedily the curvy teenager I had wed.

"Aren't you depriving Filipa and little Betty of a husband and a father's company?

"They's gonna have plenty, soon 'nuf. Ain't this ouh last day heah?"

I went with her as far as the pick-up and then the two were off in a wave of hilarity. What was it with Rus? Could it be that Rus told her stories and I had lapsed in that department?

Until that afternoon I'd successfully avoided meeting Harold East and Ellie. I'd seen them in the distance on Cup Day, but now it proved impossible not to exchange a civil word with them just before Feathers' race.

Unfortunately our stalls in the saddling-up enclosure were next to each other. Our stable lads' knew each other from Epsom's pubs, and with all their prattle we had to be polite with normal conversation.

"Hello, Ellie. Good trip over?"

"Hello. Good enough."

Harold East grumpily said, "How did you find the stables? Adequate?"
"Yes. Adequate."

That was the extent of our unwanted dialogue . .

Ellie looked prettier. Her face had softened its regal lines, and her hands fluttered girlishly. She exuded the air of a woman in love. Harold East didn't exude love, perhaps having me in the proximity dampened that emotion. He was pleased with *himself,* and confident that his filly would beat mine.

With the horses saddled we three had to move on to the paddock, we strolled under Flemington Racecourse's famous rose arches and watched our jockeys fiddle with reins and stirrups.

On the first Tuesday of every November at three p.m. all of Australia stops to watch the Melbourne Cup. Today, for the Oaks, it was a very different story. Thursday was the beginning of weekends for landowners, some of whom preferred their estates to watching fillies compete. There was no great competition like the Myers hat and men's clothing contests. Fewer helicopters brought race-goers, fewer cars jammed the car parks. Over 5 million Australian dollars were wagered on Cup Day. Less, today. Almost 400,000 spectators came on Cup Day. Nowhere near that number cared about the fillies. Many of those who had attended for the Oaks had left by the time our minor race was run.

Race-goers were not as well-dressed nor well-mannered for the Oaks Days. The shouting was worse than when a reunion of Civil War buffs give rebel yells in Kentucky.

Feathers won her race. It was a truly great moment for Hal, but also for all the Canadians at the racecourse. They waved maple leaf flags. They sang the Canadian national anthem. Hal had won for Canada, not just for himself.

Harold East's filly came Third. Ellie, with her Earl's-granddaughter manners didn't show any resentment. She did the correct thing and came up to congratulate me. Harold East did too, but with no grace.

Later, in our hotel room, when I described the scene and the trophy-giving to Happy, she wasn't disappointed she'd missed it. In our bedroom, now smelling of sex, she caroled, "Ah've had t'most won'erful tahme. Us'n went t'see t' Fairy Penguins. Wouldn't b'lieve what they does! March lahke soldiers. Ah loves t'penguins! Ah loved t'movie about 'em. They's lahke li'l boys wallowin' in a puddle."

She packed cheerfully. I noticed there was no weeping about leaving Rus. I determined in future to give her more racing stories, because I dearly hoped it was stories she had enjoyed and not sex with Rus.

Happy picked up a leaflet that offered reduced taxi services to the airport. She let out a Confederate yell. "Wait 'til y'all learns wut Ah've jus' learned. The's a charter flight suhvice from Sydney t'Melbourne 'n back, not expensive. With compliment'ry airpo't transfers. Heidi c'd have took one o' them's charter flights. She lied t'us when she said she couldn't come to Melbourne 'cause she'd miss huh puhfo'mance in t'opray. Thet makes two lies Heidi done tol' us'n."

I digested the information. I wasn't quite sure why Happy felt it was so important, but I couldn't help thinking that a charter flight would have been such a superb contrast to that horrific twenty-hour roundtrip in a pick-up.

CHAPTER 21

Filipa, Rus, and their baby Betty followed us to England. They didn't arrive immediately. Filipa was too concerned that our winter weather would affect her delicate child.

Christmas in England was a big draw, and when she read in the newspapers that England had experienced a very balmy autumn, she bought plane tickets for the two adults. Their baby went free.

A big plus was that on their arrival Fran threw out her phony count and invited them to live in her duplex. I couldn't tolerate that count. And I knew that Filipa didn't have a bottomless purse. Hotel bills would have been a big strain on her budget.

Fran and Filipa both felt they needed to cut a new record, and soon. When Happy and I returned to our cottage to be welcomed by our infants and Mrs. Rea, I made a plan to win back my wife's love. I decided to give her the horse stories she loved, night after night.

On the first of those nights I combined two of her major interests, horses, and a movie star. In this instance the horse was a small one, "Too small for its rider, Christopher Reeves," I began, once we were tucked well under our blankets. We felt the cold more intensely arriving back from 90-degree heat.

"Y'all means thet Superman guy, wut died last year, after bein' crippled fo' yeahs 'n yeahs?"

"The same. He was riding to hounds on a horse that was too small for his stature. When the horse balked at a fence, Christopher Reeves tried to release his hands from the web of his bridles' straps. Couldn't. Went head-over. Result? Paralysis."

"One wunnerful guy! Givin' hope t'so many othuh paralytics!"

"Yes, and his health seemed to be improving near the end. Such terrific inventions had come along that were applied to his case. Sad thing. His devoted wife died the following year. Cancer, I think."

Happy was quiet for a few minutes. Then she complained, "Thet's all what stories y'all tellin' me t'night? 'N just when Ah was in hog heaven thinkin' y'all had stahted in with the story-tellin' ag'in."

There was nothing for it but to delve in my memory for another story. "Happy, while you were touring with Rus, I read up on the Australian races we saw. Also, the victorious horses, and fillies. It all started way back in 1861. The prize was a gold watch. A jockey called Archer was said to have walked 800 miles from Nowra, in New South Wales, to ride in the race, but probably sneaked there in a small boat. And he won his race. By 1865 a silver bowl had been established as the proper trophy for this great event. These were made in England until ten years later when an Australian silversmith created the first of a new type. That had an engraving of a horse race set at the Flemington track. At the beginning all of the horses were Australian, until a few New Zealand horses were introduced. The race is run over 3200 meters, and as it is a handicap, that means the better the horse is, more weight it has to carry in the race."

"No fillies evah won?"

"Yes, and well-handicapped fillies too. In 2004 Makybe Diva was not only the first mare to win consecutive cups, but the first to win it with different trainers, and the only horse to win it three in a row. Her Hong Kong based Trainer, Lee Friedman said after the race, 'Go and find the youngest child on the course, because that's the only person here who will have a chance of seeing this happen again in their lifetime.'"

"No funny bus'ness in any o' the races?"

"Not exactly. But that first jockey to win, Archer, had a surprising event ruin his chance for a third cup. There had been seventeen horses to run in 1861, but when his owner's nomination form had arrived late the third time and Archer was unable to contest the Cup, it was boycotted by sympathetic owners so the race started with only seven horses competing. That's the smallest field in the history of the Cup."

"Ain't no furriners evuh won?"

"Yes. The most famous, if you count him as foreign, was the New Zealand-bred Phar Lap. Foaled in New Zealand in 1926 out of Entreaty he grew to seventeen hands. Over his career he won more than 65,000 pounds in prize money, and won 37 of his 51 starts. A New Zealand mare, Ethereal, has a story that will please you. She was trained by Sheila Laxon, the first woman to formally train a Melbourne Cup winner. But wait, there's more. She also won the Caulfield Cup, a 2400 meter race and so she's credited with the 'Cup Double.'"

"What about horses from our part o' t'world?"

"Vintage Crop in 1993 and Media Puzzle in 2002 were both brought over from Ireland by Dermott Weld to win the Melbourne Cup, and did! But I'll say that all racing people don't take to the Cup. Racing purists are wary of the unusually long distance. Also the handicap rules make the result highly unpredictable. Due to the handicap rules, mediocre horses have been known to win. They maintain that the Cox Cup, a weight for age race, is a truer indication of the best horse."

"Will them purists think bad of Feathers' win?"

"No. I certainly hope not. It was such a great moment for Hal, and his Canadian pals."

"Whut's yo' fav'rite Aus-tra-lian memory?"

"Not mine, but for many it was that great day when Glen Boss celebrated after Makybe Diva's winning the Emirates Melbourne Cup."

"Emirates! Yo'all don't mean them Arabs from Dubai got them a cup in Aus-tra-lia?"

"Can't escape them!" I laughed, kissed away Happy's pouting expression, and we made glorious love.

The following morning Happy announced she was going up to London."Oh, oh," I thought, "she's going to see Rus."

She was gone six hours, while I worked in my stables' office answering the e-mails and plotting entries for our horses' next season.

Christmas was almost upon us, and the town's main street was hung with strings of fairy lights. Carol singers came to my door and sang for money, off-key but with charm so I handed out candies as well as money.

I took careful notice of which horses had grown their furry winter coats, and guessed they'd been put out to field being considered no-hopers by the stable lads. I ordered several to return to their heated stalls, and that they be clipped on top along their backs even if that procedure left left them looking wooly on their stomachs. One week gone, and my string had suffered.

Suffering wasn't monopolized by my horses. I bit my lips, and smoked too many cigarettes worrying if my Happy was being faithful during her tryst with Rus.

When she returned late that evening, and took her favorite position by the hearth with her backside on the bum-warmer, she wore a saddened expression. "I be'n talkin' all day t'the police. They wanted t'see me. Not t'worry y'all, Ah didn't tell y'all wheah Ah was headed, but Ah needed t'see thet Inspector wut met us after Sybil's murder. He'd writ me a lettuh orderin' me up t'London soon's as Ah'd retuhn from Aus-tra-lia."

Worry me! I'd never felt so relieved! Not Rus, but the Inspector? How wonderful. I felt like using Happy's favorite saying, 'I'm in Hog Heaven.' I didn't. Instead I cautiously asked: "What did he want?"

"Ah thinks he b'lieves Ah c'd be the killuh." "What nonsense!"

"Man said Ah knew how t'git into Carla's apahtment. Ah didn't lahke Goofy for Fran. Ah was in the the-a-tre nahgt Sybil died. Ah was in Aus-tra-lia when Munchie died. All o' 'em folks Ah done knew."

"Good God!"

"Yeah man, and thet ain't all. He made me git finguhprinted, have a mug shot, 'n they's took some samples o' m'hair to match up with thet DNA they's got from unduh Carla's finguhnails."

I thought I would vomit. My Happy, suspected of murder?

Happy added, "They's said as Ah had strong hands, me bein' a jockey. Ah c'd done strangled 'em."

I sat down on the bum-warmer and cradled Happy in my arms. "My darling," I said, "I haven't wanted to upset you before, but now I'm going to tell you that I've had the same suspicions regarding Ellie. She was also in all those places, and disliked Goofy."

Happy went silent. She wept. After three long minutes, she choked saying, "Ah knows y'all thought thet. Ah c'd tell from yo'r eyes when y'all looked at Ellie in t'airport yesterday."

A clamor outside our front door drew us to peer out of our leaded windows. Ellie! She was in her mother's Rolls Royce, leaning on its venerable horn. She gestured, as if to say "Follow me."

Without judging whether it was sensible or not, Happy and I grabbed our raincoats and dashed to my old Volvo. The Rolls sped ahead. We tried to keep up. It went sixty kilometers an hour, seventy, eighty, ninety, one hundred. Our poor rattling Volvo sent up a geyser of steam, and stopped on the M-25.

I turned on the emergency flashing light and tried to urge the car on to the median's grass verge where we would be safer. Soon a police car passed us like a seagull swooping on mackerel. The officer pulled up next to my window. "Guv, what do you think you're doing? Dangerous, this. Could be killed."

"Officer, I'm calling the AA. They'll come for us and collect the car. I'm afraid I've burned out the engine."

He left us, and I telephoned for help . .

We had watched another car pursuing Ellie's. It also had a capacity for a one hundred mile odyssey. The Rolls Royce vanished in the evening fog, with the unknown car in hot pursuit, like a barracuda after a shoal of bluefish.

Now that we had a moment to ourselves, Happy asked me to lend her my mobile. "Ah wants t'call Ellie. Ah's got t'know what this is all about."

Ellie answered on the first ring. "Yes. Be quick. I'm racing my mater's car."

"It's Happy. Ah needs t'know. Did you see Munchkins in Melbourne?" "No. She was killed at her piano, I heard that. But I never saw her. When she died I was at the races watching Harold's filly come in Third. What a wasted trip!"

I took the mobile from Happy. "What color was the filly that came in Fourth in that race?"

"Gray. Why? Rick, you were there. Can't you remember?"

"I do remember, Ellie. That's why I asked you. It's okay. Get home to your mother's. Hire a detective, or a bodyguard. Good night, Ellie." Lucky I hung up because my mobile died on me at that moment due to lack of juicing while I was in Australia. I wouldn't have wanted Ellie to think I'd hung up on her. I turned to Happy, "It was a gray. The race was too unimportant to have been televised, and a Fourth's color is rarely noted in newspapers. I think it's safe to say that, yes, Ellie was at the races while Munchie was being strangled."

The AA van arrived. I showed the driver my AA card, he dealt with the Volvo and we got a ride to Epsom.

When we arrived we found Mrs. Rea in tears.

Were our infants hurt, or sick?

Mrs. Rea gulped, "Mr. Harrow, someone's killed your cat. Bumbles is dead. Strangled! Down at the stables. Go to Feathers' stall and see for yourself."

Happy and I stumbled down the manure-strewn path. We reached the stables to find both grooms weeping. Stalwart, strong, rough fellows, both were clutching wet handkerchiefs like mourners at a wake. Tom pointed with a shaking finger. We entered Feathers' stall to find her bowing her huge sorrowing head like a brown lily over Feathers. Beside her near hoof lay Bumbles, her head twisted around backwards towards her tail.

Because we'd opened the padded gate to her stall, her kittens could enter.

They surrounded their dead mother's body like flowers in a funereal wreath.

Happy started to cry, then thought that Feathers needed her caring hands and she began to stroke the filly's neck. Feathers responded. Where for a moment I'd feared that Feathers might die from sorrow, I felt relieved when the great filly's head rose like the prow of a ship battling into wind, and she took a few steps away from Bumbles' corpse. I collected the broken body and carried it to my office to find a decent box in which to bury this dear pet.

Who the hell had done this?

And, why?

Ellie? She'd been in the vicinity. We'd seen her at the door of our house. She hadn't come inside because that mystery car had been bearing down on her mother's Rolls. Who was the person in the mystery car?

As for Ellie, she had devotedly cared for Bumbles during our various trips away. I knew she felt a fondness for Bumbles, and had considered her a heroine cat when Bumbles helped us track down Feathers after the filly was kidnapped.

Those kidnappers? No, they'd left England long ago when their mission failed. I'd delved into that affair very thoroughly and learned they were naught but money-grabbers out for a big hit.

I didn't tell the local press. What for? But Virgo got hold of the story and followed up his account of Feathers escaping the kidnappers thanks to Bumbles with a small obituary that garnered more e-mails than the kidnapping had. British people love cats and a heroine cat being strangled touched their hearts.

After we'd buried Bumbles, and Happy had given Feathers a special treat of carrots, I hurried her to bed. She needed comfort, and hopefully that meant sex.

No. No sex. Happy didn't even want a story about horses or racing. She sit up in bed and used our nightstand telephone to ring Filipa.

Rus answered. "What's up, Happy? Isn't this late for you?" "Ah needs t'speak t'Filipa."

"Not here. She's doing a late-night recording with Fran at that nightclub. They're going over big, a twice-nightly show."

"Ah knows about thet show. Thet's not what Ah's callin' about. Rus, will y'all b'lieve me when Ah say Ah thinks Filipa c'd be need-in' some lookin' aftuh? Go git huh, now. Fu'st collect some clothes for huh 'n li'l Betty, 'n check in t'some ho-tel. Git outta thet apah'tment 'n don't tell nobody which ho-tel."

"Dear, darling Happy," Rus said, and I bit at each word, unable to miss out on a conversation within two inches of my ear, "Good on you, girl. I know you mean well. But we've already talked about some ghost in this apartment. There ain't any."

"Not worried about a ghost. Please, Rus. Ah loves Filipa, 'n li'l Betty. Git them to a small ho-tel."

I took the receiver from Happy's shaking hand. "Rus, she's right. Any hotel will do. Try a few on Ebury Street, not far from Fran's block of flats. There must be at least four or five there catering to overseas visitors. Or for trippers from the Victoria Line. Try the Lime Tree. I hear it's nice. After a few days, change hotels. But not to a famous one, like the Grosvenor."

"What's this all about?"

"Just believe us. I don't want to worry Filipa, but Happy's instincts are usually sound." I'd grown accustomed to Rus laughing. All those hours of hilarity in the pick-up driving to and from Sydney had left their toll. But there was no laughter at the other end of the wire tonight.

A long groan came from Rus. "I hear you. You're telling me there have been too many murders. Was there another one tonight? Anyone I know?"

"No." I had no intention of telling Rus about Bumbles. What would a rough and tumble swagman care about one dead cat? Sighing, I ended the conversation with a turnabout for his Australian expression, "G'night."

No sex for us when that conversation ended. Hearing that familiar Rus drone hadn't turned Happy on. She cuddled up in my arms, her head squeezing into my neck. But neither of us slept. I believe we were both pondering on the same subject, and it wasn't sex.

CHAPTER 22

Happy and I left for London very early the next morning. We took the train to Victoria Station and rang bells at every reception desk in the small hotels on Ebury Street until she tracked down Rus, Filipa, and little Betty.

They had checked into the Lime Tree, and were eating a spare breakfast in the minute dining room. The baby was coughing.

"Darling Happy, how good of you to come," Filipa said, her voice trembling.

"G'day, good on you girl. Do you know the name of a decent pediatrician? Baby's sick." Rus said. He didn't attempt to kiss Happy, on the lips or a cheek. I felt relieved to see that, as I'd been when I heard Happy declare how she loved Filipa and Betty, but made no mention of what she felt for Rus.

With haddock and eggs going down their gullets, Rus and Filipa didn't notice Ellie's entering the dining room. Happy did.

Frowning, Happy greeted her sourly. "Wut y'doin' heah? How'd y'find this heah place?"

"Darling Happy, hello Filipa and Rus. Baby doesn't look well. My dears, you wonder why I've come and how I found you? Didn't take much brain work. After I left the Inspector on our case, who'd asked me to come to be fingerprinted and have my photograph taken, I simply drove past all the hotels in the vicinity of Fran's flat. I saw a baby carriage parked under the big chandelier in this place's hall. Voila!"

Filipa, sniffling into a kleenex, said, "Glad to see you. Tell me, Ellie, do you know of a good pediatricians? Happy didn't volunteer any names."

"Mater will know of one." Ellie drew out her mobile and dialed her home number. She had a short conversation with her mother, wrote down a name on a pad from her key-ring, and handed the pad's top paper to Filipa.

"Oh! I know of him. He's famous. Awfully expensive."

"You must NOT worry about the money. I'll take care of it," Ellie offered, and drew out her checkbook to write out a sizeable sum.

Rus telephoned the doctor's office, made an appointment for within the hour, and then took his wife and baby upstairs to dress for the winter weather.

Left alone in the minimalist dining room, Ellie and Happy ordered coffee. They plunged into a serious chat like divers of a rescue team sent into ice-floe waters.

Ellie began, "The Inspector seemed to think I'd strangled our friends. He mentioned that I'd been to Fran's apartment, knew Goofy but disliked him, met Goofy's pal that saxophone player Jimmy Halpern, had visited Sibyl's dressing room and was in Australia when Munchie was murdered. And this wasn't like when that detective sergeant spoke of 'furthering inquiries.' It was beastly."

"Ah knows. Same happen'd t'me. Ah got t'same drillin' just yesterday."

"I imagine that the Melbourne police have been pressing our local officers to tie up the case. The coroner here, I think his name was Andrew Reid, is said to be planning to tell the jury during his inquest that a verdict of unlawful killing was the only one to be reached. Well, I'd certainly agree with that. But not when I'm the prime suspect."

"A coroner? Ag'in? Ah dealt with sever'l in the USA when mah jockey friends wuz killed."

"Coroner's inquests are conducted in all suspicious deaths in Britain and killings of British citizens overseas. I thoroughly approve of them. Someday I may want to be a magistrate myself. Some of my Mater's best friends are magistrates."

"Us'n may need o' them, soon."

"Rick thinks I killed all of them, doesn't he?"

"No. He may have rolled thet ideah in his mind, but aftuh Bumbles were killed, no mo'e."

"Bumbles? What are you saying?"

"Someone strangled Bumbles. Y'all sped away in thet Rolls befo'e us'n c'd tell y'all."

"Strangled the cat! But, why kill Feathers' friend? I understand how someone might kill Feathers." Ellie's tone lightened, she giggled suddenly. "Harold, for one, because Feathers keeps beating his fillies." Her voice dropped an octave, much saddened, she added, "I loved that cat."

"Ah thinks the cat wuz strangled as a warnin' t'lay off the case. Puhson wut done it wanted t'tell us not t'meddle. Knew we'd been involved in muhduhs helpin' the po-lice befo'e."

"That could be. Tell me, Happy, have you thought who could have done all these dreadful things?"

"Yeah man. But Ah cain't hit on no motive."

The hotel's receptionist entered the dining room. She frowned like a schoolchild held after classes. "You've overstayed the breakfast hour," she said grumpily. "Staff needs to clear up and set the tables for lunch. But there's a telephone call for Mrs. Harrow. She can take it at my desk."

It was Rus on the blower. When Happy took up the receiver, he spoke shrilly, "Happy, good on you, girl. I'll be quick. Doctor will see Betty in a few more minutes. But I've been reading magazines in the waiting room. There's an item you should hear about. It concerns your friend, Heidi."

"Rus, read it t'me."

"Says 'Miss Heidi Wahner, known for opera and operetta performances in Madama Butterfly and The Mikado, has announced that her role in the proposed production of a new re-make of *Pride and Prejudice* has been cancelled. No male lead had been found to play Darcy.' That's it. Doesn't tell you much. But I thought you should know. 'Bye. Got to go. We've been called. Our turn for the doctor."

Happy motioned Ellie to the desk and relayed the information. "P'or Heidi. Always a brahdesmaid, nevuh a brahde. Anothuh missed oppo'tunity fo' stahdom. Wut she craves!"

"What are you commiserating with her for? She never was one of our favorite people. And she would have been a disaster as Elizabeth in *Pride and Prejudice*. As Coulis would say, 'There'd be no bums on seats to hear her."

"Let's us'n go fahnd Fran. She'll be interest'd if'n we-all learns huh the news- *thet Heidi's out o' work again!*"

CHAPTER 23

We walked down Ebury Street to Fran's block. We buzzed the same old lady to let us in, and marched upstairs.

When Fran opened her door she looked like a deer caught in the blazing headlights of a car.

She was standing next to her piano in her messed-up apartment, her face contorted. There were half-finished baby bottles creating rings on its mahogany surface, there were dirty diapers and baby sheets thrown on a torn piece of plastic wrap, there were rabbit ears for luck sewn on to a baby blanket that smelled of urine.

It wasn't this chaos of baby paraphernalia that was disturbing Fran. She was shaking a wad of music sheets at us. "Oh, girls. I fucking need to talk to you. Look at these songs I'm supposed to imitate. My bosses at the nightclub where I sing, they want me to compose some shit like these.

One by Eminem.

Ripped this old lady, hung her neck by a hook.

Didn't realize it was my grandmother 'til I checked her pocketbook.

And this, by Ludacris.

The game got switched on some Ludacris shit.

So all y'all can suck my dick, Beotch!"

"Good God!" Ellie was genuinely shocked, she'd never been exposed to rap. My Happy didn't like it, but she'd heard shockers in country-music lyrics boomed out in USA car radios and on some TV stations.

Happy said sadly, "Ah guess yo' bosses don't know nothin' about Carla dyin' if'n they expect y'all to sing wo'ds lahke 'hung huh neck.'"

"Shit! What am I supposed to do? And you girls thought I used bad lingo."

"Those lyrics are worse than bad. They're wicked." Ellie pursed her aristocratic lips.

"I'm going to be out of work if I leave the fucking nightclub. And don't tell me it's easy to find singing jobs. I just heard Heidi isn't going to be Elizabeth in *Pride and Prejudice* after all. No tenor! No tenor? I could name you half a friggin' dozen who need jobs!"

Ellie said, "We've just been read a bit out of a newspaper by Rus that Heidi's show folded before it ever got started."

Happy tried to make light of the situation. "Filipa bein' heah now from Aus-tra-lia, thet can change ever'thin'. She'll make aga'n a fahne soprano fo' the Purcell Duo."

Fran started to sing. She mimicked Eminem and warbled his lyrics. In mid-vocals, she burst into tears. "Hung huh neck," she groaned.

The telephone rang. Fran answered. Her face changed like the sky after a storm can turn a radiant blue. Her voice became tinkling. "Yes, sure can. See you at your club for lunch. Bye-e-e-e-."

"New boyfriend?"

"You can call him that. Very grand. Has a title, like your cousin will get someday. Belongs to all the posh clubs, White's, Boodles, Bucks, and of course the Oxford and Cambridge, because he graduated from Cambridge."

"In what?"

"Something to do with agriculture. He'd been going to that agricultural college in Cirencester, because his family owns various estates that need modernizing. But he isn't very modern, shit no. One day I looked at his ankles to be sure he wasn't wearing spats."

"Sounds lahke Hog Heaven fo' y'all."

"Heaven? Shit, yes. But what would he think of me singing lyrics like Eminem's?"

Ellie returned to her pursed-mouth mode. "What's he think of your use of shit and those other unattractive words you pour out all the time?"

"I guess he likes it, or he wouldn't come round."

"Some stage-door johnnies get a frisson of excitement from that type of language. There were many of my cousins who married showgirls a generation or two ago because those girls excited them, being so different from the ones they met in their own circle."

"He's no friggin' stage-door johnny. And anyway, how do you aristocrats have babies if you never do it?"

"Bert, the father of the present Duke of Marlborough, told my mother that he'd never been alone with his wife-to-be – not even in a car, which had to have a driver – because that could compromise a young lady of breeding."

"And I'll bet he ended up having a mistress.' "He did. But he married Laura eventually."

"Was that the same Laura Canfield, widow of the Canfield who'd been married to a husband of Jackie Kennedy's sister?"

"The same. Look it up in Debrett's." Ellie was growing tired of fencing with Fran. "Come along, Happy. We'd best go to Victoria and try to get a train that will get us to our homes by lunch."

Downstairs in the street, walking along Old Buckingham Palace Road to Victoria Station, Ellie asked, "Do you think Fran could have strangled all those people, including her sister and Goofie?"

"Naw. She ain't a good 'nuf actress to pull off thet weepin' scene when she tried t'sing Eminem's lyrics, 'hung huh neck.'"

"She could have flown to Melbourne, strangled Munchie, and flown back again without too much ado."

"Naw. Y'all don't know nothin' about visitin' furrin countries if y'all thinks it's thet easy. She'd have had to use a passpoht, 'n thet passpoht would be stamped. Wut with terrorists 'n the lahke, them passpoht people make a turrible fuss."

Entering Victoria Station, they went to the lower level where passport photos could be taken. Ellie pointed out the booth. "Yes. I believe you're right on that account. Too complicated in today's world. But, on another subject, I'd like to ask if you noticed that the bowls of cocaine had disappeared?"

"Ah noticed."

"Perhaps she was worried that with all that baby paraphernalia the bowls could be tipped over and her costly coke lost."

"Naw. Ellie, she luhned huh lesson when she dated yo'r cousin. Jeremy didn't want chillun thet c'd be scarred by huh cocaine habit. This fancy guy, he wouldn't want a baby hooked on dope, either."

The roar and dust of their train entering its berth for the return trip to Epsom drowned out further comments from Ellie. The girls went into the stand-up serve-yourself dining car and ordered the drinks that Fran had neglected to offer.

CHAPTER 24

When Happy arrived home she found turbulence at the stables. Up and down the stable lads jumped, acting like puppets in a show. "Hal Murphy's coming to see Feathers tonight. He's arrived from Canada."

I was jumpy too. I groaned, "And he wants to run Anchor! How can I do that?"

Happy placed her arms around my shoulders. "Wut 'bout t'all weather tracks at Lingfield and at Kempton?"

"Need prior registration. I'm going to try to pay a late registration fee. Might work."

"Anchor should beat any hoss runnin' theah. He's got great condition." Not exactly laughing, but speaking in a lighter tone, I asked, "Did Anchor tell you he'd win any race we put him in?"

In all seriousness, Happy replied as ever, "When a hoss tells me he's bustin' t'race, he ain't lyin', any mo'e than Ah is."

By evening we were prepared for Hal's arrival. The house had been tidied of baby paraphernalia, Mrs. Rea had put Tim and Dorothy in their beds, and hopefully to sleep.

Happy cleaned the kitchen of fry-ups and I swept the chimney-place to have a fresh fire.

Like a procession to the music of Pomp and Circumstance we trailed Hal through the manure to the stables and showed off Feathers and

Anchor. The stable lads had done a magnificent job in short order. Both horses looked superb.

Hal congratulated them, and better still he tipped them handsomely. He startled us later over dinner when he said, "I want to give a ball. Not a dance. A real ball."

I smiled to placate him, "Your party at Spencer House last year went down a treat. That should be enough to keep your head above the social waters for now."

"No. I want a ball."

"Deah Hal, how much tahme would us'n have to arrange it? Y'all means fo' next Royal Ascot?"

"Nope. I mean for end of next week. I'm leaving for Canada on that Sunday."

Both of us were silenced.

Hal continued, "I realize it must be a difficult chore to collect enough people for a ball on short notice. So, I've thought of a solution. Give a charity ball, I'll give money for several charities if necessary, and the ladies who run them can produce the guests. I'll underwrite it of course, nothing to pay for those who come."

I chuckled. "Plenty of people glad to cadge a good free meal and fine wines. But where are you going to hold this ball? Most of the major hotels will have have their best rooms booked. After all, Christmas parties are coming soon."

"Don't I know! My own office party's due for the week after next. But I've got a longing to give a ball, and it's a ball I want."

Happy had remained quiet. Now she turned to me with a winsome expression. "Rick, Ah knows how y'feels about Harold East and now Ellie. But she's mah bestest friend, 'n she'll arrange a ball if'n anyone c'n."

What could I do? For two years Harold East had been my nemesis, and now that he's having an affair with Ellie I have to accept them as a couple.

"Call her," I said wearily. I didn't suggest she bring Harold East. Ellie came in a flash to share our meager dinner. I hadn't had time to go shopping for food. There were only remains of what Mrs. Rea hadn't eaten during our absence. What a dreadful feast to give my principal owner! He'd brought a case of superior wine with him as a houseguest present, and we drank a few bottles of that. The wine definitely saved the tone of that meal.

The conversation centered on the idea of giving a ball. Ellie was full of suggestions. "We can use one of Mater's clubs. They are far superior to any of the hotels. The Cavalry and Guards has two good reception rooms on the first floor. The one overlooking Piccadilly has great old oil paintings and a space for a dance floor. The other room would be good for pre-dinner cocktails. Then there's Brooks, with its great barrel-vaulted ceiling in the ballroom, hung with the collection of portraits of the Dilettanti Society by Sir Joshua Reynolds. I personally like the atmosphere at Buck's, but you have to pay extra to shore up the floor if there's to be dancing, and anyhow it's a bit on the small side for a charity ball."

"We can't get Spencer House?"

"Not at this short notice. And it's better for cocktails."

"But how are we going to get a guest list? I don't understand about a charity list."

"My Mater will tap her friends for their lists. She's a member of the Ladies Committee of St. John's Ambulance; very top drawer. Her best friend heads the Red Cross and will drum up assistance from her ladies. With twenty members on each Ladies Committee sending out twenty invitations we should manage."

We stopped planning for the event after brandy and coffee. I drove Ellie to her mother's home and was relieved not to see any sign of a waiting car belonging to Harold East.

Ellie returned to our hearth the following morning after stables. She had a list of other projects. "We need take-home gifts. Estee Lauder Company are always very generous with perfume and toilet water. We need a tombola, and that takes lots of gifts. We should try Harrods, Selfridge's, Harvey Nicks and those small boutiques on Sloane Street. We'll wrap the gifts here, and save by buying the paper wholesale."

Hal's idea for a take-home wasn't too clever. He said, "I own a refinery that makes maple syrup. I'll have a dozen crates of the stuff sent over by air."

Great! But messy if the bottles break, and does everyone who goes to a ball want to take home maple syrup?

We got the Cavalry and Guards Club. To save on expenses Happy and Ellie decorated the room with boughs of pine trees from around our cottage that—if very simple—had a delicious country smell. One of my old school chums gave us a discount on the champagne and table wines. Estée Lauder came through with the take-homes. And we got a cut-rate on the band which was made up of society kids who were pals of Jeremy's.

Happy e-mailed Dolly Parton by getting the address from a Kentucky colleague and she agreed to come sing. "She's a great gal, Ah knows," Happy chirped, "She has a cookbook thet sells lahke huh own banana puddin' and she gives the money fo' the Dollywood Foundation, wut suppo'ts the Imagination Library, givin' a free book a month fo' chillun aged two t'fahve. How about thet! Ah wuz raised to huh 'Stand By Your Man.'"

Fran and Filipa had hurt feelings because they hadn't been asked to perform a duet. On the final day of planning, when the program had already been printed, Happy softened and agreed that they could warble a tune each by Rodgers and Hart, Oscar Hammerstein, and Cole Porter. Old stuff, but I felt it would go over better than Dolly Parton's American country music.

Thanks to Ellie's Mater, the ballroom was filled to capacity on the night. It was a mild one for mid-December. Guests could stand out on the balcony outside the ballroom and gaze down at the vanishing tail lights of cars cruising Piccadilly, while tourists in the cars stared up at all their finery with dazed delight that they had managed to peek inside the top crust of London society. There was a sprinkling of Ambassadors, Members of Parliament, and a Cabinet Secretary. I learned that even such as they do not scorn a free meal in superb surroundings.

Happy had fussed about what to wear, but she chose the right frock and I was proud of her in a swirl of silk as she came up the great stairwell that leads skylight-wards from the marble main hall. The gown was an original by Bellville Sassoon, a favorite couturier of Ellie's Mater, and Happy's hair had been swept up into a chignon by the famous Walter of Mayfair.

My little Baptist had come a long way from her Pappy's homestead.

Of course something had to go wrong. Isn't that Murphy's Law? What happened was a robbery. All the takings for the tickets, tombola and surprise auction of an antique car were stolen when the charity lady in charge of them left her purse in a taxi going home. The taxi's driver vanished. The charity lady had used a minicab to save money, and the driver had absconded. He was no doubt on a ferry on his way to Morocco by dawn.

Oh well, the dancing and dining part of the evening went superbly. Nobody knew about the robbery until the next day, and then Hal promised to cover the entire amount stolen and the story was kept out of the newspapers.

Hal was ready to return to Canada once he'd seen Anchor in action.

I like Lingfield. It's been good to me and its all-weather track suited my late horses. We took the train to meet our head groom at the course, and we shivered together in the jockeys' changing room because there were few bars that had been heated for this late program. Even the speckled fish, camouflaged over the pebbles in that stream that flows near the station's tin-roofed walk, seemed too cold to survive.

Anchor won his race. Hal was extremely pleased. He received a small trophy and treated all of our group to champagne. We crowded into his limo for a ride back to London, having ice in our veins and unable to tackle another train ride.

We met Happy and Ellie there to stay overnight at the Lime Tree with Filipa and Rus.

Happy made the mistake of inviting them to live with us in our country cottage.

Their baby cried all the way to Epsom, and seemed to be sniffling again. I worried how we could handle a sickly infant when our own children were notably boisterous.

Rus and Filipa took over our tiring guest room. The baby was tucked into Dorothy's room near her crib.

Mrs. Rea pursed her lips and scowled. House guests were the bane of her existence. Like a hostess who has only eight plates and ten people show up for dinner, Mrs. Rea showed her displeasure by slamming down the two extra chairs around our kitchen table.

There was a Boxing Day aura as we ate. The fun had taken place the day before, the important guest had left, and the take-home gifts stored away to be recycled as Christmas presents.

Happy, to lighten the atmosphere, said, "Ah wonders how many ladies at t'ball kept their Estée Lauder take-homes fo' presents to give when the'es nothin' else in t'drawers!"

There was a small titter of laughter, but that was interrupted by a phone call.

I could hear Ellie's voice loud from the receiver when Happy took it up to answer. Ellie sounded hysterical.

She howled, "I believe something terrible has happened to Jeremy. My aunt called to say he never came home from our ball. She HAS telephoned all over, including a call to the local police, and no one has seen or heard from him. That's so unlike Jeremy. He's always considerate. Always gives notice of where he's going to be."

A vital question hovered in the air like a hawk circling to locate a prey.

I looked at Happy, she looked at me, but it wasn't until after she'd tried to calm Ellie with a promise to drive to her home that I whispered, "Could Jeremy have bolted to avoid arrest? Have we been fingering the wrong person as the strangler?"

Filipa, in a subdued tone, said, "Could there be a connection between Jeremy's disappearance and the fact you didn't want us to live any longer in Fran's apartment?"

While I hesitated to reply to that, Happy marched in like a rookie soldier entering a mine field. "Mah gut feelin' tells me Jeremy ain't the puhson wut made it impo'tant t'keep y'all out o' Fran's flat. But, havin' said thet, Ah must admit the'es somethin' smells wrong about Jeremy's disappearance."

I added, "Jeremy's an Arabic don. He speaks several dialects, knows people in both Iraq and Iran. God knows what that could mean in today's political climate."

"Ah aims t'find out mo'e at Ellie's house," Happy left the table and pulled a quilted jacket from its peg in the hall. "See y'all later. Won't be long at Ellie's. Just long 'nuf t'git some info Ah needs."

Happy was back sooner than I expected. Her face looked drawn and weary. She shrugged. "Didn't git much outta Ellie. She c'd hardly talk. Cryin' so much." She shook petals of snow from her hair and jacket. "No sign of Harold East there up at thet house. Mebbe he ain't so hot aftuh huh no mo'e."

When we'd done the washing-up to give Mrs. Rea a little reprise, we saw Rus and Filipa to their bedroom door and went to our own. We found Tim in our bed, shaking with fever.

"I'm sick. I can't breathe."

Happy rushed to find a thermometer. He had a temperature of one hundred.

She gave him baby aspirin, and put his head under a towel to pull in fumes of steam from a pot of boiling water enriched with Vicks.

He slept in our bed all night. The next morning Dorothy also had a fever, hers was one hundred and one. Happy spent the entire day ministering to our sick infants, and that evening she began to sneeze. She took her own temperature, one hundred and two. Filipa complained of a sore throat, and Mrs. Rea developed a cough. Rus and I were the only people in our home not hit by the bug that tiny Betty had brought from London.

Of course, no sex. Happy was beyond wanting anything except to feel well. Her face had shriveled, her breasts were like spaniel ears. A crimson complexion shrieked with her blond hair and freckles.

Rus and I ran a courier service to the Epsom pharmacy, and to the supermarket. He fed his lot, I tried to cook for mine.

The days grew shorter and autumn turned into winter. We were three days before Christmas before the bug gave up and left our house. I kept up the fuel level for our central heating, and brought in a new supply of logs for our chimney's gorge.

Outside there was a layer of snow like sugar coating the branches of the willows in the garden. A lonely robin searched unsuccessfully for nourishment. I scattered bread crumbs from the sick folks' trays. My business sense had warned me to keep the stable boys away from our pest house, and they had weathered the epidemic. Not even my delicate foals and two-year-olds had caught the virus. That bug was a people bug, not – thankfully – also a horse bug.

I knew that Happy was entering convalescence when she asked me for a story. It was on the night before a Christmas party I needed to go to in London, and I'd been worried about leaving her unattended by anyone other than Rus.

Happy said, "Ah wants one o'them hoss stories. Ah knows as Ah won't be hearin' nothin' from nobody all day t'morrow. Rus tol' me he's goin' t' London too."

Great news, that! I'd be going up to town a much comforted husband knowing my rival won't be in my house.

What story? I didn't think it was appropriate to give with some cheerful-earful. We'd had no news of Jeremy. There had been no closure on the strangling cases.

I did my best. "This is what happens to jockeys when they're at the top of their game and nothing seems like it can go wrong. Last year, just before the Kentucky Derby, Edgar Prado was shining his derby boots preparing to take the roses. He'd recently won at Gulfstream in Florida on Barbaro, a colt undefeated in five races. So? Just before the roses race Edgar Prado breaks a shoulder at Keeneland and is out of commission."

"Thet happens. Nothin' mo'e?'

"There's much more. Barbaro, the undefeated horse was trained by Michael Matz, at Palm Meadows in Boynton, Florida. Metz has a history you wouldn't believe. A hero's. It all began in 1989, with a plane crash. Matz, now 60, was a show jumper at the time who was good enough to be in three Olympics and eventually won a silver medal."

"A show jumpuh? But Ah wants a raceho'ss story."

"I'm getting to that. First, I'll tell you more about that plane crash. The plane was a DC-10. It weighed 350,000 pounds. A bang at 3:16 was the first indication of trouble. It lost an engine going from Denver to Chicago. The flight started to go rough, but for 45 minutes the plane flew on. Matz was seated next to two children, Melissa Roth and Travis Roth. Their brother Jody was elsewhere. The children were traveling alone without parents or a family friend."

"Ah'd hate fo' our chillun t'have t'do thet."

"Without that engine, the plane became uncontrollable. It cartwheeled making an emergency landing in Sioux City, in Iowa. Landing at 250 miles an hour, it skidded for 3000 feet before coming to a stop upside down. It split in half, killing 112 of the passengers. Among the 184 survivors was Matz and those three Roth kids. Matz helped Melissa and Travis out of the plane, told them to run and then went back inside to rescue Jody and an eighteen-month-old baby. Is that a hero or is that a hero? Afterwards Matz shielded the Roth children from knowing the full horror of what had happened to those 184 who died. Travis said later, 'the worst we saw was a cut on someone's arm. He'd told us to run and not look back.' Melissa added, 'We all unbuckled our seat belts and fell to the ceiling. There were lines of people walking very orderly out the airplane, just like you exit an aircraft. But, of course, they were walking upside down using the ceiling for a floor."

"The ceilin' a floor!"

"Metz alerted the children's grandparents. Those two were enormously grateful because they'd been told by the airline that not all the children survived. It wasn't until the following day that the kids' parents arrived. A year passed, and the Roth family went to visit Matz. Year after year the grandparents sent him maple syrup from their supply. He became an olympic star. Then, finally he turned to training racehorses."

"Yeah man, racehorses now."

"By 2006, Matz had Barbaro, sired by Dynaformer. It so happened that at Dynaformer's stud farm – called Three Chimneys – the man in charge of market development was John Hamilton, the uncle of Melissa Ross's husband Hamilton Radcliffe. By then Melissa was 29, and the mother of two infants. She still felt gratitude for the way Matz had guided her to safety and then shielded her from the horror that could have blighted her psychologically. When, like the shape of some racecourses, their lives came round full circle to where they found each other again thanks to Barbaro, the Roth family made a point of traveling to Churchill Downs to urge Barbaro to run his best."

Happy murmured in her sleepy voice, "Nice story. Except that Ah knows Barbaro broke his leg and died. Now tell me wut y'all thinks about Jeremy. Could he have killed all the people close to Fran?"

I felt sleepy too. The enigma had to be probed. "Jeremy could have done some of them. HE was Fran's lover. He dumped her but could have resented that she took up with Goofy so soon after the end of their affair. During their love affair she could have given him a key to her apartment. That's par for the course. Sybil? She could have known too much, learned it when she was part of the duo. Jeremy could have slipped into her dressing room saying he was just ahead of Ellie. Munchie?. As I said before about Fran, Munchie could have been strangled by someone who traveled overnight to Melbourne and returned the next day, or even the same day. What makes the scenario unlikely is that Jeremy hadn't met Fran at the time of her twin's murder. Carla's death ignited this whole mess."

Again, a night without sex. To tell the truth, I was so undone by nursing three sick Harrows, I could probably not have been able to perform.

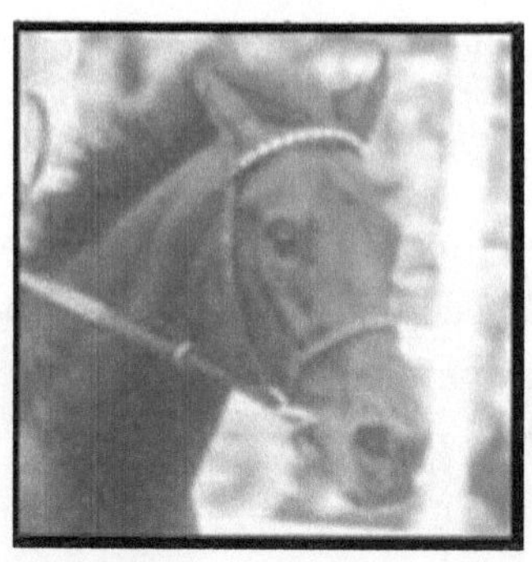

CHAPTER 25

Christmas with infants is immeasurably superior to celebrating it without children.

I chopped down a fur tree on my property, and Tim helped me set it up near our hearth. We strung it with lights in the shape of candles, hung swathes of popcorn, and I used forty-year-old ornaments my father lent me from the trees we'd decorated when I was a boy.

Tim was keen to find presents and went around the cottage like in an Easter-egg hunt trying to find in which closet we'd hidden them. Being Happy's son, he didn't believe in Santa Claus. He knew we'd bought the Christmas gifts. Little Dorothy still had her look of total innocence and a lack of greed in her wide sapphire eyes.

Dorothy's greatest thrill came each evening when I turned on the tree's lights. She reached out her pudgy fingers to try to grasp the multi-colored candles and I had my work cut out to stop my child from being electrocuted.

Rus and Filipa had less joy from their Betty. She was six months younger than Dorothy, and in any event was too feeble to participate in Christmas cheer. Carol singers came to our door in waves. We fed some, others we sent on their way with candies and cakes. We went to the town green to watch the Morris Dancers, and listened to their merry bells that winked and called from their socks.

Not so pleasant was a visit Happy was determined to make to Ellie's home. She drove there by herself. None of us wanted to further that relationship. Happy walked past the tall front door that this year did not sport its traditional wreath of pine cones and greenery. She walked into a hall barren of a Christmas tree or flowers spiked with holly. There *was* a minimal fire in the hearth, but no garlands of leaves decorating the mantel. Ellie and her Mater sat alone, with no guests or attendants. Ellie was crying.

Happy cuddled her with comforting pats. "Y'all's got t'snap outta this." Between gulps and sighs, Ellie croaked, "Not possible."

"'Sho is. Git up 'n git the Christmas spirit. Fix this room with Christmas doin's. Bake some cookies or gingerbread men. If y'all don't want 'em, the village children will eat 'em. Pack baskets with turkey 'n plum puddin's fo' the parents."

"You haven't seen the beastly evening newspapers. Mater has just come down from London. Look! Look what the *Evening Standard* has had to say about Jeremy." Lady Agatha, shivering next to the meager fire, rustled the paper.

Lady Agatha handed the *Standard* to Happy. It was open to an inside page where *Londoner's Diary* was headlined.

"Earls' son implicated in recent murder. It has been established that the Hon. Jeremy was in Melbourne when the singer known as Munchie was strangled seated at her piano. After a brief sojourn at his Surrey home on his return from the Antipodes, the Hon. Jeremy has vanished without a trace. The police have issued a notice that he help with inquiries."

"The bit about helpin' with inquiries, thet mean he's gonna be arrested?" "Almost certainly." Lady Agatha, always calm and dignified, shrieked and began to weep loudly.

Happy tried to defuse their agitation. It was like throwing a wet towel into the molten lava of a volcano. She strode to a tray where a teapot and a plate of cucumber sandwiches remained untouched. She tested the teapot. It was cold. The edges of the sandwiches had curled. She rang for the butler. No one answered the bell.

Ellie moaned, "We're here on our own. All the staff have gone to do their Christmas shopping. Late, but they'll get something with money we gave. They must, because we haven't much for any of them."

Lady Agatha surprised Happy by snarling, "You should go to Chelsea to that Fran person's flat and give it a thorough once-over. I'm certain you'll find there's a tie-in with that flat which could exonerate poor Jeremy. He's innocent of all this. Of course, he is."

Happy, feeling bewildered by the change in Lady Agatha, decided to slip away from that lugubrious house. She served a cup of the cold tea with a biscuit each for Lady Agatha and Ellie, then collected her Husky jacket to make an exit. Ellie caught her half way out of the long hall.

"If you're going to London, I'm coming with you."

She pulled a Barbour from its hanger in the hall closet and strode toward Happy's car.

There was little need for conversation on their ride into the city. Both had said all they could pry out of the other as regarded the crimes and Jeremy's get-away. Happy didn't find a parking space near Fran's flat. Christmas shoppers had overburdened the few parking lots, and it was necessary to leave the car at Victoria Station. "We might as well have come up by train," Ellie sniffed. They walked together to the Ebury Street block of flats where Carla and Goofy had been strangled. Again, they rang the push button to be admitted by the anonymous tenant who greeted her hoped-for visitors and invited them to come out of the cold.

Again they sneaked up the stairs. Again they pounded on Fran's door. Fran opened up to give them a huge welcome and show off her new décor. Again she had changed all the cushions, and pictures. Extra chairs had been added, as well as a medley of modern Christmas decorations, some very risqué. Condoms in different colors hung on the tree.

Again she led them to her bar, but this time there was no bowl of cocaine on view.

"Ellie," Fran began, "You're the fucking expert on Debrett's stud list. What have you to say about Lord Snodgrass?"

"First of all, Snodgrass isn't a peer of the realm. He may have been knighted for services to the crown, but I rather doubt that. More likely he bought the title by furthering the career of some government lackey who put him on the honors list. Really, Fran, you must get these things right."

"I met him with David Blunkett. He was Home Secretary. He'd know who was a phony."

"David Blunkett has been twice in Blair's government. Certainly he's a very able and intelligent person. Must be, since he's blind and yet managed to attain those positions. But that doesn't mean he screens all the people who hover around him. Snodgrass, in particular, is known to be dicey."

"Sour grapes. You say that because Harold East has dumped you. I heard all about it from Heidi."

Happy heard this news with mixed feelings. She felt sorry for Ellie, and now understood why all the doleful looks and a home that seemed in mourning like for a road-victim's wake. Privately, she rejoiced that Ellie's affair was over because she knew that I would be gladdened by the news. Happy said, "Is this true? You've finished with Harold?"

"He finished with me," Ellie wailed. "When I returned from being fingerprinted and photographed by the London police, Harold made a very quick dash out of my door."

Fran laughed sourly. "That son of a bitch was running like a greyhound pursued by the rabbit. His kind never fucking want any notice taken of them or theirs by the police."

Happy reviewed Fran's earlier remark. "You heard about this from Heidi? You've seen Heidi?"

"You're friggin' right. Poor thing. She came to me in her misery. She burned her hands in her fireplace when she was trying to light a bloody Yule log. She'd hoped to sing in another musical rumored to start soon. But with her hands bandaged, she didn't think she'd look the part of a fucking temptress for her audition."

Listening to Fran, my Happy wondered if Fran would ever improve her use of the English language. Happy knew that her own abuse of it was all too noticeable, but she had the excuse of having been "raised in them Kentucky hills."

The two visitors were served whisky, although it was dinnertime. Fran downed two doubles.

Fran's doorbell rang.

"Shit, that's Snodgrass and I'm not dressed yet to go out. You get the door, Ellie. And Happy, you can damn well come into my bedroom and help me find something to wear."

Happy had never been in Fran's bedroom. She found it in an awful mess, used clothing strewn on the floor, broken tights hung on chairs, and worst of all an open safe.

"Y'all don't close yo' safe?"

"Forgot. And anyway, there's nothing important in it. Friggin' junk."

"Did Carla's room have a safe?"

"I suppose so. She never told me. I think she hid it behind a picture. I bloody well never looked. None of my business."

"Wut makes y'all think her jew'ry ain't in theah?"

"Because she'd been wearing the best pieces before she was strangled. We couldn't find any of it afterwards."

Happy picked up a navy silk shift from the floor. "How 'bout this'n?" Fran didn't answer. In a hurry, she slipped on the narrow dress and preened before a full-length mirror. "It can bloody well do." She added a pair of four-inch-heel shoes and strode to the living room to greet the newcomer.

Sir Arthur Snodgrass stood there, frowning. He failed badly in the looks department. Two inches shorter than Fran, he was now six inches shorter because Fran was wearing high heeled shoes. He was balding, had a paunch, and a stutter that would keep him out of politics.

"You- you – you are late!" No kiss, friendly or passionate.

No kiss from Fran either. "Bloody sorry. But as you can see, my two best friends surprised me with a visit."

"We –we –we've got- got- got t'leave. Mi- mi- miss the curtain. Thi- thi-this show's a sell-sell-sellout." As he spoke, he gave them a thorough once-over and Happy got the impression Snodgrass was not impressed. Were these two women the best Fran could find? "I-I-I tho-tho-thought Heidi was co-co-coming. Have a ti-ti-ticket for her."

"Heidi's burned her hands. Doesn't want to be seen by the friggin' public."

"And Fi-Fi-Filipa?"

"She's in the country. Has a bad cold. Laryngitis. We weren't able to cut the demo we need."

Happy had a twinge of remorse. Drowned in worry for our children because of their fevers, she'd given scant consideration to Filipa and how her laryngitis could affect her vocal career.

Fran was pulling on a mink wrap when the front door opened and Heidi entered.

"Am I on time? Can we still make the curtain?" she asked Snodgrass, without a greeting for any of the others present.

Happy stared at her in shock. Heidi looked very changed from when Happy had seen her in Sydney's opera house. In her Japanese kimono and the obi with its wide silk band minimizing her waist, plus heavy make-up, she had seemed quite beautiful. Heidi's big nose, big hands, and big hips had all but disappeared. Tonight, here, Heidi's ugly features were very apparent. She and Snodgrass made a suitable couple, far more so than delicately graceful Fran. But her use of the English language was better. No swear words from Heidi.

Fran snapped, "You bloody well know you are. If we leave right now!" She had a parting shaft for Ellie, "Too bad Harold East dumped you, or the two of you could have joined us."

The five left together in order to give Fran the chance to lock her door. She did.

Downstairs, Snodgrass had a taxi waiting. He hadn't gone to the expense of a limousine. Because London taxis will only accept four passengers, he didn't offer to give the two women a ride to Victoria Station.

A fine drizzle permeated the night as the two friends made their own way to the station, getting thoroughly soaked by the time they reached their train's platform. On the return journey they were more talkative. They found the cafeteria-style dining car, stood at the counter, and chatted over the filthy coffee.

Fran started the touchy subject of her rift with Harold East. "He dumped me, that's true. But I'd been having second thoughts about him for some time. He was cheap on our trip to Melbourne. And never considered whether I was comfortable or having fun. He's such a poor sport: furious that Rick's filly beat his into third. He'd have been a respectable second if your husband hadn't brought Feathers to Australia."

Happy tried to soothe her friend. "Rick was only doin' his job. He don't hate Harold. Fact is, he wuz warmin' up t'him fo' yo' sake."

"I knew that. But Harold's one of a kind. Gloriously charming one day, and absolutely beastly the next. Thank goodness I haven't had to know many people who are hot and cold like that."

"Dear Ellie, y'all will meet some'un who c'n appreci'te yo'r value."
"Thanks for the kind thought. But to tell you the honest truth, it's his horses I'll miss more than I will Harold. I was learning how to talk to them just as you do yours. Those horses were the babies I've never had. How will I ever find that someone who has great horses too?"

CHAPTER 26

Ellie did find her knight-on-a-white-horse. His name was Steven Cowles. He didn't have a title, hadn't gone to Eton, nor belonged to a renowned regiment. He was a broker in the City who kept horses in the livery stable where Feathers had been held during her kidnapping. Ellie's Mater liked him. She'd never approved of the Harold East affair.

They met during a heavy rainstorm that had forced them to take refuge in a local pub. It was the day before Christmas when the pub's customers sang carols. It was "Silent Night," and "God Rest Ye Merry Gentlemen" and "Hark the Herald Angels Sing," but neither Ellie nor Steven could sing a note because they both had awful voices. They both had croaked a few notes to join in the merriment, and because they shared the embarrassment of not singing in tune they began to speak and by Christmas morning hadn't stopped. Steven was her Christmas present. Ellie was his.

They didn't have a one-night stand. Ellie shared his bed for a week at a local bed-and-breakfast until New Year's Eve, when they went to London to celebrate their love.

Happy and I met up with them at The Dorchester, where we'd been invited by the Ainsleys. That formerly Scrooge-like owner, had become with Hal Murphy the most generous of all. The Ainsley wins had transformed them, because now they weren't dependent on his military salary.

After a first-class holiday dinner there was a fanfare from the bandstand. A solitary spotlight beamed in on a female figure slouched upright beside the piano. She began to sing "Summertime," the Gershwin classic written by a Jew based on a Negro spirituals' style.

That singer was Fran. No duo, just that one girl who knew her notes and was in great voice.

Looking around the darkness, Happy saw Snodgrass. She went over to his table, used the patent Happy New Year cue, and asked, "Wut's with Fran? Why she singin' heah? Why now?"

Whispering, he stuttered, "Fr-Fr-Fran re-re-refused to sing rap. She-she-she lost her other job."

This WAS a one-night stand for Fran. Following her show, she and Snodgrass joined us at our table. Fran looked sickly. She'd lost too much weight. Why? Cocaine, or dieting? Snogging Snodgrass? Or all three?

I felt genuinely glad to see her because I'd missed Fran's last visit to check on her horses when I was in Australia.

"Great song, great delivery," I said, as if I was a bona fide music critic. Fran reacted in a surprisingly modest way. "I didn't think I was very good. Bloody awful pianist accompanying me. Why the hell couldn't my agent produce better than that fuckin' jerk?"

Snodgrass leaned across the table and took her hands in his in a proprietary manner. "Fr-Fr-Fran d-d-darling, you were won-won-wonderful." Captain and Mrs. Ainsley, our host and hostess and among my principal owners, looked dismayed by this scene. At first they'd been pleased to be in the presence of a star, but her gutter language came as too much of a shock.

I couldn't afford it, but as a diversion I called for a bottle of champagne.

"Pommery, your best," I ordered a waiter.

"So y'all out o' any singin' job?" Happy whispered to Fran.

She nodded. Fran didn't favor that subject and didn't want to expand on it.

Mrs. Ainsley made the mistake of touching on it like a mother probing the cut on her child's arm checking for ingrained dirt. "But you will be bringing out a new album?"

"If and when Filipa gets her friggin' act together. And I've still got a fan or two willing to pay thirty bloody pounds for a Purcell Duo album."

The table went silent until the bubbly appeared. When it had been served and we'd toasted Fran's performance, Snodgrass announced,

"Ch-ch-champagne ri-ri-right thing. Fr-Fr-Fran and I are engaged t'be ma-ma-married. Kept it a se-se-secret."

As the table's host, Captain Ainsley rose and lifted his glass in a time-honored manner. In a parade ground voice that commanded attention from other tables, he saluted the couple, "To Fran, the future Lady Snodgrass."

I rose too. I said, rather abashed, "To Fran and Arthur."

We all did the correct thing and downed our champagne with big smiles. Snodgrass leaned across the table to kiss Fran on the lips, husband-style. He refrained from struggling through his stutter to say a few words. Fran spoke for both of them.

"A friggin' secret. We plan to get married when my album's been cut. And this will be the last ever of classical music. I'm switching to Gospel. Have any of you heard of Carrie Underwood? About my age, and she has already sold over 3 million copies of *Some Hearts*. Her first single 'Jesus Take the Wheel' won CMT's Music Awards for Breakthrough Video of the Year."

Happy interrupted, "Ah knows thet Carrie Underwood. She's a real country music gal."

Fran continued, "Last Christmas, the CD sold over 400,000 copies. Listen up. Even though she put a sexy song in *Some Hearts*! A dark ballad: 'Before He Cheats.' Goes like this: 'While he's in a bar showing a bleach-blonde tramp . . . how to shoot a combo,' Carrie digs her keys into his paint job, smashes his headlights with a Louisville slugger, carves her name into his leather seats and then sings 'Cause the next time he cheats . . . Oh, you know it won't be on me!' Snodgrass, you listen-up!"

In military parade tones Captain Ainsley admonished Fran, "You'll have to correct your language if you intend to sing Gospel music."

"For my professional life, sure. But my private life is my own. No crap will change that. Tough times don't last. Tough people do."

It was one a.m. by then, and the Ainsleys had a long drive back North.

They used that excuse to end their hosting the table.

Happy looked tired, and I wondered if that meant no sex to tie-up New Year's Eve.

We left the future Lady Snodgrass with her petulant fiancé and rode with Ellie in Steven's car to our cheap digs at the Lime Tree.

No sex.

New Year's Day meant a legal holiday for my two grooms. The Head Lad and I would have to deal with all our string. Happy and I hurried back to our stables and did what had to be done. I mucked out manure, and gave the horses their daily grooming, cutting hairs from nostrils and otherwise tidying them. Happy did her part, loading hay nets. The Head Lad pitchforked straw into the boxes. A hard day for all of us. When nightfall arrived, Happy and I returned to our cottage to give Mrs. Rea a few hours respite and babysat our kids until they finally fell asleep. Not easy.

And again, no sex.

On January 2, I'd planned to run a horse on the all-weather track at Kempton. That was a poor decision. I'd always revered Kempton as the racecourse designed for King Edward VII to save him from journeying to Newmarket, but that day everything went wrong for my owner's colors. Our jockey got a a total ban of eighteen days for careless riding. He would have received worse, if the Stewards had seen him interfere with his rivals. A heavy fog had developed that prevented the cameras from recording that event.

It was glum driving back to Epsom in the horsebox with my Head Lad. Although customarily a taciturn fellow, he jolted my memory with a remark about an incident I'd almost forgotten. I'd tucked that memory into the deepest recess of my mind, where it lurked like when a Senior has a lapse due to Alzheimer's.

He said, "When Miss Fran were down here, she declared as she would be around a long time seein' her horses."

And I recalled that afternoon, when Fran had arrived breathless at the stables. She'd laughed, "I'll outlive these friggin' horses!"

Happy had laughed too, in a comradely but careful way "A hoss c'n live twenty even fo'ty yeahs."

"So what? I'll bloody well outdo that! I'll only be sixty, at most."

When I returned from Kempton, had my hot bath, and snuggled next to Happy in our double bed, feeling worried I whispered, "Strange thing about Fran. Everyone close to her has died. She hasn't. Did you ever wonder why?"

"Sho' have! Ah says we sh'd keep a close eye on Filipa. But don't have t'concern us'n about thet now. Let's us'n make love."

Her suggestion threw out every other feeling. We had great sex. Happy tried something new instead of her routine strip act. She'd bought a book about sex and it had enlightened her like when a switch turns on a bulb.

The next morning, when we were still enjoying the afterglow of last night, I suggested a repeat. But now Happy wanted serious talk.

Still in the privacy of our bedroom, Happy said, "Ah thinks we'd best keep close watch on Filipa."

"Any special reason?"

"M'Baptist Min'ster, he said remembuh the *Bible*'s good commandments, 'n thet includes not bearin' false witness. Ah got it right othuh tahmes when we-all finguhed murd'rers. But this tahme Ah's got suspicions, but no proof."

"Proof is relative my darling. Do you know that DNA has only been accepted in courts for the past twelve years?" "Sho 'nuf?"

"Would I lie to you? Do I lie when I say I love you? And that I love making love?"

"Ah knows wut y'all's up to. Y'all wants as Ah should tell mah suspicions!"

"Don't change the subject. We were talking about my love for you. And while I respect the "no false witness" ideal, I *want* you. And I mean right now!"

We made love again, and again the subject of murder went the way of any other thoughts, like billowing clouds before a clear wind wipes them away.

Later, Happy suggested we return to London. "Ah wants t'see Fran's apa'tment ag'in. Somethin' as Ah don't und'stand theah."

After morning stables I drove her to Chelsea in the Volvo. Traffic was intense because holiday crowds were using their day off to plunge into the shops' New Year sales. We couldn't find a free parking space. Again I settled for a parking lot.

What was Happy searching for? Not the décor! Fran had done her usual when changing boyfriends. She altered the look of the place totally. For Sir Arthur Snodgrass it was gold leaf and crimson on Louis XVI chairs, an extremely uncomfortable Louis XV sofa and a Charles X dining room set up. The paintings on the walls were by Watteau, Fragonard and Boucher nymphs and flowers, fakes, of course. Because who knew how long Snodgrass would last?

Fran was dressed differently, wearing what my mother called "a tea gown" with an ankle-length skirt over an embroidered silken top. Her hair was pulled back into a chignon. What a transformation! It added twenty years to her age! She looked like a portrait of her mother that hung over the chimney piece.

We were offered sherry in Bohemian crystal goblets. Happy made a disgruntled face. She wasn't "into" sherry. "My Paw's moonshine would put this puke t'shame," she whispered to me.

Fran's doorbell rang. She went to open it, probably expecting someone different because her expression of welcome faded drastically when she saw Ellie with her shoulders heaving and tears tumbling like the hectic waters of rapids. Fran was in the mood for fun, not for someone else's troubles.

"What the fuck's the matter with you?" she spat out at poor Ellie.

Happy went to her friend, placed an arm around those heaving shoulders, and led her to Fran's bedroom. She closed the door, leaving Fran to entertain the dreadful Snodgrass.

Ellie shook her head several times before she could speak. Then, pouring out like the Mississippi from a broken dike, her words came fast, "Preggers, I've joined the club, in the family way, I'm going to have Steven's baby and I'll lose him if I don't get rid of it."

"A baby! Y'all should be in Hog Heaven. This ain't no ways t'act. Rid of it? Wut y'mean? Down the terlet?"

"He's told me he doesn't want children." Ellie gasped for breath. "I've been waiting, hoping for an engagement ring. Nothing. I don't even dare to ask if he's married to someone else and would have a divorce. Oh! Happy dear, how will I ever tell my Mater? There has never, ever been a bastard in the Grace family."

"Ellie, darlin' y'all c'n make a great mothuh. Y'all so good with ma chillun. We c'n figuh out a good way 'round this."

"I've thought of writing to Somerset House and ask to have his records checked to find out if he's married."

"Easier t'ask him."

"I can't. Haven't been able to, tried to get the words out, couldn't."

"Tell him straight out y'all' is havin' his baby and if he don't want it, y'all don't want him no mo'e."

"He's a lovely man, but difficult. My Mater, who likes him, says I–" Ellie interrupted herself, she couldn't continue.

I learned about this conversation later, after I knocked on Fran's bedroom door and was admitted. "What's going on?"

"Rick, this ain't fo' y'all. Us'n got woman talk in heah."

"I can't stomach another minute of Snodgrass. I'd like to leave, but Steven Cowles has just arrived. Ellie, you'll have to come out into the drawing room and deal with him."

Ellie blushed. She looked like she'd prefer to jump out of the window LSD-addict style.

My Happy took her in hand, removed a compact of freckle-concealer from her purse and applied it heavily to Ellie's tear-splotched skin. She fluffed Ellie's messy hair and pulled her toward the bedroom door.

"Oh! I can't see Steven just now," Ellie wailed.

Fran opened the door. An eager-faced Steven glimpsed Ellie. He rushed to take her heaving shoulders into a huge hug. He said, "Ellie, my final decree came through. I'm a free man. We can get married. What kind of a ring you want? Emerald? Sapphire? Or just a plain diamond?"

Ellie stopped trembling, her eyes lit like they were reflecting sunshine on wet leaves after rain.

She kissed Steven with the delight of a bride at the end of the wedding, a flawed kiss because this bride-to-be had the anxiety of revealing her pregnancy. She winked at Happy over Steven's shoulder.

Happy did the donkey work for her. "Stev'n, y'all's a real lucky guy. Getting' two-for-one, wut with Ellie carryin' yo'r baby. Hog Heaven, Ah'd call thet."

Steven had the grace to blush. He reddened from the forehead oozing color slowly like lava going down a volcano. Silenced. While Fran, Snodgrass and I crowded around him with congratulations, he lost his color, and ended with a face as drained as a bridegroom's on the twelfth night of his honeymoon.

Finally, urged to say something, Steven gulped out, "Fran's the love of my life. I'm thrilled she's going to have my baby. We'll be married in plenty of time for that."

The relief in Ellie's face was wonderful to see. She said quietly, with enormous emotion, "My Mater will be so pleased. She'll give us a wedding party to end all wedding parties."

Fran went pink with jealousy. She'd expected to be the first to be married. She growled, "What the hell are you going to wear? Your bump is sure to show in anything except a hoop skirt."

Snodgrass, not knowing what all the excitement was about, said sententiously, "Empress Eugenie of France promoted the hoop skirt when she was pregnant with Napoleon III's son."

"I'll open the friggin' champagne and we'll toast the future bride and groom. What the fuck!" Fran opened her bar, and in delving for a bottle of champagne, she knocked over a small bowl containing cocaine.

Snodgrass looked shocked. "Frances, what are you doing with an illegal substance?"

"Not mine!" Fran answered quickly. "Left over from when my dead twin took a line every few hours."

Snodgrass, who usually looked street smart, nevertheless swallowed this big lie.

Fran craftily put the incriminating bowl into a cabinet with a box of oatmeal and bags of sugar. She opened the bottle of champagne with a ' 'Ta-Ta' trumpeting it was time for hilarity. A show-business aura bathed the room with the feeling the curtain was about to go up.

We drank the champagne, and asked the usual questions about where they would live and would they have a church wedding or just go to the Registry Office. Nothing more was said about the baby Ellie was expecting.

Discreetly, we left after a second cup of champagne, with Happy slightly tipsy. We had some trouble locating which car park we'd used to berth the Volvo, but when we eventually found the car we just sat in it and talked for a while.

Happy asked, "Wut y'all think o' this?"

"I'm hoping that Ellie will be very happy, but she doesn't know much about Steven."

"Not talkin' about Ellie. Ah's in Hog Heaven fo' huh. Ah means t'apartment. Wut we come t'see. Wheah the muhduhs began."

"I noticed Fran still keeps a stash of cocaine."

"Yeah man. Sho do. 'N did you see she has a safe in huh bedroom?"
"No. But is that important?"

"Could be. But wut int'rests me is the comin's 'n goin's all the tahme. So many visitors, folks as may have a key. 'N thet could include interior decorators, wut with huh changin' t'décor with every new boyfriend."

"She didn't have a decorator before Carla was strangled. The apartment was furnished still as their mother had left it to the twins. Don't you remember how old-fashioned it was, and how we wondered why with all the money they'd earned the twins hadn't brought in a decorator?"

"Yeah Ah does recall thet. It wasn't no decorator followed Munchie t'Aus-tra-lia. Wus someone who c'd git t'Aus-tra-lia, either 'cause they wus wukkin' theah o' was rich 'n c'd affo'd the fare."

"We've ruled out Jeremy, although he could fit into that category. And where the hell is Jeremy, anyhow?"

"Fo'get Jeremy. Fo' t'moment, anyways. He'd nevuh have strangled Bumbles. No way. Ah thinks he's doin' some good, somewheah. Hero stuff. Lahke in *The White Feather*."

"Still enamored of the movies?"

"Wut's with enamor'd? Don't know wut it means."

"Means love. Like you and I love each other, only you also love the movies. Two different kinds of love. Let's go home, and I'll show you what I mean. We'll watch a movie and make love at the same time. How'd THAT suit?"

"Hog Heaven! Y'all bought me a vi-de-o machine?" "Yesterday. Delayed Christmas present."

"Will it play opry? Gran' opry lahke *Madama Butterfly*?"

"Sure. In fact there must be several versions of that from several performances."

"Don't want none o' them minimalist op'rys. No costumes, no scenr'y." "I'd have thought you'd had enough of *Madama Butterfly* after seeing it so recently in Sydney."

"Let's us'n go to one o' them vi-de-o shops 'n git us an old-fashioned *Madama Butterfly*. Take it home with us'n. Ah wants t'remembuh how long it takes."

We did. There was a shop nearby on Sloane Street. The video cost seven pounds, but when we returned home to Epsom and put it in our new machine and turned out the bedroom lights after Mrs. Rea and the infants were asleep, the glorious music brought about the finest sex we'd ever enjoyed outside of Pappy's homestead. That wedding night scene, when Pinkerton carries Butterfly across the threshold of their home, with the lights of a bay beyond being doused little by little gave us orgasms better than what Puccini imagined a geisha would have with an American naval officer. The Pinkerton and Butterfly music gave us the best value for seven pounds ever.

The next morning the mood changed drastically when a London Police Inspector arrived at our Epsom door. He was the same one we'd met after Sybil's murder. He came with her case file under his arm. "We've located the Honorable Jeremy Grace," he began, once ensconced next to the fire in our hearth. I noticed that Jeremy's Hon. was once again in play. "He's in Iran on government business. Very hush-hush. Sorry we'd given him a bad name around this area."

"No sweat," I said cheerfully. "Around here we always knew he hadn't strangled anyone."

"He's involved with a hostage situation. Delicate one. Nothing I've come here to discuss. I'm anxious to close the Sybil case."

I said, "But first let's discuss Jeremy's situation. I'm not going to let you simply dismiss the bad name you gave him. And I know about hostage taking. When I was a teenager I went with my father to Lord Rotherwick's for lunch and met Alan Bristow, of Bristow helicopters. I never forgot that lunch, because the hostage helicopter story was so fascinating. But also because I was taken to see Homing, Lord Rotherwick's Queen Elizabeth II stakes winner. While we were down in the field with Homing, I heard Bristow tell how he got his pilots out of Iran. And how he went to Washington to offer to help get out the Americans when they were taken hostage in Iran. He knew the terrain, the sandstorm season, many facets of flying over Iran."

"Oh I know whom you're going on about. Alan Bristow, the entrepreneur who got all of his helicopters out of Iran after the Ayatollah had declared them to be nationalized. How he ordered all his pilots to set their watches so they could escape out of Iran at the exact same time. Pilots of the larger helicopters flew under the radar, pilots of smaller aircraft were advised to get out by bus. But Mr. Harrow, I've given up the first day of my annual holiday to talk to you about the cat."

"Bumbles?"

"The same. I couldn't sleep last night. I kept asking myself why the cat? And why always someone or something associated with the Harrow stables." Happy answered for me. "Bumbles was strangled as a warnin' to us'n t'keep our noses outta this case."

"By whom? And how would some stranger make it into your stables to reach the cat?"

"Good questions. If we knew the answers, we'd know who the strangler is." I continued, "As matter of fact, on that hour when Bumbles died, the stable lads were off duty. The Head Lad was with me up at our house. The killer's timing was clever. Between morning stables, gallops, and evening stables. Knew about those and fitted them in to perfection. But I agree it would still be chancy to go into Feathers' box. Usually she's a sweet filly. Not sweet to people who were a threat to her pet. I'd seen her rear up and try to bite a groom who gave Bumbles a shove when the boy was laying fresh straw. Anyone harming Bumbles could have been trampled to death."

"Just so. That's what I'd imagined. Have you a list of people who visited Feathers's box over the past year?"

"Not exactly. We've had schoolchildren with their teacher on one occasion. One intrepid kid pinched Feathers' bottom. And after Feathers was kidnapped, I know that several journalists came into her box and had their photographers flash away. Not popular with Feathers, but she didn't harm them. Hurting Bumbles would have been a different story."

Happy said, "Ah's concern'd fo' Filipa. She seems t'be the joker in the pile fo' now. Let's us'n go see huh."

We gave the Inspector tea and crumpets and I drove him to the train station because he hadn't used his official car to do this personal bit of investigating.

I'd planned to ask Happy what drew her to London to see Filipa at this time. But when we were alone, with the bedroom door closed, and Happy began the ritual of her striptease I forgot about everything except sex with my wife. Tonight was Happy-time. Any visit to Filipa was put on hold.

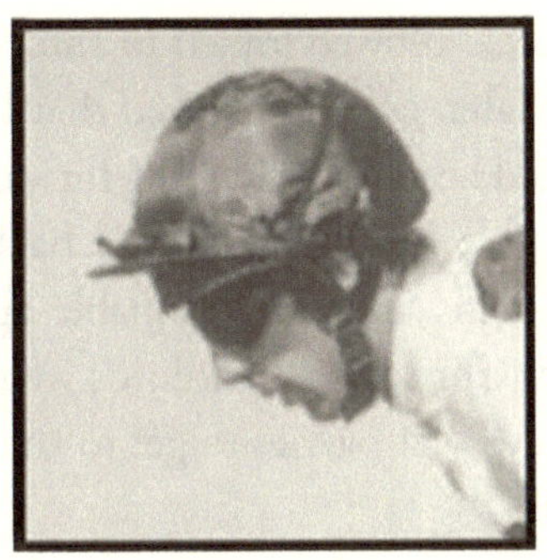

CHAPTER 27

Ellie and Steven were married as soon as possible in the Chelsea Registry Office. Happy and I stood as witnesses. Ellie looked merely over-weight around the middle in a henna colored silk suit bought off-the-peg with no fittings required. Ellie's mater, bitterly disappointed that her only daughter had not chosen to walk down the debs' society church St.Margaret's wearing a Bellville Sassoon made to order gown topped by the family tiara and accompanied by at least eight bridesmaids in matching dresses, had produced a first class reception. It took place at the Cavalry and Guards Club at 127 Piccadilly, with Ellie's uncle—the Earl—presiding to toast the couple in Pommery champagne.

Greece was the chosen venue for their honeymoon, despite recent forest fires that had devastated the region they'd selected. But I don't think they were planning to go walking in the forest. A double bed, preferably king-size, was what they really wanted.

When Steven drove Ellie down Piccadilly heading for Heathrow Airport in his 1935 Alpha Romeo, Happy shed tears of relief. "Thet's one weddin' Ah wanted t'see almost as much as m'own."

There was the usual let-down after the party ended. All of us, dressed to the nines on a formerly elegant street where blue jeans seemed to have become the norm, dispersed on our various homeward routes. I'd parked our rental Ford in the Dorchester's garage, and had a tremor of self-disgust remembering how I'd once allowed myself to enter into a flirtation with a whore there. Two years later, I felt so relieved that I'd got past that hurdle in our marriage and could head home looking forward to bedding my wife.

Filipa, Rus, and Little Betty had moved back in with Fran. They couldn't afford hotel rooms and no reasonable apartment had become available so shortly after Christmas. Landlords were too busy cleaning up after Christmas and New Year parties to get to the more serious business of letting out properties.

Ellie and Steven had changed the venue for their honeymoon. When we returned to our home we'd received an e-mail from them saying the forest fires' smoke had been too much to bear and they were heading for Vienna. Steven planned to give Ellie a treat seeing the equine ballets performed by the horses in the Spanish Riding Academy's displays of dressage.

Snodgrass had left for Dalmatia on an extended business trip to sell seaside lots.

We'd heard that Heidi had burned her hands trying to light a log fire and was on sick leave.

The very next day after we'd settled back home at Epsom, Happy wanted to check on Filipa and Little Betty. We did. We found them dressed in summer clothes.

Filipa surprised us with an invitation. "Come to Monte Carlo with me." Happy looked bewildered. "Monte wut? Wheah's thet? Why y'all goin' theah? 'N wut about Little Betty?"

"This Sheila got a contract to sing at the Monte Carlo opera house. South of the Alps, on the Med. Warmish weather. Like Melbourne this time of year. I'm taking Little Betty to ease her cough. Come with me!"

"Sing?"

"I've got the role in *Don Giovanni* of the country bride he tries to seduce, Zerlina. And guess what! Fran's agent got her the role of Don Giovanni's wife, Dona Elvira. We'll have several scenes where our voices meld and we can test how they work as a duo."

I said, "I could check out the Cagnes Sur Mer racetrack. Find out if there are races we could win there with our horses in early spring. Before racing gets started in Britain."

Happy remained pensive.

"Meet you at Heathrow in a couple of hours. You'll need to go to Epsom for lighter clothes, and arrange for your kids to be looked after," Filipa said.

Happy chimed in, "Ah's not leavin' mah chillun. We-all could come, if Rick agrees we take the chillun. Ah c'd be useful baby-sittin' Little Betty."

We telephoned the housekeeper from Fran's flat and asked to prepare the "chillun" for travel. Within hours we were on a British Midland flight across the aisle from Filipa and Little Betty.

After jetting over Paris, but not close enough to make out the Eiffel Tower, we flew above snow-powdered mountains for two hours until suddenly the whole sparkling panorama of the Mediterranean was spread out below. The wind-frothed waves' caps sent up diamond shafts reflecting the sunlight, sailboats lurched wildly to keep afloat. But our plane never shuddered. We transferred to a helicopter for Monaco, and that *was* a hurly-burly ride. Within twenty minutes, despite the heavy wind, we saw the Garnier-designed cupolas of Monte Carlo's casino and our taxi soon took us two blocks from it to the Hotel Hermitage.

Happy rubbernecked staring at its elaborate murals and painted ceilings. We were given two adjoining bedrooms off a corridor with ornate plasterwork.

"Ah loves this place! Nothin' lahke Pappy's homestead, thet's fo' sho.'" But the sex in our terraced bedroom was almost as good as at Pappy's. Long day. Interesting day. Educational day. We were both tired, but not too tired for sex. Especially when a huge platinum moon hung full over the Med, causing a gold streak on its twinkling waters, that seemed to come right into our bed.

The next morning we did the tourists-with-kids' rounds. We took the "chillun" to see its "exotic gardens," miniature zoo, dolls collection for Dorothy and antique cars for Tim. I never got into the ornate casino, but there were one-arm bandits at the rear of an ice-cream spot at the Café de Paris, and at the Fairmont. I lost a few euros, not enough to worry about. In the afternoon we sat in on the dress rehearsal for *Don Giovanni*. Filipa's and Fran's voices melded perfectly.

I tried giving the "chillun" another excursion to gardens in nearby Menton, but they howled. They wanted to go swimming, but Filipa's predictions of warm summer-like weather were off the mark. We were freezing in our cottons. Happy bought sweaters for all of us. It was Little Betty who suffered the most. Her cough not only persisted it threatened to grow worse.

Our final evening in Monte Carlo was the gala performance of *Don Giovanni.* The opera house's great architect Garnier, who'd also designed the world-famous Paris Opera House, provided a magnificent royal box for the reigning sovereign, Prince Albert II. Said to be a devotee of classical music, the prince looked very handsome, a male version of his late mother Grace Kelly. He drew Happy's glances away from the stage. "Yeah man, don't he be just lahke his movie-stah Mammy,"she repeated several times until our close neighbors in the audience told her to shush.

Fran hadn't bothered much with us. She'd never been one to enjoy the company of infants, barely tolerating Little Betty in her flat. Fran had taken a suite at the less expensive Hotel Alexandra, penny-pinching.

I did do the noble thing, however, and bought matching bouquets for the usherettes to present to both singers as they took their bows at the opera's end. Fran did look pleased. I reckon she toted up the cost of the flowers and recognized that in Monte Carlo they didn't come cheap. But then, she may have thought, "What with my training fees, Rick can well afford a bouquet for me."

Filipa had one more surprise in store. For our last few hours on the Riviera, Filipa hired a taxi to drive all of us into the hills to a sanctuary known for its miracles, Laghet.

"I'm one Sheila who believes in miracles," she said. "Don't care if produced by catholic nuns, Buddhist monks or a Delphic Oracle, my faith remains strong. This Laghet place, I'm told, is full of primitive paintings done by folks that were either cured of something nasty or saved during storms at sea. I've offered to sing Gounod's "Ave Maria" at the High Mass in the church there in thanks for Betty's cure."

Happy echoed, " 'Ave Maria', lahke wut Mario Lanza done sung in thet film on Caruso."

"The same. Only I'm no Joan Sutherland, to give it all a Sheila should give."

Filipa wasn't a Joan Sutherland. But in that musty, ancient church the acoustics provided a patina to her voice that thrilled its parishioners.

I've rarely heard people clap in a church, but those parishioners applauded Filipa.

We reloaded our restless children into the waiting taxi, and barely made our British Midland plane for the return flight to Heathrow.

No murders interrupted our stay in Monaco.

CHAPTER 28

Unpacking at our Epsom home was fairly easy. We hadn't worn any of the clothes we'd so hurriedly selected for what had been expected to be balmy weather. Again we felt tired after our trip, but again Happy delivered the goods. I told her a racing story, she did her stripper act peeling off the winter clothes that had been exchanged for summer voile.

The sex was good.

After morning stables I found Happy dressed for London.

She was wearing high-heeled boots, not the kind she chose for mucking out the horses' stalls. Her worsted jacket had a nipped-in waist. Her ankle length plaid skirt would have had manure on the hem had she worn it for walking down our path.

"Ah's still consuhned fo' Filipa." She rearranged the mess in one handbag transferring it to a more expensive one suitable for lunching at Claridge's. "Ah wants t'go up t'London. Not alone. With y'all. Will y'drahve me?"

No contest. I changed into a London suit, traded boots for lace-ups and looked for the car keys.

I drove Happy to Ebury Street, and for once found a metered parking space. We separated, she headed for Fran's flat, while I went shopping for our infants and for Little Betty.

Happy discovered that Fran had carefully stored her new décor pieces to protect them from Little Betty's sad little destructive games. When Happy entered the flat she smelled the sour milk and dirty diapers that were a given around Little Betty.

Towels covered Fran's new sofa and chairs. All porcelain and glass ornaments had been boxed for future use.

"I'm so pleased to see you, darling Happy." Filipa handed Happy the baby, who immediately spewed formula on to her blouse. Rus had gone out, and the women were alone in Fran's kitchen with the baby.

From her bedroom, Fran called sourly: "Fucking awful day. Our agent cancelled our date with the manager of Covent Garden's opera people. Heidi's got *her* audition. But not us. I wish Heidi hadn't moved in on our agent."

Happy asked, "Why don't y'all go to the au-di-tion anyways, Fran? Y'all move in on Heidi. Tell them opry people y'alls been part of a duo with Heidi and want t'join in on the au-di-tion."

"Thanks, but no thanks. You don't know friggin' all about how these things work. But, well, on second thought okay. I'll give it a try. I'll head for Covent Garden."

Fran mucked around in a closet, found a raincoat and left the apartment. Happy warmed up to Filipa and talked new-mothers talk with her, until the baby howled so loudly that she knew something was wrong.

Filipa, her face creased with worry, said, "Darling Happy, would you be an angel and run to the local pharmacist's for me? I have a wonderful prescription for Little Betty, but I'm out of it. She'll ease up on the coughing if you go get it for me."

Happy agreed. She collected the coat so newly removed, and hurried down the stairs. She knew where the pharmacist was located, and walked there briskly

She gave the pharmacist Little Betty's prescription to fill. She went to the shelves that offered special foods for sickly babies and studied labels. She looked out through the plateglass window, and noticed that rain had begun to fall. She was paying for Little Betty's readied prescription when a familiar figure caught her eye. She saw Rus walking past pushing Little Betty in her stroller. Its plastic protective cover was still open. Rain was splashing into Little Betty's face. Rus proceeded along Elizabeth Street.

He passed the children's wear shop. No new dress for Little Betty. He crossed the street and hurried beyond the chocolates shop. No candy for Little Betty. He paused a moment in front of a down market liquor store, but shook his head and continued along to the snobs' wine shop, the most expensive in Chelsea.

He dallied straightening his Aussie swagman's hat, then pushed Little Betty inside. Happy watched while Rus downed several free samples of thimble-sized freebies. She saw him call over a salesman and buy a bottle of wine. He had the salesman open it and produce a wine goblet. He proceeded to empty the bottle. No wine for his guests' supper either.

Happy headed back to the flat. No need to rush now. There would be no Little Betty at home to give medicine to.

She was half way up the stairs in Fran's building when she realized she hadn't had to press the buzzer to enter the building. The front entrance's door had been unlocked.

When Happy's intuition came into play, there was a change in timing. She flew to Fran's front door and banged. It opened without pressure. In the center of the room, Filipa was being hit hard with a wooden coat hanger. Blood was spurting from her nose and mouth, marking walls and the carpet. Filipa managed to place herself behind the sofa, but in reaching it she'd become vulnerable and the wooden hanger was now pressed against her throat. Filipa was being choked.

Her attacker was Heidi.

With her burned hands still bandaged, she'd chosen to use the wooden hanger as a lethal weapon.

Baptist Happy broke with her traditions and screamed, "Gawd!" She tore across the room, hit Heidi's burned hands hard with karate chops, then kicked her with a horse's hoof-punch.

Heidi yelled in agony when Happy's jockey-hard knuckles hit her bandaged hands.

But she didn't release the coat hanger. Using her wrists, Heidi still retained pressure on the hanger pushing down on Filipa's throat.

Happy tried two new strategies. She bit Heidi, tearing a piece off her ear.

She used a knee to batter Heidi's venus mount. After a few seconds of this double strategy, Heidi suddenly released the hanger and gave up.

She sat down on the floor. "Go on, call 999. I'm through. Now you know it's been me all along." Like an infant in a play school who has been reprimanded for peeing, she began to cry.

Filipa took deep breaths, like the ones taught to her in her prenatal clinic. She swallowed hard, testing the mechanism, "I'm all right," she croaked to Happy. "I'll do it. I'll dial 999."

Happy intervened. "Let's us'n find out mo'e." Happy sat on Heidi to restrain her further, and began sopping up the blood stains on the carpet. Fran cleaned her face with a fresh diaper.

The baby began to howl. Filipa took her up in her arms. Little Betty had wet her early-morning diaper and soiled Fran's sofa. "All right. Ask her why. Why did she kill so many good people?"

With her free hand Filipa dialed 999. Happy squatted on the floor beside Heidi, using the belt from Fran's discarded housecoat to tie her wrists. Heidi continued to sob. Happy gave her a shove.

"Listen up! Wut y'all tells the police and wut y'all tells us'n ain't gonna be the same. Ah knows thet. Us'n wants t'know the truth."

Prodded, Heidi began to string out a few sentences. "I wanted Carla's job. I wanted to be the soprano in Fran's duo. Carla was home alone. I killed her real easy."

"What did you do with the bling?" Filipa put in a few words between the bouts of howling from Betty.

"Nothing. I never saw her jewelry. She must have hidden it somewhere. But I never bothered to look for it. What would I want with Carla's famous jewelry? Thousands had seen it on TV. Nobody could hope to peddle it."

Happy made no comment. She knew that stones can be pried from settings and sold abroad. She asked, "Why Goofy?"

"I wasn't sure he hadn't seen me come into the building. I'd seen him going out. I couldn't risk him fingering me."

"And Sybil? Dear, wonderful Sybil?"

"She had a job I could have done easy. I knew I'd be a natural to be Daisy Mae. So, after the performance I waited until the dresser went out for a cigarette and slipped my hands around Sybil's neck. I think I broke it from its base on her spine. And all for nothing. I didn't get the job. Her Understudy did, and later when I did get my chance at it the damned show folded."

"'N Munchkins?" Happy's voice broke.

"I cadged a flight from Sydney on a private jet. All the other passengers were going to watch the Cup. I took a cab to Munchie's suite. Again, it was real easy. She was playing the piano and didn't hear me come in."

"But, why? You were singing at the Opera House. You didn't need to kill Munchie."

"Munchie was practicing for her new role in *Pride and Prejudice*. My contract in Sydney covered five performances. I needed to get that part of Elizabeth. But again, I didn't."

Happy couldn't bring up the subject of Bumbles' death. It was still too painful. Filipa took on that job. "Why Bumbles?"

"Because she'd become famous by ending Feathers' kidnapping. Seen on TV, headlined in the broad sheets. But I should have killed Feathers. Like in *Godfather*. You'd have taken more notice. Nobody wrote up Bumbles' death."

Rus arrived with Little Betty. He stared, perplexed at Filipa's blood.

A commotion at Fran's front door drew away our attention from Heidi's tale. In the doorway stood two helmeted policemen, old-time bobbies, of the type that used to be a familiar sight on London's streets.

They acted like the Inspector Clouseau of Peter Sellers' movies. "There's been a complaint," one droned.

"A lady downstairs as has said there's too much screaming up here." "Also, same lady has been advising the station that strangers ring her to open up the lobby door," the second bobby announced with a vaudeville flourish.

Heidi came alive. From despondency she emerged to snicker with a professional lilt. "Officers, you've simply interrupted a practice session for a stage performance. Act I, I'm a singer, and I'm supposed to be assaulted by two hookers. Act Two, the hookers get me on to the floor and use a tie-belt to bind my wrists."

The first bobby fell over the entrance carpet and ended up on the floor next to Heidi. He undid the restraining belt. From his position on the floor, he said, "You ladies best do your practicing elsewhere. And what's a baby doing here? We'd been advised this is Fran Purcell's flat, and she has no baby." Filipa cuddled Betty and defensively croaked, "You going to take my baby down to the station?" She laughed lightly, like an audience that's heard a joke before.

Happy saw the humor, but looked ahead to a possible escape strategy for Heidi. These two bobbies were never going to make it into Scotland Yard, and obviously could be outwitted by that street-smart woman.

Heidi took full advantage of their naiveté. Rubbing her back against her policeman provocatively, like a stripteaser, she said, "Officer, let me help you up. And, as you can see my hands have been bandaged, perhaps you'll do the same for me."

The two got up from the floor. Heidi started to exit. That ploy was stopped by the sudden arrival of four flat-hatted policemen, men of obvious ability. Like sentinels on duty at a palace, the four created a strong line in front of the door.

Their leader said, "No one goes anywhere. We've had a 999 call. What's brought us here?"

Filipa spoke out, far more sensibly. "I made the call. This woman, Heidi, has just confessed to the murder of the four victims in the Carla Purcell case. Carla, Goofy, Sybil, and Munchie. Forgive the nicknames. She has just attempted to choke me with a coat hanger. The one over there." She pointed to where it had fallen. "I'm sure you'll find her fingerprints on it."

Filipa developed the explanation. "Heidi is a soprano. She'd been angling to have a job as Fran's singing partner, and that's why she killed Carla. Goofy may have seen Heidi entering the building, so he was strangled later. Sybil had been tapped for a singing role that Heidi wanted, and she got murdered in her own dressing room backstage after a performance. Munchie, in Australia, was practicing for the part of Elizabeth in *Pride and Prejudice* which role Heidi coveted, and poor Munchie was caught unawares at her piano. I was about to be murdered for Heidi to replace me as Fran's duets partner. You'll notice, all the women were sopranos."

The four new arrivals listened attentively. Three looked skeptical. Their leader said, "I've been following the Carla Purcell case. And the Munchie case. We've had endless faxes and e-mails from the Melbourne police. Those Aussies don't like giving up. Hold on like terriers."

He came forward, drew out a pair of handcuffs, and manacled Heidi.

"Just to be sure," he mumbled and then led her away.

Fran met the six policemen and Heidi on the landing. "What the fuck?" she asked.

She whirled through her doorway like a tornado and broached Happy. "What the hell's going on?"

"Heidi was the strangler. She confessed. Ah's arrived jus' in time to stop huh from killin' Filipa."

"Heidi! Of course. Why hadn't we seen it? And what a fuckin' fool! She came here to kill Filipa when she could have landed a great contract! SHE was the number one candidate for a different duo, and when she didn't appear, my agent wrapped up the jobs for Filipa and me."

Filipa rushed to her. She hugged Fran, and with a tearful voice, she thanked her. "God in heaven, we've made it! And on the dotted line!" With some cunning, she added, "I hope we got the money we asked for."

"Shit, yes! Not all at once, but over a period of some months and then there's a final engagement in Las Vegas with a huge dollop of boodle."

Forgetting the wet spot on Fran's sofa, Filipa sat on it in wonder. "Las Vegas. God in heaven, isn't that where Sir Elton John's been making millions?"

"An' Celine Dion, too," Happy intervened.

I arrived at that moment, my arms filled with the packages of necessities for my Dorothy and Filipa's Betty. "What's happened here?" I asked. My eyes took in the bloodstains, the discarded belt on the floor and the urine splotch on the sofa.

"Ever'thin' Ah's imagined. Heidi tried t'choke Filipa with thet coat hanger. Ah arrived and stopped huh. She confessed, 'n the police come 'n done took huh t'the station."

"She confessed?"

"To us'n. Yeah man! But don't know how it's goin' t'play in no court o' law."

"Our Detective Inspector friend spoke to us about the DNA taken from all the victims. Useless before. Now the police will be able to match them to Heidi's DNA. That should do her for a life sentence."

Filipa, a trickle of blood oozing from one battered nostril, said, "I think I left the phone off the hook. It's on the Answerphone mode. Maybe it caught Heidi confessing to us."

We played it. Heidi's voice came over loud and clear, confessing.

"I doubt that would be admissible in court. But we'll give it in to the station. The more incriminating evidence, the better. You know that all the do-gooders will come forward in Heidi's defense, some claiming her father must have abused her as a child or that her mother preferred a sibling. Heidi may plead insanity. She'd get a few years in a modern mental facility, and then before she's even thirty be back killing people in the theater district."

Happy pouted. "Insanity, mah foot. Was nothin' but greed. Greed, n' sick ambition."

"Fuck all," Fran said, interrupting. "I've just thought of where Carla's jewelry could be. It's probably right in her bedroom safe. Nobody looked because it was friggin' assumed she'd been murdered for it. Police said the stones could be in Saudi Arabia or some such place."

We three followed Fran into the flat's second bedroom. Used for house guests and possibly for sex, the room had a closed-up smell. It needed airing. Fran threw open the nearest window, and marched across the dusty carpet to a wall where a self-portrait hung. "Carla painted this herself. Bloody awful picture, but she was proud of it. Her safe's hung behind it because nobody would ever want to steal the damned picture."

"Do you know the combination?"

"No. But I do know how Carla remembered things. Told the friggin' phone company her birth date, *our* birth date, when asked to give a secret number. Same to banks. And being a twin, I certainly do know our birth date. Let's try. You unhang the picture. I'll dial."

Fran used the numbers and twirled. Nothing happened. She tried again, this time spelling out the numbers, One for January, two for the Second, one hundred and eighty three for the year. Presto, the safe's heavy steel door swung open.

Inside were bags of jewels and some loose stones. Fran unwrapped the bling. The goods were dazzling, if not truly beautiful, being too modern and heavy.

The entrance bell rang. Fran answered, "Who the shit are you?" "Police. Your local police."

In a temper, Fran pushed the entrance unlock device and minutes later the same Inspector Clouseau bobbies arrived."Are you Miss Fran Purcell?" they asked, totally unnecessarily. Their glances fastened on Carla's bling.

"Yeah, and who the fuck wants to know? That friggin' old woman downstairs who complains all the time?"

Wrong reply.

Clouseau bobby Number One withdrew a pad from a chest pocket and read, "Under Section Four of the Public Order Act you must accept a caution for using threatening words. A caution means that said person must accept responsibility for the offense and a record will be made. No further action will be taken if said person complies with this. You are accused by Miss Agnes Templeton of Cundy Gardens, Ebury Street, London. You will please accompany us to the police station."

Number Two Clouseau bobby was frantically shoving his elbow into his colleague's near arm. He pointed to the bling on the bedside table in Carla's room. Clouseau One took no notice. He'd already seen the jewels, dismissed them as not part of his morning's duty, and pushed forward to take Fran to the police station.

Happy yelled, "Y'all gonna make a felon outta Miss Fran Purcell? Cain't do thet! She be the sister o' the girl wut got mu'dered in this heah apa'tment."

Officiously, pedantically, Clouseau One said, "We are aware of Miss Carla Purcell's murder. Miss Fran Purcell will accompany us to the police station now, or else we will add resisting arrest to the charges against her."

"What the shit!" Fran collected her sister's jewels, returned them to the safe, clanged shut its heavy door, put on her raincoat and stoically followed the two Clouseau bobbies.

Filipa said, "Rus, can't we do anything to stop this?"

"Search me! I'm just an Aussie from Down Under. What do I know about English law?"

"Rick," she turned to me. "Please stop those two idiots."

I said, "They'll get their just come-uppances when they turn Fran over to their superior. Happy, isn't that what you'd say?"

"Sho is! 'N Ah hopes it be real tough come-uppances, too!" She collected the parcels of baby paraphernalia that was due to Dorothy.

Filipa separated hers from Little Betty's. The two women hugged in an amiable way, and I got the signal we were off and out of Fran's apartment. I hoped this would be the last time we'd be here and that Fran would finally see sense and move away.

We headed toward Harrods because there was one item on Mrs. Rea's list that I'd failed to find in the Ebury Street neighborhood. Dorothy was suffering from the change in the weather and needed sweaters. We bought them in the Infants Department at Harrods, peeked at the elaborately eerie memorial that owner Mohammed Al Fayed had created in memory of Princess Diana and Dodi, and outside, started down a different way to find the street of the car park. We never reached the Volvo. Happy gesticulated wildly in front of a shop window. "Lookee, theah. Cats!"

In a clean environment, with neatly arranged kitty litter and cups of water, three kittens played with one another. They used their paws like boxers. The kittens were tiger striped with flat white faces and white paws. Their ears were almost transparent with pink insides and fine lines tracing the veins. One kitten had shoved out its pink tongue.

"Gawd! They looks the spittin' image o' Bumbles. All three o' these kittens. Y'all thinks they got stolen from Bumbles littuh?"

I said. "Nice kittens, but no, I don't think they were taken from Bumbles' litter. You know we placed all of those in good homes. These are similar, but they're certainly not Bumbles' babies."

"Ah's got t'know fo' sho. Lets us'n go inside."

I had no choice. I followed Happy into a shop full of cages with various cats and dogs on offer. Only the three in the window had been kept together as a family.

"Yes. May I help you?" An immaculately turned-out assistant came from behind a counter to smile and greet us. She had hope in her eyes that we would buy one of her charges.

No doubt she recognized a legitimate prospect when she saw one.

Happy leaned over a glass pane and reached into the front window to clutch one of the kittens and cradle it in her arms. The kitten, very well-behaved, cuddled up to Happy's chest. I think the kitten, like the salesgirl, could recognize a prospective sucker.

"This one's just darlin', Ah loves it," Happy crooned.

"The little boy one," the salesgirl crooned, echoing Happy's enthusiasm.

"The other two are little girls."

"But Ah wants a little girl," Happy said, and added one of the other kittens to her chest. Now all three kittens lost their former good manners and began to mew unhappily.

I said, stupidly as it soon turned out, "These kittens don't like being separated."

"Sho 'nuf. Ah wants all three!" Happy leaned over the glass divide and grabbed the third kitten by the nape of its plump neck. She cradled the third kitten next to the first two.

Happy glanced in my direction, sending me one of those ecstatic looks I sometimes got during sex, and moaned, "Can Ah have all three?"

What can a man do when his wife gives him the sex note?

I succumbed, and promptly. "How much they cost?" I asked the salesgirl. "One hundred pounds each." She altered that when she saw the negative look on my face. "But I can give you a discount when you take all three." Removing my credit card from my wallet, I shrugged. We were already way over our budget's limit, but I handed that dangerous piece of plastic to the salesgirl and she wrote up a receipt.

"Will you be buying a cat carrier?" she asked in a more pedantic tone. "You can't carry them away in your hands."

"Add a cat carrier."

"And kitty litter? You'll need to start out with at least two bags." "Yes. All right, kitty litter."

"We sell the best quality cat food."

"Four cans of that, please."

"Collars for all three?"

"Yes."

"Leads?"

"What do you think? That I'm going to take them for walks in the park? No. No leads."

"Baskets to sleep in?"

"No. What is this? Just write up my bill, and I'll sign it. But stop the selling act or we're going somewhere else."

"I've already wrung up the sale of the three kittens. They aren't returnable unless a vet signs a certificate that they were sold diseased."

"Okay, okay. Just ring up what else I've already said I'll take. We have a long drive ahead to Epsom."

"You'll need water for the kittens if you're going far. I sell cups that don't overturn."

"Ring up, young woman, or I am out of here."

All during my dialogue with the difficult saleswoman I'd noticed that Happy had remained very quiet. She was stroking the kittens and whispering into their ears as she sometimes did with our horses.

She didn't want to 'rock t'boat' by interrupting us.

When the three kittens were safely stored in their carrier and all my other purchases were wrapped and placed in bags, I felt as if I'd met the salesperson character portrayed by Rowan Atkinson in *Love Actually*. This saleswoman was similar in her molasses-slow approach to the finalizing of my sale. When we were standing in the doorway she was still barking, "The kittens have had their rabies shots, they have a chip in the back of their necks to prove that."

The cat carrier was heavier than I could have imagined. It seemed a long distance to walk back to the car park. Happy held on to all the purchases, the earliest ones made that morning, plus the two sweaters from Harrods, and now the kittens' trousseaus or whatever the saleswoman would have called what we'd bought.

No more mewing from the kittens. They were surprisingly docile. They seemed to know they were going to a good home. Maybe they'd felt like prisoners in a concentration camp being released by United States tanks. Their torture had been to be stared at in the show window by every passerby.

All the way back to Epsom my Happy cuddled those kittens. She would place one after the other against her breasts. Lucky kittens.

She said, "Ah thinks they's jealous when Ah favuhs one 'stead 'o t'othuh two." By the time we drove up the High Street my Happy was cuddling all three against her breasts.

No jealousy surfaced at our home when our children saw the kittens. They loved them at first sight. Mrs. Rea frowned, and I worried she'd quit at the thought of cleaning up after three kittens. But they charmed her within minutes.

My clever Happy was quick to point out that the kittens were to live in Feathers' box in the stables. She didn't want the children to be disappointed later when the kittens left our house. Simultaneously she calmed any reservations Mrs. Rea still felt about the kittens.

We fed them the food we'd brought with us. Mrs. Rea said, "I'll give them scraps. No need to spend good money on fancy cat food."

I placed a log basket near our bed, thinking they could sleep there in our room for one night. On second thought, I rescinded on that plan.

With Happy and our two infants in tow, I led the way to the stables.

Happy still carried the blissfully engaged kittens.

When we entered Feather's horsebox it was as if they knew they'd really arrived home. They jumped out of Happy's arms and began to play near Feathers mighty hooves. With one small swipe she could have killed them instantly.

She didn't.

Feathers remained perfectly still. After a full minute she let her graceful neck curve down and she placed her velvety nostrils against each kitten in turn. When her head came up she looked into Happy's eyes and they did their fancy bit of communicating.

"She done said 'thank ye kindly'. Ah thinks she already loves these kittens."

"I see that." I took Happy in one arm and pulled my children to us with the other."What shall we call them?"

"Ah's be'n thinkin' o' names all the way from London." "And what have you come up with?" "How's about Cozy, Nosey, 'n Posey?"

"They'll do. I just hope that Cozy's the name for the male." "Y'all knows it be."

When night came, and our home was silent except for the crackling of burnt-out logs in the hearth and a few creaking rafters, I led my Happy to bed. I thanked God I'd taken the kittens to the stable. I had no intention of sharing our bed with anyone other than HAPPY, animal or human.

We had great sex. There was no need for a Scheherazade-like story.

MURDERED MOTHERS

CHARACTERS IN
MURDERED MOTHERS

Rick Harrow, a British racehorse trainer having a struggle to find and keep owners.

Hillary a/k/a Happy Harrow, his wife, an apprentice jockey and talented sleuth

Timothy, Dorothy and Irish, the Harrows' children

Hal Murphy, Canadian multi-millionaire who is an owner in Rick's yard

Clara Murphy, Hal's semi-crippled wife

Marylou Whitney, Socialite multi-millionairess who breeds and races winners

Theo, Hal Murphy's Canadian groom sent to Kentucky to help out Rick

The Misses Carrington, sisters who run Caring For Tots, a nursery in Kentucky

Dr. Waller, a semi-retired physician who uses the Honeyville Gym

Amah, a nursemaid from mainland China

Mrs. Wright, a county Englishwoman employed by the Harrows as housekeeper

Joanne, a friend Happy met at the Derby, who has a three-month-old daughter

Bart, Joanne's bad-tempered husband

Beverly Shaw, an employee at the gym

Fran Purcell, world-famous rap singer, millionairess in pounds sterling, a VIP owner in Rick's yard

Sir Arthur Snodgrass, an MP, who courts Fran

Rhett Gordon, the gym's accountant

Rona Blossom, Brooklyn-born friend Happy finds at the gym

Dubber McDonald, a member of the Canadian Olympic equestrian team, an expert at dressage

Colonel Flyte, a perennially disgruntled owner who changes trainers frequently

Filipa and Rus Grant, a married couple from Australia, she doubles as a partner for Fran's duets

Una and Al Probit, a married couple in Honeyville. Una is the wealthiest member of the gym

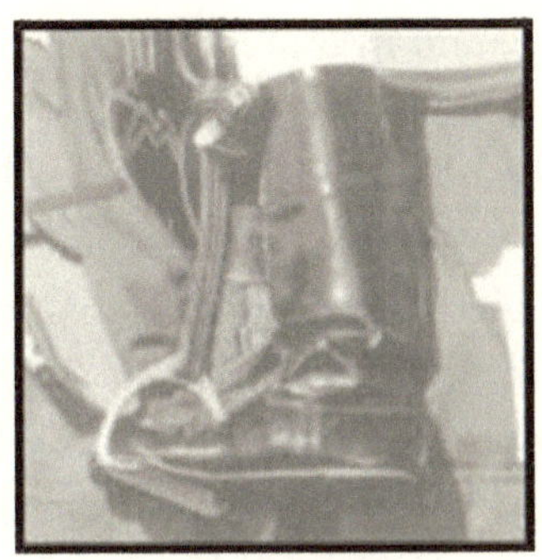

CHAPTER 1

Kidnapped! Our three year old little son, Tim, kidnapped!

Was it our fault because we'd left him with our English housekeeper, Mrs. Wright, who'd volunteered to join us in Kentucky to help with our three infants? Oh, we'd taken up her offer very quickly, relishing the prospect of escaping from housework and baby care for the three nights we would stay in Miami for the horse sales there.

Happy, my darling jockey wife, had been smothered with all the mothering she'd done. I'd felt horny, wanting to have time in private with her, preferably in a king size bed in a far away hotel.

There'd been practically no opportunities for lovemaking what with me commuting sixteen miles back and forth to Louisville every day to oversee the gallops of the two horses we'd brought from England on the orders of my kindest owner, Hal Murphy.

It had been my miserly owner, the multi-millionaire rap singer Fran Purcell, who had e-mailed me to take advantage of being on the west side of the pond to attend the Miami racehorse sales. Crafty Fran had worked out that Hal had paid our round trip airfares, saving her the money. She had been known to run alongside a bus to avoid giving sixpence to its driver, would our Fran, but when it came to buying horseflesh she could be amazingly open handed. Her e-mail had instructed me to buy two horses for a total of $4 million, and informed me that such a sum had already been deposited in my account.

I'm a British racehorse trainer, based near the Epsom racecourse. My status in the racing world had been uncomfortably low until an old Etonian school friend had invited me to be his assistant at his Epsom yard, then promptly killed himself thinking he had incurable cancer when a competing trainer had poisoned him with cyanide. His owners elected me to carry on at the stables. I'd managed to win some races for them.

Why had I agreed to do Fran's bidding and leave Kentucky for three nights in Miami? Oh, I'd checked with Hal if he'd object. And, of course, dear Hal didn't put up any opposition. By then the Kentucky Derby was over and done with, I'd managed to cure Hal's two horses of their "miseries" and I'd felt I could rely on the groom, Theo, whom Hal sent from Canada to take care of his horses.

When I look back at the last two months, everything seemed to be going my way. By mid-April all the travel arrangements had been made for our move from Epsom to Kentucky . . I'd been advised by Hal that he'd leased a house for my family of five in a town called Honeyville, about sixteen miles from where his horses were stabled in Kentucky. Our airplane tickets were electronic, so I didn't have them in my wallet, but they were for a date that fitted in well to give me time to accustom the horses to Kentucky water and its famous blue grass.

It was on Easter night in Epsom, after a day of egg hunts and exchanging fluffy toy rabbits for the children, that I decided to break the news of our U.S.A. trip to Happy.

I'd hurried upstairs. Happy was on the landing with a finger to her lips. "Got the babies t'sleep. How about us'n goin' to bed too?"

No argument from me! I'd done with evening stables, cleared my desk in the tack room. Yes, yes, yes. Bed! Right now, before our housekeeper called us down to the kitchen to observe a broken pipe or a similar often occurring disaster.

With three small children always squalling, we had to grab our time together whenever and however we could.

I have become a careful husband. I'd had one adulterous liaison, a one-night stand in Paris, that had cured me. Sure, I've heard that famous remark by Tallulah Bankhead: "Darling, if it happens on tour it ain't adultery." But my over-active conscience doesn't agree with that nowadays. I left that sort of shenanigans to my singing star owner.

But to be fair to my Happy, once under the sheet I delayed for sex, and told her the news that we'd be going to Kentucky. "The first Saturday in May, to give Mighty Moron his chance there." I had a devious purpose. I knew how my Happy responded in bed whenever she heard she was heading home for Kentucky. Responded gloriously.

No mention of a side trip to Miami. That hadn't developed as yet.

"Yeah man, Ah knows all about the trip to Kentuck!" She surprised ME. "Miz Murphy done e-mailed me them par-ti-cu-lars 'cause bein' a mother' herself she understands not t'leave it too late fo' me t'git the kids ready fo' the trip."

I was getting painfully horny, but managed to grunt, "Hal didn't say anything about bringing the kids."

"But Miz Murphy did."

No contest. All three kids had to travel too.

CHAPTER 2

Kentucky brought me such a variety of benefits, starting with sublime sex with an ecstatic Happy.

The Murphys had selected a charming many-columned Tara-style house for us, lovely even though there were eleven more absolutely identical to it on our street in the golfing community where we landed.

Dogwood in bloom, daffodils raising yellow bonnets to the amiable sun, and cherry blossoms erupting in pink petals: totally beautiful, except there were no residents of our age in this community. At least two of the largest buildings were dedicated to assisted living facilities for the very old. We saw elderly ladies in battered hats pushing their walkers for short spurts of medically-recommended daily walks. Their spouses, worn out from a lifetime working to afford these facilities, were more often in electric wheelchairs. The Murphys had been accepted as buyers, and had managed to get the housing association to agree to make an exception for my family to stay temporarily although we were young and had children. It had been made very clear that we were merely houseguesting, and would not be long in Honeyville.

The southern manse we entered was in need of a housekeeper. The Murphys had never personally inspected the place, and it showed certain amount of neglect. There was an inch of dust everywhere. In the fridge there were scabs of grey mould on wrinkled fruit, different black mold in opened pots of yogurt, green mold on half-eaten bread. The bedrooms hadn't been made up. I sat down on the bed in the master bedroom and something bit me: I looked for bedbugs, but instead saw a fat flea scurrying under the messed-up blankets. The couple with children who had earlier occupied our mansion had kept dogs that had fleas. I reckoned they tended their animals on the same low level as they tended their living quarters. But I had no intention of complaining to Hal Murphy. That was based on another of my Tips For Trainers: never complain to an owner about anything provided by that owner.

In spite of jet lag caused by having to transfer to three different flights to reach our base at Honeyville, Happy and I set to and cleaned the place and fumigated the beds. We couldn't wait around for the promised arrival of a Polish maid hired by the Murphys for us.

We went into Honeyville in our rental car, bought disinfectant, sheets, food and dozens of diapers. The latter to be used until we could connect with a diaper service that would supply us with weekly deliveries.

"Lookee theah!" Happy pointed to a former shop where an old sign said 'Fast Food', while underneath that a newer sign offered 'Caring for Tots' while I paid for our various purchases, Happy investigated the Caring For Tots premises. "My lucky day!" she proclaimed joyfully to me when we were in our rental car returning home. "Them two nice Kentuck gals, wut run thet place, said they c'd take all three o' ourn chillun. Yeah man, even Irish. Take any tot over three months 'n Irish be four months old t'morrow. Ah c'n goes with y'all t'the derby. Ah c'n leave the chillun with them gals, once Ah's made a real thorough investigation of how trustworthy they be."

No contest. I knew that Happy had a case of smothered mother. She'd coped fine with one son in Texas with no help. But after her transfer to England, her abduction in Dubai and giving birth to three babies in three years she was finding the mothering thing less attractive.

I asked, "Did the equipment look new? Did the other kids look happy and well cared for? Did those two women mention if there were set story times, and snacks a part of the program? What about naps? Did they say they have set opening and closing times? And how about clothes? Do we have to buy more clothes?"

"Yeah man, more clothes. Them women said as they like t'see all the kids dressed in white. Like they was goin' to play tennis. Yeah, I checked the equipment. Yeah, most of the kids looked happy enough. Story times, naps, snacks, yeah those too. Opening times is nine a.m., closing time five p.m."

I'd given the two women a down payment to gain entry for our kids. I felt a little more pleased about that payout after hearing Happy's gleeful plans to go to the derby.

I recalled days at home in Epsom when all three kids were hollering and poor Happy's only out was to escape to ride with the stable lads to exercise our string, leaving the "chillun" with our Epsom housekeeper Mrs. Wright. Happy might have a long wait to have household help or babysitters in the golfing community until the Polish *au pair*—promised by Mrs. Murphy—arrived.

Now that she'd found Caring for Tots, how could I ask her that she not go to the derby when horseracing was the zest of life for her?

She'd once described horseracing as Hog Heaven. I'd asked, "I thought your Hog Heaven was sex with me?"

Stupid question, got a stupid answer. "Sho 'nuf, the's lots kinds o' Hog Heaven."

Next morning, when Happy was preparing for the Kentucky Derby, she certainly looked radiant, She'd unpacked last season's best Royal Ascot outfit, a well-cut Bellville Sassoon silk suit with a saucer-shaped mini-top hat trimmed in the same silk. She found her one pair of high-heeled shoes, which added a feminine change to her jockey-shaped legs. Happy could have passed for an aristocratic county deb if she'd kept her mouth closed. She'd come a long way up from the teenage waif hanging around the Louisville track looking for a job exercising racehorses.

We dropped off our "chillun" at Caring for Tots and headed away from Honeyville to launch on to a highway for the sixteen mile trek to Churchill Downs.

Entering the racecourse to find the trainers' parking lot was even worse than that challenge at Australia's Fremantle Course on the day of its great cup. I was beginning to fear I'd be late to help Hal's lad to prepare his Mighty Moron in the stalls behind the pre-parade ring. But suddenly a car pulled out of a convenient space and we got into the area leading to a top restaurant where now we'd have time to see Hal before the race.

I knew that Hal would like to give detailed instructions for the race. I trailed through the litter of no-good losing tickets left scattered from yesterday's Oaks meeting, wondering why the hell the racecourse authorities couldn't hire enough help to clear up the mess. We reached the restaurant, and immediately Happy let out a minimal rebel yell. She'd seen Mrs. Marylou Whitney across the dining room, and that great lady of American racing had waved to her.

Mrs. Whitney had been the catalyst person who offered Happy her first job. Happy had stayed with her all through the horseflesh murders when my boss, a phoney Baroness, was killing girl jockeys. When Happy unmasked the Baroness, and I fingered her to the police, I lost my job. My boss, Burl Smithey didn't want to keep me on after I'd lost for him and all of us in his stable the huge commission available to syndicate her winning horse if I'd kept my mouth shut. But the damn Baroness was killing girl jockeys, and by that time my Happy had her apprentice jockey license and I hadn't wanted her to be the next dead jockey on the Baroness's list.

Mrs. W. had remained fond of Happy, they exchanged Christmas cards, and in the Churchill Downs main dining room I could see that my Happy had pulled out photographs of our three "chillun" to show them to Mrs. W.

But Marylou Whitney was busy chatting with TV celebrity, Joan Rivers, apparently a longtime friend. When Mrs. W. finally put out a hand for the photographs, she gave Happy a wide smile, and then gave her a hug before leaving the dining room with Joan Rivers.

Slightly crestfallen, Happy rejoined me while I stood next to Hal listening to a story his lunch guest, a Russian with no noticeable accent, was telling him.

"Da. I was in Laos, trying to sell your machinery Hal, when I had this disagreeable experience. Make sure it doesn't happen to you when you go there."

"So? What experience?" Hal didn't stop from listening to take much heed that Happy and I were there.

"Da, and what an experience. I'd taken an ordinary razor with me to the local hotel, because I was not sure about what voltage was used in Laos for electric razors. After I arrived, I went immediately to eat. I came back and noticed I had five o'clock shadow, and tried to use the new razor. Nothing. I couldn't rid myself of a single hair. I opened the razor to look at the blade.

What did I see? Black curly hairs, mixed with my shaving cream on the blade. Some hotel employee had a key to this room and had used my razor. I took it down to complain to the hotel manager. He shrugged. Said that sort of thing happened all the time. He couldn't get good hotel staff. What he could get, used guests' hair brushes, combs, toilet water and even toothbrushes. Da. Watch it, when you go there."

When the Russian ended his story, Hal looked up and said, "How's my horse?"

I didn't want to have to admit that I hadn't seen him yet that morning, so I changed the subject and asked, "Where would you like to run him next?"

He grunted, "Depends. Depends on how he does today. Where would you suggest?"

"Belmont, if he manages to place today." I didn't say "win" because even Hal must have realized that was beyond his horse's ability.

There was a precedent of a horse winning the derby after only minor success. Canonero II had taken the Kentucky roses after winning only one race in Venezuela, but that was a very rare case. "If Mighty Moron trails in next to last, I'd say we school him some in Florida at the Calder."

Arthritic Clara Murphy, who usually sat very silently in her husband's company, piped up, "We could take Mighty Moron to Hong Kong, or to Tokyo. Big money prizes at their tracks."

Poor woman, always on two crutches. I never knew if she'd had polio as a kid or suffered from old peoples' arthritis, and hadn't dared to ask. But she was certainly game. She'd joined us in Australia for the Melbourne Cup day. Never complained, never explained.

I swallowed hard. I knew nothing about the races in Asia. "How about we take him to Canada for the Queen's Plate day?"

That went down very well with Hal. He grinned like a kid who got a computer game on Christmas morning. "Yes. Well, I've been hoping you'd suggest that sometime soon. All my pals could cheer my Mighty Moron to the finish line."

"Finish line!" I realized we could be late for the race, forget the saddling up!

I steered the Murphys and their Russian storyteller to the Owners' stand. My Happy, delegated to help out the lad with Mighty Moron, did the right thing and checked girth and stirrups, led the horse to the main paddock, and gave our jockey a leg up. Hal and co. strolled from the Owners' stand in time to rub shoulders with the other Owners of horses in the derby, and glowed with pleasure as if he thought his contender really had a chance.

CHAPTER 3

Happy couldn't join us to go to the Owners' stand. She tried to find a good vantage point to watch the race. But she was pushed by rude crowds to a stand where other spectators had climbed on to benches creating a human wall over which my five foot in heels jockey wife failed to see what won and where Mighty Moron had ended.

After abandoning that hopeless stand she ran towards a fence where the contenders could be observed as they slowed down after passing the finish line.

Crack!

A horrible sound washed across the racecourse. The sound which means a nightmare for an owner. Didn't I remember hearing it at Belmont when Barbara Vanderbilt Whitney's Twist The Axe broke a leg while exercising?

It was the same sound that Happy heard as she leaned over the fence. Panting, she asked a nearby groom, "Is that hoss wut broke its leg wut won the Derby?"

"No, ma'am," the groom said sadly, close to weeping. "Thet be Eight Belles, the filly wut came in Second. Looks like she may have broken both legs. But an ambulance is coming up the field, stopped now, and is coverin' up my view. Can y'all see anything?"

"Sho do. Ah sees a be-au-ti-ful brown filly raisin' her neck, pleadin' fo' someone to stop her pain."

The racecourse vet arrived and gave orders. The ambulance covered up the scene, but Happy just managed to hear his hangman's command to euthanize the filly.

Her head sunk between her shoulders, Happy sloped away from the fence and wandered in search of me. She found me in the open stall where I was supervising Mighty Moron's after-racing care. I was trembling still, from that terrible sound and the sight of the euthanized filly with the vet on the field. But I knew my own duty lay with Hal's horse, now that the defeated animal was sweating and panting and oozing mucus from his inflated nostrils. I didn't believe it was the time to give horses a drink, preferring to wet muzzles with sponges. With Mighty Moron's background, bred in England, shipped as a two-year-old to Dubai, shipped back to England and as a three-year-old crossing the pond to Kentucky, I felt he deserved a blanket. That's what he got, after his nostrils were sponged.

Together with Hal's lad, we walked Mighty Moron to his horse box. "No prizes for this boy," I said quietly. "Came in next to last. That means we'll be heading soon for Florida to Calder for a few days."

The travelling lad, Theo, brought by Hal from Canada, spoke in a pronounced Maritime's accent, "Aboot time. I've been thinkin' of takin' myself oot to Florida on a holiday." He tipped his Panama hat respectfully at Happy. "Nice to have met you, ma'am. Hope you come to Canada."

Theo wouldn't have guessed he was about to be fired.

We didn't see Hal or Clara again that day. I avoided them because I guessed Hal would be in a foul mood.

I'd invited Happy to have a coffee in a small bar, but she suddenly looked horrified at her silk jacket that was oozing with milk. "Ah's missed the feedin' time. This maternity bra's no good." She tucked into a nearby ladies loo, her face red with embarrassment.

CHAPTER 4

Minutes later she emerged, smiling, with a girl who also had milk stains on the bosoms area of her silk dress.

Happy introduced us, "This be Joanne. She done had a baby three months ago too, and she'd been nursin' huh. She done left huh baby at Caring for Tots. Her husband's gone off in a tizzy cause she let huh boobs shoot out milk in public. Ah said as we'd give her a lift t'collect her baby 'n then we'd drive her to her home."

Joanne was older than Happy. Unless she'd had a facelift I guessed her age at thirty-five but she could have been forty-five with a little surgical help. Her silk dress had been an expensive buy, her hat too. Her shoes looked shabby, as if her budget had only gone so far as a dress and the hat. Or maybe they'd been a present from someone other than her husband.

"Sure, we'll take you to Honeyville," I agreed. The two girls sat together in the rear of the car, but I caught bits of their talk.

"Great little gym, perfect for new mothers. Lots of us there," I heard Joanne say.

"Cost a lot? Us'n cain't affo'd no fancy gym."

"Not fancy. Just made out of some shop that went bankrupt. Two women run it. Two are sisters, the younger sister will give you a massage or a pedicure, if you can afford that."

"No, don't want none o' thet massage stuff. Mah breasts too full o' milk fo' thet."

"I'll put you up for membership tomorrow. Not expensive, you pay $25 for the membership. Pay as you go after, according to the amount of time you use their machines."

"Family membe'ships too? Ah'd like fo' my husband to use this gym place too. It is fah from Caring Fo' Tots?"

"Practically next door. And I think a family membership will set you back only $35. Not bad! Go for it."

When we reached the child care facility it was past closing hour and the two owners looked furious. "Ah've got a husband t'feed!" One Carrington sister complained to Happy. "And Joanne, you ought t'know bettah than arrivin' late as this!"

I looked at the four children that they turned over to us and thought the women hadn't done that much caring for these tots. They were all in dirty diapers, except Tim, who had wet his pants.

During the ride to Joanne's house, both nursing mothers pulled out breasts and proceeded to glut their infants with the milk that would have spilled over onto their silk dresses if they hadn't been quick about it.

Joanne's grumpy husband met her at their door. The house was an authentic southern manse, with ancient pillars from the antebellum era. Expensive. The husband bellowed, "High time! What you giving me for dinner? Yesterday's garbage?" He didn't bother to let himself be introduced to Happy and me, stalking back inside without offering to carry their howling baby.

What a relief to get to our own home! There would be no yesterday's garbage, because yesterday Happy hadn't cooked dinner. We'd gone to a McDonald's.

That night of the Kentucky Derby we huddled in our 1990's kitchen. Happy and I shared a can of sardines and a bag of chips. Dorothy had her formula and baby food from a jar. Tim had ordered four different goodies at McDonald's but ate nothing there, so we asked for a doggie bag and that's what we offered him that night. He played with the toy given as a freebie and seemed quite content to down the frozen TV dinner Happy microwaved for him when we discovered that there were ants in the doggie bag. No TV dinners for Happy and me, we hate them.

All three infants went to sleep the minute their heads hit their pillows. Caring for Tots had worn them down.

Finally, I could have sex with my wife. I love trying out new beds, in hotels or wherever. And that night, tired, Happy didn't ask for a bedtime horse story. She'd had her fill of the real thing that day. She did her learned-from-TV burlesque trick, though. And the sex was great.

CHAPTER 5

After I left for early morning stables, which meant that sixteen mile drive again, Happy did the housework, fed and tidied our "chillun" and went looking for adult companionship.

Carrying Irish, pushing Dorothy's stroller, with Tim hanging on to her ankle-length skirt, Happy strolled along the nearest fringe of the golf course. Meeting no one who belonged to her own generation except for a twenty-something grounds man, she helped him trim bushes framing the golf course. "This ain't really a golfing community? Ain't it really just lahke a new fangled old folks' home? Just mo'e ex-pen-sive?" She asked him, trading shears.

"Miz Harrow, some o' the men still c'n play golf. Maybe not the full eighteen holes. Not even nine. But they come out, mornings. The putting green's popular."

"Y'knows nowheah round heah wheah Ah kin mix with folks mah age?" she prodded him.

"Honeyville has a community center. But it's also mostly fo' old folks. Bingo games, scrabble, an outdo'r space fo' shuffleboard. Down the street, a liberry, but no gossiping allowed theah. Ladies give it a miss. Fo' meetin' women yo' age, how's about the gym?"

"Yeah man! Ah knows about thet gym. Ah's got me a new friend wut goes theah. Says how it's fahne. Cheap. 'N Ah gits a fam'ly membuhship for $35."

"Thet's the one. One glamourpuss 'n one cranky ole biddy run it. The glamourpuss be Bev, the ugly one be Soledad. Mind y'all, wut gen-rally happens is folks joins up 'n nevuh much goes back to thet place. No refunds."

"Why? Why not go back?"

"Don't rightly know."

"Well, Ah thinks as Ah'll join theah."

"Suit yo'self, Miz Harrow. But som'pins wrong about thet theah place. Ah's bin willin' lahke t'tell yo' about it, but Ah's not recommended it."

Happy repeated this conversation to me when I arrived back from evening tables. she's made the awful grits and fried chicken I'd so often choked on in Britain, yet somehow here in Kentucky they didn't taste that bad. Maybe the chickens were reared specially for this Kentucky recipe, and the grits were ready-packaged so there was not that much that Happy could do to ruin them.

I told her about Hal's plans for Mighty Moron. "Definitely, Calder in Florida: an easy race. All depending on the weather. Early hurricanes will rule that one out."

"Do y'all think lahke Ah c'd join the gym? Mebbe the fam'ly membuhship 'n y'all come too?"

"Not if you want to travel to Calder with me and see how Mighty Moron performs there. You know how tight we are for money. Three murdered owners. And the Ainsleys moved on: they made so much money off Feathers they could afford to go to a really great trainer: four times Derby winner Henry Cecil. Billandbea's owners decided to retire him and he's lolling around their fields in Norfolk, near Sandringham. Major Flyte, as you guessed would happen, has taken his mudder to my nemesis Harold East. That leaves us with Fran and Hal. Got to get Hal's string in top form."

"Yeah man! Ah knows y'can do thet. But put outta yo'r mind all the bad things wut happened, think o' good things t'come."

"My darling, I'm trying to do that. But I can't help dwelling on what a waste of money that was: putting Mighty Moron in the derby. but worse, what a tragedy to wear out a promising horse."

"Yeah, but y'all moves on."

I returned to her idea of joining the Honeyville gym: "Well, I suppose you could join. And for ten bucks more, I'll join, if that's what you want.

CHAPTER 6

Until that race week ended, I had to leave Happy alone at home while I drove the sixteen miles to where our string was stabled. She hadn't been able to find household help or babysitters among the ancient residents of our community. Any regular helpers were bitterly fought for by our needy neighbors.

Anchored at home with our "chillun" Happy was feeling so suffocated by the smothered-mother thing that she went in search of the grounds man and pleaded to borrow his pick-up truck for the ride into town. "Ah promises y'all will have the truck back long befo'e yo quittin' hour."

Within minutes she was off with the "chillun" to Honeyville.

She paid for a half-day's Caring for Tots, parked our "chillun" there, then swept down the street searching for the gym. It was practically next door, located between a laundromat and the library.

The first person she found at the gym was her friend Joanne. Although dressed in standard gym wear, Joanne wasn't using any of the machines. Joanne appeared to be waiting for Happy to arrive.

"There you are! What took you so long?"

"Had t'git transpo'tation. Wheah do Ah sign up? Who takes m'money? Happy's voice carried. The glamourpuss manager showed up, hurrying into the make-shift office that was separated from the gym's machines by a see-through plastic screen. This was one good-looking gal, tall as a model, thin and yet curvaceous, with long silky blonde hair and big boobs.

She could have posed for the wartime Petty girls calendar. Through the cut-outs of the screen Happy could see the second manager, Soledad, a tired wrinkled biddie. She slouched chatting with a portly older man who was trying to shed his extra pounds on a treadmill.

"That will be $35," glamourpuss-Bev briskly handed out a bill, while the old biddie joined in to give Joanne a form to sign as the member recommending us into the club.

Within minutes Joanne was lending her gym clothes to Happy, while she changed into a chic town dress and grabbed her handbag. Joanne whispered, "Got to go. Please do me a favor, if my husband calls here, you take the call."

"What-all should Ah say?"

"Anything. Tell him I have a bad tummy ache and I'm holed up in the toilet. I'll call him in an hour."

"What if 'n he thinks y'all got 'ppendicitis and he should take y'all t'the hos-pi-tal?"

"Never. Not my husband. He'd love it if I really got appendicitis, it burst, and I died from peritonitis."

"Y'all cain't mean that?"

"I can. And I do. But I'm wasting time here. I've got to go." Joanne high-heeled her way out of the gym's door, sped into a Mercedes convertible parked directly outside, and was gone to whatever appointment she thought was so urgent.

Watching the time, knowing her half-day at Caring for Tots was ticking like the meter of a taxi, Happy took a stance on the treadmill next to where the portly older man was sweating away his morning.

"Hi, Ah's Hillary Harrow," Happy called from her treadmill to his. "Jus' call me Happy. Please, c'n y'all tell me how t'slow down this thing?"

Huffing from over-exercising, the white-haired white-bearded gym member forced out two words: "Can't say." He ogled Happy, apparently liked what he saw, and released one pudgy hand from his treadmill's bar to wave over the grouchy boss. Pointing to Happy's machine, he gestured that it needed adjustment for short-legged tiny Happy.

Silently, parallel to each other, the older man and Happy spent close to an hour on the machines.

When the old man finally eased himself to the floor to sit down on a steel chair, Happy asked him, "Don't y'all think mebbe yo' should see a doctor? Y'all seem terrible tired."

"I am a doctor," white-hair-white-beard snapped. Then his voice gentled, and panting for breath, he added, "My name's Dr. Waller. Dr. Adrian Waller. And exactly why have you joined this gym, Miss Hillary?"

"Misses Harrow," Happy corrected. Gently, because she knew she wasn't wearing her wedding ring at the gym, she explained, "Ah's wedded. Ah's had three babies, quick-lahke. Lost mah figure. Ah'd thought thet nursin' mah baby Ah'd lose weight. No such luck!"

Waller digested the information. When he could walk, he went to a vending machine, paid for two Diet Cokes, and offered one to Happy. "You're the one who might need to see a doctor, Mrs. Harrow. For a first time visit to a gym, I think you overdid it on that treadmill. Here, have a Coke."

Obediently, Happy left her treadmill, accepted the Diet Coke and relaxed into a matching steel chair. Unheeding that her morning payout for Caring for Tots was dissipating, she asked Waller, "You bin a membuh heah long?"

"Ever since it opened," he looked up toward a tired space skirting the ceiling. "See those posters up there? They are left over from the time when this locale was leased to a shop for women's intimate apparel. Apparently those posters advertising brassieres were up too high to get down."

Waller eyed the posters appreciatively.

Happy hadn't noticed them. Now she studied them. "Strange so't of bras."

"Oh, those brassieres were sold to nursing mothers." "Not lahke wut Ah weahs."

"Good quality brassieres. Special make." "They be lots o' nursin' mothuhs heah about?"

"Not enough to sustain the shop, apparently. But this gym is thriving. Full of nursing mothers. In my day, they'd be home doing housework and that would have slimmed them down."

"Why y' say thet?"

"Because. Exercise won't shift the fat in one out of six people. It's a question of how they process oxygen. Ten to fifteen percent of volunteers who offered to have experts test their ability to pump blood around their bodies found they could rid the fat only up to forty percent. But other folks who did the same amount of exercise simply don't get the same results."

"Wut c'd them folks do?"

"It appears that much of weight loss depends on your genes."

"Don't know nothin' about m'genes. Mah Mammy died when Ah was bo'n. Mah Pappy don't talk about genes."

"Fitness trainers have harsh words for folks that slack off. They say it's motivation that makes the difference. Some folks go to a gym four times a week but they don't push themselves. I push myself."

"Ah sho' noticed that."

"Folks with heart conditions need to try harder. I try harder because my heart skips a beat."

"Mah heart's fahne. Still, Ah'll try harder too."

"I recommend half an hour moderate exercise five times a week for you, Mrs. Harrow."

"Will you gimme a pre-scrip-tion fo' slimming pills?"

"No. And anyway, I can't. I'm semi-retired. Kept my medical license, but only work half days. Afternoons. You aren't a patient, I'd need to examine you thoroughly, before I could write you a prescription for anything. Right now I'm not taking any new patients."

Happy looked at her watch, and realized she'd have to pay Caring for Tots for another half-day if she didn't scoot over to collect our "chillun."

"Got t'go," she echoed Joanne, wondering why Joanne had not returned but knowing she absolutely had to leave the gym.

Still in Joanne's gym outfit, Happy rushed to Caring for Tots. To her surprise, Joanne was there.

"Did my husband call?" Joanne asked.

"Nope. Nothin'. Ah didn't have t'tell 'm no lies." Happy went into the ladies loo and stripped out of Joanne's outfit. She'd carried her own clothes with her and proceeded to dress herself. From in the loo she could recognize Irish crying for her meal. Happy opened her blouse and her maternity brassiere to give a nipple to hungry Irish.

Joanne joined her, opening the top of her embroidered dress to offer a nipple to her three-month-old daughter.

"How long y'all goin' t'nurse?"

Joanne looked slightly abashed. "Maybe another month or two. Gives me a reason not to share my bedroom with my husband."

"Not share yo're bedroom!"

"That's right. Can't stand having Bart near me." "Bart?"

"Bart. Nickname, he's really Bartholomew. Doesn't deserve such a grand name. He's such a louse."

"Ah cain't follow wut y'all's sayin'! Ain't he be yo'r husband?" "Bard has E.D. Erectile dysfunction. Can't get it up. Can't get it hard." "Don't know nothin' about thet."

"He blames me. Says as I won't do it the way he likes, I'm a poor excuse as a wife. Truth is, he's a diabetic and didn't always take his insulin. Or, if he did, maybe that's what contributed to this. I just can't stand him any more."

"Ah's real sorry t'heah thet. At least, does he love yo'r little girl?" Joanne shrugged. Totally noncommittal. Happy was in too much of a hurry to return the groundsman's pick-up to give any more thought to Joanne's family.

That night, when we were in our kingsize bed, when Happy interrupted her account of what had happened to cause her to ease off on her friendship with Joanne, she told me, "Joanne, she made such a hound-dawg face when Ah asked if Bart loved their daughter. Ah couldn't help wonderin' if she *is* Bart's daughter."

"Your new friend seems quite a dicey lady."

"Don't know what thet means. But Ah suspect she went t'see a man when she left the gym. And thet man wun't no butchuh, bakuh nor candlestick makuh. She was dressed up mo'e fancy than fo' the derby. She smelled awful purty too. Ve' fahne per-fume. But she took a shower at the gym. Said lahke she needed t'wash off the per-fume 'cause Bart hates per-fume. She changed her dress, put on a T-shirt and jeans 'n locked the fancy dress 'n high heel shoes in her locker."

I hadn't heard enough to come to a judgment. I felt relieved, though, that my Happy wouldn't get any ideas from Joanne.

Could be that Joanne's ideas might be contagious.

CHAPTER 7

The next we heard about Joanne, she was dead.

Our local coroner said she'd been murdered. Her killer used Paraoxon, a nerve agent. It had been put on her clothing, specifically on her underpants. We heard this from the local policemen who came to interrogate Happy after they learned that Joanne had recommended us as new members at the exercise club.

Happy's clever unmasking of three serial killers was something these local policemen didn't know about.

Coroners in Miami, Long Island and Saratoga had her name on their computers, but these Honeyville officers hadn't bothered to check her out.

On the afternoon that they came to visit, Happy was trying to cope with all three infants after learning that Caring for Tots was temporarily closed out of respect for Joanne and her brutal passing.

Honeyville's representatives of the law were more determined to find out how a mother in her twenties could be living in a retirement community restricted to sixty-year-olds and over.

For Happy, that was easy to answer. "Mah Husband's em-ploy-ed bah Mr. Hal Murphy of Canada. Him and his wife are in their seventies. They bought this place."

In stentorian tones, the handsome young buck bursting out of his police uniform said, "Children are not allowed here. No dogs, no children."

Happy didn't offer to enlighten this officer that the last occupants of our pseudo colonial manse had kept at least two dogs in our bedroom, leaving their fleas behind for us.

Smiling sweetly, the perfect southern mother of three howling infants, Happy did her best to mollify her uninvited visitors. The older policeman scribbled her name in a notebook, but took no further action. He smiled in return. "We'll leave you. The housing association will deal with the problem."

Happy's contribution to the memory of her short-term friend, Joanne, was to take up a collection from the gym's other members to buy a wreath for her funeral. Everyone gave some change, except for Grumpy. The doctor wrote out a check for ten dollars.

Joanne's husband didn't attend the funeral. Instead, in the first pew, usurping the role of chief mourner, was a middle-aged man in a lawyer's pinstriped suit and narrow tie. No relation. Joanne had told Happy she had no living relatives.

Happy took a determined look at his face, but she could find no resemblance there to Joanne's three-month-old daughter.

After the funeral Happy suggested we stop at Bart's house to ask if we could help with babysitting his daughter. Happy meant well. My little Baptist had been taught to love her neighbor, and although Bart lived in a far grander area than we did, she must have counted him as a neighbor.

"What the hell! Go away! Don't need any of you nosey people butting in here. I'll take care of my daughter myself. God knows I did most of that when Joanne . . ." His angry voice petered out. Half-sobbing, he headed for a magnificent flying staircase to hurry in the direction of his daughter's lusty squalling.

We watched him go up to the second floor. Happy said, "At least, Ah c'd wash them dishes," she pointed to piles of dishes on the dining room table, their centers coated with congealed grease. She led the way into a dirty but still impressive new kitchen, with a central counter for dishwashing. She scrubbed off the grease, stacked the dishes into a dishwasher conveniently positioned alongside, turned it to On, and hurried me out to our rental car before Bart could return to treat us again like lepers.

For the five mile drive to our house, Happy grilled me about how men react to marriage. She told me about Joanne's alleging that Bart had erectile dysfunction. She told me he wanted sex in an abnormal way that would not have produced any babies. She suggested again that Joanne might have been having an extra-marital affair. Only she didn't couch her remarks in exactly such precise terms.

I tried to sound well-informed. "Happy darling, maybe we're looking at Joanne's murder from the wrong angle. You seem to be hinting that Bart must have murdered her because she couldn't help him have sex, or out of jealousy because she was giving it out to someone else. From a man's point of view, I must offer some other pointers."

"Sho' nuf? Go ahead. Be my guest."

"I'm not saying I like Bart. He's a disagreeable lout. No social grace whatsoever. He ignored us the first time we came here. Although we'd driven five miles out of our way to give his wife a lift. Gave her funeral a miss. But I'll bet he paid for it, and for that extremely expensive coffin. Swore at us when all we wanted was to help him. But none of that makes him a murderer. Somehow I get the impression he loved Joanne, and was deeply hurt by the obvious fact she was having sex with another man. A man who could satisfy her sexually, something very difficult for a husband to accept. Yet, accept it, he did. Although in a highly obnoxious manner."

"He did buy huh a humongous car: Mercedes, a convertible. She couldn't have gotten thet from a boyfriend and driven it up to huh house."

"Now you're making sense."

"But Ah'll bet yo' five-to-one the boyfriend gave huh the fancy dress she changed out of at the gym, and the per-fume. Specially, the per-fume. Said Bart hated per-fume."

"I smelled perfume in their house tonight. It was coming from a dress draped on a chair."

"Yeah man! Thet same dress lahke Ah was sayin' about. He must have cleaned out huh locker at the gym and found it. Too bad."

"Tough on a man when he has to hide his love for his wife. And darling, don't think he couldn't have given Joanne a baby. Even with erectile dysfunction a man can eject his semen. Get that semen in the right location and—bingo—he could become a father. In the old days most judges would have accepted that possibility and granted custody to Bart, believing he had more opportunity to get Joanne pregnant than some one-hour lover. Now, of course, there's DNA testing. Bart probably had a

DNA test, knows he's the baby's father. This whole horror story tears his heart out."

We'd reached our street of twelve identical pseudo colonial mini-manses. I kissed Happy long and hard in front of ours. "Tomorrow night we'll be in Miami, and can try out a new bed at the Fontainebleau. How about it?"

Happy snuggled close. "Sounds fahne t'me."

CHAPTER 8

Miami in mid-May gave us the lilt we expected. The Murphy family had reserved a small suite for the two of us, and sex was delicious. I was primed for it thinking of all the nights naughty Frank Sinatra had slept there, and also that philanderer Jack Kennedy before he was President.

I was up for early morning stables, checked on the Murphy horseflesh, and hurried back for a matinée with Happy.

But her mood had soured. "Ah's bin 'memberin' how the fust murder in mah lahfe happened right heah in Miami. On thet theah picnic we gave fo' Evelyn Cohen."

I recalled only too well how that particular picnic had turned out.

Evelyn Cohen at that time was one of the top women jockeys in the USA. She'd flown from California to look for rides at Calder. Too irresponsible, to my way of operating. Happy was thrilled to meet her, and almost fainted with joy when Evelyn Cohen offered to give her some pointers to improve her jockey style.

There was a small shop in Fort Lauderdale that sold British food stuffs and I'd gone there to buy some goodies that might entice Happy to look forward to visiting Britain. I didn't know that Evelyn Cohen was an orthodox jewess and wouldn't eat the sandwiches I made of York ham.

Evelyn Cohen had opted to get sandwiches from a beach-side delicatessen. I'd provided mustard, and she didn't shy away from the can of that. She spread it generously on her sandwiches. She ate while we were still unpacking the picnic gear: chairs, a blanket, wind-breakers and the food I'd picked up in Fort Lauderdale.

When we sat down with smiles to tuck into our food and looked around for Evelyn, she was dead. She'd collapsed under the beach umbrella and we'd thought she'd been resting. I'd got an ambulance by using my cell phone to call 911, but that was only of use to spare the little children's bucket-and-spade brigade from being spooked by a dead woman. There was nothing anyone could have done to have saved her. Or so we were informed later by the Miami coroner, who explained that the poison in the jar of mustard was potent enough to kill a regiment. Lucky we both hate mustard.

All that talk of poisoning should have predicted to Happy that she was about to be involved in yet another murder. No sooner had we left our two losing horses in Miami to return home to our "chillun" than we learned that another of the girls in our gym had died, poisoned.

Isn't it true that in some of Africa's primitive tribes the mothers deface good-looking babies so that the evil spirits will pass them by? Would that we had known of some way to protect Polly Elsbeth.

She was one of the girls at our gym who had given most generously for the wreath for Joanne's funeral. Polly, a large girl with large hands, buttocks, and—of course—breasts, had been about to stop breastfeeding her infant within a week. Polly had been extremely beautiful.

"She died, poisoned with organophosphate," I was told by the gym's two managers, who had already started to collect pennies toward a wreath for Polly. This time there had been only small contributions toward a wreath. Polly, a single mother who as a waitress worked for a minimum wage and tips at an all-night café, didn't rate anything better than the cheapest wreath the local florist provides. Most gym members who had given a dollar or two for Joanne's wreath gave twenty-five cents this time.

The doctor reduced his contribution from ten dollars to two.

"Why such a cheap wreath?" Happy asked.

Glamourpuss shrugged, "Don't know. Seems like the richer you are, the more folks spend. Joanne was plenty rich." Glamourpuss had warmed up to Happy. She appreciated time out from keeping books for the accountant to chat with the club's newest member. "Last year when a girl died here, she got nothin': no wreath."

"When was thet? Recent-lahke?"

"Not so long ago. Couple months. Strange girl, been nursin' her baby until he was about a year old. His teeth must have bit her by then."

"Wow! Ah sho don't plan on doin' thet. Don't have much milk. Figure to quit in one mo'e month. How'd she die? Thet strange girl?"

"Heart attack. Right over there, next to the bigger bicycle. Just keeled over. See that doctor on the big treadmill? He signed the death certificate."

"What she do fo' a livin'? Somethin' stren-u-ous lahke?" "Easy job. Part-time secretary to the gym's accountant. Easy!" "She work fo' him raght heah in this heah room?"

"Most times. Sometimes took books home. Now I do them. Can use the extra pay."

That night, when Happy and I were in our kingsize bed, she told me all of this. Happy was interested in the fact that there was such a contrast between rich women and the anything-but-rich girls sho shared the machines at the gym. "Fifty dollar wreath fo' Joanne. Five dollar one fo' Polly!"

I was reminded of a novel by Tolstoy where he described a Christmas party in an aristocrat's home, where the rich children received expensive gifts but the poor dressmaker's tot got next to nothing.

"Who paid for Polly's gym club membership? Twenty-five bucks must have bitten into her budget."

"Ah asked Bev thet same question. She said she thought it must 'ave been the café's owner."

The next day, when Happy returned to her favorite slow Treadmaster at the gym, she gave the place a thorough going over. She stared at those posters of brassieres left behind when the last occupants of this locale had left. She thought it odd that the posters were still in place considering that this was a gym for agile women who should have been able to remove them. She stared hard at the aging doctor, whose fat belly hadn't been diminished by all his peddling on the bicycle and hours on the fastest treadmill. She stared at Bev's co-manager, wondering why she acted so sullen.

Bev was quick to explain that when Happy left the treadmill for a chat. "You should cotton up to Soledad," Bev urged her. "Poor thing, she isn't all that mean. Just looks mean. Truth is she aches for love of our gym's accountant. Name of Rhett Gordon."

"Rhett!"

"Rhett, for Scarlett O'Hara's Rhett, I figure. Gordon, 'cause he's got Scotch blood. Scotch for the country, not the whiskey. Seen him yet? Good looking. Tall, sort of thin but could do with some working out on a bike."

"Nope. Ain't seen no one thet des-crip-tion. Not many men come in heah."

"True. Men are usually willing to pay more than $25 memberships for a gym."

"Why memberships heah? Why not just call this place wut it is. Ain't no club."

"Don't know. Maybe something to do with taxes. Or maybe it's just a way of keeping out people we don't want using our machines."

That night, again, Happy wasted good loving-time to talk about what she'd seen and heard at our gym. "Lahke wut the gardener who tends our golf greens said: somethin' seems not right about the gym."

"Your new friend Bev probably has told you more than she should have. Taxes! A frightening word to small businesses. Restricting entry? Could be against the constitution."

"Yeah man. Smaht girl, mah new friend. Or—Rick darlin'—y'all don't mean lahke she c'd be in danguh! Next girl as will die at the gym!"

"Come on, sweetheart. Don't fret about her. Do your little striptease act, and let's forget that gym. Let's have some delicious sex."

We did.

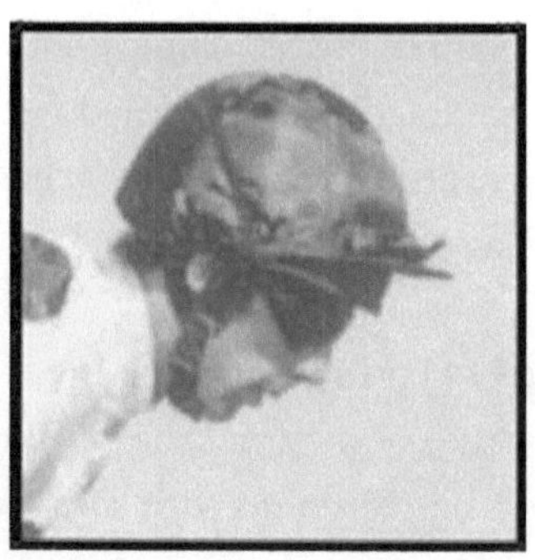

CHAPTER 9

The gym's assistant manager, Beverley Shaw, was the one to ask questions when Happy sat down at the manager's desk for a cozy chat the next afternoon for a cozy chat. "What's Miami like? I've been thinking of quitting here. Moving there. Get some action in a big city."

"Miami weren't no good fo' us this time. Hosses didn't win. Both made third, which Rick hates. He figures second, thet might be 'scused. Not third. 'N Ah suffuh'd an awful scare. Thought Ah was pregnant ag'in. With Irish barely four months last week."

"Missed your period?"

"Thought Ah'd missed it. Mebbe counted wrong. Anyways, Ah's all right. No new baby this tahme. Ah c'n still work as a jockey."

"What sort of birth control do you use?" "None. Don't knows of enny Ah'd lahke t'use." "Pill's not bad. I use that. You allergic to the pill?"

"Pill? Don't knows nothin' about no pill. Befo'e Ah left junior high, us'n had some classes, y'all knows which ones Ah mean, Teachuh calls 'em hy-gi-ene but they's really about how not t'have babies. Rubbuh plug wut y'supposed to shove up inside y'know wheah. Or a metal thing." "The coil. Teacher never told you about the pill?"

"Ah quit school t'go t'Louisville t'learn me how t'become a jockey. Mebbe the pill was bein' taught latuh. Missed thet. Anyways, as Ah tol' mah husband, Ah wanted lots 'n lots o' chillun. Yeah man, until Ah got me three in three yeahs."

Bev looked up to the ceiling as if she could get a pill from up there. She sighed, "Ask Dr. Waller to write you a prescription for the pill. That's what I did."

"He sez he don't take no new patients."

"That must have been when you first joined up here. But now, you're an old-timer. And I'll make sure you get that prescription."

I hate to think how Bev managed that. But she did. And Happy came home with a smirk on her juicy lips. I hadn't thought our nightly sex sessions could get any better: how wrong I was. Having shed fear of pregnancy, Happy surged into a new level of bliss for both of us.

CHAPTER 10

al's horses were performing below par. I knew I had to do something quickly. Hal wasn't a man to wait around long for what he demands.

I needed magic.

I decided to recruit Happy to come on the sixteen-mile drive to the stables and give me her opinion of what was wrong.

Happy made a deal with me. "Y'all come to the gym. Ah goes t'the stables."

What had happened to her all-consuming passion for our horses? Now it was stables versus gym?

I did morning gallops on my own, collected Happy and the "chillun" from our pseudo mansion, worked out obediently at the gym for one hour, then drove Happy to the stables.

Nothing, not even her budding friendship with Bev could dampen Happy's ardor for our horses when she was reunited with them.

She'd brought a basket of apples and carrots, and—naughty—sugar cubes. Bad for their teeth, but Happy fed them generous amounts and then began her whispering thing.

Happy is a kind of horse whisperer that isn't written about but who can produce desirable effects. She says the horses "talk" to her: I doubt that my

English-bred colts speak Kentucky hillbilly style. That they communicate: there's no question.

After we left the stables and were on our sixteen-mile drive to collect our "chillun" from Caring For Tots, Happy told me what was wrong.

"Them hosses has awful miseries."

"Is that why you haven't wanted to visit them before today?"

"Yeah man. Cain't stand seein' hosses sufferin' miseries. Didn't seem lahke there was somethin' Ah c'd do t'help."

"Let me be the judge of that. What miseries?" "Bellies hurt. Hooves hurt."

"Hal's horses were de-wormed before the racing season. I check the manure for any sight of new worms. Our lads check after every gallop for pebbles that might have got lodged in their hooves."

"Ah knows thet. Still, sompin's givin' them bellyaches. Heah in Kentucky we's got worms y'nevuh heard of, worms thet don't show nowheah, except fo' folks they gits pains in muscles. Pigs, wut gives 'em."

"We'll have the stable lads checked for those worms. And, what's gone wrong with our horses' hooves?"

"Don't rightly know. Them's fancy medical names pass me by. But Ah re-calls thet in England, where land sloped sharp-lahke, hosses got t'same."

By the time we'd collected the "chillun" and were at home, and Happy had taken over the changing of diapers and potty-training, I was quickly on the blower to Hal's stable lads.

Yes, Theo had been plagued with stomach pains. Pains in his muscles too. And had he been hand-feeding our string? Yes, to that too. And had the horses been worked on steep gradients? Yes! Yes! Yes! All in disobedience to orders. No hand feeding was allowed. Happy had the sole dispensation for that rule. And no working on gradients of any sort, because our two horses were not destined to be steeplechasers—I hoped—I wanted them to stand as stallions when they'd won enough top races on the flat.

Thank God, I thought, it wasn't spavins, those damned lumps on their calves caused by stress, and which never go away.

Happy asked, "What y'all goin' t'do?"

"Move the horses. Today, tonight, if possible. Fire Theo. No question of being mamby-pamby about letting him go. I can't stand over the horses twenty-four hours a day to make certain he obeys orders."

"Wheah will you send 'em?"

"You tell me!"

"What about to Mrs. W.? Such a nahce lady, lahkes me, seems so ennyways."

'She'll have gone to the Belmont races. She won the big one in 2004. Won't miss going."

"Could phone huh. Ah's got huh private numbah."

Mrs. W. came to the telephone after I gave Happy's name. I reminded her we'd met in Saratoga when she'd won the Travers, and asked if there was any chance of billeting my two horses at her farm outside of Lexington.

No luck. Mrs. W. couldn't take them but she did suggest a local horseman who took some of hers at grass.

The horseman was at home. I guess he didn't have a runner for Belmont's races. Yes, he'd take my two horses, but if I suspected worms he'd want them wormed first.

Also, he asked, "Your Mr. Hal Murphy, that Canadian, he didn't by any chance buy that pig farm no one would touch?"

"I'm afraid so."

"Mrs. Whitney, she's so knowledgeable, she turned it down fast when someone suggested she could put her huskies there."

"Huskies?"

"Mrs. Whitney won the Iditarod. That race for huskies in Alaska. Followed her team by being piloted by helicopter, and when any husky's pads bled, she'd have her pilot land and exchange that husky for one that was sound. Didn't you know about that?"

I tried to get this kind gentleman back on the subject of my horses. When send them? How much to board per month?

His answer came swift and fair. We agreed on a deal. I was able to join Happy in our kitchen where she was feeding the "chillun" and hurry her so that we could go upstairs to cuddle. And have sex.

CHAPTER 11

I didn't get my way. While we were still at our own dinner, the telephone rang; long distance. A call from Mrs. Wright in England. She was our new housekeeper, who'd replaced the ailing Mrs. Rea.

"Mrs. Harrow, I've a niece who says she'll take care of your Epsom house, if you'll have me in Kentucky. I miss your children. Could I come over for a few weeks? As a tourist? I'm not asking for you to try to get me a green card. I'll pay my own ticket."

Another miracle. Miss doing the dirty jobs for our "chillun" with their ever-soiled diapers and squalling? But that's what she said. Who was I to turn away such a marvellous offer?

But first, before agreeing, I had to consult Happy.

"Yeah man! Y'bet yo'r lahfe Ah loves thet idea. Say 'yes' quick-lahke, befo'e she done changes huh mind."

Mrs. Wright arrived simultaneously with the local vet's lab results declaring our horses to be sound. We left the "chillun" with her, after endless requests for cosseting them from Happy, and took rooms near the Lexington farm.

We might have stayed there, supervising the remarkable recovery our horses made. They were putting on condition daily, but I'd received that e-mail from my richest owner with an order to buy two horses for her at the Miami sales.

The owner was Fran Purcell, the contralto half of what had been the famous Purcell twins duet. Shortly after the twins joined my Epsom stables, the elder Carla Purcell was murdered. Her murder was followed by that of another soprano, musical star Sybil Sykes, who had employed Happy to teach her hillbilly speak for her role as Daisy Mae in *Hog Town II*. A boyfriend of Fran's was killed in her apartment. A fourth murder took place when we went to Australia for the Melbourne Cup: another soprano practicing for her role in a musical version of Jane Austen's *Pride and Prejudice* was strangled at her piano.

Happy had solved these murders with her "f'male in-tui-tion" using very little help from forensic science. Although for the eventual conviction of the murderer use of the murderer's DNA did form a part.

Fran had stayed in the Epsom stable, although I'd been moved to Kentucky by Hal Murphy. she had two sublime fillies, both with Soviet Song connections, and had not needed to depend on her cocaine habit for highs when those fillies romped to the Finish Lines often enough when they competed.

I liked Fran, in spite of her cocaine addiction, her terrible gutter language, and the rather loathsome Sir Arthur Snodgrass who follows in her wake. "To be honest, Miss Purcell," I'd barked into the telephone, "prices have gone through the roof at these sales. Sixteen million was paid by Coolmore in Miami recently."

"Pounds or dollars?" Fran knew more about finance than Snodgrass suspected. He might have a surprise one of these days if he tried a gigolo act. Fran added: "I've got a great new contract for an album with Filipa. You can go up to two million for each yearling. Dollars. Four million, for your checking account."

Returning to Miami was not as bad as Happy had predicted. No murder or rumors of murder on our horizon. Plenty of murders in Miami, but not one involving us.

CHAPTER 12

I relished the atmosphere at the horse sales. It felt great to have four million to spend for Fran's horseflesh. Colts or fillies, or one of each? I studied the sales catalogues as if they were the *Book of Common Prayer.*

Happy and I bumped into a longtime associate from The Horse Trust. He had raised money for it when it was called The Home of Rest for Horses. It was founded as early as 1886 by Ann Lindo, to provide a sanctuary for elderly horses. "You know they can live to be thirty years old, or more. Longest lived at our place got to fifty-three. But when you've got four million Britishers riding horses, without a thought for what will happen to an animal when it no longer can give you a ride, then that's when the Trust becomes meaningful."

I was listening with altered attention, because the first of the fillies came out for auction. I raised my programme several times, but the filly soon passed two million dollars.

The same happened twice again. Then a third time Happy nudged my elbow and whispered: "Not thet one. No good for nothin'."

My equine trust pal was still going on about how many horses were abandoned by owners when they couldn't offload an animal, when I spotted a filly with the breeding that most interested me: a Nureyev filly with a fine dam. I raised my paddle enthusiastically, not caring if I was pushing up her price, and eventually I outbid a faceless rival to get her for three million two. That would only leave me with eight hundred thousand for another horse, but I felt I must have the Nureyev filly.

And I did manage to get a wild eyed colt for the other bit of money: good breeding there too, with the Godolphin Arabian Line 1965 derby winner, Santa Claus far back on the dam's side.

I was gloating on my good day's work when my name came echoing down the microphones placed in the auditorium. "Harrow, please. Mr. Harrow please, this is an emergency."

Which of Hal's horses could be sick again, I wondered. I rushed to the nearest auctioneer and gave my name. I was seething with fury to be interrupted before I could take a close look at the two animals I'd purchased. What the hell had happened? Had a groom given one of Hal's horses his oats at the wrong feeding time, bringing on colic?

No. The voice on the telephone was a down-country Englishwoman's: Mrs. Wright's.

She sounded totally hysterical. "Mr. Harrow, sir. Mr. Harrow, Tim, my Timmy, your little son has been kidnapped."

That was when our personal horror began.

CHAPTER 13

Happy had accompanied me and heard Mrs. Wright's news. She'd leaned into me to press part of the telephone's receiver to her ear.

Calmly, in a far calmer tone than I could have mustered, she said: "Mrs. Wright, give us the par-ti-cu-lars." Happy, who had been kidnapped two years ago in Dubai, knew the ropes only too well.

As if from a far distance I heard Mrs. Wright's voice screaming like a WWII air raid warden. "Someone took him. No, he didn't just wander out of Caring For Tots. I'd gone to the laundromat with the children's dirty clothes. Miss Carrington came out with her hair in curlers to shout she couldn't find Timmy. Your Tim. Yes, we've had the whole town of Happyville out searching for him. Police, everybody who isn't away. Out scouring the fields. Dredging canals. No sign of him."

Happy, still calm, too calm, asked: "Any ransom note?"

"No. Not that I've been told about. Oh, Mrs. Harrow, I'm so dreadfully sorry, so ashamed."

I cut short Mrs. Wright's wailing. I wanted to get on to the Happyville police. But as I dialed the non-emergency number, as if this wasn't an *emergency*, I was thinking, "Oh God, my little Tim. I haven't paid much attention to him, living in rooms near Hal's horses. Flying down to Miami without even considering bringing him along. Dumping him on the-too-willing Mrs. Wright. Will he be psychologically scarred? I've read that kidnap victims often are. Not my Happy, because she managed her release by herself. But little Tim? If he's found alive! Will he always blame us for whatever God-awful experience he's going through? And, no, I don't have to wait for any ransom note. I know what the demands will be: give over the $4 million Fran has put into my account for purchasing her new horses, or—! Oh God, please, don't let my son die! Not my little Tim. My only son, Tim, Timothy, Timmy! What am I to do with Fran's $4 million? I've just bought two yearlings and owe that money! Fran's not easy, about money. Can be as pennypinching as Dickens' Scrooge."

CHAPTER 14

I was right about the ransom note. It was for exactly $4 million. And I was right about Fran's miserliness.

She could make $20 million with her new album. But not one cent did she offer to help rescue our Tim. And in the contract of purchase for her two new yearlings it stated that each day they weren't paid for counted toward a hefty penalty.

I paid for her yearlings. The $4 million was Fran's money.

But who knew about that money having been put into my business account? Snodgrass? Had Fran boasted about her two new buys during pillow talk with her fiancé, Sir Arthur Snodgrass?

Or had she told her duet partner, the soprano from Australia, Filipa Grant? *She* wouldn't have had anything to do with kidnapping Tim. Filipa owed a great deal to my Happy for having removed her Little Betty's iron leg braces, then found a miracle product to help that frail baby grow into a normal child. Little Betty had gone from looking like a starving orphan from Darfur, to being a plump darling who could win an infant beauty contest.

No, Filipa would never have been party to Tim's kidnapping. But, her dicey husband, Rus, was something else. If his family needed food, he was known to have blown all the cash on hard liquor for himself.

Filipa had helped Fran cut that new album as the soprano replacement for Carla in the famous Purcell duo. Filipa could have heard Fran boast about two new yearlings, for a pay-out of $4 million. Filipa could have repeated that news to her Rus, and with his devious mind plus need for money, he could have sold the info on to hard criminals he met in the lousy bars he frequented.

I was throwing a very wide net trying to come to some answer of who would have done this thing.

Happy, also delving deep into her memory, was simultaneously concerned for Tim's comfort. "Ah'd just about got him potty-trained! Will them bad men put him on a potty? If he's back in diapers, and left for hours in his own poop, he'll get diaper rash fo' sure!"

We both knew that Tim was a picky eater. Although McDonald's was his favourite watering hole, that was due to the freebie toys he got there. He rarely downed his food. What would his kidnappers feed him? Anything he wouldn't spit out?

Right away I started to develop my strategy of how to get Tim home. I began by listing all the possible sources I could tap for money.

Surprisingly, comforting me, came swift offers for loans or outright gifts. Filipa, who earned a pittance from the Purcell duo album, when compared to Fran's percentage, sent $1 million. I imagine Rus might have had a heart attack over that! Hal Murphy met that million with another from him. He e-mailed me: "Same as when Happy abducted."

The Ainsleys' came forward with a wonderful plan: I was to sell Feathers and get ten percent of the sale. They knew that if I could get such as Coolmore to bid against the Maktoums, and Feathers topped $10 million, I'd be almost at the figure demanded by the kidnappers.

With the $2 million sent, and prospects for a third, I reckoned a decent bank would loan me the fourth million. I went to three banks before I found the "decent" one. But I did find one.

Then the hate mail erupted. Misinformation from the press egged on the crazies out there who use the internet to propound hate. I was accused of murdering Tim. The confusion of where I'd been living – having left the pseudo mansion and lodged in rooms nearer Hal's horses – added to the mess. Some crazies alleged I'd sneaked back from the Miami sales, using my purchases there as a cover, and grabbed Tim.

My supposed reason? That Happy and I had grown to despise each other, and I'd snatched my son before she could get custody after an impending divorce. God! How can some people be so awful? Preposterous. I'd didn't honor these accusations by any reply. No need. There was no evidence that I'd done any such thing. Please, people, try to understand that all this is about an adorable two-going-on-three boy taken by kidnappers for lucre.

With nearly $4 million in hand, I was prepared to make a deal with the kidnappers. Didn't the big insurance companies proceed like that? The information I got was that they did, and most baddies were willing to take three-quarters or less than they'd demanded, rather than get naught.

But how to reach the kidnappers?

Waiting was excruciating. Happy was the strongest of our twosome. I'd break out weeping into my pillow most nights, strong man that I am. Happy coped. She made lists of suspects. Her amazing mind came to grips with this problem, as she had when Feathers had been taken. Her expertise in revealing the serial killers at American racecourses, and Ebury Street's, added facets. "Not Snodgrass," she declared. "He may be smaht at sellin' lots in Dalmatia, but Amer-i-can gangstuhs would gobble him up lahke a hushpuppy."

Nodding like an Atlas who couldn't bear his load, I agreed. "No, not Snodgrass."

"Rus? Too stupid. Greedy 'nuf. But this kidnappin' took military precision. Rus ain't cap'ble o' thet."

Agreed.

"Not Colonel Flyte. Too proud o' his fam'ly name." Agreed, but I felt Happy was getting to the core person. "It be Theo. Thet stableboy wut yo' fired."

"Hold on! Greedy, sure. But capable of military precision? I doubt that." "Yeah, not be smaht 'nuf on his own. He be re-cruit-ed."

That made sense. Happy's ideas always made sense. And we could get a trace on Theo. Hal had employed him, but I'd checked his credentials. In our stables we don't gamble on unknowns. Not to work with million-dollar horses!

I said. "Could be right on! If he hadn't been chosen by Hal, I wouldn't have had him near us. Theo couldn't drive in the USA, too many driving convictions. Left Canada under a cloud for fiddling the cash box at his last employment. Big-hearted Hal felt sorry for the lad: he'd gone to school with Theo's mother when he was a poor boy in Calgary. Dear Hal, his heart has often over-ruled his head."

"How we find him now?"

"Hal! Hal could reach Theo through the boy's mother." "Yeah man. Wut we be waitin' fo'?"

No waiting now. I telephoned Hal. He has lawyers on salary year round.

They got to work. Within hours Hal's lawyers had a trace on Theo.

He'd flown to Brazil. No extradition there.

I said "No extradition won't help Theo if those gangsters, he sold his soul to, decide to pay a local hitman to kill him. I hear it doesn't cost two thousand quid for one of those locals to do the job."

"Stupid, lazy, greedy Theo!"

Kind-hearted Happy could forgive Theo. Not I. If I get the chance I'll wring his lousy neck.

Hal's lawyers were less successful in getting a lead on Theo's cohorts. Hal hired private detectives. By then Happy and I had flown back to Honeyville, direct, to a small airport for glider enthusiasts west of town.

We arrived in the afternoon and went straight to Caring For Tots because we assumed that our infants would be stashed there. They were. Mrs. Wright had gone to do their laundry, again.

We discovered how easily Theo or a cohort could have slipped inside the facility and lured Timmy away with a McDonald's freebie toy, or whatever. The two Miss Carringtons were otherwise engaged from their primary task of looking after the children in their care. It was nap-time. Miss Carrington One was in the back room folding diapers. Miss Carrington Number Two had gone out the rear door to smoke a cigarette. Our Timmy had never taken easily to naps. He preferred playtime.

No point in making a complaint to the two Miss Carringtons. Too late for that to help our Timmy now. And I'm not one for suing. I decided to let Happy use her sweet talk on the women to glean what we could that might be helpful.

Happy tried. Tried hard. But these two sisters cared more for the continued success of their nursery business than to help us in any way. They shied like fillies confronted by snakes. No way were they going to truly describe that fateful afternoon. They'd given the police a skeletal description of their busy reasons for not noticing that Timmy went missing. They'd figured that was enough.

From the way they behaved, you'd have thought we were the guilty parties.

When miserable Mrs. Wright returned from doing the laundry, the Miss Carringtons treated her like a leper. As she was totally willing to accept blame, they poured in on to her as if a volcano had erupted lava all over this place. Happy and I were engulfed in their accusations like the trapped citizens of Pompeii, in the lava of Vesuvius.

No joy for us at Caring For Tots. We scooped up our daughters, Dorothy and Irish, sleepy as they were in their nap-time, dirty diapers and soiled clothes left on them by the not-so-meticulous Misses Carringtons, and went home to our pseudo mansion.

Surprise. There was a hillock of sympathy notes from our until-then-invisible elderly neighbours. Bunches of flowers too, including notes with ancient-style spidery writing pouring condolences. There were several offers to do babysitting in the long, hot afternoons to spare us from returning our babes to be hostages of the Misses Carringtons.

"Ah sho in-tends t'accept these offuhs," Happy declared, when Mrs. Wright announced that, due to the fact she had no green card to work in the USA, she would have to return to Britain.

Her stay in Kentucky had been anything but glorious. But we needed her to tend our Epsom house, and were really glad to take her to the airport with Happy's gift of local honey.

Personally, I'd have sooner given Mrs. Wright a heavy dose of laxative. Dorothy and Irish cooed ecstatically to have garnered all of Happy's daytime hours for their exclusive use. She had an endless job of buying diapers, changing diapers, washing diapers. There was no ready-to-go diaper company servicing this community of oldies. Although I imagine some of them needed diapers.

Two more days dragged on. No news from Hal's detectives. No breaks from the Honeyville police. They'd unlawfully leaked what the Miss Carringtons had told them, and the press was having a field day carving me up and Happy too.

We stopped reading the newspapers.

If we hadn't had the basic comfort of our lovemaking at night, I don't know how we'd have survived the ordeal of Timmy's kidnapping.

CHAPTER 15

As had happened before when Happy was involved in a case, she provided the break-through.

We'd had our instructions on where to make the drop of the $4 million by an SMS text message.

"Ah reckons them gangstuhs have destroyed the mobile. Broke it, or dumped it in a rivuh. But Ah knows from mah own phone how new tech-no-logy done can get a trace on thet phone. Even if broken up or dumped in wut they figuhs is a safe place."

The text message had come from near Belmont Racecourse, in New York. That was precisely in the same general area where the kidnappers had demanded we drop the $4 million. Their text message had read: "We will exchange Tim for package to be left in box Directors' Room, Belmont track." We were on a plane for JFK Airport within an hour of receiving the text message. This time we took our children with us.

A tenderness had emerged in my veins for our two daughters. I'd been spoiling them for the past two days.

Dorothy, who had a sweet tooth, craved chocolates with nuts. I knew they were bad for her, but I couldn't resist buying her favorite brand and over-indulging her craving. For Irish, who liked being rocked in my arms, I stayed up both nights with her rocking away, and every so often had been rewarded by one of her emerging smiles.

How I longed to spoil Tim!

Would we ever see him again? Could it happen that we'll pay his ransom, and then maybe hear nothing until one day a policeman will stumble on a tiny skeleton with a McDonald's toy clutched in its bony fingers. And that could be what was left of our Tim.

Happy felt optimistic. She'd got on to New York's top text message expert. He'd got on to our case straight away.

Police in the track area remembered us for solving the serial killers' murders of women jockeys, and of top Trainers. They were trying to be helpful. Trying!

The worst for Happy was her ever-pervading sense of guilt. "Ah should nevuh have stahted takin' them birth control pills. Ah should have all the babies God wants t'send me."

But she did continue taking them. I'd calmed her plaguing, gnawing pangs of remorse. "I don't think God's angry with you, sweetheart. Not for little white pills."

"They's blue," Happy wailed.

"Whatever color! The gangsters knew nothing about that, they knew that Fran had placed $4 million in my account, and that's what triggered this."

We arrived in the borough of Queens at twilight. The pressing need was to find a hotel that would accept infants: many did not. Echoes of our retirement-community golfing club of pseudo mansions.

Our friends in the police helped us locate a decent one where the cries of dozens of other infants wouldn't set off ours. Then there was the essential changing of diapers and preparation of Dorothy's food.

But there was no mother's milk for Irish. "Mah milk's done dried up," Happy moaned. "Just lahke wut happened with Tim."

Our son's name brought on a burst of tears. My optimistic Happy had broken down.

CHAPTER 16

With the hour approaching when the kidnappers expected us—according to a newer e-mail—to appear in the Directors' Room at Belmont Racecourse, we found we didn't have the correct IDs to be able to enter the place. Forget the Directors' Room: we couldn't even get past the security at the racecourse entrance.

It wasn't racing season. That had been moved to north New York State's Saratoga, in time honoured fashion from the days of pre-air conditioning, starting in the 1860s when Saratoga provided R & R for soldiers in the Civil War.

Happy's Kentucky accent didn't help. The officer in charge of admittance seemed to think she was pretending to have that accent in order to make a fool of him.

There were people viewing the racecourse's gardens. We recognized one of the policemen on duty: he'd been helpful when we came here escorting Sybil Sykes, the Hollywood actress who had caused more rubber necking than the horses in the Belmont Cup parade.

He told us we could go into the gardens. "Not one step further," his voice rapped like a tambourine.

Of course we didn't obey him. Our son's life was in the balance. Visit gardens? Hell, no! I might have looked like a terrorist carrying a heavy suitcase that could have been filled with dynamite instead of $4 million in cash. Whatever, I was going to get into the Directors' Room on time.

We did.

There was nobody there.

"How come them gangster folk could get into this raceco'se? Sho 'nuf, Ah don't ex-pect t'see them heah."

But there was a box set down in the center of this imposing room with fine old paintings of other-era horses staring down on the box. It had an open top inviting our cash.

I spoke out loud. "Whoever you are, wherever you are: you don't get a penny until we get our son Tim."

A ghostly, bottled oral message came from the wall." Your son Tim will be at the Bronx Zoo in exactly one hour. Leave the money, and make it snappy or the zoo will close."

I didn't hesitate. I dumped the contents of my suitcase into the huge open box, shut its lid, abandoned our suitcase and raced with Happy for the door. We never looked over our shoulders to identify a bagman.

Thank God our taxi driver had waited for us. Happy hadn't paid him. Kentucky hillbilly style she knew better than to trust he'd be at the gate if we'd paid the outward bound fare.

That taxi stayed just within the limits of getting a police escort to the nearest jail, what with driving five miles an hour beyond what's legal.

The Bronx Zoo? It's an enormous place. Where, oh God! Where were we to look for Tim?

Happy had the answer. "Them ele-phants is what he lahkes. Always ele-phants when the zoo animal toys got given out."

We zoomed to the elephants' area. It was huge too. So many, and some preparing for their evening naps, but one small elephant was placidly accepting peanuts from *our son*.

"Tim!"

My son! He'd heard me call out to him, but Tim merely waved with his free hand and continued to give peanuts to the elephant.

"Tim!" Happy called out. This time he waved us toward him. He was alone, except for the little elephant. There was no convoy of gangsters.

Happy threw herself to her knees to grasp Tim. He reached over her embracing arms to continue to feed the elephant.

Did he look sick? No. Did he appear to have lost weight? No. Tim was being Tim: independent, doing what he wanted.

A guard approached and sang out, "Closing time. Closing time," in the chant of my British old era timekeepers "five o'clock and all is well."

And all was well.

Tim understood the guard was closing shop. He scattered his remaining peanuts into the elephant's ground and finally *finally* turned to us.

"Hello," he said. "Where you been?"

CHAPTER 17

Tim had discovered M&M's during his sojourn with the kidnappers. He munched on them all day long, seldom offering one single candy to Dorothy. He knew she craved them, but he'd been returned to us a very self-centered young person.

We were holed up in the same hotel in Queens, waiting for orders from Hal. At least, this hotel had a babysitting service. I could make the rounds of Manhattan's loan companies to see how I could manage to extend that heavy load of the five hundred thousand I'd had to take out on short term at an extremely high rate of interest. That, to complete the $4 million ransom. And how was I ever going to repay Hal, Filipa and my other friends who'd given me those outright gifts of the rest of the money? I don't own any real estate, and not even a car to pledge for collateral. But I'm a Trainer, and I knew I'd damn well better train some horses to win big purses. Particularly Hal's horses.

Hal had selected a marvellous name for the million dollar yearling we'd bought for him in Dubai: Happy's Escape. That was in honor of my darling wife, and how she'd evaded her abductors by outriding them across the desert to the Nadj Al Sheba track's racing stables.

Happy's Escape had proved to be a slow learner. To start with, his withers didn't grow up to match his powerful backside until he was well into his two-year-old season. Also, he'd been mucked about so much during the time that Happy's abductors were trying to sell him to Hal, that he'd developed a fretful personality. Rather like our son Tim.

He was very demanding, and picky about his feed.

"Put some honey in them oats," Hal had advised.

Hal called to congratulate us on Tim's safe return. In a harder voice, he added: "I want to see Happy's Escape win in a good race, in the next few weeks in Saratoga."

"Sure, Hal. Do my best." I rang off, but which race? And how could I prepare Happy's Escape in so short a time? What with firing Theo, and moving both of Hal's horses to livery stables, winning would be a chancy thing.

And where were we going to live in Saratoga? A family of five, at the top of that resort's season. What with its music festival on, plus all of New York State's top horsemen, I was hard pressed to find lodgings. No room at the inns.

Hal came through with the answer. He booked us into the most exclusive, expensive hotel: the Gideon Putnam. Conventional, traditional, catering to the finest grandest of horsemen for several generations it was a haven for such as us but at the same time a challenge.

Happy wailed: "Ah ain't got no clothes fittin' fo' Saratoga's finest."

Both of us worried that our "chillun" might disturb elderly guests or be disturbed by late night revelers.

We were all right. The children, like pet dogs in a parade, somehow realized this hotel was not a playground and they were to keep very quiet.

I filled in all the paperwork for the two horses and myself, and was soon working both of them properly on morning and evening gallops.

No sooner had I straightened out the schedule for Hal's horses, than I received an e-mail from Fran Purcell demanding that I run her Sweet Song at Saratoga. Fran had bought the American-based two-year-olds out of the estate of our murdered friend Sybil Sykes, and along with poor dead Munchie's horse, Fran had quite an imposing stable on this side of the pond.

I flew down to Newark to meet her plane from Heathrow. Of course, pennypinching Fran had come Economy. Sir Arthur Snodgrass was on the same plane, but had arrived First Class. I drove both of them north to

Saratoga, attempting during most of the trip to explain that none of her horses were fit to challenge the finest of New York's.

"Marylou Whitney won The Travers here," Fran protested.

"Yes, after winning the Belmont, where she'd bested the winner of that year's Kentucky Derby and the Preakness. Fran, I'd dearly love to get you a sizeable prize, but realistically —"

Fran interrupted in a curt tone: "You want me to change trainers? Harold East has been telephoning . . ."

Harold East, my nemesis, always just across Epsom's green, always ready to snatch my Owners. "Fran, I'm going to tell you the bare facts. Sweet Song has developed cracks in her feet. We've fed her for her hooves internally and treated them externally to improve the condition. You didn't want the expense of a top class blacksmith. We've had to make do with a low paid friend of mine. He sent Sweet Song for x-rays which showed that the main bone in one hoof had rotated slightly. We improved that condition by choosing different shoes for her. But I don't believe I can run her on Saratoga's hard surface. Rain is forecast for late August, but we haven't seen it yet to have a bit of give in the ground."

Fran wasn't about to shut up. "What about my other horses?" "We might be able to run Verdi's Aida.

"She's important to me. My best ever operatic role was in *Aida*."

"Yeah, well if she's fit and has enough condition, I'll try to find the right race for her."

Sir Arthur Snodgrass added his stuttered comments: "I-I-I'd lo-lo-love to-to-to wa-wa-watch Fran re-re-receive a tro-tro-trophy!"

"Maybe you will." I concentrated on my driving. We were entering the high hills of Saratoga's legendary area. We passed white-railed equine estates. We saw run-down farms with pyramids of August melons jettisoned for sale on the highway under lopsided umbrellas that looked like the broken wing of a grounded bird.

Did Fran and Sir Arthur check in at the Gideon Putnam? Lucky me, they did not. Too expensive for pennypinching Fran, who earned $20 million last year for her best selling album of country songs.

I left them off at what I'd term a Bed 'N Breakfast.

Hal and Clara Murphy came over to the Gideon Putnam from their leased local mansion to visit us in the hotel's garden. Over an opulent

Canadian-style tea ordered by Clara, she questioned my Happy about Saratoga. "You like it here?"

"Ah loves it heah. This be the town wheah Rick got me mah ring 'n asked me t'wed him."

"It is a good place to bring children?"

"Sho is! And lookee there, see them chipmunks? They's so tame they think we be their guests. Watuh's awful cold in them springs, but Ah lahkes thet. Don't believe in them heated pools, except fo' hosses wut has the arth-ur-it-is. Air's pure heah, wut with them millions of trees in these heah A-dir-on-dacks. 'N evenin's Rick takes me to the music festival. We sits on the hill 'n heahs the music fo' free. At the track, we holds hands under them old shade trees near the paddock, wheah he fust tol' me he loved me."

We couldn't dally with that over-laden Canadian tea. Happy had listed some of Saratoga's best facets, but she neglected to add a downside: there were few babysitters available in a town of racing folk. We needed to go upstairs and take over the kids' never-ending feeding and changing of diapers.

As if my harvest of Owners wasn't big enough, what with the presence here of Fran, Hal and Clara, I had a long telephone call from Fran's duo partner, Filipa. "I want to buy a horse at the yearling sales. Rus says no, I don't need one. But I want one, and have enough money from my new contract to afford one. Will you go to the Saratoga sales?"

Sure, you bet I'd go to the sales. And you can bet your bottom dollar that I'd do my best for Filipa to get her a winner. A new owner, yet she'd contributed one million toward Tim's ransom money.

For Happy, this news was wonderful. Filipa was her very special friend, whom she'd helped in the cure of Little Betty. On the negative side was the fact that Filipa's controversial husband was arriving with her.

Rus, the rat who'd tried to seduce my Happy!

CHAPTER 18

Never rains, but it pours? Not only did Happy get chased again by Rus, but a new Australian seducer loomed into our lives. Happy had renewed contact with her erstwhile employer, that great racehorse Owner Mrs. Marylou Whitney, and through her had met this seducer.

Mrs.W, as she was known when Happy first met her in 2004, had invited us to her big charity do. She had formerly given it at her private estate, arriving at the party by horse-drawn carriage, like Queen Elizabeth does for Royal Ascot. This time we were invited to what was now a charity event. We couldn't afford the tickets, but were given two by Filipa.

Fran skipped the party because she wouldn't make the charity donation. Filipa introduced us to a man sharing her table, a fellow Australian. He didn't use Aussie-speak like Filipa's outback husband. He'd been educated at Eton and Cambridge, but somewhere in his life he'd learned a few tricks from brothels.

His name: Jock Hoge. Honestly, he was a distant cousin of the Hoges of England's banking family Hoges. And, he too had made his money with banks, except that he sold his Australian chain of banks and was in cash.

Jock Hoge had paid for a lot of plastic surgery. He'd had his sunken chin enhanced, his drooping eyelids lifted, his parrot neck altered into a maypole. A dentist had capped his front top and bottom teeth, but Jock stopped him there and as a result Jock's smile was like clean surf bordered by dirty seaweed.

Shrewd guy, the first thing he said to my Happy was: "Buy me a good horse. I want to be an Owner in your stable." Simultaneously, like the Welsh poet Dylan Thomas who greeted women by stretching out his hands to their breasts, Jock reached out to Happy's breasts and grabbed them!

While Happy was swivelling to get away from Jock, he swerved her to the ballroom's dance floor and proceeded to push his lead leg into her crotch like an apache dancer in a Paris lowlife *quartier bal.*

Because he was six feet four and Happy barely five feet tall, her face was too near his nether regions. I saw him trying to push her head down farther toward them.

No!

I was in a conundrum. I won't have any man grab my wife's precious breasts. I'll never permit her to be put into a compromising situation. But, as always in this business of training, I needed new Owners. Hell, though, I'd do without this Jock Hoge. I'd sooner go broke than have him around my wife, maybe for daily visits to our stable.

What was it with these Australian men that they go after my sweet little wife?

This problem started last year when I went to Australia for the Melbourne Cup but, although loving the horses as she did, Happy had accompanied me really to help Filipa with her invalid baby, Little Betty. Filipa's husband, Rus, became a pest straight away. He flirted outrageously with my Happy. She didn't exactly encourage him. However she did like escaping from Filipa's unhappy house, after curing Little Betty. When Rus offered to drive her around Australia's top tourist attractions, Happy accepted gratefully.

Rus showed her Melbourne's sights and even drove Happy to Sydney and back so she could hear the infamous Heidi sing in *Madama Butterfly* at its architecturally whacky opera house. They laughed together and sang that damn *Waltzing Matilda* until I had to buy plugs for my ears. But there was no hanky panky, not with my Baptist.

Happy had turned her back on Rus in London, after she saw him using Little Betty as a decoy to go out from Fran's flat, when Filipa moved there to become part of the Purcell duo. Happy had gone to a pharmacy to buy cough medicine for Little Betty and saw Rus pushing Little Betty in her stroller out into the rain to go to a wine shop. That spelled the end of Happy's friendship with Rus.

But now there was Jock Hoge. And how was I going to free Happy from this outrage on the dance floor? My dear Happy learned how to ride bareback as a ten-year-old but had never had dancing lessons. She had no idea of what to do not to appear ridiculous.

Happy well knew I needed new Owners. But my Baptist felt she needed to draw the line with Jock. In the days when she was a smoker and fellows tried to be touchy-feely, Happy simply burned them with a cigarette. How was she to handle disgusting Jock, who was a potential new Owner?

On that dance floor she simply did her Dogpatch-style jig, that imitated a chicken laying an egg, and hurried to the party's exit. Did I dump Jock and follow her? I certainly did.

No sweat. Jock's star dimmed the next night at the sales. Jock, who was like a fake mahogany treasure chest made of ordinary pine with a thin veneer, preened like a peacock during his moments at the sales rubbing shoulders with racing's elite and feeling one with them.

Jock's clothes were impeccable. He dressed like an English country gentleman. Suits tailored by London's Anderson & Shepherd. Shirts from Jermyn Street's Turnbull & Asser. Shoes by Lobb of St. James's. But his manners were distinctly Australian Outback.

He bulldozed through the groups of horsemen. He spoke loudly, and while his accent was from Oxford, the tone was unacceptably rude.

Jock made his mistake when he chose the horse he wanted me to buy and put in my stables. I could see that the horse was a no-hoper. Awful. In the tradition of my trade, as determined to do the right thing as would a physician who has taken the Hypocrites oath, I tried to guide him toward a useful yearling. He wouldn't hear of it. No, it had to be the ghastly monster.

Quietly, I said "There are horses for sale here that will be snapped up by an Amish Community from Pennsylvania. These people don't use cars or trucks. They have their own style small black covered wagons pulled by horses. This horse you've chosen should end up with the Amish."

Thank God, Jock insisted on that horse and I had my out. Goodbye Jock Hoge.

He didn't leave us without one more attempt to press Happy's breasts. Jock smirked to her, "I hear you're a nursing mother. I'd love to taste some of that milk."

Now that she knew that Jock wouldn't be an Owner with us, Happy gave him a swift kick not too far from the balls. He rushed from us, grabbing his private parts, groaning from pain.

Well done, my Happy!

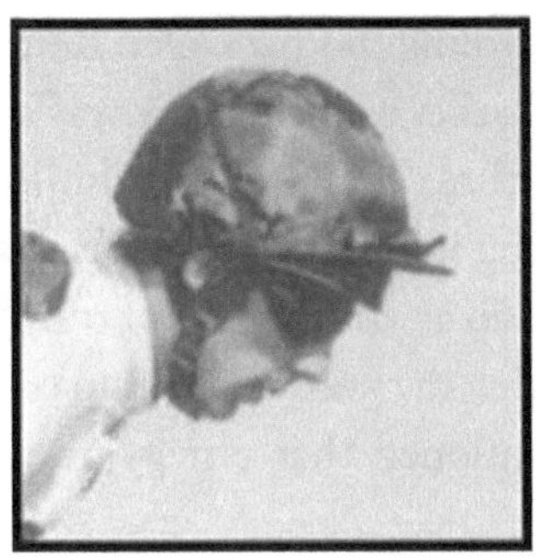

CHAPTER 19

We won two races at Saratoga. Hal went home satisfied to Canada. Fran, who also didn't need the money, did well with her Song filly because I'd managed to cure the hooves' malady.

Filipa had wasted her trip across the pond, and got hell from Rus for the expense. Her fellow Australian, Jock Hoge, fast-tracked to Sydney.

Happy and I returned to our pseudo colonial mansion. By the following afternoon Happy was back at our Honeyville gym. I returned Hal's horses to the stables located sixteen miles away, confident they'd do well there following the success of Anchor in Saratoga. After evening stables I joined Happy at the gym.

She'd parked our "chillun" with one of our friendly elderly neighbours. Now we had a list of them who'd offered to help us during our ordeal over Timmy.

No need for Caring For Tots by the uncaring Miss Carringtons. Will I ever forget that all those two harridans wanted was to keep their business going despite their publicized too obvious lack of supervision of our Timmy? And neither sister had offered to help in any way towards Timmy's rescue?

The atmosphere at the gym had improved since we'd last been there. The pall caused by two murders of the members no longer dismayed *prospective* club members. We saw several attractive new faces.

Happy warmed to a young mother called Rona Blossom, who brought her tot to the gym in a basket as if the baby was a bushel of potatoes.

Rona spent two to three hours on treadmills every afternoon, only interrupting the exercising in order to bare a breast and feed her child.

Quite content to gossip across the rails of treadmills, Rona told Happy the story of her own life, she wanted to know all about Happy's, and then—whispering—mentioned that our gym's co-manager was in love with the accountant.

"Heard thet," Happy whispered in return. "No surprise. If he'd lose his paunch he'd be as good-lookin' as a movie star."

Rona returned to the subject of their own early years. Rona, a brunette, had a Brooklyn accent with ethnic overtones. "Once when I was a kid playing in the park, I saw Barbra Streisand. Come back to Brooklyn visitin' her family. No shit. Now *she's* what I'd call a real movie star, not like these cookie cutouts we got nowadays. All look alike. Same make-up, same dark roots to their hair, nothing special about any of them."

"Ah tol' y'all thet mah husband's a racehoss trainuh. He gits all kind o' rich folk wut c'n affo'd a hoss. Mostly they be singin' stahs 'cause one brings in anothuh. But Ah found him a movie stah. Real one. Sybil Sykes. Could sing, could act."

"I remember her. She bombed in *Hogtown*, played the Daisy Mae character as a hooker."

"Yeah man. Ah's got the video. Played it 'n played it till it done wo'e out. She wanted t'hire me. Honest to Betsy, t'teach huh how t'speak lahke a Kentucky hillbilly. Ah didn't take money: she came into our stable."

"You mean she had a horse with your husband?"

"Sho 'nuf. A filly, and man can she evuh run! Fran Purcell has thet filly now. Not 'cause Sybil didn't learn no Kentucky styles. She sho did. In London, near wheah we's got us a little house in Epsom, Sybil made a big success of the stage musical."

"No shit? I wondered what happened to her. Haven't seen her in any new movies." Rona never was told by Happy that Sybil had been murdered and that we'd been in Sybil's dressing room only minutes after the strangler used a bathrobe's belt to choke her. Happy was distracted by another member's complaints.

Una Probit, the best looking of the nursing mothers, was loud and arrogant. Her roar carried all through the gym's three rooms. "I've paid my membership in full, and now you're telling me I'm getting the heave-ho? The hell I am. I'll get a lawyer. You can't throw me out. I believe in litigation. I'll sue."

The very plain, overweight co-manager, Soledad, crouched in a corner as if machine gun bullets were spraying the room. At the best of times she kept well away from Una, aware that the contrast between her own unattractive face and body looked worse when near Una's gorgeous attributes, waited without answering back. Why? What was she waiting for?

Not for her co-manager. Our pretty friend had left early for the afternoon to go to a ball game where the pitcher on the local team had recently become her boyfriend.

Not for the ever-present doctor: he blandly continued wide-stepping on the biggest treadmill.

It was the gym's accountant who dealt with Una and came to the manager's rescue. He said in a placating tone: "Una, you've paid your membership, but I think you haven't read the club rules. The way I understand them, this gym became a club in order to be able to choose its members."

Glamorous Una didn't become sullen or make a face. She'd learned long ago that smiling was her stock in trade. She widened her mouth, ran her tongue very provocatively over her enlarged lips. She brushed herself against the accountant, her breasts grazing his left side.

The accountant reacted as many men would. He grinned. He said: "Una, go home. I'll come around and see you later."

Una stripped off her gym suit, fully aware that the doctor was ogling her, and calmly dressed in her loose maternity clothes. She fastened a tight bra over her breasts, donned the skimpy bikini pants, hauled a loose shift over her head and laughed her way out of the gym.

"Good riddance," Rona said. "Never could stand her uppity ways, coming into this place as if she owned it."

"Ah wonduhs how come she lets huh kid breast feed? Ain't she feared she'll git them outta shape?"

"Those breasts? If I didn't know that kid of hers was ten months at it, until he's as fat as a piglet, I'd of been believing those breasts were made of silicone."

Both girls laughed, and the aura improved in the gym.

Rona said: "Listen, kiddo. I think I can improve the way you been speaking. Just down this street we got a good library where there are linguaphone machines can teach you to speak correctly. I been using them myself."

Happy didn't comment on the fact that Rona's use of those linguaphones hadn't improved *her* accent. She wasn't one to criticize: Happy liked to build up people's self-esteem, not knock them when they were down. She said: "Sho 'nuf. Ah'll come with y'all. But Ah thinks them machines is fo' furriners, 'n Ah was bo'n raght heah in Kentucky."

The manager dimmed the lights. Like at a country dance, dimming the lights meant it was Good Night Ladies, and gentlemen too.

The doctor and I left with the women, but the accountant stayed back with his books.

For some reason I looked over my shoulder as I shut the gym door.

Our gargoyle of a co-manager, Soledad, had a look of total contentment.

CHAPTER 20

Hal Murphy was on the blower that evening. He wanted to know if his horses had travelled well returning to Kentucky. And then he hit me with a big one. "Rick, I want you to head for Hong Kong—the Sha Tin and Happy Valley racecourses. Their names are about as much as I know about the racing in what's now Red China! Haven't been to Hong Kong since it ceased being British. Find out when the races are run, and when my Anchor and Happy's Escape will have their best chances of winning."

His wife Clara came on the blower too: "I'd love to go to Japan. Could you make some inquiries about running our horses there? You'll remember, I did say I wanted to go to Nakayama."

Dear, crippled Clara, always a good sport. Ready to go halfway across the world with her elbows in those crutches. But why Japan? I could well understand going to China in this Olympics year, but would the Hong Kong races take place at a convenient time to take in some of the Olympic games?

I went to my computer, got on to Google, and did my research.

CHAPTER 21

Arriving at its airport, we found that Hong Kong was certainly a busy place. In our section of its huge airport were the horsemen who'd chosen to run their stars here rather than in the Breeders' Cup, but there were also all the Olympic equestrian competitors jostling us for their luggage from two planes that had arrived simultaneously with ours.

Happy held on to Irish and Dorothy, while I struggled to control Timmy as I gave over our passports to the waiting officials.

It was worse in the Customs section, because all of us had bridles, girths, and bits while the equestrian chaps were collecting similar gear and swearing these were not new nor had originally been purchased in China.

While waiting in an impossibly long queue for taxis, I had the pleasant surprise of bumping into an old school friend, Dubber McDonald. And I do mean bumped, we almost pushed each other over into the alley. Fatter, his moon-shaped face very red, and his heavy arms flailing, he gulped out, "If it isn't get-up-and-go Rick!"

"I thought you'd emigrated to Canada. What's that gear you're carrying? Surely not for a racehorse."

"Always the curious bugger! I'm going to change your name to Skinny. How'd you stay so thin?"

"Riding out morning and evening gallops. I'm a racehorse trainer. And you?" I didn't add that daily sex had something to do with being thin.

"I earn my pennies by being a banker. Ride show horses for pleasure. Dressage doesn't keep you thin."

"Where you housed?"

"Hong Kong has no Olympic village as such. That's in Beijing. I'm to be quartered in the Penfold Park area."

"We are too. Shall we share a taxi there?" Dubber looked at Happy and our three infants with their mountain of luggage. He shook his head. "No. Promised I'd do that with three of my dressage buddies. Here's one coming now," he yelled across the taxi queue: "Gopher, meet my school buddy. Went to Eton together. Used to get free gallops by working the horses at the Windsor equestrian center."

Gopher, a hairy individual with a clipped beard but whose short-sleeved shirt showed hair sprawling down his arms and hands, waved heartily but he didn't relinquish his place in the queue.

I waved in return, but wouldn't have recognized him later except for all that hair. But once I'd settled Happy and the "chillun" in our small apartment, I went down to the building's lobby to look for a bar for a whisky. In the bar I was approached by this same hairy equestrian rider, who shouted out my name. He had a large voice, like Hal's, and Hal's Canadian accent. "You! Rick, I need to talk to you aboot Dubber." He pronounced about "aboot."

"What about Dubber?" I raised my glass inviting Gopher to a drink. His was a martini, not scotch.

"He's sick. Came down with a terrible fever tonight. A vicious cold, or flu. Probably something he picked up on the plane. So many people do catch flu on planes. He could hardly speak, but asked me to find you to ask if you'd exercise his horse."

"A dressage horse? But I haven't done that since I was at school." "Please! Dubber said he couldn't trust anyone but you to not mess up his horse. Famous horse in Canada. Has a fan club there. The Wonder club. His horse's called Wonder. And for good reason. He's a wonder."

"More reason for me to not get involved." I poured two fingers of whisky into my waiting glass. "He must be very valuable. If anything happens to him while I'm on board, I could get sued or worse."

"No. He's insured. And Wonder knows what to do. All you'll need add is that he gets his fresh air and goes through his paces."

I remembered how red in the face Dubber had been this morning. I thought I recognized the onset of the flu. I understood how important it was to Dubber that his Wonder be exercised by a reliable friend. Wonder could be hobbled to order to rule him out of the Olympics.

"Fresh air?" I asked. "Why do you mention fresh air? Surely the dressage horses will be exercised at Sha Tin where they'll compete."

"Sure, exercised at the Sha Tin course. But haven't you heard? All our horses, your racehorses included, will be stabled in skyscrapers. High up. Black hole of Calcutta in reverse."

I shook my head. Of course I'd read in the pamphlets sent us that conditions would be crowded for racehorses: but weren't all of us, people and animals, crowded in Hong Kong? I said: "Sorry, but I'm awfully busy. I've got three racehorses here that have to win."

"We're all busy. We all have to win at our particular sports. Give this a think. You might even enjoy yourself. It's a privilege to have a ride on Wonder. He really is a dream of a horse."

"The owner of my horses, Hal Murphy, is coming in tonight. I'll ask him how he'd feel about my exercising Wonder. That's the best I —"

Wild-eyed, Gopher interrupted: "Hal Murphy! He's one of the biggest financial supporters of our Canadian equestrian team. You're on! For sure!" He downed the rest of his martini and left the bar. I sipped thoughtfully at my drink. I knew that my main concern at the Hong Kong races was to please Hal. I sucked at the ice from the bottom of my glass.

I determined once again that I'd do my best for Hal.

CHAPTER 22

When I joined Happy upstairs in our three-bedroom apartment, she was trying to communicate with an aged, very worn Chinese woman who spoke no English. Over her shoulder, Happy said: "Rick, this be Amah. She be a live-in babysitter hired by the Murphys fo' our chillun".

Happy held up a diaper, folded it lengthwise, and took two diaper pins from a collection. The aged Chinese woman shook her grey head, refolded the diaper into a triangle, disposed of one diaper pin and proceeded to remove an old diaper and wrap the triangle around Irish, who was very wet and screaming.

Screaming stopped.

Dorothy held up a cut finger to Amah. It had a dirty Band-Aid. Amah understood. She produced a clean Band-Aid from a pocket and put it on Dorothy's finger.

Timmy watched these proceedings with intense interest. He didn't approach Amah. He went to Happy's open suitcase and found a package of M&M's, which he devoured. When Amah seemed not to notice *he* was being naughty, he gave her a huge smile.

Happy wasn't smiling. She seemed anxious and nonplussed. When Amah took over the unpacking of our suitcases, Happy went to the fridge and found a bottle of orange juice. She was about to drink her juice straight, but Amah produced a small bottle of vodka from another of her many pockets. She poured the vodka into the orange juice with a toothless grin.

I said: "Darling Happy, d'you remember when we first arrived at Epsom and we watched our housekeeper Mrs. Rea take over? I've a feeling this Amah's going to give us a repeat." I laughed, hugged Happy, took a sip of her spiked orange juice and relaxed on our kingsized bed. All I could do for the moment, with Amah still in the room, was to relax on the bed. No sex, not in front of Amah.

"Wut took y'all so long downstairs?" Happy curled up beside me: she wasn't going to sit in a chair just because a new housekeeper-cum-nanny was present.

"Met that friend of Dubber's, the fellow he called Gopher. The fellow wants me to exercise a famous dressage horse for Dubber. Gave as an excuse that Dubber has the flu. From what I recall of our student days, it might be that Dubber has a hangover from drink or drugs. I do admit, though, I thought his red face indicated he could be coming down with a cold."

"Yo'r Dubber cain't be in the Ol-ym-pics if'n he takes drugs."

"That's right. I don't know what I'd be getting myself into if I promise to help out with this horse until Dubber feels better. And how do you feel, after that long, long flight?"

"Ah's lookin' fo'ward t'tonight. Y'all gits so romantic in a new bed. But, now, tell me about this hoss o' Dubber's. And, what's dressage?"

"A term for specialty motions by a horse. Makes them seem like they're dancing."

"Dancin' ain't fo' hosses. It's speed y'all wants from a hoss."

"Yes. From a racehorse. But darling, remember there are so many kinds of horses. In ancient times they carried men in armour, and in chariots, to battle. Strength rather than speed was what was needed. Strength and endurance. In business, there were the cart horses. Huge horses were needed to pull trolleys, to pull vans loaded with steel rods or beer kegs or whatever."

"Ah knows thet. Pappy had him a hoss what pulled the plow in our fields or pulled the cart wut took us'n t'chu'ch. But he didn't do no dancin'. Rick, can *you* make a hoss dance?"

"I used to. At the Windsor equitation center. Long time ago."

"Yeah man! Rick, Ah wants t'see thet. Ah wants t'see this hoss wut dances."

"Tomorrow morning, my love. We'll take a peek at Wonder. I must do that before the Murphys arrive. I don't want to jeopardize my job with Hal if the horse is hopeless. The Murphys are due to arrive at noon. And, we may want to take the kids to explore Hong Kong's sights, in good time."

Forget Hong Kong's sights. First I wanted to use that welcoming kingsize bed. Happy was glad to order in room service, so we could stay on our kingsize bed. Amah fed the "chillun" and we two had a great night of lovemaking.

In the morning I did my stables thing. Not easy, unboxing our horses and escorting them into and out of the skyscraper's elevators. Then box them again to move them to their gallops. I managed, but I dreaded having to do this twice a day every day during our stay in Hong Kong.

Having done my duty toward Hal's horses, I went in search of Wonder. Happy had been with me all the way. She helped ride out Happy's Escape, and that filly adored her.

Wonder didn't adore me.

He neighed and rose on his hind legs and carried on as if his stall was on fire. It took some doing to calm him, but Happy's magic hands did the trick. We boxed him and led him out to the practice ground for the dressage horses which would compete in the games.

And Wonder danced.

My dressage skills were very rusty. I felt like a virgin on her wedding night: I knew what to do, more or less, but hadn't a clue how to do it with panache.

Happy watched; her rosebud mouth wide open, her sky-blue eyes narrowed. "Rick, y'all looked be-au-ti-ful. Ah thinks y'all should do this all the time. Fo'git racin'."

Working Wonder as best I could, I didn't put much credence to Happy's suggestion. Would I ever quit racing? Please God, no! Before I left Britain I'd read an account of that famous jockey, Pat Eddery, and how he'd missed racing so much that in 2007 he'd returned to it as a Trainer. After thirty-seven years in the saddle, when he'd won over four thousand races in England, and took the jockeys' title eleven times, he was satisfied to come back into racing as a Trainer.

Eddery had plenty to say about horses: "The trick is in keeping the horses sound, healthy, and their minds right. Horses are like glass. They break easily."

Wonder didn't look like he'd break easily. But that could prove deceptive. I treated him as if he was as valuable as Anchor, and gave him some of the water and hay I'd brought by airfreight from Kentucky.

"I could get into serious trouble if anything happens to this horse," I said when we'd brought him back up to his box. "I'm playing with dynamite, helping out Dubber with Wonder."

There wasn't much time for Hong Kong sights. In the end it was only Timmy who wanted to leave the apartment. Dorothy and Irish were content in their room with Amah.

"Let's us find a McDonald's," was Timmy's idea of seeing the sights. When I pointed out a traditional sampan in the harbour, Timmy wrinkled his nose. "Pretty boat," he said. "But the water, it stinks. This whole city smells awful."

Happy laughed that away. "Mah Paw's Chick Sales smells wo'se than the harbour. Thet othuth stink? Ah thinks as it's just dried fish. Should have fried 'em, like we does our'n catfish."

Timmy did like the swimming pool at The Peninsula, where the Murphys were booked to stay. We'd barely made it to the lobby when Clara called out to us from above her crutches: "Rick! Happy! We made it! We're here, and raring to see all there's to see."

We didn't go touring. We bought a swim suit for Timmy, and one for Happy. The two of them splashed around while we three had drinks in the shade of a splendid fountain.

Clara likes her whisky. She belts down a tumbler-full quicker than a reformed member of Alcoholics Anonymous who's just broken the pledge.

She said: "I do want to go on a tour that takes us to see the largest seated Buddha in all of Asia. Huge bronze Buddha. But not right now. Let's go shopping, Happy."

I thought that idea would suit Happy, but she shook her head. "Dear Miz Clara, Ah thanks y'all fo' ever'thing. Sho nuf, Ah'd love t'go shoppin'." She meant particularly if Clara was paying. "But fust, Ah needs t'send a fax to mah friend Rona in Honeyville. Will y'all let me use yo'r Business Centuh in this heah ho-tel? And git faxes back?"

Hal said, reassuringly. "Come on, Happy. You don't even need to ask for something like that."

"Ah's so grateful to y'all, fo' so much. Fo' this swim we just had, fo' the big apahtment, but most of all fo' the nanny: Amah."

Clara interrupted. "I thought you might need someone to help with your children. I remembered in Epsom you had that good housekeeper, Mrs. Rea before that incorrectly-named Mrs. Wright. You'd never escape the little ones to do all you need to do in Hong Kong, if you didn't have a nanny. Is she any good?"

"She's great. Ah knows how to feed, keep clean and love mah chillun. But Ma'am, Ah sho don't know nothin' about dis-ci-pline fo' chillun. Amah do. Ah's got lots t'learn from huh." Happy left us to send her fax to Rona. When Happy returned she kissed Timmy goodbye and left The Peninsula with Clara.

Hal ordered a chocolate ice cream to keep Timmy contented while we talked business. "Aboot Anchor, I think he's such a great horse that he should win any sprint race we put him into."

"No, sir. I mean, no, Hal. Really, I truly appreciate these years I've had training Anchor, but he can't win the big ones."

"Then find a race he can win."

"I intend to do just that. And, uh, Hal, there's something else. A school pal of mine Dubber McDonald, asked me to exercise his dressage horse, Wonder. They're here for the Olympics Games. To compete."

"No problem with that. I know Dubber. I've seen him on Wonder. He could win a medal for Canada. But, why has he asked you to exercise his horse? They're a duo. Dubber's a zephyr when he's aboard Wonder."

"Dubber's sick. Says he has flu. I don't know what's really the matter with him, but there'll be no medal for him if he doesn't get well in time to do his bit."

"I'll ask this hotel to recommend a good doctor for Dubber. Meanwhile, I want to show you the Happy Valley racecourse. That's where Anchor will win. I know it well. It's a jewel. Some people think it was placed in the center of downtown Hong Kong. Not at all, it predated those skyscrapers by well over a hundred years. This city was an insignificant fishing port until 1842, when China ceded it to Britain in the Treaty of Nanking, marking the first of the opium wars between China and Britain. In 1898

Britain took control of Hong Kong Island, the Kowloon Peninsula, and the New Territories and held on to them for ninety-nine years. I came here in the 1950s and made my first dollar gambling at Happy Valley."

It was almost dark by the time we reached the race course. We'd fed Timmy at McDonald's and he'd gotten his share of freebee toys. We'd passed parks where the evening groups of Tai Chi experts were going through their graceful motions.

Happy Valley glowed from the neatly spaced overhead lights that illuminated its tracks. Able to accommodate thirty thousand spectators, it was merely a quarter full for tonight's events. But Hal, as he so often does, soon recognized some friends from the racing world.

"Good on ye Hal."

"Come to win some of Happy Valley's prize money?"

Hal's two acquaintances were Australians. He introduced them. "Meet John Ridley and Stuart Mitchell. They're members of Australia's Jockey Club. Hey fellows, you among the top execs for the Olympic events?"

"We're playing hooky tonight, coming to Happy Valley's racing when the Olympic games will be played out at Sha Tin."

"Our Sheilas stayed home so far. They won't arrive before the final medals are given out. That will probably be at Sha Tin, although some distribution of prizes might take place at the Beas River facilities, near the golf club, on the Hong Kong Jockey Club's property. Could happen. Sha Tin's so huge: with its seventy acres or more."

We strolled through the nearly empty stands, and every so often I bought a treat for Timmy, which invariably he threw into garbage cans.

Timmy just had to make an untoward remark. In his shrill baby talk voice, he asked: "Why do the people here have slit eyes?"

Hal showed himself to be ultra-understanding. He was only too familiar with Timmy's psychological problems cued by the kidnapping which ended with Hal paying some of the ransom. "Some folks are always different. But this is China's land, and here we're the ones who are different. Here we're called the Round-Eyes."

"I like my eyes," Timmy said, sulking.

The Australian Jockey Club members left us. Who could blame them? If this wasn't Happy Valley on a non-racing day, Timmy would have been banned at any racecourse where age eighteen is the minimum age.

"See the Turf course?" Hal pointed it out. "That's where Mighty Moron should run in the ten furlong handicap."

"Got you!"

"We won't aim for the Queen Elizabeth II Cup. Too late in the year. Can't wait around for that. With seven hundred races in Hong Kong every season we'll find another sure-thing for Happy's Escape."

Timmy wet his pants.

Nothing to do about that except to head home.

In the taxi, Hal said: "Maybe you should move here to this Wan Chai district. Closer to the course. And Happy could shop for groceries at the Wong Nal Chung complex. I'll look into this tomorrow. The ideal place for you would be The Trillium boutique apartments. You'd be near Causeway Bay. How does that sound?"

I nodded, gratefully. I couldn't say much because Timmy had started to whimper, then bawl. I truly love my son, but just the same I felt very relieved to return to the Penfold apartment and hand him over to Amah for dry, clean clothes.

CHAPTER 23

Happy had accumulated another mountain of goods in Hong Kong's markets. With what we'd already brought with us, I began to think she was trying to make our baggage look like the Himalayas.

"Lookee at wut all Ah got!"

Like most women she wanted to show off her purchases and win applause for the bargains.

Lamely, I said. "Lot of stuff." I asked: "What's singing?"

"Thet be a nightingale. Ain't it purty? Lookee at them flowuhs wut Ah's got. All them dozens fo' two dollahs. Don't miss seein' the jade. Thet's a lucky stone in China. Ah bought lots. Cuff links fo' y'all. A pendant fo' Amah. Didn't fo'git Rona none: she gits a ring. Aftuh it got dahk, Clara an' me we went to somethin' called the temple market. Yeah man! We sho got bargains theah too!"

Happy had that female glow that women send as a signal they shopped well. I've seen that same glow from a filly when she'd won her race

Tell me a story," she ended, snuggling up to me again in our bed. "Somethin' t'do with these heah Ol-ym-pics what's comin'."

I thought a minute. Not easy. I've never been a fanatic where the Olympic Games are concerned. Followed them, of course. As any sportsman does, I suppose. I took a deep breath. "This one concerns

Winston Churchill. And Darling, don't ask 'who he' because you must have heard of Churchill."

"Sho have. He owned a good hoss called High Top."

That brought out a smile. "Yes. But this story relates to the 1923 Olympics, when even your Pappy wasn't born. These particular Olympic Games were made into a film called *Chariots Of Fire*. Maybe you saw it on Turner Classic Films."

"Sho did. Ah loved thet theme music."

I cleared my throat to begin the story:" If you recall, the story mainly concerned two rivals who wanted to win for Britain running in the Olympics that year. One of the two runners hoped to become a missionary and was deeply religious. He wouldn't run on a Sunday."

"Yeah man. Ah knows Kentucky Baptists wut won't do nothin' on a Sunday."

"Later, after the Olympic Games, this same deeply religious man was involved in a problem with the army. He wanted to be a conscientious objector. What's that? Someone who doesn't want to fight on religious grounds. At that time Winston Churchill was Assistant Secretary of the Navy, and he intervened for the fellow to get him out of trouble."

"Thet's it?"

"You expected blood and gore? I can give you that too. In 1972, during the Munich games, several Olympic athletes were kidnapped from their quarters by Black September Palestinian terrorists and taken as hostages. Those hostages were part of the Israeli team. Their main trainer was killed and so were several of the athletes. Gory enough?"

"Tell me them names."

"I'll start at the beginning. Shmuel Lalkin, head of the Isrealis' delegation, was worried about how lax security was. He'd noticed that many athletes were flaunting the rules and would climb over a chain fence late at night to return to the Olympic Village. On the night of September 4, a group of innocent American athletes did just that, and—without meaning—also helped the Palestinian terrorists gain access."

"You blamin' the 'Mericans?"

"Nobody blamed the Americans. They were in the wrong place at the wrong time and did the wrong thing. Lalkin had complained to the Olympic authorities that the Israelis were too isolated from the rest of the village. Nothing was done about that. At 4:30 a.m. on what was now September 5, as the Israelis slept the terrorists made some scratching noise that awoke Yossef Gutfreund, an Israeli wrestling coach. He shouted a warning to his compatriots, and with his huge 300 pound body tried to hold shut the door to Apartment One. He failed. The terrorists pushed in and grabbed wrestling coach Weinberg and shot him in the cheek, then forced him to show them the location of more hostages. But meanwhile Gutfreund's actions let his roommate, Tuvia Solokovsky a chance to escape by smashing a window and jumping out. Weinberg was also a hero. He lied to get the terrorists to bypass Apartment Two. But they invaded Apartment Three, and when Weinberg tried to stop them they killed him. But again the actions of a brave man saved another, because Weinberg's attacks allowed Gad Tsobari, a wrestler, to escape through an underground garage. Now the Terrorists bound up their hostages against chairs. Another hero who'd fought in the Israelis' Six Day War, Yossef Romano, a weightlifter, tried to attack the Terrorists and was shot and killed. Meanwhile in Apartment Two, the shots were recognized and more action taken. One Israeli, a marksman, Henry Hershkowitz, and a fencer Don Alan, another fencer and Lalkin with the team's two doctors managed to hide and then leave the building."

"This is terrible."

"There's more. Interestingly, because we're here in Hong Kong, it's worth mentioning that the Hong Kong delegation to the 1972 Summer Olympics was housed in the same building but released by the Terrorists. These guys had names: they included Luttif Afif, their leader, his deputy Tony Nazzal, Ahmed Chic Thaa, and Adnan Al-Gashey, most of whom had worked in the Olympic Village and knew its secrets."

"Shame!"

"You can say that again. These fedayeen asked for the release and safe passage to Egypt of 234 Palestinians and Arabs in jails in Israel. They also demanded the release of two German Terrorists held in Israeli jails, founders of the German Red Army group. The Terrorists threw Weinberg's body out of the building's front door to illustrate what they were capable of doing. It was rumoured that German authorities offered these Terrorists an unlimited amount of funds if they would release the hostages. This offer was sneered at."

"Them Terrorists should ha' taken the money."

"Five of them died at shootouts later at the airport to which they'd been transferred. The Germans doublecrossed them, broke promises. But the Germans didn't send enough experienced police to deal with the Terrorists. In the end all their hostages died; one of the hostages may have been shot by the German police in error. Anyway, eleven hostages died: two in their apartment, and the other nine at the airport, shot or incinerated by grenades thrown by the Terrorists."

Happy had grown restless. She murmured:" What happened to the Ol-ym-pics?"

"They were suspended for a day. First time in the history of the Games. Eighty thousand people attended a memorial service for the hostages, and several nations' delegations retired from the Games. Wouldn't participate. A Dutch distance runner, Jos Hermens, summed it up: 'You give a party, someone is killed at the party, you don't continue the party, you go home.'"

"Ah hopes nothin' lahke thet happens heah in Hong Kong." Happy turned over, and went to sleep. All I got for this storytelling was her warm back.

CHAPTER 24

Next morning the Olympic Games were much on her mind: Happy decided to leave Timmy with Amah, but he wouldn't have any of that. In the end, both mother and son accompanied me while I exercised Dubber's horse.

We had a surprise. Dubber, totally recovered, had unboxed Wonder and was already schooling him. Happy looked on, riveted.

"This be dressage?" She asked.

Completely alert, at home on his horse like the centaur he'd become, Dubber replied, "Dressage is the method of training horses to perform manoeuvres as a display of obedience. That's what I'm doing. Watch the reins and my heels. I give him a hint to glide two paces to the left, then two to the right. He needs to do that in the Olympic competition."

Happy nodded. She'd been reading up on Olympic tests ever since her first day watching me on Wonder. "Dis-ci-pline, wut mah chillun need." She gave Timmy a long, meaningful look. She commented: "Seems lahke Wonder he knows wut t'do without no hint."

"You've got it right. He does. Want to give this a try?"

Dubber dismounted. Happy, wearing jeans and boots for early morning gallops, stared at him in amazement. "Ah's t'rahde yo'r hoss?"

"Be my guest." Dubber was no longer flushed in the face. He looked very well turned-out in the proper outfit for schooling here. This was a totally changed Dubber.

Happy didn't just get up into the saddle. First she whispered in Wonder's ear, then stroked his neck, and placed her cheek against his long brown-maned one.

She stared at the saddle as if Queen Elizabeth had offered to let her take a seat on Edward III's throne. She said nothing, exactly as she had at Royal Ascot when I'd won a race and The Queen had presented me with the trophy for our missing owner, and noticing Happy's advanced pregnancy had asked my wife when the baby was due. Happy had whispered, "October." Now she couldn't say a word.

Dubber gave her a leg up. Happy sat still in the saddle. She got her bearings, and then made to get a feel of Wonder. Within minutes horse and rider were as one. Enthralled, Happy very gently touched Wonder's reins. No feet into his ribs. Wonder, with eloquent grace and elegance, glided a few paces to the left.

Another rider had brought along a boombox for music to help his horse perform his manoeuvres. "Someday My Prince Will Come" drifted over the ground toward Wonder. He pricked his ears and with consummate dignity began to dance.

Happy's face lit up like a Christmas tree when its lights go on. She gave Wonder his head and the two of them danced together. And this was no hillbilly 'chicken walk'; Wonder gave a sublime example of the ballet steps usually exclusively seen at the Spanish Riding School in Vienna.

Several bystanders applauded.

When Happy dismounted, she said with a glow, "Thank you, Mr. McDonald."

Timmy piped: "Dubber McDonald? Like in McDonald's?"

"Yes. Call me Dubber McDonald." He went to his long black gear bag and removed a hand-carved-in-wood small statue of a horse. He handed it to Timmy. "Made by Canadian Inuits, eskimos."

Timmy studied his present.

If he'd been seven and receiving his First Communion, his facial expression couldn't have been much different. He turned the horse and noticed it had its male organs. "Not like at McDonald's," he said. Could it be that he preferred those plastic freebies?

No. Timmy shoved a tiny hand into his pocket and brought out his bag of M&M's. With love shining in his eyes, he asked, "Would you like a candy?"

Wonder was becoming impatient. He wanted to show off again. He wanted more applause: he knew about applause. But we weren't to see any more of Wonder's amazing grace until his definitive day in the Olympic Games section for dressage. Meanwhile, Happy had been hanging around the practice ground, studying the dressage horses just as she had studied the racehorses at their gallops at that Louisville horse farm when she wanted to become a jockey.

Talk of being patient! Happy was bursting out of her expensive Chinese silk dress, while the hour long parade of participating athletes went on. When the athletes, clad in the uniforms selected by their home nations, waved and blew kisses to us, Happy finally broke down in tears.

"When's the hosses goin' t'come?" she asked through gasps, repeatedly. No horses, not yet, only more athletes. The athletes were apparently all very excited to be present in Hong Kong. It was as if they danced as they passed our stands.

We waved back.

In our stand the spectators had been given different coloured kerchiefs to wave. I hadn't got a kerchief. But I participated in that new phenomenon, *the moving wave* that was so much a feature in the 2007 memorial that the Princes William and Harry organized in Wembley Stadium.

We sat through the several days of trials.

Happy became amazingly knowledgeable about the precise moves necessary for a medal. During Dubber's event, we not only witnessed a glorious exhibition of pace and dance by Wonder, but Dubber also excelled. He was a mature rider who had dedicated a lifetime to schooling horses to perform at their best. He won a minor medal. But it was enough to set off a huge cheer from Canadians present, who waved their miniature Maple Leaf flags and shouted: "Dubber, Dubber, Dubber."

Hal had arranged for us to be invited to the celebratory dinner. There were parties all over Hong Kong for winning teams. The many nations represented had booked every major hotel, The Intercontinental, the Island Shangri-La, The Mandarin Oriental, The Four Seasons, you name them, they had every dining room filled with medal-draped athletes.

We couldn't go to any party. Dorothy was running a fever. "We'd best stay in and see if she breaks out in spots," Happy said.

I think Hal was pleased we didn't go out on the town. This was crunch time, when our horses had to win their races. He was delighted that we decided to save our energy for his horses.

CHAPTER 25

The next morning Hal was at the gallops with his binoculars. He didn't look hung-over. "Didn't drink much," he said. "Not quite my type of festivity. I raised my glass only once. When Mr. Lee said it was a good thing the Equestrian games took place in Hong Kong, far from Beijing's over-watchful eye. There had been more freedom, more jollity."

When he brought down his binoculars to his squared chin, Hal added: "Don't like the look of my Mighty Moron. I think he's sick. I got in a doc for Dubber. I think we should get a vet for this colt."

The Happy Valley doctor was summoned. He gave Mighty Moron a thorough examination. "Could be equine flu." He said gravely. "There was a break-out of that last year in Australia. Maybe one of the visiting horses brought it here."

Hal groaned: "So, I've always heard if you get a Chinese disease get a Chinese doctor. But are you sure?"

The Chinese vet spoke English very well. "Your colt has a fever. I'm going to order that he goes into isolation. We'll observe him a few days."

No argument. And the races were only a week away!

Happy visited Mighty Moron every morning. On the third day she said:

"The colt don't have flu. Got a runny nose, lahke most colts git this tahme o' year."

Dorothy and Mighty Moron both began to seem better. No coughing. No more runny noses. But I decided to give both a rest. No swimming pool for Dorothy. No gallops for Mighty Moron. Amah wanted to take the chillun to the zoo to see the pandas. Happy played down that idea. She wasn't ready to get our translator-cum-bellhop explain that Timmy had been released at a zoo after being kidnapped. Instead we took Timmy to see the giant seated Buddha. We had the service manager of our apartment complex arrange a picnic lunch. We went on a fake sampan to the island, walked the path to the monastery and gawked at the bronze Buddha along with all the other tourists.

Tired, on our return to our apartment, Happy suggested: "Let's us'n take Amah with us when we leaves heah."

"I've already put that to Amah. No way will she go to Japan, because she remembers when the Japanese invaded her province. She said she'd love to go to the USA, but I know she'll never manage to get a Green Card."

"She's so special with our chillun . . ."

"Darling, I agree. And I think you need her too. I've come up with an idea: I'll try to get her into Britain as an asylum seeker. Our friendly translator told me she'd lost all her family during the Cultural Revolution."

"Thank y'all, Rick. Ah hardly wanted t'ask. Cause Ah thought mebbe it'd look lahke Ah was tryin' t'git household help if'n Ah said Timmy behaves so good with huh."

"And so he does!" I pulled Happy gently toward our kingsize bed. "I know you're tired, but would you like a story?"

"No. Not a story. A lovely kiss!"

We had one of our last great sex sprees in that bed that night.

CHAPTER 26

Anchor won the big Hong Kong sprint. He earned us a lot of boodle. With a million dollars bet every Sunday at Happy Valley, the execs could afford it. The two tracks in Hong Kong earn 11 per cent of the area's total tax income. The purses start at one hundred and fifty thousand dollars. Compare that to similar low-budget races in the UK which give five thousand, if you're lucky. The top prizes pay millions. Even Hal's Happy's Escape earned decent money for coming in Second. Happy's Escape had done well to get a Place, because the draw had been nearly fatal, on the far side where the going was sticky.

Hal wanted to leave for Japan soonest. Clara was the one who was bugging him to get on a plane. She'd bought all she could ship home, and was giving away much of her stuff to the Peninsula's chambermaids.

Hal wanted to see the horseracing museum before quitting the city.

I went there with him while Happy packed up her shopping favorites. As Amah packed for the children huge, gooey teardrops swilled out of her slanted crinkle-lidded eyes. She was going to miss us. After all the trials and tribulations that our spoiled "chillun" had given her? Yes!

Amah came into my open arms and I gave her a hug. I also gave her a bonus over her salary, and instructions of how to go to a travel agency to collect a ticket for London.

CHAPTER 27

We couldn't just pack up and leave. Primarily because Happy had been given the ride on Happy's Escape at the racecourse outside Tokyo. I could hardly believe that Hal would chance his horse losing by putting up a barely-fit jockey who didn't have experience on that racecourse.

But those were Hal's orders.

Happy took to the job with glee. She and her namesake got on like rum and Coca Cola. Soon both horse and jockey knew the course as well as their home gallops. And, can you believe it, Happy won the race!

Several festivities were planned to celebrate her win but Happy was anxious to get back to Honeyville, having been unable to contact Rona for so many days.

The faxes had stopped. She'd telephoned Soledad at the gym, but that sour woman always hung up on her.

The Jockey Club had invited Happy to a dinner with Japan's leading jockey: Yataka Take. The dinner was scheduled to take place in Kyoto, that magnet for tourists. This was one event that even a homesick Happy couldn't turn down. I explained to my darling wife that in Japan good manners counted more than winning races and that therefore she HAD to make an appearance at the Jockey Club dinner.

Kyoto had temples, gardens, grand homes. It dates from the time of Christ, but today's Kyoto was a hymn to Buddha.

I'd insisted that our owners were invited to the party. Hal and Clara put off their return to Canada, which turned out to be very important for me. While Clara and Happy fussed over what to wear, Hal took me aside in the hotel bar. "I've decided that as Anchor is really an Ascot horse, he should be returned to England. You and Happy should wind up your time in Kentucky. Uh, tell me Rick. Have you been tempted to hire a geisha? Here we are in the land of geishas: Cooey, if I haven't even *thought* of getting one. I sure love my Clara!"

"I haven't been tempted either. And, yes, I'll be glad to take Anchor to England."

"So! You'll head back to Epsom after settling up in Kentucky."

Those orders suited me fine. I'd missed my own country, and I felt it was right to return Anchor to Ascot. He'd grown into a marvellous, mature contender. I still felt he would never be a great horse, but he was a damned good one.

The drive to Kyoto was magical. Passing the ancient villages and seeing the rural Japanese at their evening labours.

I particularly enjoyed watching the fishermen pulling in their nets. I'd got a great kick out of the morning we'd spent at the fishermen's market, savoring that incredible fresh tuna that was so unlike what you get in restaurants or shops. I loved the way the great fish were auctioned as if they were racehorses. And in this magical evening light I could appreciate further the fishermen's tasks.

Kyoto's horsemen had turned out for Happy. She was the star of the night. Executives from all of Japan's twenty two racecourses came to fete her, and she was applauded. Even cheered.

But, as always seems to happen, after that high came a very terrible low. On our return to Clara's hotel, she called after our car to come back that there was a fax at last for Happy.

The fax read simply "Rona was murdered today. Soledad."

CHAPTER 28

Returning to Honeyville brought us no joy. How could it, with Rona murdered?

Our fake antebellum mansion smelled of mould. There was no one available to babysit the kids: all our elderly neighbours had given one another the flu, and so Happy trundled our three children to the gym to ask the all-important question of what had happened to Rona.

There was no way I could help her except serve as driver to and from Honeyville: my horses needed to be unboxed and carefully examined for bruises after their long flights.

There had been no collection for a wreath for Rona. No mention or sign of Rona existed showing that she had ever been at the gym. When Happy cornered Soledad, that sour-faced woman rejected any and all queries.

Not to be put off, Happy bristled like a tomcat hosed down with icy water. She waved the fax received in Tokyo.

"Soledad, you sent me this fax. Now y'all got t'tell me what happened!" Her dull eyes sliding from side to side as if she was watching a ping-pong match, Soledad squirmed.

Like a nursing home patient who has wet her pants, Soledad whispered "Can't say. Nothin' to say. She died."

Soledad ducked under Happy's arms, escaping their cage to run outside and down the street.

"Wow!" Happy sighed.

Her eyes scoured the gym for a familiar face. But all the sweating nursing mothers working the treadmills were newcomers, who had joined while Happy was in the Far East.

She poked her head into the manager's office. Nobody. She looked into the assistant manager's premises. Nobody. Then she heard a cough. She followed it and found the accountant in his cubbyhole, pouring over the gym's books.

He leered at her. "You still nursing, Mrs. Harrow?" he asked provocatively.

"Uh, hello, Rhett. Ah means Mister Gordon. Well, Ah'm sort of nursin'. Lost mah milk when Timmy were kidnapped. It didn't come back so good after. Have to mix it with store-bought formula."

"What a pity."

"Uh, where' ever'body?"

"You mean the manager's assistant. I sent her to the basement to scour around for last year's tax returns. We're having a slight problem with the IRS."

"Soledad?"

"I saw her a moment ago running down the street . . Can I do anything for you?" That wasn't a question: it sounded more like an invitation.

Happy was spared inventing a reasonable reply.

The accountant's door banged open and a furious, spitting-lipped Una surged into the tiny cubbyhole. "You rat!" She growled at Rhett. "You promised never to call me at home." Then she saw Happy, and shut up.

Happy took in the scene and drew her own conclusions. She thought glamorous Una was flirting with Rhett in spite of her lip-spitting.

For once, she got the wrong idea.

While Una had pretended to be running this show, when she went to a mirror to freshen her lipstick, Una used her lipstick to write a message for Happy on the palm of her hand, "Save me."

Having freshened her lipstick, Una marched to the accountant's desk telephone and dialed our local florist. Over her shoulder she purred to Rhett: "You owe me flowers." When the florist answered the call, Una said, for Happy to catch her address, "Send that $10 special you ran for Mothers' Day to The Old Barn on Riverside Road."

She retuned the earpiece to its cradle and left the room without any goodbyes.

Rhett Gordon kept his eyes averted from Happy's delving gaze. He growled, "Una wants her membership fee returned, because Soledad won't let her back in. And what is it that you wanted?"

Happy invented an excuse. "Same thing. Refund. Mah husband and Ah are both returning to England. We won't be usin' this gym no mo'e."

"Sorry to hear that. Also sorry to have to say that there is no chance in your case for a refund. You've had your money's worth. It's not the gym's fault you won't be staying out your year's membership."

Feeling dismissed, Happy went to the gym's locker room to clear it of her belongings.

When I collected Happy with her mountain of gym clothes, she was bristling with the news of Una's plea for help.

Once we were inside our rental car, she groaned: "We's so tired aftuh no sleep on thet long plane rahde. But Ah feels we got t'protect thet Una. Stay in this car outside huh house t'night. Got to get a babysitter. But, from wheah?"

"You never liked Una that much. Why this, suddenly?"

"She really meant 'save me.' Please Rick, it ain't always folks what Ah likes thet Ah means t'help."

No contest. I came up with the suggestion we hire our friendly grounds keeper to babysit. He was willing as long as he could use Tim's collection of video games to help stay awake.

By dusk we were positioned in our car under trees that screened it from Una's imposing house. Her mansion was of the authentic variety. No columns, but another Georgian style that had been designed by an eighteenth century itinerant Irish architect. Its finest detail was the fan-shaped glass over the front doors. Next to it was the old barn of its name.

A solitary light shone in an upstairs window. We could watch Una moving from place to place in her upstairs bedroom. She was obviously extremely nervous. She never sat down, but paced like a tiger waiting for a meal. Hopefully not like the Seattle Zoo's Tatiana that ate a visitor last Christmas Day.

Where was Una's mysterious husband? None of the gym's members had ever seen him. And now he was still the invisible man; not even his car was in the driveway. I'd seen that car several times when it collected Una from the gym, but never the man in the driver's seat.

What drew my attention that night was Rhett Gordon's red Jaguar as it entered Una's driveway.

He emerged from the Jaguar outfitted in what for a moment seemed like an eighteenth century costume. But when I looked closely I recognized that his outfit consisted of the knee breeches and long jacket adopted by some shooting men at private shoots. On his head was the traditional deerstalkers' red cap with its ear flaps.

More sinister was the arsenal of shooting guns on the jaguar's rear seat - a 12-bore shotgun and three rifles, accompanied by boxes of cartridges.

He leaned back into that rear seat arsenal and chose a rifle, loaded it and strode into that elegant home, armed with his deadly weapon.

Seconds later we heard Una scream.

I didn't hesitate. Yelling to Happy to dial 911 and give this address to the police, I then rushed to the Jaguar, selected another rifle, loaded it and bolted for Una's upstairs bedroom. Happy, holding a handful of cartridges, followed not far behind.

Una was on her knees in front of Rhett, whose breeches had been dropped. He was tugging at her hair.

"It's one or the other," he sneered without explanation.

From her kneeling position, Una whined: "I've told you before I won't let you drink the milk from my breasts."

"And I've told you that you must."

In a corner of the bedroom a baby was crying for its dinner.

I burst into that bedroom wielding the rifle and said in all seriousness. "Enough of this. I'll take your gun and you leave now or you'll have the police to answer to. They're on their way."

Surprisingly, Rhett pulled up his breeches with one hand, lowered his rifle with the other and handed it to me, then strode from the room.

From the corridor he said, "This was all play-acting, you understand. Una and I are going to put on a scene for our local playhouse."

He smirked. "You can return my rifles to me tomorrow at the gym."

A scene for the local playhouse? Not bloody likely! Such a porno scene would never be condoned at the Honeyville Playhouse with its supporters garnered from among our sedate elderly community.

I would never know. A rifle shot echoed to us on the upstairs floor. Una called us to her window. "My God, it's my husband, Al. He's shooting at Rhett with one of Rhett's own guns!"

We watched like UN observers as Rhett dodged bullets, jumped into his Jaguar and sped down the drive. His rear lights blinked like subdued fireworks.

Al Probit revved his own engine and followed, the rifle useless on his lap.

Before we could go downstairs and get in our own car, the police arrived.

The two officers sounded like actors out of an Inspector Clouseau movie.

"You know it's a punishable offense to call out the police as a joke."

"No joke, officer," I droned.

Happy echoed me, "We wuz asked by this heah lady, Miz Probit, to come save huh."

"From what?"

Una, previously known for her immaculate hairdos and clothes, had rushed from the house in her torn negligee with her hair still down from having been pulled by Rhett.

"I'm sorry you were called out, officers. This is my home, you can check that out on your mobiles. There has been an intruder. My husband is even now chasing him down the highway. And both men are armed with rifles."

The second Clouseau woke up at the word "rifles." He got on his walkie-talkie and called his station. "Armed men driving on US.#1."

He turned to Una. "What make cars?"

"Mr. Gordon's in a red Jaguar. My husband, Al, drives a Mercedes coupe '98, cobalt blue, license plate AP2."

Next we were part of a car chase to end all car chases.

How did we know whether to head North or South? Una, who remained at home with her baby, had previously suggested we go to the South Drinks Shooting Preserve.

South.

We wound through pre-dawn fog. Ahead were the rear lights of hundreds of cars, blinking like the car in Edward Albee's *Who's Afraid of*

Virginia Woolf. Nothing sexy about them. They were occupied by workers who needed to be on the job early.

When dawn arrived we found ourselves in a carpark, alongside rows of Hummers, their interiors littered with discarded shooting apparel and unwanted lunches.

Our two Clousseau police officers had dashed into the woods. We could hear shooting, but I explained to Happy that those shots were from cartridges loaded with pellets for birds. As if to corroborate my comment, a flight of two pheasants arched simultaneously overhead.

Happy said: "Ah don't know rightly if we'uns should go into them woods. We ain't got no guns, no red jackets or caps. Mebbe not too good an idea."

We didn't need to go into the woods. The two armed men burst into the car park. Al took aim at Rhett, and fired.

Rhett went down. Not dead, he'd been knee-capped. "That will teach you to go to my wife for your vile habit," Al shouted.

The two Clousseau cops caught up with Al. One called for an ambulance for Rhett while the other arraigned Al, and read him his rights. Al offered his wrists for handcuffs.

Al said: "Self defense. Rhett Gordon's a murderer. He has single-handedly dispatched three nursing mothers from the Honeyville Gym. He'd selected my wife Una to be the fourth. After he sucks milk from their breasts, he kills the women to insure silence."

Clousseau two gave a sneering laugh, and added – like a 1920's character in an early movie. "Yeah, tell that to the judge."

My Happy intervened. "What he said is true, Officah. Ah knowed this fo' some tahme, but had no proof. Send someone from yo'r forensics lab to the Honeyville Gym and take his DNA off his telephone theah, then match it up with prints from the needle a detective found what wuz done used to kill them good nursin' women from our gym. Case closed."

We headed home to our "chillun" to release the patient grounds man.

By mid-morning, still without a night's sleep, my Happy had to appear before the Honeyville Magistrates' Court and give her deposition.

I hired a lawyer to be certain that Happy would not be kept back from accompanying me and our "chillun" on the upcoming flight to England.

She just made it.

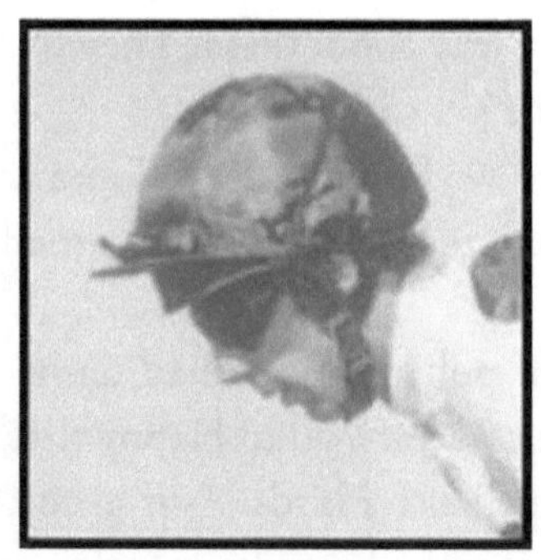

CHAPTER 29

Dear old Epsom's plumbers had failed to preserve our cottage from the rains that came with autumn. We arrived to find leaks in our thatch, frozen pipes and a worn-out fridge.

Fortunately, as I gauged it, most of the damage had hit the eighteenth century cottage and missed our modern stables. All the horses were well enough after their flight from Kentucky. There had certainly been too much flying for them this year, what with Hong Kong, Tokyo, New York State and Kentucky.

Only Happy's Escape appeared to resent his return to Epsom. He acted up about his oats, didn't take to the water, and detested the farrier. I had to find someone else to shoe him, provide bottled water and change the provider of his oats.

Every time I return from my travels to Epsom I feel a wonderful, warm welcome in my nuts to be home. And why not? With my darling Happy in it with me.

MURDER IN MARRIAGE

CHARACTERS IN MURDER IN MARRIAGE

Rick Harrow, a British racehorse trainer having a struggle to find and keep owners.

Hillary a/k/a Happy Harrow, his wife, an apprentice jockey and talented sleuth

Tim Harrow, the Harrow's 3-year-old son

Dorothy Harrow, the Harrow's 18-month-old daughter

Irish Harrow, the Harrow's 4 months old baby

Don Blair IV, teenage accuser of Rick, screaming Rick murdered his father.

Mrs. Edna Blair, Don's strange grandmother who rules Blairville

Sherill, who sells racehorses in Clearwater, Florida, a telephone pal of rap singer millionairess

Fran Purcell

The Blairville Sheriff, very full of his own importance unless there is a Blair present

The babysitter

A volunteer tour guide at the San Marcos Fort near St. Augustine

A woman who wrestles alligators for a living to rid them from hotel gardens

MENTIONED IN LORI BLAIR'S DIARY

Lori, disgruntled wife of Don Blair III

Don Blair III, Lori's cuckolded husband

Don Blair, Jr., a crossdresser who was married to the incredible Edna

Pedro, a Guatemalan sailor who is in prison for murdering his boss

CHAPTER 1

"You murdered my father!" I heard a voice yell outside our front door. Christmas morning in 2008 was surprisingly cold for Florida. My little son, Tim, had climbed out of his crib to wake his mother, and I'd followed them to the Christmas tree in the parlour where he started tearing open the wrappings on his presents. Other mornings I would have left for our strings' gallops, but while I'm usually a very conscientious English trainer of racehorses, I felt that at least on Christmas I could give preference to my growing family.

With Tim fully engaged with his presents, my wife Happy had left the parlour to collect our two baby daughters, Dorothy who's one and a half, and little Irish who's barely four months old.

The front door's bell rang. At seven a.m.! If I hadn't heard that yelp of misery from outside I might have thought one of the stable lads had left the horses long enough to deliver gifts for our kids.

I opened the door. A totally scruffy, wild-eyed teenage boy stood on the threshold brandishing a very large knife. Not a cake knife: the type that kills.

"You murdered my father!" He roared again.

I stared into the boy's eyes. I recognized desperate misery there, not danger to my family.

"Come inside," I said quietly, "and give me that knife. We could use it for cutting away the wrappings on presents."

Suddenly transformed into a meek adolescent out of his depth, the boy began to cry. Stepping into our parlour, he handed me the knife.

"I don't know you," I added, "but you look as if you could use a cup of coffee."

"No coffee," the boy bleated. "I need the truth. Your name and your picture fill the last pages of my step-mother's diary. She wrote in it that you'd said you'd kill her if she told your wife Happy about fucking with her. And now she's dead, and my father's dead too."

Now I was the one who needed coffee, or something much stronger. Looking closer at the boy, I recalled seeing group photographs where he'd been behind Lori Blair. Yes, his step-mother.

Oh no! That affair with Lori had ended weeks ago. I'd been in Miami at the horse sales, and met Lori at a party at the Seminole Reservation's hotel casino. I'd discovered that in America the Seminole Indian tribe had taken advantage of the fact that it was still officially at war with the United States and could have a gambling casino near Miami where gambling was illegal. Its hotel had since become infamous as the site where playgirl turned millionairess Ana Nicole Smith had died from a cocktail of pills. Although it had this sinister past, the casino hotel was popular for wild parties. A group of trainers had invited me to dine there, and I'd met Lori. She seemed definitely one of the wild party girls. It wasn't until we'd had an incredibly lurid night together that I learned she was the wife of a sedate lawyer, scion of an eminent middle Florida banking family, the Blairs of Sunblair.

Happy had been in England giving birth to Irish. I'd felt horny, after months of no sex. And Lori Blair had been only too eager to provide me with the type of hot sex I'd craved.

"Come back outside." That was an order to the Blair boy, not an invitation. I spoke over my shoulder, calling to Happy as I frantically closed the front door, "I'll be dealing with the boy out here."

I said to the boy, "I haven't killed anyone. And I never said to Lori that I'd kill her if she told my wife about our affair. I haven't seen her in weeks.

I've been back in England. I don't even know how Lori and your father died.

Or when. And how did you find me? We've only just moved into this cottage. Look, I'm really sorry to hear about your father. But I haven't—"

The boy interrupted my phoney condolences. "Don't try bullshitting me. I've seen the picture where you two were fucking in her bed. I found the Diary three days ago, same day they died. I got her diary out of a night table and the picture was pasted on to the last page she'd written on. Before the double shooting. Find you? Your cell phone number was in her diary. Right next to that picture."

"Oh? And why haven't you turned the diary with its picture over to the police, since you say there's been a double murder."

Speaking through deep gasps, the boy whined, "Can't. The police think that my father killed Lori, then himself. If the police saw pictures that showed she'd put horns on him, that could provide a reason to totally believe he'd killed her."

For a few moments I said nothing. This was no joke. I *had* taken pictures of us in her bed with a camera Lori provided. She'd said it made her more sexy to be photographed in full coitus. What a fool I'd been. She'd told me to rig up the camera above the bed and use a string to pull the shutter. Damn fool!

I could hear my wife cooing Kentucky-hill talk to little Dorothy. Then she broke into "Rudolph the Red Nosed Reindeer" and I knew she'd have put on the fake reindeer antlers we'd bought at the five-and-ten. Oh God, what had I been thinking of when I got into Lori's bed? And my Happy, not making a scene although she may have heard the boy's accusations.

What to do now? I scanned the pimply boy's face. Aside from all his other troubles, he was very unattractive. With his slumping, round shoulders and bent legs he'd never make his local high school's football team. He had a lean, pale face with sucked-in cheeks, and squinting eyes, already thinning auburn hair that needed a barber, his ugliness aggravated by a lack of normal eyebrows.

Finally, I choked out to him, "I'm going to try to help you. Strange to say, but my wife – Happy, she's called—is a magic hand at solving murders. Nine, so far. Lend me that diary."

I could see in his reddened eyes that he suspected I'd be burning it. Young Don Blair, who was a very young sixteen, still snivelling, drew the diary from his blazer pocket. He hesitated, but after a long pause, it was handed to me. Reluctantly. He stared back into my eyes, we had a fencing match of retinas.

He said, "Our local coroner sealed off my father's house. I'm living with my Grandma. She's Mrs. Edna Blair, in the Sunblair phone book. Not an easy lady to be with. When you're ready, call me on her phone."

Again I gave a moment's thought before I spoke. I worried that the boy was living with his paternal grandparent who might also believe I'd killed her son. Debating with myself, I finally decided to manage the situation on my own terms. I said ponderously, "I've been offered a colt for sale in Ocala. I'm planning to go up your way tomorrow. Bring my wife, Happy. Maybe take the kids to a stopover at Disney. I'll head later towards your town, Sunblair. But the deal is, don't involve me with your police. Keep my name out of this until we're ready to be of some help."

Surprisingly, the pimply boy nodded agreement.

Suddenly, I felt a tug at my innards. Good God, I'd shagged his step-mother, yet he's forgiving me the agony I caused his father.

Now, I watched, as with his narrow shoulders slumped and back curved, he lumbered toward the distant bus stop. Christmas morning! And he had no one to go to, except to some cranky old grandmother.

A bus arrived. The boy shoved himself aboard. No backward look for me. No wave, no shake of the head. I watched as he paid his fare and found a seat as the bus lurched around a corner and out of sight.

Time to face Happy. Time to explain what I was doing giving my attention to some strange boy when my wife and kids were waiting beside the Christmas tree.

I didn't have to explain. Happy stood on the threshold waving a hideous tie, saying: "If you hate this, I can take it back. Expensive, $135, from Hermes." She came forward, kissed me on that place on my neck that sends me into orbit.

Holding the tie, and making as if to put it on over my bathrobe's collar, I took little Irish from her and squatted down beside Tim. He was sulking, angry that his new mechanical toy didn't work.

"It needs a battery," I said, and rummaged in a readied box to find a battery the right size. I fitted the battery, and the toy revved to life. But Tim had lost interest in it and was laying out a company of wooden soldiers. He still looked angry. I compared his troubles to the pimply boy's, who had lost his father, now perhaps to be labeled a murderer himself if the police proved to be incompetent.

Tim had never quite forgiven his mother and me for having more children. He wet his bed every night to prove to us he was still enduring the aftermath of that anger.

His personality had altered from a sunny baby's to a resentful infant's. Happy went into the kitchen and emerged minutes later with two mugs of coffee. "Ah'd have liked to have met that young man at the door. Seemed awful troubled. Weren't he? Did Ah hear somethin' about a diary? Did he confuse you for a publisher? No. You two stopped together too long. Somethin' else. Any way Ah could be of help?"

I kissed her again. Had she heard all of Don Blair's conversation?

Coffee dribbled on to my new tie. No chance of returning it to Hermes for another one now. Shaking my head, I said: "We'll talk about the boy tomorrow, darling. Not on Christmas. What he brought was no Christmas gift for either of us."

CHAPTER 2

I'm a British-born racehorse trainer. I'd married Happy four years ago when I was working in Kentucky as an assistant trainer to derby winning Burl Smithey, and Happy was an apprentice jockey just turned nineteen.

We went broke after Happy unmasked Smiley's richest owner as the serial killer of three girl jockeys. I hadn't wanted to lose my Happy as the next dead jockey, so I'd backed her and lost my job. After being in a limbo of unemployment, I'd finally taken on another job in Texas with a small time trainer. I'd managed to buy a really good racehorse for one of his owners, called NILE. But that owner wanted to send NILE to another trainer in California, and I was selected to follow on with the horse's training there. Happy hadn't objected, she's crazy about the movies and movie stars and met two oldies who had once had their names in lights. But I hadn't got along with the new trainer, Bono Munoz, because he believed NILE to be only good enough to enter mile races while I believed that NILE should be trained for the classics at a mile and a quarter. So when a former school friend, Ivor, invited me to return to England to be his assistant trainer, I'd jumped at the chance after Happy had agreed to this move. Shortly after our arrival in England, Ivor had killed himself thinking he had cancer.

As the months went by, based comfortably at Epsom, near the racecourse for The Derby, I'd had some good wins for my owners, principally at Ascot.

Later I'd taken my string abroad when I felt a horse could win a race at Santa Anita, Melbourne or Dubai. The latter was a nightmare for us because Happy, abducted there, barely escaped from her captors in time to reach the jockeys' hospital and give birth to our Dorothy. Our eldest child, Tim, had been born in Texas, when I'd been training Nile. But for this third sprig, Irish, Happy had opted for our local Epsom midwife.

Madness, but then that's my courageous Happy! She had a difficult birth with Irish but didn't need a caesarean as with her other two babies. Again, she was delivered of a girl. We named her Irish because of the blue-purple colour of her eyes "Ah sho' ain't a know-it-all. Ah kinda thought she were special, with them eyes thet blue purple colour. Didn't cotton on 'til now most babies have 'em. Even kittens, and some hosses."

Happy had decided to breast-feed Irish, although that hadn't been possible before. She'd relied on powdered milk for the first two babies. "Irish, she be special," was her excuse for breast feeding this sprig.

"Yes. You can say that again. But all ours are special."

"Yeah man," she agreed, in her Kentucky drawl that I hadn't been able to eradicate with elocution lessons. Happy's schooling had been interrupted because her great passion for horses had led her to quit Junior High—illegally—to opt for working in the nearest racetrack's stables. "Irish, puhfect."

"Irish, perfect name, yes," I said, echoing her as I'd become accustomed to doing with whatever Happy threw at me.

Interrupted schooling, yes, but my Happy had a brain in her head that had led to the unmasking of three serial killers in the past three years. All that, and motherhood too! That's my Happy.

In England the day after Christmas is called Boxing Day, not because people box one another but because some of us put unwanted gifts in boxes for next Christmas or take them to needy families. On that particular morning the spectacular Miami sunrise was turning the sky the color of a sliced papaya. I'd walked in with Happy to the babies' room in our Miami cottage. It was a cold morning, but this particular room was on the floor above the kitchen and received the best natural heat in our house: in Miami our house had no heating just as in Epsom our house had no air-conditioning. It had started out as a guest bedroom when Tim's crib had been positioned next to our double bed. When I'd found him staring at us when we had sex, I decided Tim should have the guest room. He had to share it with Dorothy and Irish. It was a smelly room, what with Tim's bedwetting and the girls' constantly soiling diapers.

All three started howling at once. When Dorothy entered our family, Tim had been very jealous. Now both elder children were resenting the arrival of Irish. When she bawled, they bawled. I guess they figured they were bigger and could cry louder and get attention quicker.

Happy, very adept at handling this particular situation, managed to crowd all three to her breasts for cuddles. Lucky kids!

The telephone rang downstairs. I rushed to answer. I'd been expecting a call from my most generous Owner, Hal Murphy, who was based in Canada. A rough diamond, he was equally hard and brilliant. I'd lost four of my owners to the Ebury Street serial killer, and couldn't afford to lose Hal.

I didn't want to act obsequious, but short of sucking-up I did everything to please him where his horses were concerned.

When Happy, very pregnant, had been abducted in Dubai this was one owner who proved his mettle. He offered to pay out one million dollars to buy a ringer that was offered by her kidnappers in exchange for Happy. She foiled that attempt by using her jockey skills to gallop away on a loose horse. Reaching Dubai's stables for visiting racehorses her water broke and she had to enter the jockeys' hospital for her second caesarean. Dorothy had been trying to arrive feet first: a breech birth.

I don't believe that every good deed costs dear. In fact, I do believe God's in his heaven and all's going to be well with the world. Proof positive, Hal did buy another horse in Dubai, and that horse is turning out to be a miracle like the Nile I'd bought in Texas for an oil man, Sol, and lost when Sol transferred him to another Trainer. His name? Mighty Moron. Oh, the names some owners choose for their beautiful horses!

Hal sounded unusually abrupt on our early morning call. "My horses okay? When will Anchor run? And Mighty Moron?"

I delayed answering. I simply didn't know what to say. Both horses had been entered in various races at several racecourses, but so much depended on the weather. I couldn't decide where or when to send them until I got a reliable weather report.

Finally, hesitating, I mumbled: "Gulfstream, the early meeting for Anchor. We both know how he likes warm weather. But the rain has destroyed so many hopes this year: non-stop, worst we've seen in a century. Houses swept away, commuters drowned in their cars. And Anchor's no mudder. I think we'll have to wait and see how it dries here. Otherwise we should ship him back to England and run him at Royal Ascot. Nick Smith, Ascot's head of PR, has been beating the drum for the 2008 early meeting."

Gruffly: "What day's that meeting start?"

"Wednesday, April 30th. But, Hal, don't expect Ascot in 2008 to be the same old cozy place it used to be, when The Queen could walk down to the paddock through crowds that parted for her so nobly. Not on your Nellie. This is a very different new Ascot, where The Queen's so protected behind steel reinforced glass she can barely see a race."

"So? About when will Anchor be ready? In time for April 30th?"

"Could be. He's bursting out of his skin at the moment. If the ground was right, he'd fly past the Finish Line."

"So, enter him for the sprint."

"Can't guarantee what's going to happen by April 30th. Do you recall the unusual races for the 2007 Shergar Cup Day? Like at the Belmont course, all the races could be classified with the same name, these classified as Shergar Cup races. All winners got the same amount: thirty thousand pounds. Well, you know what that means: about fifteen net. Strangest day, jockeys each got five rides, and were left out for one. Jimmy Fortune – he really has the most appropriate name, such a lucky jockey—won over six furlongs with Our Faye. But the Australian jockeys, who came to the UK for this, only managed to get points. Do you still want me to enter Anchor for the very first day of flat racing there?"

"Yeah. I read *The Racing Post*. I know what you're saying. I've a reason for inquiring."

I didn't doubt it. Busy Hal rarely called if he didn't have a major reason. "Could it have to do with the Kentucky Derby?"

"Yeah, you guessed. I want you to run Anchor at Ascot in April, and then get your ass over here to put my three-year-old into the Kentucky Derby."

I whistled. I couldn't stop myself. "Hal, he's a maiden. Has never seen a racecourse."

"So? I know what a maiden is: had a few in my time," Hal roared hoarsely, "I say he's a miracle horse. Better for us punters if nobody knows just how great he is. And remember, he damn well cost me a million dollars."

Trainers' rule Number One: never contradict an owner. Never make one look a fool: which I could have done if I'd reminded him that Ireland's Coolmore people had paid sixteen million dollars in Florida last year for The Green Monkey.

I cut to the point: "You'll have to pay one hell of a forfeit price to get him in at this late stage."

"So? What's money for? If not to spend?" He rang off.

I'd heard his wife calling him back to bed, and wasn't surprised at the finalizing click. I hurried back upstairs. Happy was on the landing with a finger to her lips.

"Got the babies back t'sleep. How about us'n goin' t'bed too?"

No argument! We'd done early stables. I'd cleared my desk in the tack room. Yes, yes, yes. Bed! Right now! With three infants always squalling, we had to grab our private time together whenever and however we could.

I was a careful husband. I'd had an adulterous liaison, a one-night stand in Paris, with a Russian woman with a Putin's FSB past, that should have cured me of that type of fling. But, I'd heard that famous remark by Tallulah Bankhead: "Darling if it happens on tour it ain't adultery."

With the kids' diaper smell still in my nostrils, I flared them and said: "Why don't we go up to Disney, check into a hotel and make love there? You know how I enjoy sex in hotel rooms. The babysitter said she'd be pleased to go to Disney with us any time. We'll park the kids with her, make love and go see that colt which is up for sale."

Happy's eyes glowed with that special embers-fire that comes with the prospect of special sex. After an instant those embers faded: "Sho' 'nuf, but let's us'n go see that pimply boy while we's travellin' after we's read his step-mother's diary."

We did have a quickie before she phoned the babysitter to come around. Happy packed the usual mountain of baby paraphernalia into our rental Hummer and when the babysitter arrived we sent her to the kitchen for a case of water bottles, and then hit the road.

Murphy's Law. What could go wrong, went wrong. The Hummer was sideswiped as we left the driveway. We had a flat tire on dangerous, busy 1-95 that was packed with many holiday makers still high on whatever had been their poison for the past twenty-four hours. I had to park the Hummer on the median to sweat myself wet while changing its enormous tire. Passing drivers yelled encouragements, like: "Next time take the train!" or appropriately "Git a horse!"

Once I had the tire fixed, I'd become so jumpy that I continually found myself driving on what in America is the wrong side of the road, on the right: British style.

Of course all the reasonably priced Disney hotels were fully booked ahead for the Christmas season and without a reservation I had to pay an outrageous sum to crowd all of us into two small rooms for second class accommodation. The better Disney rides were all booked too, and extensive queues snaked forever for anything. Never mind. All our babes were too young to enjoy any of them, and even neglected to watch. the parade to see Mickey and Minnie. Timmy didn't want to eat anywhere but at a McDonald's which made dinner a little cheaper.

It was my Happy who looked disappointed. I parked the kiddies with the babysitter when they'd started to bawl from being overtired, and finally Happy enjoyed some aspect of Disney by going to the China pavilion and experiencing a vicarious trip to its mainland. She'd thought to watch a show that would enlighten her about the origins of horses in earliest times, but no such luck. She would have needed to go to a show put on by Mongolia for that. Horses had originated from Mongolia not—as she'd thought—China.

We did have sublime sex later in our down-market hotel room. It featured an electric moving mattress that accelerated our own movements. Tacky, but a first for both of us that kept us laughing as we reached for those peaks in orgasm.

Then came the reading of Lori's Diary. The pages were in a loose-leaf schoolbook binding. I read some and then passed them on to Happy. In this way we worked our way through all of it to where the pictures of me in coitus with Lori were pasted to the final entry.

CHAPTER 3

Happy read silently. No grunts. No sullen, sulky comments. Once she said: "Oh, no!"

She'd propped herself on two pillows and read with a minilight over her head.

Lori's December pages started: "I met this gorgeous Englishman after the boat show. I was on such a high after seeing all those gorgeous yachts that any stray guy would have looked good. But this one was different from most of the men I meet up here in Dullsville, our horrible boring Sunblair. First of all he has this funny accent I'd got used to from watching all those English movies on TV. Like Jeremy Irons as the Earl of Leicester in *Elizabeth I*. Or Richard Burton in *Cleopatra*. Deep voice. Promising a sexy man. Love it. I took a quick look at the crotch in his trousers, but they were too well cut to give away what was there. I'll bet he's got a great cock with the two good balls that matter so much to me. Not too tall, he'll fit in my bed just fine. Fit in me just fine."

Lori didn't write every day. She'd skipped filling up the pages until the following weekend. "Got the Englishman into bed. Not easy. Acted like a virgin on a hay ride. 'No, I can't.' And 'Really I shouldn't,'" but when push came to shove he wanted it as badly as I did. What a lay! Then lousy old Ron had to spoil everything by arriving home early and the Englishman had to hide out on the balcony of my bedroom just like in all those old

French farces. Farces, or farts? No matter, the promised hurricane hadn't hit, so Rick was okay out on the balcony. He grabbed his clothes and made a run for it while Ron was taking his shower. I guess Rick had enough sense to have parked his car in the empty driveway of the snowbirds who own the house next door."

More empty pages, where two days had passed. Then, in hurried handwriting: "Rick trains horses and he has to spend most of his time in Miami, or at the Delray training center. There was a preview yacht event in Palm Beach, and we rendezvoused there at the Chesterfield Hotel. Later, I screwed him on the deck of a divine 100 foot yacht that was for sale, and empty. Incredible! A sunset was going down behind the city's new skyscrapers, with reflections in the windows that twinkled like rubies. What a turn on. Yachts and rubies, nothing makes me feel sexier except maybe taking pictures of me having an orgasm. Rick delayed doing that, I had to press him, get him really turned on before he'd agree to pull the string that activates the shutter. Oh, man. When he finally agreed did I come or did I come!"

The final entries read: "Rick says he has to go back to England. He won't listen when I beg him to get a divorce. Says he loves his wife and children, couldn't bear to part from them. I'm super ready to divorce Don. Can't stand him or his snivelling Don Junior another day. But Don says he won't divorce me. Because he's a lawyer and knows how much he'd have to give me, he won't opt for a divorce. What is it with men that they don't want divorces? Just because Don's pressing to become a full partner in his firm and the other partners are old-fashioned evangelicals who don't believe in divorce, he can't expect me to hang around for ever. So I went to see a lawyer who does divorces. He wanted $5000 up front, but when I told him I hadn't got anything in the bank he said he could try to get the judge to force Don to pay my lawyer's fees because Don's rich and I'm not. Well, my case started out okay. The judge did rule that Don had to pay my lawyer's fees because I'm poor and he's rich. Lucky the judge didn't require me to list my tangible assets, like the ruby earrings Don gave me when we married, and my car. Last things he ever gave me worth anything. He said no more gifts until I change the way I make love. Says he doesn't like the way I do it. Then the judge made me face Don during something called mediation. Horrible. That's when according to Florida law we're to have a meeting where we must try to get back together again. Instead of a reconciliation, Don offered me a flat settlement in addition to the $10,000 I'd agreed to take when I signed that damned Pre-Nup. Stupid me, in those days $10,000 had seemed like a lot of money comparing it to my salary of $75 a week as a receptionist at my lousy job at his family's bank. I should have known how much money he earns. Didn't. Not until later when I became a member of his dysfunctional family. His mother playing at being the grande dame of Sunblair. Wearing a hat and leather gloves in winter, and carrying a parasol and wearing cotton gloves in summer. But she sneaks away to other towns to do her thing at dancing contests. And my awful father-in-law Don Senior, that asshole, with his cross-dressing, showing up in bed in a bridal nightgown and at dinner wearing something copied from Scarlett O'Hara in *Gone With The Wind*. As for that wimp, Don Blair IV, too short for basketball, too slight for football, and too stupid in school, I feel like vomiting every time I see him. Thanks to getting the idea from watching an old clip of the movie *The Sound of Music* where Baron von Trapp's would-be fiancée tells of sending step-children off to boarding school, I got him out of my way except during vacations. Nothing ever came of my divorce petition. My lawyer got paid by Don, and said he wasn't going any further with the case. I got dropped in the shit. Case got dropped. I understand that Florida's short of judges with too many cases on the dockets. This judge threw out my case when I said I wouldn't agree to the measly amount Don wanted to settle for. The hell with Don. What I need is a real guy with a big penis and who understands yachts."

That final page threw me. I've got a normal size cock, and I'm knowledgeable about horses, not yachts.

End of the Diary pages we'd been given.

Happy returned her set of pages and I clipped them back into place in their folder. We lay side by side. There was a heavy silence, except for cars screeching out of the car park beyond our window.

Finally, Happy sighed: "Reckon she got herself killed? Or is the story mo'e comp-li-cated? This Don might have shot her. But kill himself? Cain't guess at thet. We'd need to know mo'e about him. Let's us'n drive on to Sunblair t'morrow. Ah don't like this ho-tel anyways."

Tim didn't like the hotel either. He wouldn't eat the breakfast served free in the lobby. We had to make the now-customary pilgrimage to the nearest McDonald's.

CHAPTER 4

McDonald's done with, we hit US 1, heading north.

It took hours to reach Sunblair, far in the north of the state.

Entering Sunblair, I telephoned to speak to Mrs. Blair from my car phone. "Mrs. Edna Blair? This is Rick Harrow. Your grandson suggested we come to Sunblair to help him. We're just entering the town now. We'd like to find Don Blair Junior. Could you tell us where to find him?"

"Who are you? How do I know you aren't some pedophile, stalking my grandson? He's a pretty enough boy for a stalker to try his filthy tricks on him."

I thought of the scars on his face from acne, but I didn't contradict her. I tried a placating mode, "Believe me, he wants to see me."

Happy gently took over my cell phone. "Mrs. Blair? I'm Happy Harrow, Rick's wife. We done drove all the way from Mi-amah to help your grandson. Where can we find him?"

"Oh, he's at the sheriff's office. I guess he's safe enough from predators there. Turn right at the Post Office. First big building on your left."

It wasn't so easy to find the Post Office. We circled some rather grand avenues with Southern-American style houses, reminiscent of the antebellum ones I'd seen in Mississippi, garlanded with wide porches framed by imposing pillars.

On my earlier trip to Sunblair with Lori she'd done the navigating and I hadn't paid much attention to its buildings. I was there for a fuck, nothing more.

It was not until we'd entered a slum area that we did locate a Post Office. These streets were mean, crowded with Guatemalans, Haitians, and Cubans squatting on the sidewalks: one Latino pointed out the large building we wanted. It was not on a main street, and I guessed the land was cheaper here. I thought that might explain why the sheriff's office was here.

No candy wrappers or empty beer bottles on its lawn.

There was an over-spill of Latinos standing in a stationery queue on its steps. Why? I wasn't to know.

As a family of five *whities*, including three infants with a mother carrying the latest baby, we sidestepped the queue. In an oversized hallway we looked at doors spaced around its octagonal shape, The doors had labels reading: Internal Affairs. Detective Bureau, Narcotics Bureau, Organized Crime, Media Relations, Tactical/Intelligence Bureau, Homicide, Corrections, and Detention.

There was an information desk planted in the center rather like the stove in a modernized kitchen. The uniformed policewoman seated there was an African-American, the first I'd seen in Sunblair. She pointed to the doors. "All these doors belong to the sheriff's office. You got an appointment. Or arraigned? Which door you want?"

"The sheriff's. Could you point it out?"

I expected a smart-ass reply. Instead I was ushered with Happy and our infants to the sheriff's private office. No delay.

Tim, who had been kidnapped last year, had never quite forgiven his mother and me for not releasing him from his abductors earlier. Also, he resented us having more children. He wet his bed every night to prove to us he was still enduring the aftermath of his kidnapping.

I had become a permissive parent, like many other fathers around the world I'd let my child control me. Not Happy, her approach to Tim's problem was cuddles and strict orders. "If y'all gives a hoss his head he'll run out into a road and get killed. Same with kids, let them go as they pleases and no mo'e problem because the kid will be dead, killed on a road." Now, she wasn't about to permit Tim to carry on here in this police station. She held tight to his belt. He became subdued, he'd watched a lot of police movies with Happy.

We entered to find the sheriff with his shoes propped on his desk.

The white-bearded sheriff didn't look like anybody a Casting Director would hire as a cop for a gangster movie. More like Santa Claus, he was perfect for *Miracle On Thirty-Fourth Street*. He could have acted as a Santa without makeup.

He'd perched his massive behind on the front of an imposing desk. He was smoking a cigar underneath a sign advising No Smoking. There were at least five stogies in a nearby ashtray. He was nodding with compassion at something Don Blair had just said. The pimply boy, decked out in jeans and a T-shirt, was sitting on a corner of the desk as if he was the sheriff's son. Was this sheriff partial to orphans? Sorry for Don Blair? Should I have had more sympathy for Don Junior because he was an orphan?

"You're Rick Harrow?" he asked, not needing an answer. He'd surely seen the compromising photograph on the last page of Lori's diary with me wearing an idiotic expression after coitus.

To the sheriff I said, "Yes. And this is Hillary Harrow, my wife." I never used Happy's nickname in front of officials, from the Queen on down.

Happy gave the sheriff one of her huge crescent smiles that had been known to melt murderers.

His face softened. He offered Happy the only available chair. She immediately proceeded to pull out the towel she used as a curtain and began to breastfeed Irish.

Soon Irish could be heard sucking away.

Young Don Blair looked embarrassed. No doubt he'd never heard an infant sucking at breastfeeding before.

"You have some information for me?" The sheriff directed his question to Happy. Had he heard about her reputation for solving murders? As far away as in Sunblair? Possibly, what with the wonders of Google. I wasn't going to allow him to use my Happy for his purposes.

"No. We're here to comply with a promise we made to young Blair," I said.

The sheriff asked, "You've read Mrs. Lori Blair's Diary?"

Although it was too painfully obvious that the sheriff didn't require a reply, I said glumly, "Yes."

"I hope you haven't come here to waste my time," This sheriff was one tough bloke.

Young Don interrupted. His usually slightly untidy hair was now in a complete mess, the ends standing up like corn in a field; his face was racked from tear stains, gulping, he bleated "I'm the one with information! I've just learned that Lori had AIDS. Her Guatemalan boyfriend too. But not my father."

To my astonishment, the sheriff let Don take over. Why? Impressed by his name, Blair? Could it be because the information about Lori and her lover having Aids was new to him?

Sensing that this visit to the sheriff had been worse than a mistake, I gave Happy the nod, meaning we should leave. I said, "Let's go. Goodbye, Sheriff. Thanks for giving us your time."

Did this information mean I'm infected with HIV? And, now too Happy! I couldn't wait to get out of this sheriff's office and go to a clinic to have us undergo lab tests.

With all the various units behind those eight doors outside, I knew somewhere close by there must be a local Sexually Transmitted Diseases clinic.

I interrupted Happy from her breastfeeding, and again suggested we leave. Reluctantly, she detached Irish, who began to howl. I said to the sheriff: "We came to see Don Blair. I wanted to fulfill a promise I made to him to try to help solve this case thanks to my wife's very special talent. We'll be at the local hotel, if you need us."

"Wait!" Don Blair jumped off the desk to block the door. "Don't! Don't, please don't go to the Blair Hotel. And anyway, you *needn't* check in at the hotel. It's totally horrible, crawling with cockroaches. One tourist saw rats. My grandmother will give you rooms. Her address is Forty-Nine Williams Street. Ask anyone. Anyone can point it out to you." He slid away from the door, opened it gallantly for Happy, and began to cry.

I saluted the sheriff as if we were both in the same regiment and eased out into that hexagonal hall. The queue of immigrant workers had increased in size and length. We passed doleful looks leaving the building. I'd read in my Florida newspaper that several towns had suffered from the state's real estate bubble, which not only had caused abandonment of construction on new buildings but on hotels also. I surmised that these immigrants had been brought to Sunblair to work as hotel workers for a project that had been abandoned.

"Clinic, first?" Happy asked, forecasting what she knew we had to do. We went to the car park, and climbed into the Hummer where she finished breastfeeding Irish while we scoured the neighborhood for the right clinic.

It wasn't difficult to locate. A queue of Haitians stood out from its entrance like an exclamation point. Again we bypassed that queue. Inside, a surly nurse in a soiled uniform of bright printed cotton led us to a barely-clean room. Very unlike anything we'd have found in a hospital, this place was obviously down-market for locals who would have damn little money.

Sunblair was obviously on the skids. It had too many new immigrants for too few jobs. The national economy's doldrums were accentuated here. There were For Sale signs on many office buildings and empty lots where construction had halted. It didn't surprise me that this clinic for contagious venereal diseases would be so dilapidated when poverty reeked all around the neighborhood.

We both submitted to the tests. Would I need to have Tim, Dorothy and Irish tested eventually? Oh, God. Please, no! I paid, and knew it was going to be a hard road to endure the terrible wait for our results. Was it Robert Frost who wrote a poem about a "long road to travel?"

Forty-nine Williams Street was indeed easily pointed out by a passerby. He'd indicated we should leave this down-market slum area and head for a low hill that overlooked it. Probably one of the few hills before the Alabama border.

We entered a broad avenue with century old trees hung with Spanish moss.

Stately homes were set back from long driveways with wide trees sporting feathery branches that had once sheltered carriages carrying ladies with parasols wearing hoop skirts. Sunblair had been founded when great plantations had surrounded the town. The Civil War had wiped out the plantations. The slaves were long gone, leaving a vacuum to be filled eventually by today's Latin immigrants, and Haitians. But with no plantations, no factories, and little tourism, the great houses belonged to a past tense as surely as aristocrats in a republic.

The senior Mrs. Blair's house was the grandest of all. In perfect order, with newly painted black shutters and a seamless white facade, the large columned porch led to a set of double doors crowned by a glass Georgian-style fan light.

Mrs. Blair had been advised of our arrival. She stood centrally between the open double doors, a welcoming smile on her parchment face. She could have been right out of a poster by Norman Rockwell, depicting a Southern lady exuding hospitality. Her fluttering hands played with organza skirts. Her hair was in a neat white bun, drawn back from loops over her well-formed ears. She wore low-heeled lace-up shoes with elastic save-those-varicose veins stockings.

"Welcome to Blair House," she said in a very different tone from what she'd used on the telephone. "And what attractive children you have," she added. What a transformation. The moment we stepped through her wide doors she was a Southern aristocrat eager to provide comforts to travelers. Blair House? Surely that was the same name that graces the mansion where visiting dignitaries are housed in Washington D.C. For one mad moment I wondered which of the two mansions had preceded the other to take that name.

But underlying that smile was the sadness of a mother who has recently lost her only son. Her skirts were black, her shoes were black, she wore a black and white printed blouse: she was in mourning. No hypocrisy there, she was really grieving. With graceful movements, almost like a ballerina on stage, she led us up a floating staircase to the upper level bedrooms. A magnificent chandelier studded with pink light bulbs hung from a rotunda. It vied with the late December sunset to flood the walls with a rosy glow.

Happy was given a separate bedroom from mine. Did Mrs. Blair think I'd caught AIDS from Lori, and should be kept in quarantine? The clinic had told me that "the rapid test" would take about twenty minutes. It was time for me to use my cell phone and inquire whether I'd caught the disease or not, and whether I'd infected Happy. I dialed the clinic's number and got the results from the nurse.

Negative.

Our tests were clear. Lori must have caught HIV from a lover who came on the scene after me. Thank God!

From experiencing a high from the good news that we weren't diseased I went into a down by finding the room assigned to me. My bedroom was a morose, gloomy brown. Everything there was brown: the mahogany bed with its brown velvet cover, a brown toned Aubusson rug, two matching chairs upholstered in brown leather. Walls with brown based alternate stripes. Was this her late husband's bolt hole? If so, it hadn't provided a pleasant escape from whatever troubles had obsessed him. I unpacked my gear, and looked for Happy's room.

It was down the hall near a very solid bathroom, where a heavy tub on bronze feet offered a foot in diameter head shower. Apparently there was only one bathroom for the entire floor. Not surprising, considering this house dated from two centuries ago in the early 1800s.

Happy's room was a wonderful contrast to mine. Her bed had a sweeping, vaulted canopy covered in white organdy and trimmed with Irish lace. The boudoir table had a skirt embroidered in spring flowers and the two chairs beside it were covered in pastel chintz. A wooden mantel hovered over a long-extinct fireplace. Cherubs in several positions of prayer decorated the chimney ledge. Lovely.

Happy was fussing over her mountain of baby paraphernalia. She'd brought dozens of diapers for the three infants, but not enough sweaters.

"It be much colder heah than in Mi-ami," she pronounced Miami Mi-amah. "Who'd have guessed?"

Mrs. Blair entered the room carrying towels. "It's always ten or more degrees colder here than in the southern part of the state. The Gulfstream veers out to the Atlantic after Jupiter." She hung the towels on a mahogany towel rack. I hadn't seen one of those since leaving England. Another reminder of "the old ways in England" was a stand holding a basin and jug to relieve congestion in the bathroom.

I hadn't expected to have a feeling of homecoming any more than I'd foreseen the change in Mrs. Blair.

"Thank you kindly," Happy said, helping herself to one of the towels that smelled of potpourri.

"Jemima will have supper on the table in the dining room at seven," Mrs. Blair said smiling, and left us alone.

"What were the test results?" Happy asked quickly. "Negative. I don't have HIV. You don't have HIV."

"Thet means the woman Lori had another lover after y'all. Or lovers."

"Yes. I thought of that too. But, Happy —"

"Don't. We ain't goin' to fight over what happened. You got one hell of a scare. Me too. You ain't goin' to chase after other women very soon again. Seems like y'all's unlucky with adultery. Didn't thet Russian woman, Irina, work for Putin's FSB? Lucky escape y'all had, thet time too."

Irina! Happy knew about Irina? And had kept quiet all these many months, never complaining, never haranguing!

If I hadn't already loved her beyond everything else in life, I certainly did now. I could hardly wait to get through dinner with Mrs. Blair so that I could rush Happy upstairs and under her bed's vaulted canopy.

CHAPTER 5

Meanwhile I had to be the thoughtful father and locate the room where our children had been planted. They had been given one that was obviously not meant for family members. It was very plain, almost like the rooms of second rate boarding schools in Scotland. As a boy I'd been dispatched to one of those a long time ago, and was ecstatic to return to England to enter Eton, where most boys were separated into more comfortable housemaster's homes.

The babysitter's room was even more stark. It told me that the 1800s must have been a bad time to be a servant in such a household. Dinner was a painful process. Before seven o'clock it was announced by a gong.

We heard voices in the hall: young Ron's and Mrs. Blair's. There were excited notes, horrified exclamations, and then silence.

Feeling like intruders, Happy and I took our places at the long table. Our children had been allocated to the kitchen where the babysitter and a mothering Jemima was attending to them.

Mrs. Blair indicated she would say a prayer. The Grace was over-long and her son's death mentioned twice. Over the papaya salad, fried chicken and grits with avocado, not a word more was said of Don Senior. Mrs. Blair was saving the cannonball for dessert.

"You'll like our mango pie," she began. "All our fruits are grown on the place." She had a sweetly modulated Southern-American accent without the "ain't"s and double negatives Happy used. "It won't make you sick, but Don's news might. It seems that Lori had AIDS."

I answered, "We knew."

My two words hung in the air like the tip of a tornado. Had Mrs. Blair just learned that Lori had Aids and was wondering if I'd caught it too?

Why was I here, at this traditional table being entertained by Mrs. Blair? She had obviously read Lori's diary! Had young Don told her about his trip to Miami to accuse me, and that he'd come away convinced I hadn't killed his father? And that he'd heard that my wife Happy had solved nine murders?

That must be the explanation.

In the grieving tone of a mother who couldn't replace her only son, Mrs. Blair continued: "My son didn't have AIDS. Lori must never have had relations with him after she met the man who infected her. Don Junior has just left the medical officer detailed to this case. He told Junior that my son was not the carrier. Now I'll leave it up to you two to clear his name. If it's true that Hillary has solved other murders. I know that my son didn't kill Lori. You will need to prove that."

Mrs. Blair had swiveled in her chair and was concentrating on Happy.

Her every word pierced Happy like arrows.

Happy blushed. "We'll do what we can," she murmured.

Mrs. Blair's demanding tone changed. "Your name's Hillary, isn't it? Why are you nicknamed Happy?"

"My Paw thought like as Ah was happy-go-lucky. And Ah was too, until Ah made up my mind to be a jockey and give my all to thet."

"And you actually got your license to ride as an apprentice jockey?" "Yeah Ma'am, Ah sho' did. But thet took some doin', what with bein' from up in the hills and needin' t'git to Louisville fo' to work there. Lucky Ah was too, 'cause my Aunt Bessie had wed a hot-walker at a hoss farm. He taught me, so little by little Ah was allowed to ride hosses, and when Ah showed like Ah could make them go faster, Ah got my license."

"I see. And when did you start to solve murders?" Mrs. Blair spoke icily for the first time, as if testing Happy. Mrs. Blair had got to the nitty-gritty. "When a girl jockey done got killed. We was on a picnic t'gethuh. She was poisoned by some altered mustard. She were Jewish and wouldn't eat the ham sandwiches we'd brought."

"And you are a poisons expert?"

"Naw. But when two other girl jockeys done got killed, one by a dart and t'other strangled, Ah just knew by my innards who could have done them in."

"I see." Mrs. Blair was cutting short her comments. "Go to bed. We'll talk more in the morning." She rose from the table. No coffee was offered. No mint chocolates or port as might have been the case in England after such a grand dinner.

Like two orphans we scuttled upstairs to our separate bedrooms. I fell asleep listening to the two Blairs, grandmother and grandson, their voices drumming like hail stones.

CHAPTER 6

I dreamed during the night that I was at home in England at my father's house in Warwickshire. He was helping me to pack my kit when I was leaving to fight with my regiment in the Bosnia war. But in my dream it was Lori Blair who kissed me away in our driveway.

What had been my feelings for Lori in early December? There was lust for her, a shadow of her lust. Not love. I had not admired her. Lori had never shown herself to be the type of woman I'd call a lady, but worse, her heart had seemed soiled. I was awakened by Happy kissing me. She'd slid into my bed and her toes were wiggling against mine. Though born on a parcel in the Kentucky Hills, in her own way she was a true lady.

The breakfast gong sounded before we could initiate lovemaking.

I raised my shoulders, as a defeated lover, and changed from pajamas into a T-shirt that read 'Mickey Loves Minnie' from Disney, and put on my old jeans.

Happy rushed to her room to dress.

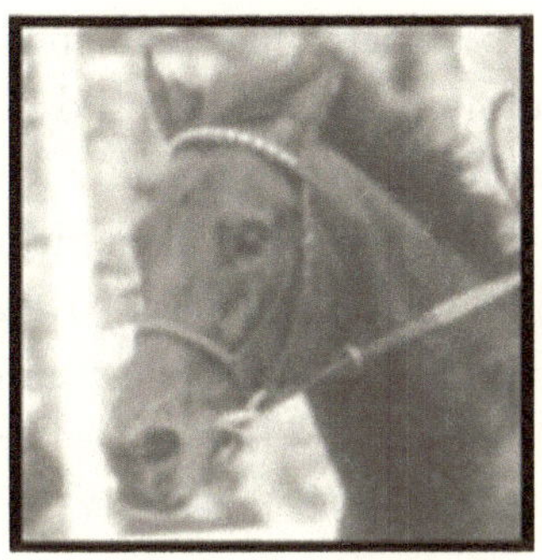

CHAPTER 7

I joined Happy at her door. Ready, we ushered our children down into the hall.

Mrs. Blair stood at the base of the flying staircase. On her face was glued that Southern Hospitality smile. "I hope you slept well," she murmured. "Do come to the table while Jemima's waffles are still hot."

The waffles were beyond delicious. I ate two, both topped with melting butter and maple syrup. Happy was offered grits with bacon drippings, which she accepted joyfully. Our babysitter, Tim and Dorothy were in the kitchen with Jemima and were wolfing her waffles.

Howls from Irish in the kitchen hurried her mother to dispatch the grits and get on with breastfeeding.

When Happy had left the room, Mrs. Blair asked questions she'd considered too delicate to pursue in front of my wife. Mrs. Blair set to with a barrage. "How did you meet Lori? Didn't she tell you she was married? Weren't you worried that her husband might cause trouble? Did you ever confront my son?"

How much should I tell her? Be truthful? Truthful yes, hurtful no.

I began by answering her last question, first. "No. I never met your son under any circumstances. And no, I wasn't concerned that he'd cause trouble. I understood that he was a gentleman, from this town's oldest and most distinguished family: so, if we met, which we didn't, I would have expected that we'd have both acted like gentlemen. Yes, Lori told me she was married, but not until our second date. I'd met her at the Seminole Hard Rock Casino and we'd gone on together to a horse sales party. At the Casino I'd gone up to her and said I liked the rubies she was wearing. Now, I rue the day and know I should never have approached her."

"No, indeed you should not. Wasn't she wearing her wedding ring?" "Not that I'd noticed. Her ruby necklace and earrings were so dazzling." I didn't add that her breasts' nipples had peeked out from her low cut blouse and they'd been even more dazzling.

Young Don Blair must have read my mind. He growled: "My father gave her those rubies. I heard him say they matched her pubic hair."

I thought: "My God, what a family! The father talked about the stepmother's pubic hair in front of his son."

The waffles had lost their appeal. I stood up from the dining room table, gave a slight bow as if Mrs. Blair was royal, and hurried up the staircase. I felt we'd overstayed Mrs. Blair's Southern hospitality. Worse, I was suffocating.

Don Blair Junior followed me. "Come into my room," he said in a whisper. "I want to show you something."

I hesitated. But the lure of discovering some facts of interest to this case drove me to chance Mrs. Blair's wrath for entering his room because she might have accused me of being double-gated. Hadn't she already shown suspicions of homosexual predators being on the trail of her grandson?

Downstairs, in the dining room, Mrs. Blair was still on Happy's biography. She looked delighted when Happy left the kitchen for the dining room.

Mrs. Blair had a lorgnette beside her plate. She raised it to stare at Happy. There was silence for a few minutes. When she spoke, Mrs. Blair had changed her tone. She was conciliatory.

"Tell me, Miz Harrow, is it true what my grandson tells me, that you are famous for solving murders? He said he looked you up on something called Google."

Shyly, Happy nodded. "Yeah, Ma'am. Solved a few." "And how did you start?"

"By reading noospapers and seein' murder movies."

While the two women exchanged biographies, I took my chances and followed Don into his lair.

The room where Junior slept was another surprise. It was decorated in high school memorabilia, but with sixties dates, obviously his grandfather's old room. "Choate Varsity" was printed on a triangular banner over a narrow bed with a coverlet in red white and blue stripes. The boy's bed could have been a coffin covered by a flag. There were old prints showing turn-of-the-century golfers, ancient bowlers from Rip van Winkle's time, and trophies for winning at sports dated 1962 to 1966. In the closet were women's clothes in the fashions of the 1920s. Had Blair Senior's father been a crossdresser?

I noticed there was something missing in this room: the normal paraphernalia of a teenage boy. There was no computer, no television, no iPod.

In fact, I could see nothing that related to Young Don. He'd brought zilch from his other home, his parents' fatal house. No reminders of that house with its double murder. And he'd been stuck in his grandfather's very dated room.

He dug under his mattress and handed me more pages from Lori's diary. "Read these. You'll understand more."

I took the pages and scuttled out of his room. I found Happy back with the "chillun" and urged her to pack and get into the Hummer, fastest.

We signed the silk-covered Visitors' Book, gave a solemn promise to Mrs. Blair that someday we would return here, and gave hugs to Young Don.

Back in the Hummer with our "chillun" and babysitter, we plunged southward down US 1.

After a few miles of thoughtful silence, Happy murmured, "I feel sorry for Don Blair Junior. Awful room he lives in, awful home. Be-au-ti-ful architecture, ugly story. He was right to seek us out. Inter-estin' that he had the in-i-tia-tive to search on Google. Mo-ti-vated, because as he told me, he loved his father."

I muttered, low, so that the babysitter couldn't eavesdrop, "Happy, I have a burden of guilt. Caused by what I did to him, and to you."

"Give me a kiss. And let's us'n drive as far away from here as we c'n git."

CHAPTER 8

We hadn't planned to make any stops on the road back to Miami. But again we'd overlooked Tim's penchant to make demands.

Having decided to return to Miami by the Scenic Route, we found ourselves in St. Augustine, home of the oldest chapel in the USA and also of a series of amazing forts. Happy wanted to visit the chapel.

"It be called Nuestra Senora de la Leche, thet's Spanish fo' Our Lady of the Milk, and as Ah's havin' trouble breastfeedin' Irish Ah'd like to stop there."

No way. Tim had glimpsed the outer fortifications of San Marcos Fort. Yelling, he pointed them out, "That's real boy stuff. I'm sick of Dorothy and her dolls. I want cannons."

There was nothing for it but to interrupt our trip, pay the entrance fees, and immerse ourselves in the history of this fort.

A volunteer guide, costumed like a British soldier of the revolutionary era, explained, "This fort is made of coquina rock, that means crushed seashells from this area. It was built by Spanish soldiers, helped by slaves. The king of Spain complained about its cost, said he should be able to see it all the way from Madrid considering the amount of money invested here. The French and British also held it for a time. The incentive was the treasure held here from ships coming from Mexico and Peru with this fort as a principal stop on the Spanish Main. Come on, we'll climb the ramps and I'll show the little boy how the cannons worked."

Tim didn't need prodding. He was up the chief ramp like a gazelle. He touched the gleaming bronze of the massive cannons. These were stood on curious bases with step-like contrivances permitting them to be made higher, or lowered.

Our volunteer continued his set speech, "These cannons were better designed for warfare than what the French had in World War II at the Maginot Line. Those French cannons were set to face Germany and could not be altered. But, two hundred years earlier, right here, these cannons were on swivels so that they could be altered to fire against enemies coming from any direction."

"Boom, boom, boom," Tim shouted out, and pretended to light a cannon's fuse. A very forward child, my son Tim.

Isn't it amazing what kids learn from television these days? Happy asked, "Are there any other forts in the area?" I tried shutting her up on that one, because I didn't want to have to visit another fort, but our guide finessed me and answered quickly,

"Oh, yes. South Southeast of here you could visit Fort Matanzas, a very interesting place. Matanzas means massacres. The fort took that name after the Spanish soldiers based there massacred four hundred Huguenots who had settled nearby. Being Catholics from the severe Inquisition era, they'd felt they had to eradicate the Huguenots in their area." He'd painted an ugly verbal picture, that I guessed meant he didn't want to lose us as his tourists. Did I look like someone who gives hefty tips?

I looked up above our heads to watch a flight of pelicans wing past. I didn't want to stare in a South Southeast direction, though, in case Happy followed the pelicans' route and got the idea of going to Fort Matanzas.

"What about hosses?" Happy queried. Horses being her favorite creatures after her "chillun" and, I hope, me. "No hosses here?"

"Of course, horses. The earliest Spaniards to arrive in Florida brought horses. In fact our Florida lawmakers are even now pushing to make the Cracker horse the official state heritage horse. Had you heard about our Cracker horses? Some folks calls them marsh, tackles, because they can tackle our marshes. They are the descendants of Arab horses brought to the state by the early explorers. Ponce de Leon made the journey from what is today Tampa to Tallahassee in 1539 on a marshtackle. They aren't very handsome horses, a light beige color usually, with small ears and meager withers. But they sure did their job here in the Sixteenth Century."

Our guide wasn't finished with the subject of forts. "There's Fort Marion too. But it doesn't have a moat around it like San Marcos, nor those wide windows that Matanzas boasts. Of course, they have sentry boxes for alerting the arrival of enemies. Those sentry boxes are based on designs used in ancient Spain, where the cry would have been *moros en la costa*. That means Moors On The Coast." He ended his act by flourishing his tricorn hat. Then he stuck out the palm of his hand in the time honored fashion of asking for a tip. I paid.

Happy declared herself to be tired. We'd walked all over that fort, and fortunately the babysitter had kept the two little girls in our car or we'd have had a demand for overtime and God knows what else from her. Personally, I was very glad to get back to the Hummer myself, and find the highway.

A charming surprise welcomed us as we passed the outskirts of St. Augustine, a parade was starting. There were Florida schoolgirl cheerleaders twirling batons, but of far more interest to my Happy were the Cracker horses on show. They were ridden by men in Spanish colonial era costumes. One rider had foregone wearing a costume and was kitted out in his everyday cowboy outfit of wide-brimmed straw hat, high heeled boots, and flannel shirt.

We watched the parade until the "chillun" grew bored, started to yell, and I had to start up the car again.

Charging down the highway in the Hummer, I glimpsed a sign advertising a hostel associated with the Florida Bed and Breakfast Inns Association. Great. One of those would be cheaper than the hotels we'd encountered at Disney and in Ocala. I turned in to the driveway of the first one we came to, and was mesmerized by the long alley of tall old royal palm trees. They had thick crowns of palms that reminded me of ballet dancers' skirts, only inverted. With a high wind starting, the royal palm trees began to sway and their fronds to dance.

In my mind I'd translated these palm fronds into the tutus of dancers in Swan Lake.

My choice of this bed and breakfast hostel paid off. Happy relaxed in the bygone era atmosphere. I could afford three rooms, so I promptly sent off Tim, leaving the girls with the babysitter. Finally I had Happy in a double bed, for sex. The bed had no tacky addition offering a rumba rhythm.

Happy and I didn't need any addition to spur our lovemaking. And in Happy's arms I could feel I was the prince who had captured the queen of the swans.

In the morning we had another Florida experience. We viewed the capture of an alligator. A crowd of onlookers from our hostel had gathered near a brook that passed under sahuarina trees laced with dripping Spanish moss. In a clearing a wiry middle aged woman was wrestling a six-foot alligator.

I held Tim's hand in a vice. No running into that clearing to get closer to that alligator for our inquisitive three-year-old.

Happy made friends with one of the other tenants from the hotel. "Why this lady wrestlin' this all-i-gator," she asked perkily.

"Damn 'gator was sashaying around the Inn's grounds. Can't have that. Some of us bring our dogs with us. Dog would be a tasty morsel, for a 'gator. This lady? She's been hired to rid the place of the 'gator. Her husband was usually hired to do the job, but he's passed on and as she'd learned the tricks he used, she's the person what folks calls when there's a gator bein' a pest."

From head to end of its tail, this alligator was as long as a horse. It had pre-historic armor-like skin on its back, but when "the lady" tipped it over we could see the very vulnerable underside that is so desirable for shoes and handbags. It had a peculiar roar, and its eyes bulged with fury. But "the lady" had snared its powerful jaws, and soon – too soon for our Tim -– she'd netted it with ropes and forklifted it onto the back of her pickup to be released far from any of the area's inns.

The onlookers dispersed. I went to the hotel's lobby, found the cashier's desk, paid our very reasonable bill, repacked the Hummer with all of Happy's baby necessities, geared up the Hummer's tired engine, and headed South. All five of us were relieved to return to our Miami cottage.

Irish stopped bawling. Dorothy found a packet of chocolates hidden away. Tim ate his favorite M&M's.

After our four-hour drive home, and paying the disgruntled babysitter, settling the infants for the night and having a stiff drink each. I slipped the pages of Lori's diary from my blazer's pocket. I didn't suggest we read them in bed. They seemed to be figuratively dripping with pus, I didn't want to sully our sheets with their venom.

We sat down in the kitchenette, handing on the pages as we read them.

In this addition to the diary, Lori had torn into the memory of her husband's father, Donald Blair II. She'd scribbled: "How I despised that old pig, Donald the Great, what with his wearing women's clothes and being such a meany about money. No wonder my husband's so mixed-up. Can't have an erection. Can't ever satisfy ME. Won't spend a tenth of his salary. Leaves me at home when he looks up his snobbish Kent School friends."

Her father-in-law had been a cross dresser. That could explain the old-fashioned clothes Mrs. Bliss had worn: remnants out of his weirdly-filled closet.

Her father-in-law wasn't the only gentleman to draw Lori's wrath. Her diary continued with more hate for another character, "How I hated Mr. Collins, such a nasty boss always snarling at my darling Pedro. No wonder Pedro killed him. Screaming at sweet Pedro as he did, accusing him of pilfering money from his safe. And after Pedro had saved his yacht from months of dry dock in Guatemala by inventing a way to change parts out of other boats to get Mr. Collins's stinking boat to work. Now the police have locked up my Pedro with his gorgeous cock and glistening balls. Arraigned him on a murder charge without bail. Pedro had been doing the world a favor when he knifed horrible old Mr. Collins. I'd have pawned my rubies to help Pedro pay back Mr. Collins, but I never got the chance before he insulted Pedro so outrageously that Pedro pulled that knife. But what am I going to do without my Pedro? I don't want to try to renew that stupid affair with Rick Harrow. The hell with that. Anyway, after tasting Pedro's sublime lovemaking, who'd want what insipid treats Rick had to offer."

Insipid treats? According to the ecstatic expression on her lips that wasn't her opinion when I was lying on top of her in bed.

Did I have to give these pages to Happy to read? I did. I'd promised to share them with her, and so sharing was a must.

My amazing wife digested their contents without a snide comment. She said, "Ah don't need no adultress to say ugly things about my husband. Don't know as Ah'd believe anythin' she done wrote."

To prove her disdain for what she'd read, Happy initiated love-making. Perhaps just to prove SHE didn't think I was an insipid performer.

The following day I devoted every hour exclusively to the horses under my supervision. Our newly bought colt showed heat in a foreleg and I had to call in an expensive vet. If we were to make the date set for us to return to England with the new colt, I had to work fast with the vet.

Returning home in the evening, longing for a hot shower and a cup of coffee, I wasn't delighted to see young Blair at our house, seated in my leather chair sipping coffee out of my mug with the word 'Dad' on it. I hadn't given a thought to Young Blair all day: I'd wiped his story from my mind.

I came into the living room to hear part of his take on the description of Pedro's arrest. Speaking forcefully now, he drummed his fingers on a small suitcase he'd brought with him. This was a very changed Don Blair, he had straightened his shoulders, making visible a long strong neck. Suddenly he seemed to have grown two inches in height. His mouth was firm.

He said in a voice that was changing from tenor to baritone, "We'd suspected Pedro as the murderer of my father and Lori. Because he'd used our local clinic and been tested positive for Aids, as had Lori. But we soon learned that Pedro had been locked up in jail for killing his boss before my father was murdered. No way could Pedro have got out of that jail. Not one of those jails that mollycoddle criminals. Do they call them open jails? No, Pedro was with the guys that are ankle shackled. He's in the one for future inmates of death row. He was refused bail."

Happy, holding the matching mug reading 'Mom,' interrupted.

"Why would Pedro kill his boss, thet Mr. Collins? Yell back, maybe. But kill? We saw Guatemalans in Sunblair standing in line for want of jobs. Pedro's job with Mr. Collins sounded mighty fine."

"Pedro lost his temper. In Guatemala a man can get off for that, something in a law under the heading of *ira y intenso dolor*.

Doesn't work that way in the USA. Didn't you read about the actress who wrote and starred in *Waitress*, Adrienne Shelly, and how she was murdered in New York when she harangued an Ecuadorean? Some guy called Diego Pillco. She'd scolded him for making too much noise in her building. He took offense, killed her, and then hung her in a bathroom to make it look like a suicide. She'd made thet great movie, *Waitress*."

"Ah loved thet movie. The last scene when the cake-maker walks away with her little girl, just wonderful. Ah DID read about her murder. What a waste of a talented woman. Killed, just fo' complainin' of noise."

"Well, she did slap the Ecuadorean after complaining. Men aren't used to being slapped by a woman in Ecuador. Real machos, the men in Ecuador. Not like my grandfather: that wimp. A crossdresser. No wonder my grandmother took up ballroom dancing and entered tango contests all over America. And with a mother dancing the tango on TV and at every whistle stop, is it any wonder that my father had a wild streak that pushed him into marrying Lori?"

"Thanks fo' thet info about Mrs. Blair Senior. Ah's been ponderin' this case o' your'n. Ah'd thought maybe the murderer could have been a robber who done went wild and shot them both when the burglary went wrong? There's just been a case in Miami where a famous football star got killed thet way. The Washington Redskins star, Sean Taylor. Four guys broke in when they noticed luxury cars parked outside the Taylor home. And one of the suspects told police he'd broken in there befo'e. That he knew Taylor kept $200,000 in a black bag in a bedroom. Had your father's home been broken into befo'e? Did he keep money in the house?"

"No," Young Blair seemed to have a load on his shoulders like a Guatemalan brick carrier, "there was no break-in. No signs of a burglary. Never a break-in before, either. What incriminates my father is that he had gunpowder stains on his right hand."

Quietly, not prodding too noticeably, Happy asked, "Where do you go to school?"

"I'm a boarder at Pils Academy, in Massachusetts. Soon as my father married Lori, they packed me off to boarding school."

"And that's where you were on the night of them killings?"

"Yes. It was exam week. I'd finished most of my tests when the news of the deaths came, so I was excused from taking the last ones to go home for the funerals."

Happy nodded. "Did you pass the tests?"

"Not all of them. I flunked again in geometry. I'm no good at mathematics. Which is terrible for me. I've seen lift-offs at Cape Canaveral. Awesome! I wanted to be an astronaut. No way, not when I'm so lousy at math. Reminds me: I've got a plane to catch. My holidays end tomorrow. I've got to leave for the airport."

I asked: "How long does it take to get from Florida to your school in Massachusetts?"

"From Miami, about three and a half hours. Direct flight to Boston, then a local takes me to the west of the state."

"And door to door from your father's house in Sunblair?"

"Duh! I know what you're thinking. That I could have killed them and flown down and back from Pils. No way. I loved my father and had got used to Lori. And I've never been able to kill anything: not even worms to go fishing. My father may have had his peculiarities, such as marrying Lori, the kind of woman the oldies used to say you fuck but don't marry. But Lori was never worse than stand-offish to me, thought I was a bore."

"Don, we didn't suspect you," Happy said, placing a friendly hand on Don's.

"So you didn't. Goodbye for now. But don't think I'm letting this go. I've got my Grandma to think of too, you know. She's going to be awfully lonely. She'd built her life around my father and his law career. She's not such a dragon as she appeared when you were in Sunblair. She was putting on an act hoping to get you to clear Father's name. I'm going to help her to find a new interest. She loves ballroom dancing. Maybe she could get on a TV program's ballroom dancing competition and that could give her more fun in the future."

Young Blair picked up his small suitcase and went to the front door. "I've got my computer at Pils, you can e-mail me there on www.blairjunior. com or text me on my cell phone: 1-617-444-0040."

The door shut behind him. I could hear him treading his way toward the bus stop. I didn't go to the window to watch him board.

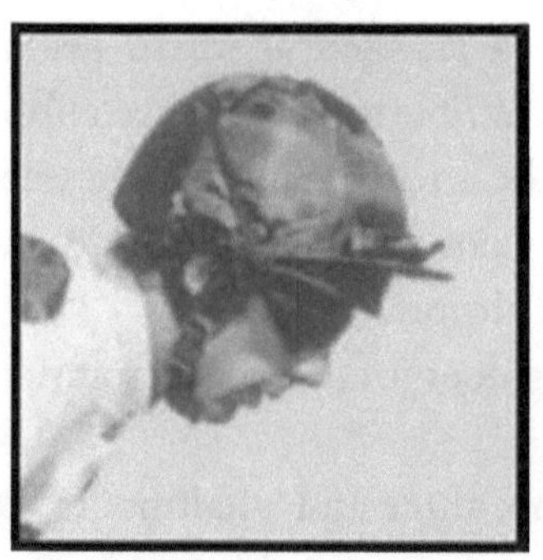

CHAPTER 9

My cell phone rang. I looked at the caller's name on the ID panel. On the line was Hal Murphy, my Canadian owner, who'd been so generous to help with ransoming Happy when she was abducted in Dubai. I'd had to forego my care of his horses to fly to Miami to look for the derby prospect colt Fran was so determined to find.

"Yes, sir? Did you have a Happy Christmas? What can I do for you?" That name, Hal Murphy, had wiped from my mind all vestige of the Blair murder.

"You can get back to England, soonest. You e-mailed me that Anchor's got trouble in a hoof. I have great new plans for that horse. I don't want him mucked about by some asshole vet poking about his hooves without your supervision."

"Yes, sir. Soonest. I'll get Happy to start packing. We're finished with looking for colts here. But there could be a small problem. Could your secretary sort out tickets for my family? Tickets may be hard to get this time of year. So many English students returning home from the holidays." I didn't go on about Anchor's sore hoof. Rule Three on how to deal with owners: accentuate the positive, never dwell on the negative.

"If Business Class is not available, I'll pay for First. Can't let any asshole ruin Anchor." Murphy rang off. He'd never been cheap when something had to be done. Supervise our English vet? Sure. And wouldn't First Class be nice!

Of course Happy had to repack all the clothing and equipment for the "chillun." I suggested we pay the babysitter to come back to us to help with the packing.

"Thet idle good-fo'-nothin' babysitter who did nothin' but complain cause we didn't stay at Disney for the whole three days so's she could go on all the rides? Forget it. We couldn't afford stayin' on at Disney. We cain't afford her now!"

Trying to help Happy pack was useless. Happy was using glass baby bottles to feed orange juice to Irish: she believed the plastic ones leaked chemicals. I broke three glass bottles before she asked me not to help "no mo'e."

Murphy's secretary called my cell phone several hours later to inform me we were on the next afternoon's flight: First Class. I was to collect our electronic tickets at the British Airways counter.

The little cottage-style house in Miami's Coral Gables had never appealed much to me, yet I felt a certain end of the school year nostalgia to leave it. In the evening, looking at the reddening sunset sky with a flight of pelicans soaring overhead with their white underbellies tinted rose from the setting rays, I acknowledged that Miami had its better moments.

From the path that led to a small dock I could see a heron preening itself, plucking at its feathers while it balanced on its stilted legs. Nearby was a puddle, ugly during the day, but quite beautiful now reflecting the last crimson rays of the setting sun. Like Miami, sometimes ugly, but could be beautiful.

Next morning we drove in the Hummer back to the airport's rental agency. Where only last week the avenues had been garlanded with lights, holly and full sized plastic reindeer now these same avenues had no reminder of Christmas other than broken strips of tinsel and the occasional still-blinking fairy lights.

Happy sighed: "What's the weather report for southern England?"

"Very cold. I read the world report in the Miami Herald. But I spoke to Mrs. Wright this morning and she promised me that she has our Epsom house well heated."

"What she considers warm is about the temp-era-ture of the North Pole." Tim, who was growing into a tall boy faster than bamboo shoots reach toward the sun, asked: "Isn't that where Santa's supposed to live?" Tim accentuated the word "supposed" to remind me he was a big boy now and didn't believe in Santa Claus.

"Yes, son." I reached Thirty-Sixth Street and noted a sign showing an airplane denoting we were nearing the airport. I recalled reading somewhere that so many visitors to Miami couldn't read English, that it would be useless to print signs in my native language. We'd gone back to cavemen's use of picturing what needed to be communicated.

We almost missed the plane for London.

Seated in the First Class section, I got help from the stewardesses to feed Dorothy and Tim, while Happy breast fed Irish. When the three children had full tummies they went to sleep. Relaxing, Happy reached for the local Florida newspaper.

"Lookee here," she said in what was an unusually deep tone: "Look at this article about a rape at Palm Beach's Everglades Club."

I leaned over her shoulder to read the headline. It blazoned, "DNA Testing On Trial."

The article concerned the rape of a twenty-year-old, Melissa Legare in April, 2006, who had been working as a pastry chef at that club. On April 2 she claimed she woke to find a man pushing with his penis to get inside her. She knew the man, he was a Guatemalan dishwasher, Esdras Cardona, an illegal immigrant. Both the victim and the alleged attacker lived in dormitories provided by the club, alongside its premises near the intersection between Worth Avenue and Cocoanut Row in Palm Beach. The Guatemalan, thirty-three years old, was one of eight siblings who worked in the USA.

Melissa Legare had previously reported to the club management that she had observed Cardona peeking through her window to watch her toweling herself after a shower. He claimed he was innocent of the rape, that during the night before dawn on April 2nd he had been playing cards with his brothers, who also worked for the club and lived in the dormitories. But the pastry chef insisted she recognized him. She said he'd left behind a shirt, in a medium size, white, made by Hale, and that a similar shirt had been found in a drawer in Cardona's room. Also, a toothbrush had allegedly been left behind by the attacker. Cardona was accustomed to carrying a toothbrush in his shirt pocket. The pastry chef's regular boyfriend swore he'd seen that same type of toothbrush tucked often into his shirt pocket by Cardona. This circumstantial evidence was enough to convict him.

Cardona was convicted of the attack in the summer of 2007.

In December, 2007, Cardona received help to re-open his case. He demanded DNA trials be made on the hairs found in the victim's bed. There had been an outcry by Guatemalans all over Florida that Cardona had not received a fair trial in 2006, and his DNA must be tested.

Happy nodded. "Ah feels that this Cardona's case could have some bearin' on the Blair couple's deaths. Any mater-i-als what don't belong to Mr. Blair's house, such as a swatch of organdy, or a piece o' string; anything, everything should have been tested fo' DNA. Especial-like anything from Grandma Blair's house, that could have had DNA of the murderer on it."

"Why are you interested in this, my darling?"

Happy used her index finger to point to the center of a column in the newspaper story. "It says here that there's a wave of prisoners insisting that they too have DNA evidence they want tested. Post conviction claims, they's called. Listen up, Honey. This could have been impo'tant if them Sunblair po-lice had wanted t'give y'all a hard time. Read this here, 'Florida legislators recently passed a law requiring that all criminal defendants taking plea deals be asked beforehand if there exists any biological evidence that may exonerate them.' Them's impo'tant words. It's the state's way of heading off a defendant's post conviction claim befo'e he even says guilty as charged. Do y'all follow? This guy Cardona, he didn't have enough money to pay for a private lab to do a DNA testing on that toothbrush. And them hairs wut were found in the girl's bed, a man's hairs that were never tested by the state for their DNA. Not befo'e the trial. A jury found Cardona guilty, he was given twenty years. Honey, y'all hear? Y'all could have got twenty years on cir-cum-stantial ev'dence in the Blair case. DNA! It sho' could mean a lot in the Blair case too. None o' your DNA on the murder weapon."

I took over the newspaper, and attentively read the entire article. By the time I'd finished it my Happy was as deep in slumberland as were our "chillun"

Except for that article about the DNA involvement in that rape case at the Everglades Club, during the flight we had no other comments relative to the Blairs' case. I was glad to oversee Happy's calm and tranquil sleep. Why should a trial about Melissa Legare's human rights have affected her? According to the article I.d read, her attorney had put forward that there were acts or omissions that contributed to the constellation of factors that brought about this particular crime. Discriminatory practices had fostered a dangerous environment. I didn't get the connection. But, apparently Happy had done so.

CHAPTER 10

Every time I return from our travels, I find that my home in Epsom has hardly changed at all.

Timeless English country life suits me perfectly. Yet, although I settle back immediately into my schedule at home, nevertheless when I receive a call sending me back to an airport, I'm always ready to go.

Fran Purcell had been lucky with the yearling I bought for her in Florida. As a two-year-old the gelding would win several races. I wouldn't give him too many runs, I was saving him to produce really great form as a three-year-old.

I'D HAD him gelded. With geldings I know you have to win as many races as possible because there's no chance of the big money from nominations. And Fran couldn't be sure he'd do well over the sticks because not all flat racing giants make good jumpers. The flat racing life of geldings spans at most nine years whereas a jumper could go on into the teens.

When Fran telephoned and ordered me to go back to Florida to buy another horse, I acquiesced although I knew that January was not the best season for the good sales. The snowbirds' season would have begun with the zillionaires present to make ridiculously high bids on so-so horses.

Fran was not to be put off her demand that I return to Florida. Had she realized that this latest acquisition was no earth-shaker?

"Shit, I've a friend in Clewiston who swears he's got a miracle horse for me. Jump on a plane, and take a look," Fran demanded in her deepest contralto. No contradicting this owner.

"May I bring Happy with me?"

"Oh, I suppose so. But I'm not paying the airfare for all those other little kids and a nanny."

It was only Tim who'd pay half-fare. The two infants would go free, but again no contradicting this owner.

With Mrs. Wright ensconced in our Epsom home and our neighbor Ellie visiting every day, I felt I could chance going to Florida leaving behind the two baby girls.

I paid for Tim's half-fare ticket. Happy packed the usual mountain of clothes for him, although in Florida he usually made do with shorts, a T-shirt, and pajamas.

We three flew into Miami skirting the edge of a hurricane. It had missed Florida's shore but its curling winds had spat fury along the beaches downing palm trees and leaving a mess of coconuts and fronds.

With the many bad memories we shared of other times in Miami, I decided to rent a car and take my little family directly to Clewiston.

I'd booked us into the historic Clewiston Inn, gracing that town of two thousand resorters and sugar farmers on the south side of Lake Okeechobee. My travel agent had guaranteed that this white-columned stately pile had been updated. It was. We drew up to the columns from the Sugarland Highway. The doorman took our luggage and showed us the way to the reception desk. Much as I would have preferred not to, I hired a double bed room with cot. That meant that Tim could observe Happy and me at our lovemaking. Not a great idea, but Fran wasn't paying for our room.

Happy and I both get extra joys by making love in hotel rooms far from home. But it was not to be tonight. We'd decided to have Tim in the same room. After observing Tim's continued problem with bedwetting, maybe spurred by fear of new places, there was no way I'd banish Tim to be alone in a strange room on his own.

When Fran Purcell's friend, Sheldon Walsh, joined us in the Hotel's bar, he seemed to be a jolly sort of fellow: heavy with beer-fat. I'll bet he'd been busy over Christmas playing Santa Claus at children's parties.

His head had strands of hair carefully skimming what would otherwise have been a large bald pate. His hands had the brown liver spots of Floridians who have not avoided the sun.

"What do you think of our renovated ho-tel?" He asked proudly, a warm grin showing that he'd capped his top teeth but hadn't bothered with the lower ones that were tobacco-stained. "The Big Lakes Corporation bought the place. Spent millions. The Everglades Lounge features a 360-degree mural painted by Shepherd, worth a million by itself, or so I'm told. Come on in there, we'll have another drink. You can bring the kid, he can have orange juice."

We followed Sheldon into the room he'd christened the Everglades Lounge. "Beautiful room," I said politely. The mural was sensational, with muted colors as if it had been painted at early dawn before sunrise.

"Did you take the Mott Suite in this here ho-tel? It's named for Charles Mott, who transformed our bankrupt Southern Sugar Company into the U.S. Sugar Company and more or less saved the town."

No comment. I could hardly tell a prospective client that I couldn't afford anything better than the cheapest double room. I said: "When can I get a look at your colt, Mr. Walsh?"

"Call me Shelley. Everybody does." He drank three straight bourbons. No branch water for this Floridian. "Tomorrow morning. Early's best. Before gallops."

Happy and I felt tired after our long transatlantic trip. I was glad to get Shelley into his Buick and watch him weave down the highway, hoping he wouldn't be stopped by a police car because he was well over the alcohol limit.

Tim whined. "Where's McDonald's?" There was nothing for it but to go to the front desk and ask for the nearest McDonald's. We followed directions, and found the local McDonald's without too much sweat. I bought Tim his favorite Big Mac and chocolate float while Happy rummaged for the give-away toys Tim so loved. Of course Tim fell asleep before I returned to the table with his food. Happy asked for a doggy-bag and we took Tim's dinner back to the hotel.

"How sound asleep is he?" I asked Happy when we were in our own bed.

I had hopes we might be able to get in a little lovemaking before he'd wake up and ask for his usual nightly drink of water.

Happy said nothing so as not to wake up our son. She shook her head. She well knew that the noises she made during sex would rouse even a very tired three-year-old.

No sex that night. And Tim did wake up too soon, He did demand his glass of water. By the time dawn streaked the morning sky I was super ready to view the colt.

I wasn't early enough. An unwelcome visitor had arrived at the hotel and demanded the number of our room.

Now young Don Blair was knocking up a storm on our door.

"Hello. Come in before the hotel detective throws us out because people complained about the noise." I showed him into our small room furnished with a desk and chair in addition to our bed and Tim's cot. Crowded!

Don Blair quickly took up a position near our desk, plunging into its chair. To my amazement, he pulled a piece of string from his pocket as an explanation for his unwelcome presence. "This isn't the one I'm going to tell you about," he began without any hello or how-are-you. "But it's about the same size and length, and from the same roll as the one Jemima found."

He was talking to Happy, ignoring me. "My school gave me leave to come back to Florida for the coroner's final say. I called your house in Epsom, and a Mrs. Wright told me you'd be at this hotel by today. I felt compelled to locate you and share with you what conclusion the coroner reached. After all, we've made this part of the murder's journey, together."

Happy, dressed in a hotel toweling robe over her skimpy baby doll nightgown, nodded sagely.

Why? What was this all about?

"String," Happy muttered, nodding, "I knew it had to be a piece of string. So, Jemima found it. Ah told her to look fo' it when Ah was stayin' thet night at Mrs. Blair's."

I roared, "When you went into the kitchen to breastfeed Irish?"

"Yeah, man. But tell us more, Don Junior, about Jemima and the string." Junior wasn't about to relinquish center stage. He intended to draw out his grand moment as long as possible. He'd traveled the length and breadth of the state to bring us his news.

But he was hungry, and kept us waiting. Don Blair had located Tim's dinner and proceeded to sip the chocolate float.

Tim lightly hit Junior's free hand. He whined: "That's my drink."

Young Blair relinquished what was left of the chocolate float. Tim, satisfied, interspersed gulps of it with snacking on his cold Big Mac.

Finally, Blair Junior continued: "My Grandma decided we must sell my father's house. The murders are still on the police blotter, but our lawyer convinced the right authorities to let us go ahead with a sale. First, the place had to be cleaned. Grandma sent in Jemima, and acting on your wife Happy's tip, Jemima found the piece of string."

I echoed, "Piece of string?"

Happy said nothing. Again she nodded, but no questions followed. "Jemima's clever about lots of things besides cooking. She recognized the string was from her roll in her kitchen and – totally careful, like – she placed it in a plastic sandwich bag and took it to the police."

Now Happy asked a question. "String *was* from a roll in your Grandmother's kitchen?"

"That's right. Lori wouldn't have had any string in her kitchen. No food either. I doubt she'd ever made a roast of any kind of meat in her life. But Jemima uses string to wrap her roasts."

Happy and I both know that Happy's culinary skills leave much to be desired. But she did know about wrapping a roast in string from having lived with her Aunt Bessie. Happy's eyes had come alight. "She said: "Tell me this, did Jemima keep thet string safe enough for the po-lice to be able to test for DNA?"

"Yes. That's why I've come across the state here to Clewiston. To tell you: the police have found a match."

"Lori?" Happy said authoritatively. Not a question: a statement.

"Yes. The police found Lori's DNA from the palm of her right hand matching DNA on the string."

I intervened in this ballet twosome of words. "Will someone please enlighten me as to what you're talking about?"

Don said, "Mrs. Harrow understands. You see, Mr. Harrow, it can now be proven that Lori killed my father. After she'd shot him in their bed and cleaned the gunpowder from her hands she'd hooked up that string to his gun, placed the gun in his right hand so there would be powder burns on it, aimed the gun at herself and pulled the string. Case closed. My father's name is cleared."

Happy said, "Ah knows y'all is wonderin' what connection Ah'd made to illegal immigrants on the Blair case. Simple. Lori's Pedro were an illegal immigrant. Ah'd understood Lori, thet as a woman so in love with her Pedro, she'd accepted she was goin' t'die from gallopin' AIDS. Knowin' thet her Pedro would die fo' killin' Mr. Collins, it don't seem too difficult to link up her idea to shoot Don Blair III and fake her own murder."

I asked, "And your interest in DNA?"

"Ah's learned thet po-lice need proof in a court o' law. When Ah read in Lori's diary how she asked y'all to use a piece o' string to work the shutter of her camera, Ah's put two 'n two together and knew string would be part o' the answer to the Blair riddle. Ah guessed thet Lori's DNA would be on the string because she couldn't remove thet once she were dead."

Distasteful as it was for me, I tried to understand how the Lori and Pedro love affair had ended in Don Blair Senior's murder partly because discriminatory practices aboard the Collins yacht had fostered a dangerous environment. Pedro killed Collins, so when Lori lost Pedro she dispatched her husband and shot herself. Like Professor Higgins in *My Fair Lady*, "I think I got it."

The boy began to weep. This was no adolescent crying. Don Blair had mutated into an adult. His acne was gone, his back had straightened and when he stood up from the desk he wiped his nose from his fully unfettered six feet height.

He was weeping from relief.

Embarrassed, I said, "Let's all go to McDonald's for breakfast. Maybe it won't be as good as your Jemima's, but it'll be my treat."

Breakfast didn't happen. The intercom rang. Sheldon Walsh was announced. He was impatiently demanding to know where I was and why was I late to test his colt.

"Happy and I want to invite you to breakfast, Shelley," I countered. "We'll be downstairs in a tick. We've got our son and a certain Don Blair Junior with us. Once we've all had some bacon and eggs, I'll be your man."

We went to McDonald's. Not with Don Blair. He got on his motorcycle and disappeared down Sugarland Highway.

A happy man.

Shelley wasn't so happy when breakfast ended and we went to inspect his colt. In spite of the yearling being well-groomed and in a well-kept-up stall, I could see at once that he was a no-hoper, with faulty legs, and that must have wiped the smile from my face.

No sale. Even Tim made a face at the sorry state of the colt's twisted legs. I had difficulty finding the right words to walk away from Shelley. Be polite? No, not after he'd brought me all the way to Clewiston from Epsom with a fraudulent call to see a yearling he knew had gimpy legs.

No wonder he'd needed three straight bourbon drinks to face me in the Clewiston Inn's Everglades Lounge.

He'd lied long distance to Fran Purcell, perhaps imagining she'd be foolish enough to buy the colt unseen. Fran Purcell? Not on your Nellie. Fran, who twisted every penny before she'd spend it was not one to be tricked easily. It had cost her to send me here to examine the colt, what with a wife and son in tow. She'd been told I wouldn't leave them behind. To be fair to Fran, she knew how much I love them.

I wanted to be fair in return. Sternly, giving his fake Santa Claus jolly-fat-boy persona a hard look, I said, "Don't ever call Fran Purcell again. You've burned your bridges with her."

Alone, the three of us made our way back to the Clewiston Inn. I paid the bill, which seemed steep even though I'd calculated it earlier. I'd forgotten about the taxes, and mandatory tips.

CHAPTER 11

By late afternoon we'd returned to Miami's Airport with Happy's mountain of luggage. We were checked in for a return flight to England.

On board our 757, Tim fell asleep promptly. There was an article in the Florida newspaper I'd got from a stewardess that had a follow-up on the Everglades Club rape story.

"Lookee there," Happy pointed to it over my shoulder. "Thet little pastry chef, Melissa, is suing fo' havin' suffered as she done has. Ah hopes she gets a couple of hundred thousand. Not all the women in Flo-ri-da be bad 'uns like Lori Blair."

I agreed. I squeezed close to her and we kissed, not caring who saw us. Later, the next night when we were back in our own Epsom bed, we made wonderful sublime exquisite love. What a lucky fellow I am. Rating good women on a scale of one to ten, my wife rates ten.